Rock Island Public Library
401 - 19th Street
Rock Island, IL 61201-8143

D171566?

# PRAISE FOR ROBERT SHEARMAN

"Thrillingly unpredictable, bizarrely life-enhancing. . . . Shearman is a great writer."

*The Scotsman*

"A writer who is not afraid to approach the big subjects, but does so from interesting oblique angles and with a light, kittenish gait. Rather profound, ingeniously plotted."

*The Independent*

"Shearman's prose is a mixture of faux-naive mundanity and breathtaking fantasy visions. Addictive. Wonderful."

*SFX*

"Corrosively funny, wistful, sharp, strange and black as a coffin lid, Robert Shearman is an addictive delight."

**Mark Gatiss, Co-creator of** *Sherlock*

"Shearman offers us haunting, nightmare alternatives to our world that are still somehow utterly recognizable as our own, thanks to the way he always picks out the comically mundane among the impossible and the fantastical."

**Steven Moffat,**
**Executive Producer and Hugo Award-winning writer for** *Doctor Who*

"His stories are like the bastard offspring of Philip K. Dick and Jonathan Carroll, but with a quirky personality that is completely their own."

**Stephen Jones,**
**World Fantasy Award-winning editor of** *Best New Horror*

"Shearman has a uniquely engaging narrative voice and he steers clear of genre clichés, injecting elements of horror and the surreal into a recognizably real world. As impressive as his quirky imagination is his emotional range: most of the stories are darkly humorous, but humour, horror and genuine pathos all make a powerful impact in a very short space."

*The Times Literary Supplement*

"Shearman's stories are hard to categorize, a unique fusion of literary and the fantastic, perhaps not surprising from a writer whose credits include Doctor Who scripts and mainstream theatre."

*The Guardian*

Rock Island Public Library
401 - 19th Street
Rock Island • 61201-8143

JAN -- 2018

# REMEMBER WHY YOU FEAR ME

## THE BEST DARK FICTION OF ROBERT SHEARMAN

ChiZine Publications

**FIRST EDITION**

*Remember Why You Fear Me* © 2012 by Robert Shearman
Cover artwork © 2012 by Erik Mohr
Cover design © 2012 by Samantha Beiko
Interior design © 2012 by Danny Evarts
All Rights Reserved.

This book is a work of fiction. Names, characters, places, and incidents are either a product of the author's imagination or are used fictitiously. Any resemblance to actual events, locales, or persons, living or dead, is entirely coincidental.

Distributed in Canada by
Publishers Group Canada
76 Stafford Street, Unit 300
Toronto, Ontario, M6J 2S1
Toll Free: 800-747-8147
e-mail: info@pgcbooks.ca

Distributed in the U.S. by
Consortium Book Sales & Distribution
34 Thirteenth Avenue, NE, Suite 101
Minneapolis, MN 55413
Phone: (612) 746-2600
e-mail: sales.orders@cbsd.com

**Library and Archives Canada Cataloguing in Publication**

Shearman, Robert
          Remember why you fear me : the best dark fiction of Robert Shearman / Robert Shearman ; introduction by Stephen Jones.

Issued also in electronic format.
ISBN 978-1-927469-21-7

          I. Title.

PR6119.H435R46 2012      823'.92      C2012-904985-9

**CHIZINE PUBLICATIONS**
Toronto, Canada
www.chizinepub.com
info@chizinepub.com

Edited by Helen Marshall
Copyedited and proofread by Kate Moore

Canada Council    Conseil des arts
for the Arts        du Canada

We acknowledge the support of the Canada Council for the Arts which last year invested $20.1 million in writing and publishing throughout Canada.

ONTARIO ARTS COUNCIL
CONSEIL DES ARTS DE L'ONTARIO
an Ontario government agency
un organisme du gouvernement de l'Ontario

Published with the generous assistance of the Ontario Arts Council.

Printed in Canada

*To my sister, Vicky*
*who's always been braver than me.*

# TABLE OF CONTENTS

# NOT REALLY A HORROR WRITER

## AN INTRODUCTION BY
## STEPHEN JONES

What can I say about Robert Shearman that hasn't been said before?

Well, quite a lot, really.

For starters, *Remember Why You Fear Me* is his first honest-to-god horror collection, which is odd because, as Rob will readily tell you, he doesn't write horror fiction. Or even genre fiction for that matter.

Yet I first met Robert Shearman lurking at the top of an escalator at the World Fantasy Convention in Calgary, Alberta, in 2008. He was looking confused (which I later discovered is an almost perpetual expression for him). But not as confused as I was.

I pride myself as an editor for keeping up with what is happening in the genre. Yet here was this fellow Brit, who I had never heard of before, who was not only up for a World Fantasy Award for his first collection of stories, *Tiny Deaths* (which, again, I had never heard of, let alone seen), but who had been additionally nominated for one of the stories in that collection, "Damned if You Don't."

That's a hell of an introduction for anyone to the genre.

It turned out that Rob was better known as a playwright and radio dramatist, working alongside such luminaries as Alan Ayckbourn and Martin Jarvis.

However, perhaps his biggest claim to fame was that he scripted a 2005 episode of *Doctor Who*, which is remembered by everybody as the one in which they brought back the Daleks.

As it turned out, Rob won the World Fantasy Award for Best

Collection in Calgary, which was no mean achievement for a fledgling author. However, his publisher didn't see it that way. They were under the impression that they were publishing a book of "literary" stories, which is why they had never bothered to send it out to the usual genre reviewers. They were horrified when he returned home and proudly announced that he was the recipient of a big-arse bust of H.P. Lovecraft!

But trust me, as I discovered a few weeks later when he sent me a copy, *Tiny Deaths* contained some terrific horror stories. These included the aforementioned "Damned if You Don't" (one of the most disturbing, funny and surreal pieces of fiction I have ever read), "Mortal Coil" and "So Proud" and "Favourite."

Two years later Rob had found a more sympathetic publisher and put together a second collection, *Love Songs for the Shy and Cynical*. Once again, the stories were an audacious mix of themes and styles, but he still managed to include the British Fantasy Award-nominated novella "Roadkill" (another personal favourite of mine), along with the popular "George Clooney's Moustache" (also shortlisted for the same award) and "Pang." As it was, the collection itself picked up the British Fantasy Award for that year, as well as winning the Shirley Jackson Award.

Whether he liked it or not, by now Rob was definitely considered a *genre* writer.

With his third collection, *Everyone's Just So So Special*, published in 2011, he pushed the boundaries of his fiction even further. The book featured "Cold Snap" along with two stories I had the honour of commissioning.

When I was putting together my anthology *The Dead That Walk: Zombie Stories*, I invited Rob to contribute something.

"But Steve," he whined over lunch, "you know I'm not a horror writer. I can't do that stuff without being funny. And I've never written a zombie story in my life."

I ordered us a couple more bottles of wine and told him to go away and think about it.

A few weeks later he delivered "Granny's Grinning," one of the most terrifyingly twisted stories I have ever published. Yes, the word "zombie" is in there, but Rob's particularly skewered tale went way beyond what anyone would expect to find in a book of stories about the reanimated dead. To my mind, it's a modern classic of the genre.

So when it came time to do a follow-up anthology, *Visitants: Stories of Fallen Angels and Heavenly Hosts*, I approached Rob again.

"But Steve," he complained in the pub, "you know I can't do horror stories. I'm no good at writing to a specific theme. And I've never written an angel story before."

I bought us several more pints and told him to go away and think about it again.

Sometime later he submitted "Featherweight," a particularly nasty story involving cannibal cherubs. Once again, it was like nothing else in the book.

Because neither of these volumes was published in the UK, I reprinted both of these stories in consecutive editions of The Mammoth Book of Best New Horror.

More recently, we were having dinner and I mentioned to Rob that I was working on two new anthologies—*Haunts: Reliquaries of the Dead* and *A Book of Horrors*—and how pleased I would be if he could submit a story to both.

"Oh, Steve," he sighed, "as I keep telling you, I'm not really a horror writer. All my stuff turns out to be weird or humorous. Not the kind of thing anyone would want to see in a horror anthology."

I asked the waitress to bring him the pudding menu and patiently explained that that was what made his stories stand out from so much other genre material. I also suggested that he might want to go away and think about it some more.

He did. The result was "Good Grief" and the British Fantasy Award-nominated "Alice Through the Plastic Sheet," two of the most blackly comic horror stories it has ever been my pleasure to publish.

All the above, plus a number of original and uncollected tales, are contained in the book you are now holding. (There are also a few more if you happen to be reading the e-book version.)

Besides the collections, Rob has also published an omnibus of his stage plays, *Caustic Comedies*, and he's been working on a novel for nearly as long as I've known him. Or so he claims.

Over the past few years we have become good friends—attending the same conventions, meeting up for riotous lunches and dinners, or simply working together on various publishing projects. So here are some little-known facts about Rob that I would like to share with you:

Rob was born in the West Sussex town of Crawley in 1970. He tells Americans that it is near Gatwick Airport, just to make it sound more interesting. Rob looks older than his age. I hesitate to say "wiser."

Rob loves eating. When you meet him, he has either just consumed a meal or is on his way to have one. Sometimes both at the same time.

And he is certain to regale you with a story about how he is about to go on a diet the following week, or is already on one and has lost several pounds. He really does believe this, and nobody has the heart to tell him differently.

Rob loves drinking. Sometimes, when we go out for one of our "lunches"—which have been known to last until dinnertime—and we have consumed our body-weight in bottles of wine, Rob will still have a few whiskies on the way home as a "night-cap." I really don't know how he does it, especially when I have barely managed to crawl back to my own residence.

Rob loves travelling. He'll go anywhere. He's been known to travel to the ends of the Earth (well, Australia) for a free convention membership. He has also been fêted around the globe by various cultural organizations with too much public money at their disposal. And, if all else fails, he'll take a cruise to teach Russian literature to little old ladies. I'm not even going to go there.

But Rob does love the ladies. No, really. Who knew? The guy is a babe-magnet. I remember that after blearily leaving a British Fantasy Awards Banquet in Nottingham, Reggie Oliver and I were amazed to observe Rob semi-lounging on a sofa, surrounded by half-a-dozen attractive women draped over the furniture or literally sitting at his feet. Personally, I put this attraction down to the fact that women think he is funny and "safe." It also helps that he looks like a big, cuddly teddy bear.

Rob loves reading his fiction aloud. I hate most authors reading their own stories, but he is apparently very good at it. At one of his book launches a few years ago, Sarah Pinborough and I were admonished by his publisher for talking too loudly—*outside* the venue! I can only presume from this that Rob must read very quietly indeed.

Rob loves writing. But not in his office. Or even his home. He prefers to work on his hand-written first drafts in museums and art galleries—and of course, cafés. I don't know if this makes his work any better, but at least it gets him out of the house.

Despite a reputation that continues to grow, Rob probably still doesn't consider himself to be a horror writer. But that's okay, because by now everyone else does and he has the awards to prove it. The creepy, disturbing and, yes, often hilarious stories in *Remember Why You Fear Me* will only add to his well-deserved esteem, and I am delighted to have been the catalyst for at least a few of them.

However, there's still one thing that I simply do not understand—just how *does* he get to hang out with all those attractive women at conventions . . . ?

—Stephen Jones
London, England
May 2012

REMEMBER WHY YOU FEAR ME

REMEMBER WHY YOU FEAR ME

# MORTAL
## COIL

On first impression, it looked like an apology. But the more you reread it—and it was reread a *lot* that day, it was pored over and analysed, governments around the world made statements about it, dismissing it first as a hoax, then taking it more seriously as the afternoon wore on, until by evening you could have sworn they had been in on the whole thing from the start, television programmes were rescheduled to make way for phone-in discussion shows and cobbled-together news reports that had very little actual news to report. . . . The more you reread it, you couldn't help but feel there was a note of disappointment to it. It was almost patronizing.

This is what the message said.

*"You've got it all wrong. And we're sorry, because it's our mistake. If we'd made things clearer to you right from the start, none of this would have happened.*

*"We gave you a knowledge of death. We thought it would make you rise above the other animals, give you a greater perspective on how to live your lives fruitfully, in peace and in happiness. But it's all gone horribly wrong, hasn't it?*

*"You obsess about death. Right from childhood, it seems to exercise your imagination in an entirely unhealthy way. You count all the calories on every single tin in the supermarket, you go to the gym twice a week, just so you feel you can ward it off that bit longer. You pump botox into your cheeks and stick plastic sacks into your breasts so you can kid yourselves you look younger, that death isn't on the cards yet. And then, when death finally does happen to someone you know, you go to long boring funerals and sit on hard benches*

*in sullen silence, dressed in smart clothes that make you itch, with only flat wine and sausage rolls to look forward to. And the growing certainty that soon it'll be your turn, the sausage rolls will be eaten for you.*

*"You're frightened and you're miserable. We can't blame you. Looking down at you, it makes us pretty miserable too!*

*"Houseflies and worms and llamas have the right idea. They understand that death is just part of the system. As much as birth and procreation. A thing to avoid when it isn't necessary, and to accept when it is. And so houseflies and worms and llamas have a better grip on what's expected of them, to be as good houseflies, worms and llamas as they can be, and not let all that death baggage get in the way.*

*"As we say, sorry. We made the mistake of giving you a little knowledge, when either none or more would have been more sensible. There was some hope we didn't need to spell it all out for you, but don't you worry, that's our fault, not yours. And so we're going to put an end to it.*

*"We did consider that taking away the knowledge of death would be the best thing. But there was a general feeling that it'd be a shame to go backwards—and that we've enough houseflies and worms and llamas as it is. They're coming out our ears! So, starting tomorrow, expect things to be different. It'll be a new chapter. For you and for us!*

*"And in the mean time, please accept our apologies for any distress we may have caused you."*

You see, that patronizing disappointment was hard to ignore. Especially after multiple readings of the message. Some very well-known intellectuals appeared on the phone-in discussion programmes that evening to complain that they'd been so obviously talked down to. "After all," grumbled one, "what do they expect? If they're going to turn the secrets of life and death into a crossword puzzle, they can hardly object when we all sit around trying to solve it."

The first message had naturally taken everyone by surprise. In every country around the world, on every television set, on every radio and in every newspaper, the words appeared. All in the language of the country in question, of course. Many people studied the different translations, just to see whether they could glean any hidden meanings, but all they could conclude was that (a) German words can be irritatingly long and never use one syllable when six will do, and that (b) French is very romantic. So no one was any the wiser.

The next morning everyone was glued to their television screens. Even the sceptics, who stubbornly insisted the whole thing was some elaborate conjuring act, waited with bated breath to see what trickery was lined up next. And in countries where casual murder had become a part of everyone's daily lives, the perpetrators surprised themselves by holding back for once, and tuning in to see whether the killings they executed so nonchalantly had any deeper meaning. In Britain, the BBC didn't even bother to prepare their scheduled programmes. And so, when a second message resolutely *failed* to appear and explain life and death and matters besides, the BBC were caught on the hop and forced to transmit a series of Norman Wisdom films. Worldwide, the excitement gave way to disappointment, then to anger. It's quite certain there would have been riots in the streets, causing more bloodshed and more death, had Something Not Happened.

So it's just as well Something Did.

Of course, it took some people a while to realize anything had. They were so intent upon the TV screen that they ignored the sound of the letterbox, of the daily post falling onto the mat. Had they stopped to consider that all the postmen were at home, the same as them, they might have shown more interest.

The envelopes were light brown, soft to the touch, and seemed almost to be made of vellum, like medieval manuscripts. There were no stamps on them—and the names weren't handwritten, but typed. And there was one for each member of the household, however young or old. Inside, each recipient found a card, stamped with his or her full name. And underneath that, as plain and unapologetic as you like, was a short account of when and how the recipient was going to die. Some poor unfortunates, either elderly or obese, found the news so startling that they died right there on the spot—and the card in their dead hands had predicted that exactly. Sometimes the explanation would be moderately chatty, and full of information. Arthur James Cripps learned that he was to die in fourteen years and six days, by "drowning, after being knocked over a bridge by a Nissan Micra; frankly, if the water hadn't finished you off, you'd have died minutes later from the ruptured kidneys caused by the collision in question." A lot of people learned that they were just going to die of 'cancer.' No fripperies, no more detail, no context—the word 'cancer' on the card saying it all, as if the typist had got so bored at hammering out the word so often that he could barely wait to move on to more interesting deaths elsewhere.

The Norman Wisdom films were interrupted, and news updates directed people to their letterboxes. The anticipation was terrible—

worse than checking your exam results, or your credit card statement after a particularly expensive holiday. Parents with large families had to be put through the torture again and again, forced to confront what would happen not only to them but to their offspring. And if, inevitably, some were appalled by the bad news—a twelve year old child to die of meningitis, a three year old girl whose ultimate fate was to be abducted after school some seven years later, raped and strangled and her body never recovered—most went to bed that night somewhat reassured. At least they *knew* now. They might only have one month—one year— fifty years—but at least they *knew*. In fact, sales of cigarettes tripled over night, as smokers and non-smokers alike realized that all the agonizing over the health risks was now redundant. If it wasn't going to kill you, why not take it up? And if it was, well—it's a *fait accompli*, isn't it? Might as well enjoy it whilst your lungs last.

Just about the only person who wasn't reassured was Henry Peter Clifford.

Harry would never have thought he was an especially special person. Even in his moments of hubris or overweening arrogance—which, for him, were few and far between—he'd have been hard pushed to have described himself as anything better than distinctly average. He naturally assumed, on that fateful morning, that his envelope simply hadn't arrived yet. This was nothing new to Harry—his birthday cards were always late, he only received postcards after everybody else had had theirs. His wife Mary read her fate with shaking hands, and all he could think was that he'd probably have to wait until tomorrow to go through the same thing. But the next day there was still no envelope for him, nor the day after. The world had subtly changed, but for Harry it all looked pretty much the same.

The Government had quickly set up a number of help centres to deal with the crisis, and so, on the fourth day that Harry *still* hadn't found out when he was due to die, he caught the bus down to the citizens' advice bureau. The streets were that much more dangerous now; cars sped along roads knowing full well they *weren't* about to be involved in some tragic accident, and pedestrians ran the traffic with similar impunity. The bus driver catapulted his eight ton vehicle of red metal down the hill with the certain knowledge that his number wasn't up, and as Harry gripped the seat to prevent himself from being flung bodily down the aisle, he only wished he could be as sure.

There was a surprisingly long queue at the help centre, which cheered Harry somewhat—in spite of the long wait he'd have to put up with, it reassured him to think others were having complications too. But it turned out these people in line were just wanting grief counselling for deaths that hadn't even happened yet. Indeed, the rather bland blonde behind the desk suggested that Harry was the only person who *hadn't* received a death envelope.

"Well, what can I do about it?" asked Harry lamely, and she shrugged as if the oversight was in some way his fault. "Is there anybody I can write to?" The woman told him that since no one knew where the envelopes had come from there wasn't much she could do. "But if you don't know anything about this whole thing, why have you set up a help centre?" The woman shrugged again, and called the next person in the queue forward.

"Maybe you just lost it somewhere?" said his secretary brightly. "It fell behind the sofa cushions or something. I'm always doing that." The secretary had been saying *everything* brightly after finding out that her death, in sixty-seven years' time, would be a painless little thing, her heart giving out in the throes of sexual congress with a South American toyboy. "I should check under the cushions again," she said, not a little unhelpfully.

The trouble was that everyone seemed to share his secretary's scepticism, and expressed it much less complacently. They were perplexed at first by Harry's outrageous claims he'd had no envelope, that he had been left out of a global miracle that had changed them all—as if he were the one man still claiming that the world was flat when everybody else had accepted it was a bloody sphere now, thank you very much. Then they'd get angry with the idea that he was trying to get attention. "Why *wouldn't* you get an envelope? What makes you so special?" Typically, Harry hadn't thought of it in this way at all; on the contrary, he had wondered why the universe had deemed him so insignificant that he was the only one to be ignored. He vaguely mused whether he preferred the idea of being singled out because he was the most important person in the world, or because he was the *least* important. And decided he wasn't fond of either much, frankly.

"I'm afraid I'm going to have to let you go," said his boss. "You know, it's not my decision. But I have bosses, and they have bosses, and, you know . . ." He gave a smile. "You know how it is."

There had been some controversy about just how much employers had the right to know about their employees' life expectancy. Companies would argue that it was surely relevant whether or not they could expect their staff to go on providing good service, or whether they had to accommodate for the fact they might be dropping dead left, right and centre. At job interviews prospective employees lost out to candidates who could demonstrate they had longevity on their side, and those already in work found their bosses would rather ditch them quickly before they were subject to expensive health plans. The Government said something non-committal about the data protection act and employee confidentiality, but also that any organisation had the right to expect full productivity from its staff. None of which helped anybody very much. When Harry was first asked to show his death envelope at work, his inability to do so was taken to mean he had something terrible and contagious and doubtlessly fatal to hide.

His boss gave him another one of those smiles. "Really, you're lucky," he said. "Getting out of work is the best thing that can happen to you. Enjoy yourself. Enjoy the rest of your life. I wish I could," he said with apparent regret, "but it seems this old ticker of mine has another forty-seven years to go. Bloody thing!" He held out his hand to wish Harry goodbye, and in spite of himself, Harry shook it.

And later that night his wife told him she was leaving.

"I can get another job," said Harry. "Nothing fancy, I know. But there's lots of casual labour, they don't care whether you snuff it or not. We can make it work, Mary."

"No, we can't," said Mary. And she told him how when she'd held that death envelope in her hand, scared to open it and find out how long she'd got, she'd made herself a vow. If I've only got a couple of years, she thought, if that's all I've got. Then I'm out of here. I'm not going to waste anymore of my life. Because we only go around once, and I'm letting it slip by, I should be climbing mountains and exploring deserts and scuba diving and sleeping with people who'd do it with the lights on. That'll be the present to myself. If I've got two years or less, I'm leaving, Harry.

"But," Harry pointed out gently, "you haven't got two years. You've got thirty-eight. The cancer doesn't get you for thirty-eight."

"I know," said Mary. "And I was so disappointed. And then it dawned on me. If I'm *that* disappointed, that I'd rather be dead than living with you, then I shouldn't be living with you. Goodbye, Harry."

He couldn't argue with that.

Mary wasn't a cruel woman. She recognized that Harry wouldn't easily be able to earn money, whilst in her robust and not-yet-carcinogenic state the world was her oyster. She left him the house and a lot of the money. She also left him the cat, which Harry thought rather a shame as he'd never much liked it—he'd simply never got round to telling Mary that. And Mary said she wanted to start the rest of her life as soon as possible, and was gone by morning.

And, of course, a lot of people out there were following Mary's example. Those who realized that the end was in sight decided that this was their last chance to see the world. Thousands of elderly English people flew to America, and thousands of elderly Americans flew to England—until, at the end of the day, roughly the same number of the diseased and the dying were roaming the streets in both countries, just sporting different accents. With typical brilliance, Disney decided to exploit this new trend in end-of-life tourism. They used a motto— "Make the Last of Your Life be the Time of Your Life," which had a certain catchiness. If you could show proof you had three months or less, you were entitled to discounts to *all* the theme parks, and V.I.P. treatment once you were through the turnstiles. There was a special queue for the nearly dead, and a soberly dressed man-size Mickey Mouse or Goofy would respectfully show them to their rides. As it turns out the venture was so wildly successful that the Nearly Dead queue was often longer than the regular one, but that didn't matter— the ticket holders still felt they were being given special treatment. And attendance went up all the more when the elderly, who had always sworn that being spun through the air on a rollercoaster would be the death of them, now had concrete evidence that, in fact, it wouldn't.

Harry wouldn't have much wanted to visit Disneyland, but if his time were soon to be up, he'd certainly have wanted to have gone *somewhere*. But he couldn't afford a holiday. Unemployment benefits hadn't exactly been *abolished*, but it was hard to justify why you should be given a free hand-out when your death envelope demonstrated you had another fifty years of health in front of you and weren't just about to die in penury. And any attempt Harry made to get some money was thwarted by the absence of that envelope. So when, one morning, it came through the letterbox, Harry was delighted.

At first he couldn't believe it was really there. He'd given up hoping it'd ever turn up. But there was no mistaking it—that off-brown colour that you just didn't find anywhere else, the softness to the touch.

He opened it hastily. He didn't care *when* he died, or *how* he died. Just so long as he had proof he did, in fact, *eventually* die.

**"HENRY PETER CLIFFORD,"** said the stamp.

And then, typed:

"Awaiting Further Information."

Harry stared at it. Unable to believe his eyes. He turned over the card, hoping for something else. Something telling him it was a joke, not to worry, he was due to be impaled on a wooden stake that afternoon, anything. But instead, in ballpoint pen, someone had written, "Sorry for the Inconvenience."

As the day went by, as he did what he normally did—had breakfast, fed the cat, watched afternoon TV—Harry wondered whether the scrawled apology might even be God's very own handwriting. Still, probably not. He'd probably use one of his underlings, some saint or angel or vicar or someone. He'd always imagined the handwriting of a Divine Being would be a bit more ornate. And that he'd be able to spell "inconvenience."

The next morning he thought there might be another envelope, a follow-up to the last. There wasn't. But there was a knock at the door.

At first Harry saw the envelope rather than the man who was holding it. "I think you should read this," he said, and he held it out to Harry nervously.

Eagerly Harry read the name on the top, was immediately disappointed. "Jeffrey Allan White. That isn't me."

"No, it's me," said Jeffrey Allan White.

"I don't understand," said Harry. He held out the card for Mr White to take back. "This isn't me," he repeated uselessly.

"Please," said Jeffrey. "Read the rest of it."

And Harry did. Then he read it again. He stared at Jeffrey for a few moments, and saw a man in his late fifties, a bit unkempt, shorter than average, plump, and just as scared as he was.

"Can I come in?" said Jeffrey. Harry nodded, and got out of his way.

Harry didn't know what to do with his strange visitor. He led him into the kitchen, wordlessly indicated he should sit down. Jeffrey smiled a thanks awkwardly. The cat was excited that someone new was in the house, and jumped up on to Jeffrey's lap. "Sorry," said Harry. "Do you like cats . . . ?"

"I'm a bit allergic," replied Jeffrey. "But it doesn't really matter anymore."

"Can I get you a drink?"

"I'm fine, thanks."

"A coffee or a tea . . . ?"

"A coffee then, thanks."

"All I've got is decaf . . ."

"Decaf is fine."

"Milk?"

"Yes. Thanks." And there was silence from them both as Harry busied himself with the kettle. It wasn't until the water was nearly boiled that Harry thought he should say something.

"But I don't even know you."

"No, I know."

"But I don't. So why . . . ?"

Jeffrey smiled, but it was a nervous smile that had no answer. "Thanks," he said as he took the coffee. "Thanks, this is fine," he said again.

"Why did you come here?" asked Harry. "I mean, I'd have run away."

"But really. Where would I go?"

Harry shrugged. "Well. Anywhere."

"I almost didn't come," said Jeffrey quietly. "When I first found out how I was going to die . . . I almost laughed, it was so specific. My wife, she's one of the cancer ones, how can she avoid that? But if you know you're going to die at the hands of Henry Clifford at 23 Sycamore Gardens on 16th September, it seems such an easy thing to prevent. If you'd asked me last week," he said, as he took a gulp of his still too hot coffee, "I'd have said this was the last place in the world I'd have visited."

Harry waited patiently for Jeffrey to go on. Jeffrey couldn't meet his eyes, looked at the floor.

"But if it *isn't* true . . . if I *could* prevent it . . . then it's all meaningless, isn't it? Isn't it? I'm not sure I could go on like that. I'm not sure I could cope with tomorrow, when I'm not supposed to see tomorrow in the first place. What would it all be for? My son," he added. "My son and I never much got on, we hadn't spoken in years. Once he found out I was going to die, he got back in touch. We've been going to the pub. Chatting. Like friends. Not as family, but *friends*." He looked up at Harry imploringly. "You've got to help me. You've got to do this. It says . . ." and he fluttered the envelope at Harry weakly, "it says you do here."

"I don't know how to stab someone. I'm not sure I could go through with it." Silence. "I mean, it's the actual sticking it in . . . I think I could do it if I had to shoot you, you know, from a distance. . . ."

"It says stabbing."

"Yes, I know."

They both finished their coffee.

"Maybe," suggested Jeffrey at last, "you could just hold the knife. And I could run on to it."

"Okay," said Harry. "We could try that."

Both Harry and Jeffrey were shaking as Harry pulled open the kitchen drawer and looked at the knives. "Do you have a preference, or . . . ?"

"Best get one that's sharp," said Jeffrey.

The first time Jeffrey ran at Harry's knife, Jeffrey kept his eyes closed. The problem was that Harry did the same. And so they didn't collide correctly, and the worst Jeffrey sustained was a cut on the arm.

"Ouch," said Jeffrey.

"Sorry," said Harry.

"There's no way that's fatal," said Jeffrey. "We should try again."

This time Jeffrey, at least, kept his eyes open. Harry *tried* to, but at the moment of impact he couldn't help flinch. So all he felt was Jeffrey's body groan against his, and a strange sucking as the knife was pulled out. When Harry dared to look, he was horrified to see there was blood everywhere, on his hands, on the floor, and on Jeffrey's stomach, of course, which was the point at which the knife had obviously entered.

"I'm sorry," said Harry. "I'm sorry. Does it hurt?"

Jeffrey laid on the floor, sobbing, clutching at his wound. "Again," he said. "Again."

Harry looked at all the blood, at Jeffrey's agonized face, and balked. He left quickly, closing the kitchen door behind him.

An hour or so later he pushed the door open gently, as if trying not to wake his guest. "Jeffrey," he whispered. "Are you still alive?"

"Please," said Jeffrey, his voice now guttural. "Finish me off."

Harry stared. And then—"No!" he said to the cat, as it poked its way into the kitchen, and began to lick at the blood with curiosity. "Out of here, come on! Shoo! I'll close the door," Harry said to Jeffrey gently. "Leave you to it."

Harry tried to watch the television, but it was hard to concentrate. Later that evening he went back to see how Jeffrey was holding up. Jeffrey couldn't speak, but looked at him with big desperate eyes. Harry hesitated. Then picked up a heavy rolling pin, stood over his victim, took aim at his head.

"No," croaked Jeffrey. "Stabbing. Says it's a stabbing." And Harry left once more, determined to watch whatever was on the telly, and *make* himself concentrate on it.

Sometime before midnight Harry braved the kitchen again. He was relieved to see that Jeffrey was, at last, dead. And had indeed died on the 16th September, even if the actual process had taken rather longer than either of them had anticipated. Harry looked at Jeffrey's eyes, as if trying to find some truth in his death, but all he saw was a glassy stare. He thought about moving the body, but realized that with all the worry he'd put into the actual killing, he'd not given a moment's thought to what he should do afterwards. And so he decided to go to bed, face that problem in the morning. After all, it wasn't as if Jeffrey Allan White was going anywhere.

That night Harry slept rather better than he thought any murderer had a right to—so soundly, in fact, that he was only woken up by frantic hammering at the door. He opened it in his pyjamas, so bleary that for the moment he forgot about the corpse on the kitchen floor.

Outside there were five people, each of them holding death envelopes.

"No," he said. "No, no, no." And he closed the door on them.

But they didn't go away. They were staring death in the face, they were frightened—but each of them knew that their lives had to end somehow, and destiny had chosen them to be at the hands of Harry Clifford. The cat was very excited when he showed them all, one by one, into the sitting room, and with heavy heart read the grisly instructions within their soft little brown envelopes. There were two drownings, which Harry conducted in the bath one after the other—only realizing as he lugged the swollen corpses into Mary's bedroom afterwards how heavy bodies became when full of water. Another one had his head caved in with an electric iron, and since Mary had been the one to take charge of all the practical details in their marriage, it took Harry a full half hour to find the right cupboard in which she'd kept it. There was another stabbing to be performed, but this one was quicker than the day before's; Harry had learned to keep his eyes open this time. And there was a hanging, which caused both Harry and his victim no end of problems.

"Did you bring a rope?" asked Harry.

"I didn't know I needed one," said the rather shy teenager, blushing through a wall of spots.

"I don't just have a rope lying about," said Harry. "If you want me to hang you, the least you could do is bring your own equipment."

In the end they decided that the shower curtains could be taken down, wrapped tightly around the youth's neck, and with some care he could be suspended over the upstairs banisters until he expired. Then Harry cut the body down, dragged it to Mary's bedroom, and laid it alongside the five people he had already killed. Mary's room seemed the best place for all these strangers; it was a place he'd had little cause to visit over the last two years of his marriage, not since Mary had asked if he could move into the spare room. He surveyed his handiwork for a moment, all six bodies lying higgledy-piggledy across Mary's bed and by the dressing table at which she used to do her make-up and hair. Then, without a hesitation, he closed the door tight, went to his own room, packed a rucksack, and left the house.

The next day he was on the Cornwall coast, walking along the cliffs, watching as the sea crashed into the rocks. He began to feel normal, human. He waved politely at the passers-by, managed a smile, as if he too was simply out for a gentle stroll without a care in the world. One kindly looking old man, walking his Jack Russell, said good morning.

"Good morning," said Harry.

"Here on holiday?" asked the old man.

"Yes," said Harry. "I think so. I don't know. Maybe," he said decisively, "I'll live here. Yes."

"Well, it's a beautiful part of the country. I've always loved it, man and boy. I say," said the old man confidentially, "I do believe you're supposed to push me off the cliff." And he produced the telltale envelope. "I'm sorry," he said, with genuine sympathy. "I can quite see how that would disturb your walk."

Harry pushed him over the side, and his body span all the way down, glancing off the odd rock. Neither of them were quite sure what to do with the little dog, so the old man kicked him off the edge before he took his own fall. "He loved me, I know it," he said with tears in his eyes. "It's what he would have wanted."

If these death envelopes were going to follow Harry wherever he went, he supposed he might as well go back home and live in comfort. The cat was pleased—he hadn't been fed for nearly a day, and was starving. And the people *did* keep coming. Sometimes as many as twenty could be found in the morning, sick with fear, clutching their little death sentences. "It's all right," he said to them, soothing, calm. "We'll make it okay. There's nothing to be afraid of." And, as the weeks went by, and the corpses began mounting in his ex-wife's bedroom, he realized that he meant it. All this death, there really *was* nothing to be afraid of. If he'd found a purpose in life, at long last, after so many years of not even bothering to look, then this was it—he could make sure that these poor souls shuffled off this mortal coil in as humane and tender a way as possible.

He decided to charge his victims a small fee. They were all too eager to pay, he discovered—it wasn't as if they could take their money with them. And with the cash he bought lots of painkillers, the strongest that could be purchased over the counter. When all's said and done, if your way out of this world is by having a hammer turn your skull to splinters, then a preparatory swig of a couple of aspirin is unlikely to do much good. But Harry realized it was a *psychological* help, that his patients felt it was altogether a far more professional operation. "Thank you, doctor," said one gratefully, just before Harry bludgeoned him with a saucepan, and Harry felt an indescribable swell of pride.

He even hired a secretary to take care of them all, to ensure that he disposed of them in order and in good time. He chose the secretary he'd once worked with, the one who so brightly had realized her death was at the thrust of a toyboy. She was no longer so bright or cheery. "I've not even had a sniff of sex in ages," she complained. "What if this toyboy in sixty-seven years' time is the next bit of sex I get? It's a mistake," she concluded, with a wisdom that Harry had never expected of her, "to see in the way you die an explanation of how you live. The fact I'm going to die bonking a Brazilian does not mean I'm a great lover. Death is just another bit of stuff that happens."

And then, one day, just suddenly, it all stopped.

"A quiet day today," the secretary told Harry, when, by noon, no one had knocked at the door. But it was a quiet week as well. At the end of the month, with no patients calling, Harry paid her off. She said she was sorry the job was over. "I felt we were doing some good." Harry told her he was sorry too.

But, surprisingly, sorrier still was the cat. The ginger little tabby had been a great favourite with all Harry's victims, taking their minds off the operations ahead of them. It'd enjoyed parading around the waiting room of a morning, checking out all the newcomers, and allowing itself to be stroked and petted and made a fuss of. Now the cat would stare out of the window, eyeing anyone who walked up the street—and visibly sagging with disappointment when the passer-by wouldn't stop at the house. The cat's fur grew matted and coarse, it no longer washed itself. It had no interest in eating, it had no interest in anything. It was beginning to pine away.

Harry could see his cat was dying. And it seemed to him an

extraordinary piece of cruelty that he should never know exactly when the cat was to die, when its suffering was to stop. The cat would lie, listless, looking at him with pleading eyes. Harry recognized the look; it was the same expression he'd seen in Jeffrey White's when he'd bled to death in the kitchen all those months ago.

Harry cradled the cat in his arms, and stroked its fur. He'd never liked the cat, and the cat had never much liked him—but it purred for Harry now, and Harry was touched. The cat heaved with a huge sigh that seemed to echo down its thinning body, and then gave the gentlest of mews. And Harry knew there was no person more humane than him to end the poor cat's life, and that the cat knew it too, he'd seen the fact of it countless times in this very house. Because Harry was the greatest killer of all, and he *was* special, and that's why he'd been singled out, that's why he couldn't die, why they wouldn't let him die, he had a job to do. He wrung the cat's neck so quickly the cat would never have known. And he carried its frail little body up to Mary's room, and left it with all the other corpses.

And then he sat down and cried. He hadn't cried for any of these deaths, he hadn't found the time. But he cried now, and he cried himself asleep.

The next morning he started when he heard something at the door. Still dozing in the armchair, he sprang to his feet. Ready to welcome another client, to practise his expertise with gentle care.

But instead, lying on the doormat, was an off-brown envelope.

Numbly he picked it up. And opened it. And read it.

"**HENRY PETER CLIFFORD**" said the stamp.

And, underneath, just the one word:

"Cancer."

And that was it. Not even a date. Not even the recognition that there should have been a date. Just this one word, this ordinary death, this trivial death, laughing at him.

He turned over the card. And, in the same handwriting he'd seen before, in ballpoint pen: "Sorry. We lost this behind the sofa cushion."

Harry sighed. He put the card back in the envelope for safe keeping, laid it gently down upon the hall table. He wondered what he should do with the rest of the day, the rest of his life. He couldn't think of anything.

So he went upstairs to bed. Drew the curtains. And, lying in the darkness, explored his body for a lump.

# George Clooney's
## Moustache

I tried writing this on toilet paper but it's hard writing on toilet paper because the paper's so thin it breaks. And you can put some sheets together to make it thicker but that's not much better and you have to write so slowly to keep it from breaking that by the time you reach the end of the sentence you forgot how it started and you forget what it was you wanted to say anyway, and anyway you get through a lot of paper like that. XXXXXXXX **He** caught me, I knew he would, he's smart like that, I was taking so long in the bathroom that he began to bang on the door asking if I was all right and I said I was all right, and I flushed, but he said if I didn't open the door he'd break it down and so I did. I should have flushed away my writing first while I was at it but I just didn't have time to think and he picked it up and he read it and I thought he'd get angry because a lot of it was about him, well all of it really. But XXXXXXXX **he** didn't say anything bad and he said if I wanted to write he'd get me some proper paper if it meant that much to me. And a pencil too, not a sharp one, he'd seen a film once about how a sharp pencil could be used as a weapon and stuck into someone's neck and that was funny because I think I've seen that film too but I couldn't remember what it was called, neither of us could, we laughed about that. And I told him I'd never do that to myself, I'm scared of blood, and he looked a bit shifty and said he'd been more worried I'd do it to him actually, and I hadn't even thought of that and said I wouldn't, we laughed about that. So XXXXXXXX **he** gave me this pad and this pencil. And told me I could copy out what I'd written on the toilet paper if I liked. But I didn't want to, he'd been so nice about the whole thing and what I'd said on the toilet paper wasn't very kind.

I didn't want to write anything for a while, I didn't know what to say anymore, and he'd ask me sometimes about it over dinner, have you started writing yet, but he said it nicely, it wasn't a nag and didn't come out sarky. And so eventually I thought I'd better write something after he'd gone to all that trouble, and so I did, and this is it.

---

Over breakfast he read what I wrote last night. He said it was very good, but that some of the grammar needed a little work, that it wasn't always easy to read, and I asked about my handwriting, and he said that was good, and about my spelling, and he said that was good too, it was just the grammar, I could do with a few more full stops. So I'm going to do that. When I remember. I'll try. He said he'd have to change just one thing, and he crossed out a few words with a pen, and handed it back. And he'd crossed out all the times I'd used his name, he'd put 'he' instead, he said that he should never have let me know his name in the first place that was a mistake. So I could carry on writing, but no more names. And I said could I use another name instead, it'd get a bit much calling him 'he' all the time, and he said that was all right. And George told me that he was glad I enjoyed the pad and the pencil, that they'd been a present. And that I'd get more presents, so long as I behaved, so long as I did what I was told. I told George I would and he was so pleased. He asked what I was going to write next and I couldn't think what, and he said I should write about what I know. But I don't want to write about my life before, if you're reading this you probably know it already, it's probably not much different from yours. So I'm going to describe where I am. I don't like descriptive bits, I'd rather tell stories, but here goes. There are three rooms. (Actually there are more than three rooms, but I only get to go in three of them. There's the kitchen, but I'm not allowed in there because it's full of sharp things, George keeps it locked with the bolt he took from the bathroom. And there's the room which has the front door in it, I don't go there.) But there are my three. There's the sitting room which is where we eat our breakfast and our dinner and it's got a television in it and George watches the news a lot, and sometimes he watches other things too, sitcoms I think because I hear laughter and it isn't George's. Then there's the bathroom, but you know about that, it's only different now because he took the lock off. And then there's the bedroom which is where I am now, I spend most of my time here. George keeps it locked but he lets me out when I need to, when it's time for breakfast or dinner or when I need the bathroom. The walls are a bit old and have wallpaper on which is a bit old and when I get bored I can count the stripes but I don't need to be bored now because I have the pad and the pencil and I can use them instead. And that's enough for tonight and I'm going to sleep now, night night.

----

He asked me why I'd named him George. But he wasn't angry, he was smiling. Puzzled though. And I told him it was because he looked a bit like George Clooney. And he laughed and said he did not, and I said he did too, and I laughed as well. And actually I suppose he doesn't look much like George Clooney, not really, what I mean is that George Clooney has nice eyes and my George had nice eyes just like his, and you know how George Clooney has got a sort of square jaw, well my George has nothing like that but it's a nice jaw anyway. And the real George Clooney doesn't have a moustache the way my George Clooney does but still never mind. So if you're the police and you're out there looking for him then they're not that alike really, to be honest there's no point going after George Clooney. And George said that I was right, he did watch sitcoms, he couldn't only watch the news it'd do his head in. He was sorry if it disturbed me, he could turn the volume down if I liked, and I said that was okay, I liked to hear the laughter. And he said that if I was very good that could be another present, he'd let me watch a sitcom some time, not now but soon. I thanked him for that. And he said it was very odd there was nothing on the news yet, it'd been over a week now, you'd have thought there would be something. I said I didn't know, maybe they were keeping it a secret, and he said it just didn't make sense. Then he told me he'd wash up breakfast and he put me back in my room. And a bit later he came back and said why not, we'd watch a sitcom that night, he'd come and get me when one was on. I'd been very good and I deserved a present. (And I think he liked the fact I'd called him George.) And it's funny, I suppose I'm writing this for George now. I thought at first it was for Daddy, or Paul, or Jessie, although Jessie couldn't read it she's only two, but Paul could read it to her, he's a really good dad like that. But this is for George now, isn't it? Hello George. You really *do* look like George Clooney, I was being silly before, except for the moustache. And George came and got me and took me into the sitting room, he had the lights off and there was only the light from the TV screen, it was like going to the cinema! And I said that, do you remember, and you laughed, and we sat down on the couch and watched *Friends*. And it was an episode I'd seen before but that was okay, I pretended it was new and laughed anyway, I didn't want to hurt George's feelings. Although of course you've just read this, George, you know that now, sorry. Sorry. It was a great evening, a bit like a first date, and I hope we can do it again soon.

---

I'm in love with George Clooney! I am. I'm shaking as I write this, can you tell, I hope my handwriting isn't too wobbly, but I'm so relieved too. Just to let it out. I love you, George. Let me tell you why I love him. I love his body, no not like that. I love his eyes. I love his teeth. I love his neck. I love his nose. I love his face, it's a kind face, and I know George has had to do some bad things, I know that's why I'm here, but you can tell from his face he doesn't really want to, and there are some people out there who don't do bad things but their faces aren't kind and you can tell they'd *like* to do bad things but can't get round to it and I think that's worse somehow. It's a nice face and I love the way it smiles. I love his arms. I love his chest. I love his stomach. I love his hands. I love the way he's got bits of hair growing on his hands. I love his legs, I haven't seen much of his legs yet, but it's February and it's cold and I can't wait for summer when it gets hot and he'll get into his shorts. I love his hair, I want to run my fingers through it, I bet it tastes like butterscotch. I don't just love his body. I love his voice. I love his smell, it's a nice smell, I can't work out what it is yet I'll come back. I love the way he cuts up all my food for me in the kitchen. I love the way when he locks me in my room he smiles first and says good night and then he turns the key quite slowly so that it feels like he doesn't want to say goodbye yet. I love the way last night we watched *Friends* again and it was a better episode this time, Chandler and Joey were funny and it didn't have the monkey in it. And George didn't laugh at it, and nor did I, we let the TV do the laughing work for us. And after *Friends* George turned over and we watched the weather and then a documentary about plastic surgery, I don't know how people can go through that. And there was a late film and George said did I feel like staying up for it? And I said yes because it was nice just sitting there with him and being close to him and smelling him and I bet his hair tastes like butterscotch. And during the film George leaned over and he kissed me and he said sorry sorry was he being too forward and I said no he wasn't and he gave me that smile I love and took my hand in his hand with all the hairs on it. And he took me to his bedroom. And I thought it'd be like mine with all the old stripy wallpaper but it wasn't, there were silks and rugs and mirrors on the ceiling and a big four poster bed. And he put me on the bed and it was the softest bed I'd ever felt and the sheets were like velvet they were like butterscotch. And we made love right there and then he was gentle but not too gentle and he was rough but not too much, he was in me and through me and George was all around me and all about me and there was nothing but George. And then he kissed me on the lips gentle and rough and that was the nicest thing of all and told me I was the best he'd ever had and that was a nice thing to hear because he is George Clooney after all. And then he took me back to my bedroom and said good night and did that slow key thing and I wrote all this. I love you, George. I'd marry you if I weren't married already.

---

I remember what he smells like. It's sweat. But a nice sweat, I love it.

---

George is a bit cross with me and making me write this. He wants me to say that what I wrote last night wasn't true. Well, some of it's true, watching *Friends* was true and it didn't have the monkey in it is true and the plastic surgery documentary is true. But nothing about the sex. George wants me to point that out. He said he'd be in enough trouble as it is for what he'd done without lies, and I said the sex was very loving and he said he didn't think the police would see it that way. So sorry I made that part up. And he wants me to say I made up the bit about being in love with him too. So sorry I made that up. (But I didn't, it's true, I love George Clooney.) And he said what was this about August, it'd all be over long before then, it should be over by now, why wasn't there anything on the news about it? And that he thought I should take out my pad and my pencil and write a letter to Paul or to Daddy and say what George wanted. He'd written one but they'd just ignored it, from me they'd know it was real and he meant business. And I said no. He looked surprised. So was I. I couldn't imagine saying no to George Clooney. But this pad and this pencil are for writing to

*George*, these are love letters to him only. I'm not going to write to my husband with them, that would be cheap and nasty. And George got cross again and said that if I didn't write the letter he'd punish me, I wouldn't be allowed to watch TV anymore and I said good, that plastic surgery thing was horrible it had given me nightmares, doing things to their breasts and to their lips, I don't know how people can go through that. And he promised if I wrote the letter he'd buy me some butterscotch, he thought I might like that, and I said I'd write it if I got the butterscotch first and he thought about it and then said yes. So I'm locked in my room again and he's at the supermarket and I'm having a nice dessert tonight and I'm meant to be writing the letter now but I'm writing this instead and I'm telling you now I won't write the letter even so. I don't love Paul anymore, I love George. When George took me I wanted Paul at first, and Jessie, and Daddy, but if they wanted me they'd have come and got me by now, they wouldn't have let this happen. They don't deserve me the way George does. And I'll try and eat all the butterscotch before George reads this or he'll know I was breaking my promise and take the butterscotch away, sorry George sorry. But what we have, George, is good and pure, and I can't let you spoil that, George, I'll doing this for you, George, it's for you, George. When I think of what I wrote about you at first on that toilet paper it makes me ashamed. Hurtful things. I'll never do anything to hurt you again.

---

I've been a very naughty girl, and I'm sorry, properly sorry this time not like last time. And George was quite right to be angry and do what he did, and to be fair he only hit me the once and that was to get me to shut up. It's not entirely my fault, though, I'm not trying to get out of it, but I'd never have thought of the pencil if he hadn't put the idea in my head in the first place. But then George points out that I must have been writing with the side of the pencil, trying to sharpen it to a point, I must have been planning it quite on purpose, so I don't know what to think. After I stuck the pencil in his throat I didn't wait around, he was making a strange squealing noise I didn't like at all, and there was blood everywhere. Besides I was trying to escape. I rushed for the front door and I think that's where I made my big mistake, because it's in a room I hadn't seen before, I'd arrived with that blindfold on, and I wasted too much time looking around and taking it in. Then I remembered that George was behind me, I could hear the squealing closer, and I got the chain off the door and got to turn the key but didn't get to do the bolts before he reached me. And I suppose if I hadn't been distracted by that new wallpaper and stopped to count the stripes I might have got outside. As I say he only hit me the once and he didn't break the skin, and I think that was fair because I'd certainly broken his there was blood everywhere I don't like blood. And we didn't watch *Friends* for days, and he didn't let me have my pad and my pencil either, not for days. But the pencil hadn't been that sharp, I hadn't killed him or anything, and George is such a kind man he forgave me in the end. He gave me back my pad, as you can see, and he gave me back my pencil, but he makes sure that I only write when he's there to watch, but I like that better, it's nice to have his company. And we were watching the news tonight and something lovely happened, it said that Paul was dead. Paul was dead, and so was Jessie, and so was Daddy, and it was okay, it was all quite painless, they wouldn't have felt a thing. This meant I was a free woman I said, and George turned to me and smiled and said that was all he was waiting for, and he took out a ring. Diamonds I think yes, and he got on his knees and proposed and of course I said yes. We went to his room and made love again, and it was even better this time now we were engaged, it was official and everything. And I told him I was sorry I had tried to run away. And he said it was okay, and he kissed me, and told me that if I ever tried anything like that again with the pencil he'd be forced to kill me. And then he held me in his arms, all night long in his arms around me, never leaving me, except for the bit in the middle I got up to write this.

---

George has started smoking. He'd stopped years ago he said, but he's been feeling tense. He looks tense too. And at night I can hear him walking and making the floorboards creak, I don't think he's sleeping much. I wasn't sure at first how I felt about the smoking. Daddy used to smoke, but stopped when they made it bad for you, and Paul doesn't smoke, and Jessie doesn't smoke, and I don't think Paul and I would have let her anyway. But I don't know, I think I like it with George. It makes him look rugged. He's asking me why no one's reported my disappearance, don't my family want me back? And I said that Paul probably knew I wasn't in love with him anymore and was doing the decent thing. That didn't make him any less tense, not one bit. I asked him if I could cook dinner for him to help him unwind, and he looked at me a bit strangely then sort of shrugged and said why not. It was lovely to see the kitchen, all the saucepans and spoons and knives and sieves, all silver and gleaming, it quite took my breath away. He wouldn't let me do any of the sharp stuff, but it was nice us doing the meal together and I made him my specialty. We ate our beans and chips in the sitting room and I think George enjoyed it as much as I did. Afterwards he lit a cigarette and I asked if I could have one, a little shyly actually. And he said he'd nearly finished the packet he needed them, but he'd get some more tomorrow, a lot more, I could have one of those. And I told him they made him look rugged. And that I loved him so much, I loved his hands and his teeth and his neck, I loved his arms, all I didn't love was his moustache, George Clooney didn't have a moustache, the real George Clooney, it spoiled the effect, it spoiled everything. He didn't say anything for a while, just sat there and smoked. I asked him if he was all right. And he said he was just working out what to do now. What should he do now? And I told him not to worry, I'd take care of the washing up for once. And I did.

----

I'm worried about George. He's behaving very oddly. He hardly said a word when he let me out for breakfast, and he didn't touch his Rice Krispies. He smoked the last of his cigarettes, then said he was going out to buy some more, and locked me in my room. When he let me out for lunch I told him he'd promised me I could have a cigarette today, and he didn't say anything for a while, then handed me the packet. He lit it for me. I'd never smoked before and it was pretty horrid but I worked out it wasn't quite so bad if you don't put it in your mouth. I asked him if I looked rugged and he said he didn't know, so I asked if he could take me to the bathroom so I could look in the mirror, and we went and looked and I don't think I looked especially rugged, not like George does. But then I'm not sure I want to look rugged, so long as one of us is rugged that's all right with me, I asked George if he could do the rugged stuff on his own and he said sure. I told him that when we had a baby we'd see how it went, if it were a Jessie we wouldn't let it smoke, but we would if it were a Jimmy, he could be rugged like his father, we'd start him young, we'd start him right away. I asked him when he thought we could get to work on that, the whole baby idea. He didn't say anything for a while again and then said he needed to go out.

I asked him why and he said he needed some cigarettes. I pointed out he'd only just bought some and then asked if he was getting extra in for Jimmy and he said yes that was it. He took off in the car so quickly it didn't dawn on me for a while he'd forgotten to lock me in my room. That was very exciting. I could go to the bathroom when I liked, I could turn on the TV and watch whatever I wanted, there was nothing good on though. I even opened the door to his bedroom, I hadn't been inside and my heart was pounding, I was so excited, and it was everything I hoped it would be, it had the silks and the mirrors and the four poster bed, I couldn't wait for George to come home with his cigarettes so we could start making babies there. And eventually it occurred to me I could open the front door if I wanted to, and that the bolts weren't drawn and the chain wasn't on, I could get outside if I wanted to. Get some fresh air maybe. But I didn't want to. Not really. It wouldn't smell of George out there. I wanted George. I want George. I hope he's back soon. He's been gone hours, I hope he hasn't got lost. If he's not home soon he'll miss *Friends* and his beans and chips are getting cold.

---

George woke me up with a shout. He didn't scream of course, George Clooney wouldn't scream, but it was a definite shout. I went to see if he was all right. He seemed very upset. He told me that he'd been in Belgium. I said that was nice, what had Belgium been like and he said he didn't give a shit about Belgium, Belgium was just as far as his car had taken him before he needed to sleep for the night. It was impossible, how could he be back here? I said that maybe he'd only been pretending to be in Belgium, I did that sometimes, when I got bored I made up stories and sometimes they seemed almost real. Though, as far as I could recall, never stories about Belgium. And why was I still here, he asked, didn't I realize it was over, he'd set me free? and he shouted a bit. He went to the front door and opened it and told me that I could go, what was I waiting for? It was over. And I hadn't wanted to go outside yesterday when George was gone, I certainly didn't see the point now he was here. And I told him that wasn't how love worked, you couldn't just open someone's heart and close it again when you'd had enough, I would always be waiting for him, I was his life now, there was no escape. He told me to leave and I said I wouldn't. He called me a stupid bitch and I forgave him, I forgive you George I know you're very tense right now, but I'm not sure you should be encouraged, I may have to punish you for that. He went to the kitchen, came back with a knife, kept on jabbing at me with it. He said he didn't want to hurt me, he'd never wanted to hurt me, had he? He hadn't hurt me, not much? I agreed, and said that it was his very tenderness that had captured my love, his very distinctive rugged tenderness. I'll kill you, George said I'll kill you if I have to, and I told him that Paul had killed me once, or maybe he'd just tried to kill me, it was so long ago this was before we had Jessie and became a proper family and Paul realized he loved me after all and George would feel the same when we had a proper family George just you wait and see, and then George killed me.

———————————

George Clooney screamed. I thought that was disappointing. I do hope he doesn't disappoint me again. I poured him his breakfast cereal but he wasn't hungry. He told me that this time he'd nearly made it to America, after he'd killed me he'd locked my body in the bedroom then gone straight to the airport then caught the next flight out, he'd only shut his eyes for a little nap and here he was again. He was very upset by this and I felt very sorry for him. He asked to be freed. Please let me go, he said. I'd let Paul go, hadn't I? But Paul was a special case, I said, how many times do you get gazumped in your affections by George Clooney? I couldn't just *stop* loving George, I told him, it wasn't like a tap, it was real this love it wouldn't be denied. But if he did everything I told him to, I'd do my very best, I promised, I'd harden my heart to him, I'd try to get bored of him and let my passion for him die. What did he have to do, he asked. Convince me that you love me, I said. That you live for me, that you live only for me, you won't try to run again, will you George, that isn't love, but I'll lock you in your room anyway from now on, I know how hard it can be sometimes to do the right thing and listen to what your heart wants. Love me blindly love me desperately love me entirely love me without end or hope of end. And maybe I'll get bored of your love, what's more boring than that? And finish your breakfast. I'd made him his breakfast, the least he could do was to finish it. He ate his Krispies, and then I poured him a second bowl, and then a third, and then more, I could have made him eat those Krispies all day but then I got bored, you see George, I can get bored, there's hope for you yet. Then I kissed him, hard on the lips. I told him he was allowed to respond. I loved him, I said. I loved his hands and I loved his eyes and I loved his teeth but the only thing

I didn't love was his moustache. In fact I disliked it. In fact I hated it. In fact the very sight of it made me want to hurt him. George Clooney didn't have a moustache, my George would be better off without one, my George would be safer. And he said he'd shave it off right away, and I said no, I couldn't trust him with sharp objects, not anymore. I'd have to shave it off for him. I fetched a knife from the kitchen. He asked for shaving cream and I said there was no need for that and he began to cry and I told him that he had to keep still he mustn't flinch, if he kept still and didn't flinch I wouldn't cut him, but he was crying so much he flinched so I did cut him, I took off his upper lip. I don't like blood, I'm scared of blood, but sacrifices have to be made. He looked a bit funny now without a lip but at least he was also without a moustache, it's not such a bad trade off. And now I told him I wanted us to make love, I wanted to have butterscotch love. I wanted him inside me, not one scrap of him could get away, and to make the point I took the gobbet of flesh that had been his lip and popped it in my mouth and swallowed it down. And he threw up, and I'm sure I don't know why, I was the one who had eaten the disgusting thing. We had sex, and it wasn't as good as I remembered it, and I made allowances I knew he was scared and confused, and bleeding quite badly actually—but it was all right, I closed my eyes and I pictured the four poster bed and the mirrors and even a fountain, why not, a little fountain in the corner, and I smelled him and he smelled of sweat but it was nice, it was a good sweat really, I love it.

---

I'm not convinced yet but he's at least trying hard. The effort he puts in is quite touching. I cut up his food for him and he always looks so grateful and says please and thank you, and I keep his hands tied for the meal so I have to feed him every single mouthful and he always remembers what I told him and to smile after each bite. If I'm stricter with him than he was, it's just because I love him more than he did me, I see that now, but he'll learn, there's so much time to learn. Sometimes I'll let him out of his room when *Friends* is on, though he hasn't actually *watched* one yet, I keep the blindfold on, he doesn't mind, he's lucky, the best bit is hearing the audience laugh and wondering why. And I light him cigarettes and let him puff away, he looks rugged like that, and I don't let him hold the cigarette because it might burn him, and I suppose that having it fed to him like a baby cuts down a little on the ruggedness but I can pretend I'm good at pretending I'm so good at it. Sometimes I get him to smoke a whole pack in one go to see if he'll be sick, and sometimes he is. And at other times we'll make love. And when he's not busy with the eating and the smoking and the sex he's got a job to keep him occupied. He sits in his bedroom and writes me letters. Just to let me know what he feels for me, to show me I'm his one and only. This is his latest:

*I love*

*you*

and they're getting better, I don't accept them unless they're neat and tidy. I haven't given him a pad yet, and I'm not sure I ever will. Writing on toilet paper is slow work, but it makes you really think about what you want to say. And you have to be careful, because toilet paper breaks so very easily.

# Damned If You Don't

"I want to make a complaint."

And Martin felt a thrill of courage, and for just a moment the first sensation of actual happiness since he'd arrived in this God-forsaken place. Here he was, always rather a timid man—both in the bedroom and in the boardroom, which is why he'd never accomplished much in either, but Moira had never complained, bless her, and even if he'd never had the smarts to rise to managing director like everyone else his age at least he'd never been sacked or demoted or what was the word they used now, yes, *reassigned*, no, they'd always kept him on, he was just too solid to lose. Solid, that's what Martin was, steadfast, reliable. But timid. Never one to rock the boat. And yet, here he was, all five foot three of him, squaring up aggressively to someone who must have been at least eight foot tall. And that wasn't even counting the horns.

Of course, Martin realized, in that split second when he felt so brave, he wasn't being as brave as all that. He'd chosen this demon specifically. Yes, he was eight foot tall, but that was distinctly diminutive for a demon since the rest of them were much larger and more ferocious. And there was a blond tuft around the demon's horns which made him look almost endearing.

The demon turned both of his red rheumy eyes on to Martin. He didn't encourage him to go on, but neither did he *discourage* him, which was all to the good. Martin floundered anyway. He'd been so intent on summoning up the nerve to start complaining he hadn't given much thought on how to continue.

"It's my roommate. I'm not happy with my roommate," said Martin.

"I didn't even know we'd be *getting* roommates. I haven't shared a room with anyone in forty years, not counting Moira. And Moira was bad enough with her snoring, I used to have to wear ear plugs. I don't suppose I could have a room to myself? No, okay, too much to hope for. But if I'm going to be here for a long time, and I think that's the idea, I should at least get a better roommate. Not that one. It's just . . ." and here he ran out of words for a moment, and then found a feeble conclusion, ". . . not on."

The demon looked as if he were going to say something very cutting, then changed his mind, deciding that eternity was long enough as it was. "Martin Travers," he boomed.

"You know my name?"

"I know everyone's name. Your roommate has been especially selected for you."

"Right," said Martin. "I see. Right. And how . . ." and he felt a bit of the old fire coming back; he'd come this far, he might not get the courage again, "how exactly was he chosen? A lucky dip or, or, or what? I mean, I'm just saying. I don't think there was much thought to it. That's all."

"Your roommate is very clean," said the demon.

"Yes."

"Doesn't smell. A friendly personality. Snores much less than this Moira of whom you speak."

"Right. Good, I'm sure . . ."

"Frankly," said the demon, dropping some of the booming cadence from his voice, "you're in Hell, and you could have done a lot worse, mate."

"But he's a dog."

"He is indeed."

"I'm not trying to make a fuss," said Martin. "But I deserve a human at least. Surely. I mean, I could do better than a dog. I'm not a, for God's sake . . . I'm not a murderer or anything . . ."

The demon shrugged. "Everyone's equal here. No segregation based on gender, race, age, sex . . . or species." He grunted and leaned forward confidentially—Martin felt a little nauseous as he was caught in an exhalation of fetid breath. "Personally, I preferred it in the old days. Lutherans on one side, Calvinists on the other, and never the twain shall meet. What we've got now . . ." He waved a claw disparagingly at nothing in particular but the whole denizens of Hell, "It's just political correctness gone mad."

"The thing about dogs is they make me itch."

The demon sucked air through his teeth in what was actually intended to be a gesture of sympathy, but sounded instead like a terrifying death rattle. Martin recoiled as if he'd been struck.

"I'll see what I can do," he rumbled. "Okay? But I'm not promising anything."

"Thanks," said Martin. And unsure what else to do now, nodded, made an attempt at a friendly smile, and went back to his room.

The demon watched him go. He wished all the damned would leave him alone. All the bigger demons laughed at him about it. It was that tuft of hair over the horns that did it. Every night he'd shave it off, but by morning the bloody thing would always have grown back.

––––––––––

The dog was waiting for him.

"Are you all right?" he said. "You just took off without a word. I was worried."

The funny thing was, it was only if you looked at him full on you could tell he even was a dog. Try out of the corner of your eye, or stand to him sideways, he seemed to be just another faded soul bouncing around in eternal damnation.

"I'm sorry," said Martin. "I was just a bit . . . you know."

"I do know," said the dog. "It takes a while to get used to! Don't worry about it." And he gave a friendly little smile, then panted cheerfully with his tongue hanging out. "What's your name?"

"Martin," said Martin.

"Nice to meet you, Martin," said the dog politely, and offered his paw to shake. "My name's Woofie."

"Vuffi?"

"No, Woofie. I'm German."

"Ah."

"Yeah."

They smiled politely at each other.

"I've never been to Germany," said Martin.

"Oh, it's nice," said Woofie. "Well, bits of it."

"Yes."

"Rains sometimes, mind you. And gets a bit nippy in the winter."

"Same as anywhere, I suppose."

"Yeah, I suppose," said Woofie, and smiled. "Still, I liked it."

They smiled politely at each other again, and Woofie even affected a friendly tail wag. Martin would have done the same, had he had a tail.

---

"Anyway," said Woofie. "I don't want to get in your way. You know, but if there's anything you need . . ."

"Thanks."

"Make yourself at home. Well, it *is* now. Do you have a preference . . . ?" he added, nodding at the bunk beds.

"Oh, I don't want to impose," said Martin.

"It's no problem. Whichever one you want. All these years here, I've been in both. I'm happy either way. Don't worry," Woofie said, perhaps seeing the involuntary look of disgust on Martin's face, "I don't moult. And they're clean sheets."

"Well, I suppose the top one might be more fun," said Martin. "If you're sure you don't mind."

"Hey," said Woofie generously, "I know what it's like to be the new guy. We've all been there. Anything I can do to make it easier. There's a spare wardrobe over there, it's all yours. Washbasin in the corner."

"What about the toilet . . . ?"

"We never need to go," said Woofie. "Funny that. First couple of days I was here I was frantic looking for a litter tray or something, til I realized I didn't need one. And yet they give us a washbasin. I've never quite worked that one out."

Woofie politely offered Martin use of the sink before they went to bed, but Martin let him go first. He watched his new roommate wash his fur, and brush his fangs, and a part of him thought he was about to scream and the scream would never stop, *I can't be in Hell with a dachshund*. Woofie wiped the sink clear of his gobbets of toothpaste, looked up at Martin. "It's free when you want it."

As Martin washed, he looked into the mirror. He stared at this timid little dead man, standing at five foot three. And if he tilted his head all the features he recognized vanished, and he saw a soul like any other. Every day, he realized, he'd look in this mirror when he washed, and he'd never be able to forget that he was dead, that he'd only ever been meat hanging on a frame, and that the meat was now rotting and the frame could be seen underneath. That's why Hell came equipped with washbasins. Not because of the sink, but the mirror. Martin sighed heavily, and all the stale meat of his face wobbled, and the soul framework dimmed a little. He heard Woofie let out a little snore, already asleep and dead to the world. And he didn't know why, but it reassured him, just a bit.

---

For the next few days, Martin waited for the tortures to start.

"It doesn't quite work like that, though," said Woofie. "I'm not saying there *aren't* tortures, but I've been here for ages and no one's started on me yet. I don't like to say anything in case it reminds them."

In the mean time there were the shopping malls to wander around. None of the shops were ever actually open, but Martin didn't have money to buy anything anyway, and it was reasonably good fun to look through the windows. There was a nice local cinema which screened films every evening, some of them even only a few months after general release. And Woofie kindly invited Martin to join his bowling team. They'd all go bowling three or four nights a week, and some of the players were really rather good. They were all dogs, and seemed a little reserved around Martin because he was a human. Martin felt a bit offended by that—if there were any qualms to be had, he should be the one having them. But none of the dogs said anything for Woofie's sake, and after Martin bowled his first strike, after a week of practice, all their congratulations seemed genuine enough.

"It's like the holiday village I once stayed at in Lanzarote," said Martin. "Hell isn't so bad."

But of course it was.

"What are you in here for?" Martin asked his roommate once, as they were getting ready for bed. He wasn't especially curious. Just making conversation.

It was the first time he'd ever seen Woofie irritated. "That's not a very polite thing to ask, Martin."

"Oh. I'm sorry."

"It's okay."

But a few days later, as they were riding the mall escalator up and down for kicks, he asked him again.

Woofie sighed. "Tell me what *you're* in for first."

Martin was more than happy to do so—in fact, he'd just been waiting for the excuse to let it all out. "It's because I don't believe in God, apparently. They told me that when I arrived."

"Uh-hum."

"The thing is, I thought I *did*. I went to church most weeks, you know. Always thought there was some sort of higher presence or something."

"Uh-hum."

"Turns out I only believed I believed. But actually I didn't."

"They hate it when you're wishy-washy," said the dog. "You'd have been better off not believing in God at all. They'd have respected that."

"I wouldn't have gone to Hell?"

"Oh yes. But you'd have been able to sleep in on Sundays." And then Woofie told Martin the reason why *he* was in Hell.

Martin was surprised and impressed.

"Don't be impressed," said Woofie. "It's nothing to be impressed about."

"It seems a bit unfair," suggested Martin gently.

"It *is* unfair. Most dogs go to Hell because they weren't kind to their masters. They bit them. Or wouldn't come when they called. Or wouldn't chase the sticks they'd throw. Dogs not doing what dogs are meant to do."

"Yes, I can see that."

"And I'm here because I *didn't* bite him. Frankly, I was damned right from the start. If I'd been lacking in my dogly duties, straight to Hell, no questions asked. But as a good dog, loving and patient to my master, I was serving Adolf Hitler."

"So, really," said Martin, "it's just guilt by association."

"Yeah," said Woofie. "When he told me to fetch a stick, I was just following orders."

"Did you tell them that?"

"Of course I did. They said that's what *everybody* said. Throughout history, the same feeble excuse. So," and he gestured with his paws at Hell, "this is where I finish up." As it turned out, he was gesturing at the time towards a Virgin Megastore, but the point was still made.

"I can see why you'd be bitter about that," said Martin.

"Oh, I don't know," said the dog, and he shrugged. "If I'm going to be damned anyway, it might as well be for something impressive. . . . It *is* impressive, isn't it, really?" he asked shyly.

"It is impressive."

"I said you looked impressed."

"You did and I was."

"You know Strudel the poodle, who won the bowling last night? He'd belonged to Goering. I mean, just think. Bloody *Goering*. How embarrassing." Woofie allowed himself a proud smile. "If you're going to be in Hell because you were once the prized pet of a Nazi, better to be Hitler's than some jumped up SS Kommandant with ideas above his station."

"I take your point," said Martin, and for a moment felt embarrassed that the evil which had sentenced him had been so banal in comparison.

"I can't stop looking back," said Woofie. "I feel guilty. Of course I do. I think, if only I had been a better dog, maybe I'd have been a more calming influence."

"No," said Martin.

"If I'd distracted him for just one more hour with my squeaky toys, that would have been another hour he wasn't dreaming up death camps . . ."

"You can't think like that," said Martin. "What could you have done? Nothing, you could have done nothing."

"I hope this won't make a difference between the two of us," said Woofie. And he reached out for Martin's hand with his paw.

Without thinking twice, Martin squeezed it. "Of course not," he said. "It doesn't. Really, really."

Martin didn't bring the matter up again. They bowled together as usual, watched the same movies, took turns to use the washbasin. And, if anything, Woofie seemed more relaxed around his roommate. The polite friendship was replaced by something warmer and more honest; Woofie let down his guard and beneath the affable doggy exterior there was a really sharp sense of humour. His mocking impersonations of the rest of the bowling team, all done behind their backs, used to have Martin in stitches—they were cruel, but so accurate, especially the way he imitated Rudolf's stutter or Ludwig's limp. And it all helped single Martin out as his *special* friend, the one he would never laugh at privately, the one that he truly took seriously. Martin felt quite proud of that.

"You may as well get it over with," said Woofie one night. The lights were out, but Martin couldn't sleep, and he was pleased to hear the voice of his friend rise from the bunk beneath him. "Ask me what he was like."

"Who?"

"Who do you think? Come on. Everyone always wants to ask. It's all right."

"All right. What was Hitler like?"

"He was okay," said Woofie. "Quite generous with treats. Didn't like me lying on the bed, but was usually good for the odd lap. Even as I got older and fatter, he never minded me climbing on to the lap for a cuddle. He wasn't a bad master at all. Of course," he added reflectively, "he had his bad days. When he got things on his mind, and he did a lot, actually, as time went on. Then sometimes he wouldn't find the time for walkies. But, you know. He did his best."

There was silence.

"And at this point everyone asks whether I knew I was being fed and petted by an evil man. Go on, ask it."

"I don't want . . ."

"It's all right, really."

So Martin asked the obvious.

"I was his first dog, his childhood pet. So you've got to bear in mind that when I came on the scene he hadn't done anything yet. Well, anything that was particularly *evil*. He'd done a few things that were *naughty*, but really, refusing to eat your greens, or reading under the bed covers after lights out, or graffitiing over pictures of Otto von Bismarck . . . I mean, you wouldn't say that was especially untoward. I know what you're going to say. That surely I could have seen *something* there. The seeds of the man to come. Say it, you might as well."

"Did you see the seeds of the man to come?"

Woofie paused. "Do you know, Martin, no one's ever asked me that before?"

"Really?"

"I'll have to think about that." And so he did. And then, at last, the voice gentle in the darkness:

"It's not as if he ever had the chance to discuss matters of state with me. But I don't think he'd have been ashamed. I dare say he'd have explained the need to burn the Reichstag, or invade Czechoslovakia, he'd have explained the concentration camps. I'd have only had to ask. I honestly think he was just doing his best. Muddling through, like the rest of us. Trying to be a good person. I'm not saying all his decisions were *good* ones. And that he didn't get carried away. Who wouldn't, you or I in the same position, who wouldn't? But people think of him as a demon. And he wasn't. Well, we know what demons look like. And he was just a man, you know. Just a man with his dog. Like you and me. Well, like you, anyway. Yes," Woofie said softly, as he thought about it, "Adolf Hitler was a lot like you."

"Thanks," said Martin, and meant it.

"Why didn't you want to ask? No one else has left it for so long."

"I just supposed," said Martin, "that it must get a bit irritating.

Always being in his shadow. People never asking you about *you*, only the famous person you hung out with."

There was silence for a while.

"But I was in his shadow," said Woofie. "I was his dog."

More silence. For a while Martin thought Woofie had fallen asleep. And then:

"Thanks, though. That's really thoughtful of you. Thanks."

"That's okay."

"You're my best friend."

"You're my best friend too, actually."

"We can cuddle if you like," said Woofie. "I don't mean anything funny," he added hastily, "just cuddling. If you like. I mean, there's nothing funny about a man and his dog sleeping together, is there? If you like."

"I'm not sure there's room," said Martin slowly.

But there was room, if Martin leant into the wall a bit. And Woofie wasn't very big, he curled into the spaces left by Martin's body as if they'd always been designed to fit together like this. If Martin laid against Woofie sideways he was rubbing against his soul, but face on he could feel his fur, and the warmth of it was more comforting than he could have believed.

"Good night, Martin," said Woofie softly.

"Night." And within minutes Martin heard the snoring that told him his new best friend was asleep. And he had only a few moments to realize how reassuring that snoring was, how much gentler than Moira's, how much more *right*, before he was fast asleep too.

---

"Good news," boomed the demon. "You're being transferred tomorrow morning."

Martin tried to work out how he should respond. "Oh," he said eventually.

"Well, don't look too bloody grateful," muttered the demon as he stomped off. He was having a rotten day already. Since he couldn't shave the tufts of fur round his horns, he'd set about plucking them out with a pair of tweezers. This only succeeded in drawing attention to them still further, and the overall effect made him look a bit camp. He rather suspected—accurately, in fact—that behind his back in the staff room the piss was being ripped out of him quite mercilessly.

Martin wondered how he should break the news to Woofie. But that was the one thing he needn't have worried about. He was waiting for him when he got back, the body unnaturally tense. Martin thought he might have been crying.

"Hello," said Martin, for want of anything better to say. Then, "I'm sorry."

"Was it something I've done?"

"No. No, that's not it."

"What is it? Just tell me what I ever did that was wrong."

"It's not you, Woofie. I'm sorry. It's me. It's my fault, it's *me*, I'm sorry."

Woofie looked so sad, with his big dog watery eyes boring into him. Martin wished he'd be angry—bark at him, nip at his ankles, *anything*. Anything other than this quiet and this hurt.

At last Woofie said, "Is it because of the whole Hitler thing?"

"No," Martin hastened to reassure him. "It's because you're a dog."

Silence.

"It's nothing personal."

Silence. For the first time since he'd met him, the dog made Martin itch.

"So it's not because of what I've done. It's because of who I am."

"Well. Yes. Sort of."

Woofie stared at him. "That's sick."

"Yes," said Martin. "It is. I'm sorry. Is there . . . is there anything you'd like? Anything I can do, or . . ."

"No," said Woofie. And then he changed his mind. "Yes," he said gently. "I'd like my bunk back. The top bunk. My favourite bunk. And all to myself. Please."

So that night Martin slept on the bottom bunk. Woofie hadn't spoken again all evening, and he stared up at the little sagging mound from the bed above him, and he wanted to touch it, *prod* it, just to get some sort of reaction, even to have an argument, just so there could be an ending to this. But he didn't dare. In the morning, Woofie seemed kinder, even to have forgiven him.

"Best of luck, Martin," he said, and offered him his paw.

"And best of luck to you too," said Martin warmly. "And thank you for everything." He made to give him a little pat on the head, but Woofie stepped backwards instinctively. He'd gone too far.

Martin's new roommate was a human called Steve. Steve was very polite and almost friendly. He didn't give Martin the top bunk, but really, why should he have? It turned out that Steve was a rapist. But, as he told Martin, it had only been the once, and it was a long time ago, and he felt very sorry about it. And besides, Martin didn't know the child in question, so he decided not to be bothered about it.

And Steve let Martin hang out with his friends. At the shopping malls, at the cinema, at the bowling alley. It had been a long time since Martin had spent time in the company of humans, but he soon adjusted. Inevitably there were occasions when he'd almost run into Woofie: the first time was a bit awkward, and he could see that Strudel would happily have jumped at his throat. But Woofie barked something in his ear, and with bad grace Strudel turned his back on the fair weather human and got back to his ten pin bowling. And that was the worst of it. After that, whenever Woofie or Martin realized the other was near, they'd simply not make eye contact as discreetly as possible. It was never not embarrassing—but it was an embarrassment that Martin could handle with increasing ease as the years went by.

It may have been on his third or fourth Christmas in Hell that Martin received a card. "Something addressed just to you," said Steve with a sniff, as he handed it to him. Most of the cards would say "Steve and Martin," and one or two might be for "Martin and Steve." Never Martin on his own.

"Dear Martin," it said. "Long time no speak!" And the exclamation mark dot was a happy face, just trying a bit too hard.

Martin took a breather from hanging the tinsel—Christmas decorations are always very popular in Hell—sat on the bunk, and read the card properly.

> Dear Martin,
> Long time no speak! How are you? It's been ages.
> This is just to wish you a merry Christmas, and let you know an old friend is thinking of you. Because we are old friends, aren't we? I know we've lost touch, but I didn't want you to think there were any hard feelings. There really aren't. I only want the best for you. I only ever did.
> I catch sight of you every once in a while, and I keep meaning to say hi. But either you look very busy, or I'm very busy, so it never happens. Which is so silly! We must catch up one day. That'd be lovely.
> All the old gang are well, and send you their best.
> Lots of love, Woofie.

And the "love" had been written with a hesitancy that made it all the more emphatic. And then, in a different pen, there was a P.S.

> *P.S. Look, if you're up for it, and I'm sure you have other plans anyway—but still, no harm in asking. We're thinking of having a party at New Year's. Nothing very fancy. If you've nothing better to do, and I dare say you have, do come along!*

And then, same pen, but written later:

> *I miss you.*

Martin reread it. He wondered if he should send a card back, but really, Steve took care of all that.

"Shall I hang it with the others?" said Steve, reaching out for it.

"Sure," said Martin. "Why not?"

And then, some time in January, the announcement came.

Hell was getting too full. There simply wasn't the space for many more damned souls. So someone had decided they had better send an emissary to God, and find out what should be done about it. And when he came back, the emissary said that he'd looked long and hard, and it turned out there *wasn't* a God after all. He wasn't sure there had never been one, but if there had, he certainly wasn't around any longer. And this had caused a bit of consternation—who was going to solve the overcrowding problem now?—until it was realized that his non-existence solved the problem in itself. After all, it seemed hardly fair to be damned for not believing in God if it turned out you were, embarrassingly enough, absolutely right.

Martin was told he could leave immediately.

"Where am I going now?" he asked. "Heaven?"

It turned out he was going to Surrey.

---

The day the dead came back to Earth was one of mixed emotion. Everyone seemed overjoyed to see their loved ones return; there were a lot of tearful reunions and a lot of street parties. The government weren't really sure how to react until they realized that on the whole everyone was very happy about it, so decided in the end they were happy about it too, and acted as if it had been their idea somehow.

But no one had quite anticipated that the dead weren't going to go back again. Had it just been a flying visit, then fair enough. But by the end of the week most people really felt that they'd outstayed their welcome. The government picked up on the prevailing mood and quickly asserted that they'd *never* been happy about this, that they'd had nothing to do with it whatsoever. And even that new measures would soon be taken against this unwanted invasion of the immigrant dead.

When Moira first saw Martin again, she hugged on to him so hard that he thought she'd never let go. She'd still kept all his clothes and belongings, suitcases full of old nick-knacks that she couldn't bear to part with. She said everyone had told her to give them all to Oxfam, and when she'd refused well-meaning friends had got rather angry with her and worried about her mental health. "So I got rid of them. I've been very lonely. But I knew you'd come back for me." Martin was touched. He didn't want to point out he wasn't back because of her at all but a bureaucratic quirk. "Thank God you came back." And that there was no God to thank, and if there had been there wouldn't have been the bureaucratic quirk in the first place. They made love that first night, and for several nights afterwards, something they hadn't done much even when he'd been alive. And it was surprisingly nice, but not so nice that he minded when they sunk back into their usual platonic domesticity. Within a week he was lying in bed next to her, blocking out the snoring with ear plugs. And in the dead of night, when all was still, he could almost believe that he'd never died and been to Hell at all.

At work, however, they weren't so accommodating. For old time's sake, the boss generously gave Martin ten minutes out of his hectic schedule. "And it is hectic at the moment!" he told Martin. "Busy, busy, busy! Well, I needn't tell you. You know what this job's like, you've lived it!" Martin was told that they would *love* to take him back, they *really* would, but they just *couldn't*, not in the present climate. "You can hardly expect to take a leave of absence that long, without any warning, and expect your job waiting when you get back." And besides, the boss admitted when pressed, not everyone felt very comfortable working alongside corpses. Not the boss himself, of course. But even Martin must admit, being one himself, there was something funny about the way they looked. Whereas once he'd been respected for being so reliable, so solid—now, in a very real sense, he wasn't solid anymore.

See the dead face on, and you could just about pretend they were normal—that they were living and breathing like all right-minded people. But turn your head to the side and you could see the soul, that all of this skin and bone and individuality was just a façade. It wasn't a thing anyone liked to be reminded of. And it meant that the dead were instantly recognisable. By and large the living would ignore them, some would glare at them with obvious hostility; there were even incidents of target beatings by gangs, but outbreaks of violence became rarer when it was realized you couldn't do anything to kill them. Within weeks the worst that a dead man walking the streets might expect was to be spat at.

Once upon a time, if you'd wanted to separate a race from the rest of society, to make a people stand out and be judged, you'd bring out the yellow badges, you'd start shaving heads. Woofie's masters had done it. But no one had to isolate the dead; with their souls flapping about for all to see, they'd done it to themselves. And the worst part of it was that they felt ashamed of each other too. A dead man seeing another dead man would turn his eyes in the same way as a living man would; once in a while there might pass a look of sympathy, of understanding, but they'd hurry on, not daring to talk to each other, not daring to reach out and say 'I am one of you'. As if for fear that the vacancy in their eyes, the deadness that had so much more to do with the heart no longer beating and the lungs no longer filling, might be what you looked like too.

Moira didn't like to mention to Martin the fact that he was very nearly two-dimensional. But even her discretion used to irritate him. She'd try to ignore it at first, then to make it go away. She'd make him his favourite meals, fried and fatty, and she'd say it was because she loved him, that she'd missed cooking for him, that she just wanted him to be happy. But he saw the truth.

"You're trying to fatten me up!" he said.

Moira blushed, and admitted that she thought he could do with a little padding out, his body might lose some of its *flatness*, if only if . . .

"But the food doesn't go anywhere. I eat it, then it vanishes. It doesn't stay in the stomach, I don't have a stomach. For God's sake, I can't even shit."

Moira cried, and said he'd changed, he'd never used to be like this, he didn't love her anymore since he'd changed.

And he wanted to say of course he'd bloody *changed*, he'd died, hadn't he? He'd died and gone to Hell, and she *hadn't* died, she'd just stayed cosily alive, what had they got in common anymore? He'd gone to Hell and fallen in love with someone else, he'd fallen in love with Hitler's dog. But he couldn't say this, even Martin couldn't be so cruel.

It gave him no pleasure to see his widow crying all the time, it just revolted him. "I can't even shit," he repeated numbly. And then, as an afterthought, "I want a dog."

Moira pointed out he didn't like dogs. He was allergic. They made him itch.

"I want a bloody dog," he said, "that's all I bloody want. Get me a bloody dog."

---

They called the new dog Wuffles. Martin had wanted to call it Woofie, but couldn't quite do it, it was all a bit too raw. Maybe in time he'd rename it, he didn't suppose the dog would mind. Moira had wanted to name him Snoopy, but Martin calmly pointed out that was a bloody stupid name, Snoopy was bloody stupid. Besides, Snoopy was a bloody beagle, wasn't he, and this wasn't a bloody beagle, it was a bloody dachshund, you stupid bitch, it was a bloody sodding buggering dachshund. And then he kissed her gently on the forehead and told her she'd done well, it was a lovely dog. And if she could now bloody well leave him alone to play with it.

The thing was, Wuffles didn't like Martin. He *loved* Moira—he'd wag even at the sound of her voice, wait outside the bedroom door for her, was never happier than when she was petting him or stroking him or touching him. From Martin he'd just recoil. Martin supposed he could see his soul, the same as everyone else. And he quite respected the dog for it—at least it wasn't a hypocrite.

Still, he'd try. He'd take Wuffles out for walks—*drag* Wuffles out for walks, pulling the resistant pet by the leash until it had no choice but to follow. They'd go to the woods. Martin would find a nice fat stick, and throw it.

"Fetch," he'd say.

Wuffles would just stare at him blankly.

"Fetch," Martin would repeat. "Fetch the stick."

Wuffles would look to where he'd thrown it, look back at him, then lie down. He wasn't going to chase after a stick. Not for *him*. For his mistress, anything. But for this flattened dead man, the dog refused to follow orders.

One day Martin dragged the dog to the car instead. They drove far far away. He opened the passenger door. Threw the stick he'd brought with him.

"Fetch," he said.

But Wuffles made it clear that if he wasn't prepared to chase a stick in the woods, he certainly wasn't inclined to do so on the hard shoulder of a motorway. So Martin pushed the dog out of the car anyway, and drove home without him.

Moira was distraught. "It's all right," he reassured her. "He'll be fine. There are lots of rabbits for him to chase out there, probably. And if he *isn't* fine . . . He was a good dog, he never bit or scratched. He loved his mistress. So at least he can be sure he's going to a happy place."

Martin never saw Wuffles again. But when a few weeks later he opened the door to a dachshund who had rung his doorbell, he thought that his unwanted pet had tracked him down. That he'd have to take him on an even longer journey up the M1.

"No, no," said the dog. "It's Woofie. How are you, Martin?"

"Woofie," repeated Martin. "I didn't recognize you."

"Well, it has been a long time. Can I come in?"

Once inside, Martin asked his old friend whether he wanted anything to eat or drink, wanted to sit down, wanted anything, really. "No, I'm fine," said Woofie. "Nice place you've got here. Very cosy."

"It's not mine, it's hers," said Martin. "It's nothing to do with me. How did you get out of Hell?"

"Oh, they're letting all sorts out now. I wouldn't be surprised if the whole thing hasn't shut down before too long."

"And how did you find me?"

Woofie smiled. "A dog can always find his master. If he wants to hard enough." He let his words sink in. "You do know you're my master, don't you?"

"Yes," said Martin.

"I only think sometimes. That if I'd met you. Right from the start. If I could have given my love to *you*, and not to Hitler . . . I'd never have gone to Hell in the first place. I could have been great. And I think, too, that with me there beside you, you wouldn't have gone to Hell either."

"No," said Martin.

"We could have been great, you and I. We could have been great."

And Martin kissed him. And he knew that what he was kissing was a dog, and that it was a *dead* dog, but it was all right, it didn't matter, it was all all right.

"Let's get out of here," said Martin. And he got his coat, locked the front door, and put the keys through the letterbox. He considered leaving a note for Moira—but really, what would he have said?

And man and dog went out together. They had no money for food, but that was okay, they had each other. They'd sleep when they got tired, on park benches, in shop doorways, wherever they could cuddle up. And people would avoid their gaze on the street as always, and some would still spit at them. But together man and dog had a strength. They would stare down their persecutors. They showed they weren't ashamed.

Early one morning they were shaken awake by an angry farmer. They'd decided to spend the night in an empty barn—the straw was scratchy but warm.

"Get out!" screamed the farmer, with a fury that was mostly fear. "Get off my property!" And he jabbed at them with the handle of his pitchfork.

"There's no need for that," said Martin. "We're going."

"You're filth!" the farmer shouted after them, as Martin and Woofie walked to the door with as much dignity as they could. "You dead bastards. You dead perverted . . . and on my property! You're filth!"

And, quick as a flash, Woofie turned round, leaped up, and tore out his throat.

Martin looked as surprised as the farmer, who, eyes bulged in shock, reached out for a neck that largely wasn't there, before pitching forward on to his face. The blood sprayed across the straw.

"Oh my God," said Martin, bending down. "He's dead."

"Good," said Woofie. "Now he knows what it feels like."

"Oh God, oh shit," said Martin.

"Come on, let's go," said Woofie.

———————————

They walked in silence for a while. Martin kept looking at his hands, and every time he did—yes—they were still smeared with blood.

"Oh God," he said at last. "It was an accident. It was an accident."

"It wasn't an accident," said Woofie. "I all but bit his head off."

"Oh God."

Nothing more was said for a few minutes. A man walked towards the pair down the footpath. He gave them the customary glare of hatred and contempt. And then he saw Martin's bloody hands, and the way Woofie openly snarled at him, and there was blood there too, right on the jaws—and he hurried on.

"What's going to happen to us?" Martin moaned.

"What are they going to do? Send us to Hell? Been there, done that."

"Oh God."

"Hitler was like this, you know," said Woofie. "The first time he had a Jew killed. Well, that's it, Woofie, he said. If I'm right, then I have made a blow for justice and the common man. But if I'm wrong . . . If I'm wrong, I'm damned forever.

"And do you know what I said? What I whispered into his ear. Oh, he couldn't hear me, of course. Dogs can't talk. But I whispered it anyway.

"If you're going to Hell for one Jew, then why not for a hundred? For a hundred thousand. For six million. If you're going to be damned anyway, at least be damned for something impressive. I'd rather be damned for being Hitler's dog than Goering's. Do you understand?"

"Yes," said Martin. "Oh God. I understand. Oh God."

"There isn't a God," said Woofie. "Stop saying that."

"Sorry."

"Do you realize by how much the dead outnumber the living? Do you? Thirty to one. And yet *we're* the outcasts. We're the ones who are spat at. How long do you think that can go on for? How long *should* it go on? Martin?"

"What?" said Martin weakly.

"How long?" demanded Woofie.

"I don't know."

"Then think about it," said Woofie sternly. "For once in your life, just think."

And Martin thought.

"But we mustn't hurt them, Woofie," he said eventually. "We can't do that. We should just put them . . . I don't know. Out of harm's way."

"For their own good."

"For their own good, exactly. Somewhere safe. Promise me, Woofie. Promise me, whatever happens. That what we'll be doing is good."

Woofie promised, Martin smiled, and on they walked. A man and his dog, making plans.

# SO
## PROUD

It had taken her long enough to get used to the idea he was her boyfriend. She kept on expecting him to open his eyes, realize there were other girls out there, prettier, smarter, go with them instead. And then that day he'd proposed, right out of the blue, and amid the excitement and the pride she'd also realized she'd have to start thinking of him as a fiancé now, it'd be another adjustment to make. But now here they were, they'd done the registry office, both families had got together without incident, there'd been none of the clashes they'd been expecting—hey, even the weather had stayed bright for the photographs. And as the cameras were trained on them, she looked at him, and thought, *husband* now, got to think of him as *husband*. That sounded good to her, the most right so far. He smiled at her, and she could see in that smile that he loved her; she'd got him now, *husband*, he wasn't going to get away. And in the relief of that moment, in that triumph, she realized at last that she loved him too.

There wasn't to be a honeymoon, they couldn't afford it. Maybe one day, he said, when they were rich. And she'd agreed, and pictured that in a few years' time, in a hotel in Marbella, somewhere with a beach, they'd look back and say, *this* is our honeymoon, and laugh, because by then they'd be rolling in money, *every* holiday could be a honeymoon. But there was still a treat in store, far better than a honeymoon could offer. His parents had spoken to her parents, and together they'd bought them a flat. It was a small flat, there was no point in pretending otherwise, but it was theirs, and they wouldn't be in anyone's spare rooms anymore. They climbed the stairs, unlocked the door, and they stood on the threshold of their new home. He asked, jokingly, if she wanted to be carried over the threshold, and she, jokily, said yes. And because neither of them could quite be sure how much the other was joking, they did it anyway; she lay back in his arms, and he heaved her bulk into the tiny kitchen. They both felt a bit self-conscious afterwards.

He said it really was *very* small, this place. Not enough room to swing a cat! And she laughed, and said they'd just have to make sure they didn't *get* a cat then, and he laughed, and said he didn't like cats anyway, he was allergic, and she laughed again, but realized with some little shock she'd never even known that, were there other things about him she didn't know? He looked at the hand-me-down furniture and the hand-me-down wallpaper and said it would have to do for the moment, they'd do better later. And he took her to the hand-me-down bed, and there they made love. And it *felt* like making love, too, she'd always thought of it as just sex before, something you did guiltily in the spare room hoping the parents wouldn't hear, but now he was her *husband*, wasn't he, and this was their home, wasn't it, this was Making Love. As he bounced around on her she imagined this was what Mummy and Daddy got up to, how they'd done it all these years, mature, legal, sanctified by wedding contract and local registrar. She squealed with pleasure throughout the whole thing, even when she really wasn't feeling very much anymore, even when frankly it was all over and the two of them were spent.

Maybe it was the squealing, or maybe the added frisson of being newly wed. But within a few days she realized she was pregnant. She called her mother to ask her advice, but her mother wasn't much help—she said the whole wretched business had been rather a long time ago, and she was really doing her best to forget all about it, thank you. The wife didn't mind; she liked the idea of another life inside her, and she wondered whom it would most look like, herself or her husband. The husband didn't look too happy when she told him though. He pointed out there wasn't even the room to swing a cat, hadn't he said they couldn't swing a cat? And a baby was even bigger than a cat, most likely. And the wife laughed and said they'd just have to take care not to swing the baby, and he sulked a bit and said it wasn't funny. And he asked her whether she really intended to go through with this, to alter their marriage so drastically even before it had started. Wasn't she thinking of aborting it? And she hadn't been, actually, but now she *did* think of it. She made herself a cup of tea in their hand-me-down kitchen with the hand-me-down kettle, and applied her mind to the notion. And she concluded it'd be rather a shame, wouldn't it?—and they'd never find out which of them the baby most looked like, she was looking forward to that, that would be the best bit. It'll be all right, she assured him, trying to coax him out of his sulk, they had each other, and they loved each other, and this baby was a *result* of that love, they'd love it too and care for it and not swing it around the cramped flat. They made love again that night, and the wife had to give him credit, the husband certainly put in as much effort as he normally would, you would hardly guess he was so angry.

The leaflet she got from the library was packed full of information and lots of colourful pictures. The wife thought the cartoon drawings made it all look very exciting, and could hardly wait to see what she was going to enjoy the most—the morning sickness, the strange hunger cravings, or watching her own belly button pop out. But she didn't have to wait the nine months she'd been promised. That Friday evening, as the married couple sat in front of the portable television, her waters broke. She told her husband she felt the most extraordinary urge to *push*, but he told her she was being ridiculous and went into the kitchen for a Diet Coke. But she pushed anyway, she lay on the floor and pushed and pushed, and she did it all very quickly; he hadn't made it back from the fridge before she gave birth. She felt it suck out from between her legs, and then the sort of physical relief she associated with having a really good belch. And she got to her feet to see what her new baby looked like. Her husband, on his return, almost dropped his Coke can.

It wasn't what either of them had expected. It wasn't a baby, or not a human baby, at any rate—instead, they were looking at a Chesterfield sofa. The wife couldn't help but wonder how something so big had been hiding in such a small place—because this wasn't one of your *small* Chesterfield sofas, no, this one was at least six foot long and three foot tall. It was covered with some strange thin gloop, and the wife worried that it might stain the leather upholstery—but it was all right, it was like cellophane wrapping, it came off in one easy tug. Now both husband and wife could see that it was a very good sofa indeed, high quality stuff, that—and the leather was coloured a fashionable dark green. Neither of them quite knew what to say for a while, until the wife remembered the leaflet she'd been reading, and suggested they cut the umbilical cord. So the husband dutifully went back into the kitchen for the scissors. And as he cut away, the wife looked her new baby over, from every angle the cutting would allow, and couldn't help but feel a little disappointed. The Chesterfield sofa didn't much look like *either* of its parents.

At first it was pleasing to have such a fine quality piece of furniture. The hand-me-down pieces they'd been left by the flat's previous owners were serviceable, but not at their best—the single armchair was fraying at the sides, and if you sat too close to the left armrest you risked being jabbed by a loose spring. The Chesterfield sofa, on the other hand, was luxury indeed. It was far more comfortable even than their bed, and one evening the husband began to make love to the wife on it, and only stopped when she pointed out it made her feel slightly weird having sex lying on her own offspring. But the richness of the green leather only showed up how drab everything else in the flat was by contrast—it looked strange and alien against the peeling pink wallpaper and the threadbare stained carpets. And it was clearly too big for the sitting room; the only way they could position it was diagonally from one corner to the other, and even then it was hard for the wife to see the television screen; it blocked so much light from the window it made the whole flat seem dark, small, and dingy, even more so than it really was. So the husband told her that they'd have to get rid of it, such class simply wasn't for them, and the wife reluctantly agreed. Late one night he brought some of the lads home from work, and they heaved it out of the flat, down the stairs, and into a skip they'd found further up the road. The sofa all but filled the skip, but the lads had done it under cover of darkness, no one had seen them do it, so it was all right. And the wife noticed immediately that her husband's mood lifted, he seemed more relaxed than before. They made love that night and it was passionate and it was good, she squealed for all the right reasons this time, and she thought as she lay in his arms afterwards that she could get used to this. She could get used to not having a baby after all if this is what marriage could be like. And she told him that, and he looked so pleased, and even though he was very drowsy he put his tongue in her mouth and they made love all over again.

So when she found out she was pregnant once more he nearly hit the roof. He asked her what on earth she thought she was playing at. And she told him she hardly thought she was the *only* one responsible here, and burst into tears. And he said sorry, sorry, and put his arms around her, and said it was okay, it was *nobody's* fault, they'd just have to take even more precautions in the future, that was all. And maybe it would be all right anyway, maybe it was just another bit of furniture they could chuck in the skip, they must keep their fingers crossed. And it *was* another bit of furniture. Some time on Wednesday, whilst her husband was at work, she became the proud mother of an escritoire. She didn't know it was called an escritoire, mind you, so she had to be a bit vague when she called him on his mobile, and when he came home early he didn't know it was called an escritoire either. The husband sighed, and asked what they could want with a writing desk, he never wrote anything anyway. And she showed him all the drawers, and the place you could put your pens, and the lovely design on the mahogany, but he wasn't impressed. He said that if she was going to propagate furniture, couldn't she at least come up with something that was actually *useful*? They needed so much stuff, why not just pop out a couple of chairs or a table? He said he thought it was embarrassing anyway, he'd better call the lads from work, see if they wouldn't mind carrying the desk to the skip, but if they began to suspect all this unwanted furniture was coming from his wife's belly he'd be a laughingstock. He went as far as to say that had he known he'd been marrying someone who was a bit abnormal in the baby department, he might have had second thoughts. She cried and said that maybe *he* was the abnormal one, not her, it might be his sperm not her eggs, and he said no, he knew *perfectly* well that he could produce babies, did she really think she'd been his first? There was tons she didn't know about him, *tons*. And they both fell silent because they'd said too much, and then she asked him if he had a child she didn't know about, and he reassured her that it hadn't got as far as that, they'd dealt with it, it was okay—but he went on to mutter under his breath, just loud enough for her to hear, that he was pretty bloody sure all that palaver he'd been through hadn't been for a king-size sofa or some fancy writing desk. And then the lads came.

As the lads were about to lug the offending escritoire down the stairs, one of them asked the husband whether he'd be prepared to take twenty quid for it instead. The husband narrowed his eyes suspiciously. Why would a spot welder want a writing desk? What was in it for him? And the lad buckled and admitted he knew someone—not that well, mind, so this was a bit of a gamble—who liked to buy up posh furniture once in a while. The husband went very quiet. The lad asked if he wanted the twenty quid, and the husband said no, he didn't want his twenty quid. And the lad said, all right, should they put the desk in the skip then, and the husband said no, he thought he'd hang on to it after all. And the lad said, sod you then, and that the husband mustn't think he'd come out late at night again and have his time wasted like that, and the husband rudely assured him he wouldn't want him to. There was a banging of doors as the lad left, taking all the other lads with him, and had the escritoire been a human baby it would undoubtedly have started crying—but, because it was an escritoire, it didn't. The husband looked at the desk thoughtfully, as if for the first time. He pulled out the drawers one by one, turned them over, gave them a proper inspection. It almost made the wife tear up with joy to see him being so paternal at last. And then he said he was going to phone in sick for work the next day—he had things to do.

When the wife woke the next morning the husband had already left—and the escritoire had gone too. But he didn't bring it back with him. Instead he brought back a Chinese takeaway for them both. A bit of a treat, he called it, he thought they deserved to splash out. He announced that he'd sold the writing desk for three hundred pounds—three hundred!—and he beamed at her as if expecting a round of applause. The wife didn't want to let him down, so gave as congratulatory a look as she could muster. Her husband explained that their son turned out to be a genuine antique from the reign of George III—that was the 1700s, you know—and the dealer had been very keen to get his hands on it. The wife asked how it was possible their son was from the 1700s when he'd only been born yesterday, but the husband huffily asked her what she thought he looked like, a furniture expert? After she'd polished off her sweet and sour prawn balls, the husband led her to the bedroom. She started to get out their precautions—one for him, one for her—and he shrugged, and said he didn't think they needed to worry about precautions *too* much.

The next time she fell pregnant he didn't get angry at all. On the contrary. He brought her cups of tea, kept asking how she was, wanted to make sure she didn't overexert herself. And he'd nuzzle her swelling belly, kiss it, and whisper to it—what are you going to be when you grow up? What are you going to be? Over the next few weeks she produced a grandfather clock, two sixteenth-century tea chests, and an ornate dining table designed to seat a party of twelve. Every time they'd appear, pushed and pushed, after so much *pushing* the wife thought she'd burst, he'd unwrap the covering gloop and snip the cord like a kid opening a Christmas present. There were many more Chinese takeaways, and the wife began to associate the taste of sweet and sour with the nausea she always felt after giving birth. And it wasn't just Chinese takeaways the husband would buy; bit by bit, the hand-me-down furniture was replaced with fresh items he'd get from Argos. But every new item she'd produce from her stomach still somehow made them look as drab as the hand-me-downs, and a bit more plasticky to boot. In the bedroom the husband would become more experimental— wonder if they'd produce different types of furniture if they had sex in different positions. They did it standing up and were soon blessed with a Victorian standing lamp. They did it on all fours, and out came a whimsical framed portrait of four dogs playing poker. He invested in a lavish edition of the Karma Sutra, and was delighted with the gold statuette of Vishnu she delivered, so very exotic.

One evening, in a daze of sweet and sour, she told him that she missed the set of brass toasting forks he'd sold that day to buy their dinner. He looked perplexed. Told her patiently that they had no *need* for toasting forks, brass or otherwise. She agreed; but added softly that they were their children, weren't they? Right down to their little brass handles they were their children, and she missed them. He told her that she couldn't possibly *miss* something she hadn't even had until one o'clock that afternoon; she was being illogical, it was just her post-natal depression playing up again. And she supposed that was true. In the same way that she couldn't help but feel there was something different to their lovemaking now. She'd lie beneath him, watching as he bounced around on top—well, whenever the Karma Sutra allowed bouncing—and she'd zone out a little watching his face, the gritted teeth, the rolling eyes, the spit, all that effort, all that work. It didn't seem like it had anything much to do with her anymore. She no longer felt the urge to squeal; if there was any squealing to be done, he'd be doing it, and it'd be a squeal of avarice. But when she tried to bring this up, as delicately as possible, she'd be told the same thing. Illogical. Post-natal Depression.

And then, one day, something truly miraculous happened. She'd just given birth to a four-poster bed, and thought little of the fact— she coolly admired all the frills and drapes, but she'd long ago taught herself not to get too attached to things like that. It was a big bit of furniture, it all but filled the room, and the wife wasn't sure how her husband could get it to the dealer. But, she considered wearily, that was *his* problem, *his* part of the job, let *him* deal with it. She tried to swallow down the inevitable taste of sweet and sour sickness that took her after a delivery, no matter what she ate before it. And was about to go into the kitchen, make herself a cup of tea, when she felt something fall out of her body and hit the floor with a dull clang.

It was a kettle, she saw. Not an especially nice example of kettledom, the stainless steel a little rusted. Not antique either—her Mum's one was just the same, and she doubted that predated the seventies. Under normal circumstances, the kettle would be a disappointment, you'd be lucky to get a fiver for it. But sitting on the floor next to the opulent bulk of the four-poster bed, it looked laughably banal. Probably no better than the hand-me-down kettle they had in their hand-me-down kitchen.

But it looked like her.

She'd all but given up looking at her children for any signs of resemblance, to see whether they took most after mummy or daddy. However impressive it might have been on its own terms, the four-poster bed was really just another four-poster bed; she knew intellectually it was of her flesh, but she felt no bond to it. But the kettle was something else. She couldn't work out why they looked so similar; the spout didn't look like her nose, the handles were nothing like her ears. Maybe it was just because it a bit tarnished, a bit dirty, and it wouldn't go for much in Oxfam.

"Peek-a-boo," she said to the kettle, and smiled. "Peek-a-boo!"

And she knew then that she was going to be all right. She could cope with all of this. Produce children who weren't going to be her children. Live with a husband that she knew less and less day by day. Make love that wasn't love at all. If she could just have her little daughter by her side, see her face whenever she needed to, remind herself what this whole family thing was supposed to be about. Was she a daughter, maybe he was a son . . . ? She picked up the kettle gently, ever so gently. Daughter. Definitely daughter. How lovely! Up to now all the furniture had been boys.

She'd got her now, *daughter*, she told herself, *daughter*, and she wasn't going to get away. She cradled her in her arms, and the baby kettle gave a sigh of calm that quite broke her heart. She wouldn't tell the husband, this was all hers, she was all hers. And she took her into the kitchen, kissed her softly, and shut her in the cupboard.

# ROADKILL

## i

He'd said he liked companionable silence, that was a sign of friendship. But when it came down to it, what they had was just silence, really, wasn't it? As they sped down the motorway in the dark, no sound except the low roar of the engine and the occasional grunt of the windscreen wiper, she felt drowsy, she thought at least that she might get some sleep. But she didn't dare—it'd seem rude—they *weren't* companions, not really, in spite of what they'd done—and he kept on stealing little looks at her, throwing her awkward little smiles, and saying, "Sorry I'm being so quiet, sorry." If he wanted the companionable silence then why did he keep popping up with such stuff as, "Oh, look, only twenty-two more miles to the nearest service station," or "Oh, look, cows"? Always with that apologetic grin she'd found rather endearing only a day before.

"Do you want some music?" he said at last, "would some music be nice?" He fished around for a wad of CDs with his spare hand, "I think some music would be nice," he said, "I'll see if I can find Elton John." And then she didn't so much hear it as *feel* it, there was a thud, and a quick streak of something very solid against the windscreen. "Jesus," he said. He didn't drop the CDs, she noted, he put them back safely into the glove compartment. "Jesus, what was that?"

"Pull over," she said. And he looked at her with bewilderment. "Pull over," she said again, and he did so. The car stopped on the hard shoulder.

"Jesus," he said again. "We hit something."

You hit something, she thought. "Are you all right?" she asked.

"I think so," he said, "yeah. Yeah, I'm fine. Are you all right? What do you think it was? I mean, it just came out of nowhere. You saw that, didn't you? There was nothing I could have done. Jesus," he looked up at the windscreen, "I hope it hasn't damaged anything."

"You should check," she said, and he just gave her that bewildered expression again, so she sighed, undid the seat belt, and opened the door. She wondered whether he might be in shock, but she'd seen him look bewildered a fair amount that weekend, and it couldn't *always* have been shock. She wondered whether she might be in shock too. "Fuck," she said, as she stepped out into the dark and the rain, "fuck fuck," but actually she felt good, some fresh air at last, and something was happening, there'd be no need for a companionable silence now, she didn't feel like saying 'fuck' at all. She gave the windscreen a cursory inspection, and from inside the car he gave her a hopeful thumbs up. She gave him a thumbs up back, but she hadn't looked, not really, there could be shards of glass all round for all she cared. And then she turned and walked back down the hard shoulder to look for a body.

It wasn't rain, not really, just a bit of wetness in the air, and it was refreshing. She liked it out here in the black, on her own, and she wondered how long she could get away with it, with not returning to the car, returning to him—pretending instead to look for whatever it is they might have hit, she'd never find it now. And then she saw it, maybe about two hundred yards behind the car, a little mound that had been knocked into the middle lane. She stood parallel to it, but couldn't make out what it was. She thought it might be moving. She waved back, indicating he should reverse the car. For a moment nothing happened and she thought she'd have to walk all the way back and tell him what to do, "fuck," she said, and then, slowly, surely, the car began to back down the hard shoulder towards her, he'd got the message.

"It's just there," she told him, as he wound down the window. "Try to angle the car a bit, so we can see what it is in the headlamps."

"What is it?" he asked her.

"I don't know," she said. "Try to angle the car. You know. So we can see what it is in the lamps."

He did his best. She still couldn't identify it, it was sprawled in such an odd position, she couldn't even see if it had a head. But there had to be a head, because it was definitely alive, whatever it was it was twitching, you couldn't twitch without a head, could you? "Probably a bird," he said, and she jumped, she hadn't heard him get out of the car, "you saw the way it flew at me, probably a bird." And he sniffed. But it looked a bit large for a bird, and besides, surely that was fur? "We should go and get it," she suggested, and he looked horrified. "It's in the motorway," he said, "we can't walk out into the motorway." But there were no cars coming, no headlights in the distance, and the creature twitched again, for God's sake it was *twitching*. "It's not as if we'll be able to help," he said, and she gave him a look, said a "Sod it" under her breath, and then ran out into the road.

Up she scooped it into her arms, and she made to dash back, but as she did so she felt that the creature had been stuck down on to the tarmac, she fancied there was resistance as she pulled it up, and she was suddenly terrified that she'd left bits of the body behind, that she'd make it back to the safety of the hard shoulder with only half an animal and the rest of it trailing after her. "Are you all right?" he asked, and his arms were out wide, and for a moment she thought absurdly that he wanted to *hug* her, after all that had happened, and she thought, no, he wants to take the animal from me, he wants to *share* this—but not even that, now his arms had dropped uselessly to his sides, he was doing nothing to help, nothing. And as she reached him she had a sick urge to drop the creature to the ground, but what would be the point of that, why bother rescuing it in the first place? And though she suddenly felt such revulsion to it, she kept it in her arms those few seconds longer, she knelt down and laid it out gently on the hard shoulder. And she realized at last that it *was* fur, matted fur, and she wondered whether it was matted with blood or with rainfall. "There," she said, as she pulled away from it at last, "there you go," and, stupidly, "you'll be all right now." And it did have a head she saw, thank God, and it turned that head and fixed her with its eyes.

"It's a rabbit," she said.

"Yes," he said. "Or a hare. I always get the two muddled up. Aren't hares supposed to have longer ears? Or is that the other way round?" He thought for a bit. "Do you think those are long ears?"

"I don't know."

"Nor me. If we had another rabbit here, you know, side by side. You know, we could compare."

They stood there for a good half minute, just looking down at it. And it lay there, for the same length of time, just looking back. "It's not moving much," he said.

"No."

"Do you think it's dying, or what? There isn't much blood. I mean, unless there was in the road. Was there a lot in the road?" She didn't answer. "What do we do now?"

"I think," she said heavily, "we have to put it out of its misery."

"Right," he said, "right. And are you sure," he went on, licking his lips, "that it's actually *in* misery? I mean, it's not making much noise. It's not squealing or anything. Surely if there were misery, there'd be squealing and stuff."

"Help me find a rock," she said. And they both went up to the embankment, scrabbled around in the grass. It didn't have to be a rock, anything sharp or heavy would have done, but it was rocks that they found. Hers was better than his. When he saw that, he dropped his to the ground.

"How are you going to do this?" he asked her.

"I'm not going to do it," she said, and she'd never been more sure of anything. "You're going to do it." And she gave him the rock.

"You could have just left it in the road," he said. "Why didn't you just leave it in the road? Some car would have come eventually, squashed it, there'd be no need for rocks and shit." And she felt such a flare of anger at that, but she didn't raise her voice, "Go on," she said. Go on, finish it. Finish what you've started.

So he stood there, all five foot six of him, weighing the rock in his hands, aiming downwards. "You're going to have to get closer than that," she said. "Jesus," he said. "What, right down in the, you want me on my, right, Jesus." And he got down on his knees. "I hope you're happy," he said. "I hope this is what you want. Jesus."

"You're going to have to hit it pretty hard," she told him. And she almost laughed at the look he threw her then, and it wasn't funny, not really, she really *mustn't* laugh. But he'd tried so hard all weekend to accommodate her, to keep smiling no matter what, and here on his face at last was something like fury. "Go on," she said. And he muttered something, and lined up the rock to the rabbit's skull, as if he were taking a snooker stroke, for God's sake, as if he were swinging a golf club. "You might want to hold its head," she added.

"I'm not *touching* it," he said. "I'll kill it, but I won't touch it. Oh. Oh. Wait. Look."

And she'd had enough suddenly. "I'll do it," she said, "if you can't." I just want to get home, she thought.

"No," he said. "What's this?"

She stooped beside him.

The rabbit had a wing. It was thick and black and leathery. And *wide*, it lay stretched out to the left, a wider span than the body from which it had unfurled. The rabbit blinked at them, as if it was as surprised as they were.

"It can't be real," he said. "It must be stuck on." And he hadn't wanted to touch the creature before, but now his fingers were all over it, feeling the wing, prodding at where it met the fur. "I can't see any join," he said. "I thought it must have been stitched on or something, but it just comes out of the skin." The rabbit gave a little cough, almost politely—and from out of its right side a second wing unfolded. It spread even wider, and it fluttered a little under the drizzle.

The rabbit shuddered and gave a single grunt. It was only for a beat, it was very quiet, but they both heard it. "I don't see what difference it makes," she said.

"Maybe there's some sort of scientific base nearby," he was saying. "You know, where they put ears on mice and things." He was on his feet now, looking about, as if expecting to see a laboratory on the horizon. "Do you think that could be it? I mean, maybe it escaped. Maybe they want it back."

"Give me the rock," she said.

"What are you talking about?" And for a moment he genuinely didn't know. Then he grinned at her, talked very slowly, very patiently. "But, no. But we can't kill it now. That would be terrible. I mean, look at it," although he was doing nothing of the sort himself, he was beaming with a big smile now and his eyes were bright. "I mean, what if this is even *better* than an experiment from a lab? I mean, this could be a new *species*. Can you just think of that?"

"No," she said.

"Look," he said. "Look." And then he was silent for a moment, as if trying to work out what she should be looking at. "Okay, look. We came out here for something magical. Didn't we? I mean, that was the whole point. And maybe this is it. This is something magical."

"It's in pain," she said.

"We'll get it a towel," he said. "There's one on the back seat, I think. Yeah, we'll make it nice and comfortable. Go on," he said. "Go and get the towel. Go on then," and there was just a touch of impatience in his voice now, and as she looked at him his eyes were gleaming in the rain, it was raining for real now and it made his face look shiny and alive.

And she fetched the towel, and he wrapped up the rabbit within it as gently as he could. Lovingly, she thought, almost lovingly. She tried to help, but he waved her away. He stroked the wings and he stroked the fur, and told the creature it was going to be okay. The creature looked at him a little doubtfully, but at least it didn't make that grunt of pain again, that was something. And they carried it to the boot, they shut it in, and then they drove away.

## ii

And on the way up all they'd done was talk. After a few hours, halfway up the M5, he'd admitted to her he'd been a bit nervous, what if they hadn't found things to chat about? And she'd laughed, and said fat chance! The words had just spilled out of both of them, sometimes there were about three different conversations going on at once—she thought it was rather exhilarating and laughed every time she lost her train of thought only to find another altogether. First off, of course, they'd talked about work—he'd only been at the office for a few weeks, whereas she'd been there for *years*, she could tell him all the gossip—and he said he was relieved, that the people he thought he was beginning to like were the ones it was safe to like, and those he hadn't taken to were precisely the ones to steer clear of. It was good to get such inside information! And they'd discussed their family, why it was he didn't get on with his mum, why she didn't get on with her dad. "It's the same sort of thing," he told her sympathetically, "but in reverse. Jesus, what's wrong with our parents anyway?" They'd even touched on politics, and although she rather suspected the views he held were just watered down versions of her own, at least they weren't going to argue, at least they were in the same general ballpark. He'd picked her up from the top of her road first thing that morning; as it turned out, he could have done so from the house, she'd sorted everything out, but he said it might be safer his way. "Is that all your luggage?" he'd said, and she'd smiled, and said she didn't think she'd need much. And she'd sat in the passenger seat beside him, and there wasn't any crap lying on the floor, and there was a smell of lemon. She thought he must have cleaned the car especially—and then thought, why not just ask him? So did. And he blushed and said he had, actually, was that really pathetic? "No, no," she said, "it's nice, it's nice." And meant it.

She navigated. He told her he didn't have a satnav. "Well, I do," he said, "but I don't like it, I think the voice is a bit creepy." And she'd laughed, and agreed, those voices *were* a bit creepy, weren't they? Although she didn't find her satnav creepy in the slightest. And he'd said that maybe they only hired actors to record those satnav things if they had creepy voices, and he'd tried to picture the auditions involved, even acting it out, turning down Mel Gibson, Jack Nicholson, because they didn't sound enough like axe murderers, and the joke must have been run on for over half an hour, and somehow never quite stopped being funny. She was pleased to see he didn't mind when she gave the wrong directions, when they came off the motorway at the wrong junction. "It's a holiday!" he said, "it's not as if we're in any hurry!" They pulled into a service station, and he bought them both a coffee. He noted how she insisted it come with soya milk, he told her with mock grimness that was important knowledge he would store away for future reference, and then grinned.

"Look," he said. "Silly to ask. But just so I'm sure. What we're doing is what I think we're doing, isn't it?" And he played with his plastic stirrer. "You know. We are shagging, aren't we?"

"Yes," she said.

"Oh, good," he said. "Oh, that's what I thought. But it'd have been embarrassing if . . . I mean, I only got us the one room. Good."

She leaned forward across the coffee and the soya milk. And the detritus of how many other travellers, maybe they were all going down the M5 for a spot of shagging, why not. He looked surprised, and it took him a few moments to realize he should lean in too. And she kissed him on the lips. He responded very well, actually. There was a bit of movement on his part, a sort of nibbling, but not too much, he didn't get carried away. And although the tongue did make an appearance, it didn't hog the party the way it sometimes could, it was just a push against her teeth, a quick hello and goodbye, a quick see you later maybe.

"You've done this before," she said.

"What, kiss?" he said, and was puzzled. Then he realized she was teasing, and said, "Oh yes, kissing, I've kissed a few times, yeah."

"Good to know," she said.

"But never," he added, as they got up and put on their coats, "someone who tasted of soya. That was a new one on me."

"It's a lovely part of the country," he told her as they drove on. "I grew up there as a kid. And I hope you like the hotel. It had a nice website. It's a family hotel, you know, nothing posh, but I don't like those posh hotels much, do you? They're not very personal. I like personal, personal's nice. This one looks nice, the pictures are nice, it has off street parking."

"So long as it has a bed," she said, "we'll be fine."

The landlady was waving at them from the front window. "This must be it," he said, and they pulled up in the driveway. "Hello, hello!" said the landlady, opening the door to them. "And welcome! We spoke on the phone, yes? I'm Marcia. I hope you'll be very happy here." Marcia was fiftyish and grey haired, with arms thick enough to churn butter.

They introduced themselves. "Married?" asked Marcia. "Yes," she said. "No," he said. "Only the one of us," she said. Marcia laughed. "Say no more!" He looked embarrassed, but she didn't mind—she'd rather he'd been mistaken for her husband than her son. Marcia led them through to the back of the house. "And here's your little part of our home," she said. "Here's the key, and there's a separate door through the garden, you see, if you want to come in late at night. Just so you won't worry about disturbing me or my husband." She watched them take in the room, the wardrobe, the TV mounted in the corner, the bathroom door, for some reason a painting of a goose. And the double bed, big, bold, bloody unignorable, right there in the centre. "Have fun!" she said, and left them.

"I like her," he said, "she seems nice." She put down her bag on the bed, kissed him from behind on his neck. "Oh!" he said. "What are you doing? We haven't even unpacked yet."

"I'm sorry," she said.

"No," he said, "I'm sorry. Sorry." He opened his arms, and she thought, a hug, he wants a *hug*. She stepped into the embrace anyway, and he held on to her gingerly as if she were cut crystal, and he rubbed his cheek against hers, and gave her a peck. Then he thought about it for a moment, grinned, what the hell, and kissed her full on the lips. It was for longer this time, and the tongue gave more than its cameo performance. "Okay?" he asked.

"Oh yes," she said. "It's very nice here."

"It is, isn't it? I love hotels!" He released her, went to open drawers, cupboards. "There's a kettle here! And an ironing board. And look!" He'd found a little folder, right by the Gideon Bible. "They do room service. Just like a proper hotel. Shall we order something?" She assured him she was fine. "Oh, it'll be fun. We can have breakfast in bed! I think we should! Hang on," he said, winked at her, and lifted the receiver. Dialled a number. Waited. "It's ringing," he told her. And then,

"Hello! Yes, we thought we'd order breakfast in bed for tomorrow! We thought, why not, it's a holiday, if you can't do it on a holiday . . . ! . . . No, we're staying in your house. Yes. In the guest room. Yes. Yes, at the back." She lay down on the bed and waited for him to stop talking. "Yes, then would be fine. Looking forward to it. Thank you." He hung up, smiled at her. "Breakfast in bed, what a treat!" And she smiled back. "Come here," she said to him.

He lay on the bed next to her. "Okay if I take this side?"

"You're fine."

"It's quite soft, isn't it?"

She made to shrug, but she was supported by one of her shoulders, so it came out as a twitch. They snogged for a while. "You're really special," he told her at one point. "Whatever happens this weekend, I want you to know, it's just great to have such a good friend at the office." They snogged a bit longer. "I should unpack," he said. "Do you want to unpack?"

"We're only here the one night," she told him.

"I know," he said. He got up, unzipped his suitcase. Took out three, maybe four, shirts, and a spare pair of trousers. He opened the wardrobe. "Okay if I take this side?"

Marcia recommended them a restaurant in town. They wouldn't need the car, it was only ten minutes' walk, and besides, the weather was lovely. "Neil swears by the crab," she told them, "you must try the crab!" They found the place easily enough, it wasn't too busy, they got a table for two, and a waiter lit a candle for them.

"I don't like crab," he confided to her, and she agreed, she couldn't abide shellfish, so they giggled, ordered a steak and a lasagne, and joked that they'd *tell* Marcia they'd had crab when they saw her. The house red had no label, but was rather good, and they got through two bottles of it.

"Coffee?" asked the waiter.

"I won't, but my girlfriend here will, but the milk has to be soya." Girlfriend, she thought with surprise, it almost sobered her up.

"I'm not sure we have soya milk, sir, I'll check." "It has to be soya, that's what she drinks."

"Listen," she said to him, and touched his hand gently, "I can have other milks, it's just soya for preference." But no, no, he was adamant, it'd be soya or nothing, only the best for her, for his girlfriend—if there was no soya milk to be had he'd bloody well go out and get some, leave the restaurant, find some supermarket, and bring back his own.

And fortunately the waiter returned and said there *was* soya milk, so no one had to find out whether he'd back down or not. Mind you, she thought as she sipped at the coffee, it didn't taste like soya. By the time he'd paid—his treat, he insisted—it had begun to rain. Just a drizzle, really, they were both so hot after the wine it was welcome. And he told her he'd protect her, and did his best to hold his hand flat over her head as they walked back to the hotel. It did nothing to keep her dry, of course, but it made them both laugh.

When they got back they snogged again for a little while. As soon as she'd stepped into the room he whirled her around, and caught her mouth with his. It was quite nice, but as she stood there straining her face up to meet his, she couldn't help feel there were more comfortable ways to do this. "I'm going to get ready for bed," she said gently, and indicated the bathroom, "all right?" Of course, he said, did she want him to come with her . . . ? No, no, she assured him, she just wanted to clean herself up a bit, nothing sexy or complicated like that. He said okay, and she thought he looked a little relieved. "I'll only be a minute," she said, kissed him again, stepped into the bathroom, and closed the door behind her. As she washed her face she noticed that he'd carefully laid out all his toiletries side by side at the top of the sink, toothbrush, toothpaste, shampoo, a pair of tweezers.

She opened the door, and nearly laughed. He was standing there naked. Arms to one side, as if presenting. It wasn't that there was anything funny about his body, not in the slightest, it all seemed to be present and in roughly the correct dimensions. It was just the surprise at the whole reality of it. He looked down, smiled a little awkwardly. "Sorry about him, he's got a bit excited."

"So I can see," she said. "No, it's very flattering."

"Thanks."

"Do you want me to strip off, or . . . ?"

"Oh, absolutely. Yes."

"Okay," she said, and did so.

"Wow," he said. "You're really beautiful."

"Thanks."

"No, really," he said, with utter sincerity, his face was frowning with so much sincerity. "Really beautiful."

"Well," she said. "That makes two of us."

He smiled at that. "Look," he said. "This is the sort of last chance to turn back, isn't it? I just want you to know that's an option. We don't have to do this if you're not ready . . ."

"Oh, shut up," she said, kindly. "We might as well, I'm here now."

"I think I'll just use the bathroom myself," he said. He wasn't in there for long, she heard a couple of bursts of deodorant, and he was out again. "Right," he said, with an entirely new confidence. There was a ribbed condom slightly weighing down his penis. "You lie on the bed. I'm going to make love to you as you've never been made love to before."

"Okay," she said.

He knelt at the foot of the bed, looked at her feet, narrowed his eyes, *inspected* them. And then, with a suddenness that was probably meant to look very dramatic, but came across as just a bit too deliberate, he darted his head forward. And began to suck at her toes.

"What are you doing?" she asked.

"I'm going to lick you all over," he told her, very earnestly. "Every single inch of you, you're going to be kissed on every inch. From head to foot." He corrected himself. "Foot to head, I'm working upwards."

It was quite a pleasant sensation, she found. And, thank God, mostly dry. He only dabbed at her with the tongue, and then any little spittle he left was hoovered up by his lips. That was fine, actually, she wasn't quite sure how well she'd have suffered lying there glistening and soggy. As he poked his tongue between her toes, she actually allowed herself to be aroused. "You've done this before," she teased him.

He stopped, looked shocked, serious. "No," he said. "No, really. All of this . . . this is inspired by you. This is what you bring out in me."

"Okay," she said, and closed her eyes. She lay back and blissed out, as she felt his tongue climb ever higher up her body. "It's okay," she breathed at last, "that's lovely. You can enter me now."

"But I've only reached the knees."

"It doesn't matter, I'm ready." And she pulled him up closer, and looked him full in the face, and it wasn't a bad face, she thought, a little bewildered but it was trying hard. And she fed him inside of her.

"Jesus," he said. "Oh, Jesus." "Yes, I'm Jesus, baby, I'm Jesus," she said to him, "now keep going. Go on. . . . Oh."

"Oh," he said. And then, "wow." And then, "I'm sorry, I got a bit overexcited."

"That's okay," she said. "I was excited too."

"Did you come?" And however politely he asked, the question sounded so blunt that she wasn't quite prepared for it. She had to hesitate before saying yes. "You didn't, did you? I'm sorry."

"I'm pretty sure I did," she said.

"I'll stay inside. He's been hard all day, I know he'll wake up again."

"If you like," she said, and they both lay there, not saying anything for a while. He smiled down at her. She smiled back. It was all very friendly, really. And then he began to start thrusting again. "Look," she said gently, "if you're not ready . . ."

"No, something's happening down there," he assured her. And then began to grunt along with each thrust. Come on, he seemed to be saying with those grunts. Wake up. Wake up. And she thought she should do her best to help, she began grunting too, just to chivvy him on. The grunting got louder and louder, it was like some caveman metronome, his light boyish voice given up as he growled ever lower in pitch. Her own grunts sounded embarrassingly tinny beside his, she thought, and she tried to deepen her voice too. And then, "Can you hear that?" he panted.

"Don't stop," she said.

"Next door," he said, "listen!" And he was right, through the thin walls she could hear their hosts having sex too, Marcia and Whatsisname. Neil. "Don't stop," she said, "use them. Use them to help you keep time." And on they grunted, all four of them, until at last with a sigh of relief and an exhausted gasp of "Jesus" it was all over and he was able to roll off her.

"Well done," she said, sincerely.

"Thank you." He looked very pleased with himself.

Next door the grunting went on. Her lover smiled indulgently. "Listen to that," he said. "We probably inspired them. Do you think?"

"Maybe," she said.

"Old married couple like that. We probably reminded them what it was all about."

"Yeah," she said, "look, I'm quite tired now, do you think we could get some sleep?"

"Sure," he said, and he seemed so serenely smug, she could probably have requested anything, he'd have said yes. "I'll just pop to the bathroom, be with you in a tick." She was asleep before he came back.

A few hours later—the neon alarm said it was gone two—she stirred. For a moment she forgot where she was. Then she saw the picture of the goose, and she saw him too, sitting on a chair in the corner, right beneath the TV set. She saw the red glow of a cigarette. She didn't even know he smoked.

"What's wrong?" she said.

"I'm surprised you can sleep," he said softly. "They're still at it. It's been going on for *hours*." And she hadn't noticed it, it'd been so regular that she'd screened out somehow, but now she could hear it. The same grunts from next door. Keeping rhythm, keeping time.

"Jesus," he added, and sucked on his cigarette.

"I don't think you're supposed to do that in here," she told him.

"Sorry," he whispered, and stubbed it out.

## iii

They didn't talk about the grunts. She might even have thought he couldn't hear them over the burble of his own chatter, but she watched his face, when there was a grunt she could see him *flinch*, he could hear them all right. They were very erratic. At one point there wasn't a grunt for a good three or four miles, and she thought, it's dead, it must be dead now, and *thank God*—but then it came again, just as clear as before. It's still hanging on, she thought. What's it hanging on *for*?

He'd given up any pretence at companionable silence. He was lively, told jokes even. She didn't have to pretend to respond, he kept talking anyway, she could have been in the trunk as well for what difference it made. "We ought to think of a name for it," he said suddenly. "Scientific discovery like this, it'll have to have a *name*. Won't it?" He paused for a moment. "They don't name animals after the people who discover them, do they?"

"I think that's inventions."

"Yeah," he said, and was disappointed for a while. But he quickly perked up. "Half bat, half rabbit. What about 'babbit'?" They drove in silence for a few seconds, then he laughed. "Even better! 'Rabbat'. I like that, what do you think?"

"You said it could be a hare."

"Oh yes." He thought about this, weighed up the permutations of syllables. "I hope it's not half hare," he said. "Let's keep our fingers crossed."

He'd already rhapsodized about the legacy of their achievement, the great worth of what they'd found. Not that he meant financial worth, he quickly assured her, although actually, why not, why shouldn't there be a bit of money in it? The two of them would be famous. They'd be on the news, and in programmes for the Discovery Channel. That had made him pause for thought. That could be a bit complicated, he'd realized. You know, considering what they'd been up to.

"Oh," she'd said. "I suppose."

Maybe, he'd gone on, only one of them should step forward. One of them should get the attention, the media coverage, whatever. And the other one, of course, wouldn't be left out. The other one would be fine. Any money that came his way, he'd split it with her fifty-fifty.

"I wouldn't worry about it," she'd said.

No, no, straight down the middle. He wouldn't cheat her. They were friends, weren't they? Good friends. Look, it was up to her. I mean, *she* could be the one. If she really wanted to be. She could be the one to step into the limelight. . . .

"No," she'd said. "I think this is your discovery. You're the one who ran it over."

He'd laughed at that and said, yes, he had, hadn't he? He'd been the one. He'd do all right by her, though, she'd see. He'd take care of her. And he'd reached for her with his spare hand, tried to give her a friendly squeeze. And she hadn't been sure what part of her body he'd been aiming for, but what he'd found was her knee, he was at it for what seemed like ages, squeezing away down there like there was no tomorrow. She'd felt her flesh crawl.

"Oh, look," he said eventually. "Eighteen miles to the next service station." About six miles from it, he said, "What do we reckon? We could stop for a coffee. Stretch our legs."

"I'm fine," she said.

"Okay," he said.

Three miles from the service station he said, "I might get myself a coffee, though. Stretch my legs."

They pulled into the car park. It was mostly empty, just a few overnight lorries over in the corner. "Last chance," he said. "Can I get you anything?"

"I'll just stay here," she said.

"I won't be long."

"Okay."

He disappeared into the darkness. She sighed with relief. And for a couple of minutes she just sat there and enjoyed it all. The peace of the car. The rain against the windscreen. The grunting from the trunk. Then she opened the glove compartment, rummaged inside. Travel sweets, a few CD cases, they weren't much use. She picked up instead the book from which she'd been navigating, a hardback road atlas to Great Britain. Not perfect, but the best there was. She reached under the steering wheel, felt the trunk door release. She hesitated, then got out of the car.

She swung open the trunk. "I'm sorry," she said, she was apologizing already and she hadn't even seen it yet, she couldn't have told you what she was sorry for, for what she was about to do or that it had taken her this long to do it. For a moment she thought it wasn't even there—the towel was empty, it had been scuffed aside. And then she saw it, hiding in the corner. It shuffled forwards, to the light, to the rain, and to her. "Hello," she said, and felt a bit stupid.

It gave another grunt—quieter this time, as if it knew it no longer had to make itself heard through layers of aluminium and plastic. It blinked, and fluttered its wings uselessly. She looked for a wound. The stomach was all but bare, the rabbit had nibbled away at its fur, and the skin beneath looked thin, like cellophane. Something moved beneath it, bulged.

"Oh God," she said. Warily she put her fingers to the belly. And then she was ashamed of herself somehow, that she was being so squeamish, this poor animal wouldn't even be in a Welcome Break car park if it wasn't for her, she put her fingers to the belly and *pressed*. And the belly pressed back against her, a kick, just a little kick.

The rabbit grunted again. And then it just lay back, its distended stomach waving up at the woman brandishing the atlas. It almost made her laugh. Go on, the rabbit seemed to be saying, displaying itself. I'm ready, love, take me. She got a sudden insane urge to lick at the rabbit's toes, I'm going to lick you all over. And then she really did laugh, out loud and barking, and the rabbit tutted impatiently.

The skin was so thin, it just needed the littlest help to break. She wasn't one to grow long fingernails, they were a bugger to type with at work, but they were sharp enough anyway. Just one little slit, and that was it, there was something a little wet running over her fingers which she supposed might have been blood but felt different somehow—and the skin pulled back of its own accord from the puncture, opening out into two flaps. And poking free, a little nose, no, several noses behind it, all trying to jump the queue. They were all pushing through the open door at the same time, if they were only that little more patient there'd have been plenty of room, but the babies were blind and stupid. So she put down the atlas, and with both hands held open the flaps a bit wider. And flop—out came the first. And then there was more space, out came all the others, mewing and cooing as they hit the bottom of the car trunk with a bump.

Five came out altogether. She waited for a sixth, wondered if she should pick up the rabbit, try to squeeze one out. But at last the mother relaxed, it was all over. Her head lolled back against her own fur pluckings and a couple of empty crisp packets. Her babies kept bouncing around, into each other, into her, chattering away for all they were worth, but she didn't seem to mind. The eyes stared upwards, fixed upon her human midwife. One of the children took a jump right over her head, but she didn't break focus, it didn't distract the severity of that look. Well, lady, the eyes said, what now?

The first baby out, clearly the most entrepreneurial of the bunch, took the leap to jump back over its mother. It jumped higher this time, and as the woman watched, she could see a tentative flap of something small and leathery. A tiny wing slid out from the baby rabbit's side, then back in again, as if it didn't know whether it belonged on a rabbit or not.

And as the rabbit mother stared at her, so she stared at the babies, all of them starting to stretch their wings, to realize they had wings in the first place. And they, of course, didn't stare at anything, their eyes still sealed tight, crying out not in distress but obvious bewilderment.

The expression on their faces reminded her that her lover would be back soon.

"Come on!" she urged them, out loud. "Come on, quickly!" And she flapped her arms by her sides. They couldn't see her, of course, and even if they could have done, and had had even a *glimmering* of what she was trying to encourage them to do, they'd have found the demonstration somewhat impractical. The mother rabbit grunted at her, and even seemed to roll its eyes.

She picked up one of the babies, the one that seemed to be the genius of the litter. It was soft and wet and seemed composed of nothing but clay skin and those ridiculous tiny wings, she felt its little heart beat as it sat confused in the very palm of her hand. "Come on," she said to it again, "please," and it bounced around as if summoning up the nerve for a test flight. And then it *did* it, it did, it actually flew, it made the jump out of her hand—and she thought it would simply drop to the ground, and it did drop, that's true—but before it hit the surface it rallied, steadied itself, gained height again. She watched it fly, it was flying, not in a straight line, with no confidence, it was like a drunkard tripping his way home, but flying all the same.

And she turned back to the trunk, and saw its siblings, all of them too, jumping about, taking experimental little hops into the air. "Please," she said again, as if that would do any good—and then, one by one, each of them rose up out of the car, and took to the night sky. They *soared*. Only a minute old, two minutes, out in the wet, and the cold, and with no mother to suckle them: what chance could they have? And for God's sake, they were blind, they were flying *blind* at a motorway. Their eyes were still glued tight, she ought to get them back, she could catch them and stick them back in the boot, anything would be better, surely? But she couldn't see them anywhere. She looked up at the lamp post, there were creatures buzzing around the light—but they'd never have made it that high, they must be gnats.

She looked back to the mother. She couldn't see the wings, they must have slipped back inside the body, it didn't look special anymore. She knew it was silly, but she couldn't help it, she studied that rabbit face for something—gratitude? blame? But there wasn't anything to be seen, it was just a rabbit, that's all. She supposed she should finish what she'd started. She ought to bludgeon it with the hard spine edge of the A to Z Great Britain Road Atlas (2002 edition). But as she picked up the book the rabbit closed its eyes, gave one shuddering breath, and was still.

She got back into the car.

She really thought she'd like to cry now. She really thought that would be nice. She gave it a good go, too; she scrunched up her eyes, tried hard to force something out. The effort made her head smart. It was no good. She clearly wasn't the crying type.

There was a knock at the glass, and she started. He was there, grinning, motioning for her to wind down the window. She did.

"Sorry I've been so long," he babbled, "I made a couple of phone calls, they were very excited. Don't think they minded I woke them up." He passed her a plastic cup, she accepted it dumbly. "And I got you some coffee anyway. And yes," he laughed, "I know, I know, it's soya milk, don't you worry, I got you the soya, don't you worry about that."

And she told him she didn't want any fucking coffee, if she'd wanted any coffee she'd have fucking got some for herself, what did he think she was, an idiot? What did he think she was? Because he didn't *know* her, he didn't have a clue, he didn't have the faintest fucking idea. And how *dare* he talk to her about soya milk, as if it were some private fucking joke between the two of them, he hadn't earned the right for that, he hadn't earned the right for anything—some joke about soya milk they could be nostalgic about one day, do you remember the time we first met and you'd only drink soya milk, blah blah, that was the same weekend he'd run over the rabbit, how hilarious, she *liked* soya milk, that was all, okay, and it hadn't got the slightest fucking thing to do with him.

And they drove off. If he noticed the fact the grunting had stopped he didn't say anything, but then he hadn't bothered to react when there *had* been grunting, so there was no surprise there. In fact, he didn't say very much at all, and if it wasn't companionable silence, it was at least silence, so thank God for small fucking mercies.

## iv

He'd clearly gone to bed eventually, because when she was woken up at half past eight by a knock at the door he was fast asleep next to her. He wasn't exactly at the far end of the bed, he could have moved further away from her had he really put some effort in, but there was still an appreciable gap between her naked body and his. In sleep his face was utterly without expression, turned towards her. He was cuddling a pillow tightly.

"Just a second," she called out, and got out of bed. She looked for her nightie, then remembered she hadn't actually packed one. She thought to get a towel from the bathroom instead.

He stirred. "What is it?" There was another knock at the door. "Oh!" he said, and his eyes were open, he was wide awake, and he bounded to his feet. "You go back to bed," he told her, "my treat, this is my treat. . . . Just a second!" he called out, and hurried over to the wardrobe. He took out an ironed pair of pyjama trousers, struggled into them.

"Good morning," he said, as he opened the door. "Is it breakfast?"

"Breakfast ready," said a man.

"Do you want me to take it from you, or do you . . . ?"

The man came in, pushing a little trolley in front of him. On it was a couple of plates of steaming food, she thought she could smell bacon, and a mound of toast. "I'll leave it here," said the man. He was short and ugly and had a sort of beard, although she couldn't be sure whether that was intentional or simply because he hadn't bothered to shave for a few days. He looked across at her, now safely back under the duvet, nodded. "Morning," he said.

"This looks nice," said the vision in pyjama trousers, flapping after him. "Lovely. Are you Neil?"

"Yes."

"You're married to Marcia?"

"Yes," said Neil.

"Your bedroom is just through there," and he pointed at the wall.

It wasn't really a question, and Neil could have ignored it, but he confirmed that this was the case. "And you were there last night." Neil didn't reply. "Nice."

"Enjoy your breakfasts," said Neil. Formal to the end, no hint of a smile, he gave another nod at them both, first to him, then to her. Then left.

"So," he said. "That was Neil."

"Yes," she said.

He looked over the trolley. "Quite a feast here," he said. "Sausages, baked beans, mushrooms, egg, fried tomato. Are you hungry?"

"I don't really do breakfasts," she said.

"No," he said, "nor me. But breakfast in bed. How could we not?" He brought her over a plate. "There you go," he said. She held it in both hands, it was uncomfortably warm. "Oh," he said, "and you'll be needing . . ." and went to fetch her a knife and fork. "There you go," he said. He went to get his own plate, got into bed beside her.

It was hard to eat without a surface to lean on. She'd have rested the plate on the duvet, but she'd have worried the tomato sauce from the beans would have washed over the side. She speared anything that was small, she made short work of the mushrooms. "Do you want my sausage?" he asked her, and she said no, she hadn't even started thinking about the mechanics of eating the one she already had. "Fair enough," he said.

They ate there in silence for a while. She wished she could turn the television on, just for a bit of company.

"What do you want to do today?" he asked her. "We're on holiday, it's up to you. There are some quite nice things around here. I was looking at some of the leaflets last night. There are some underground caves, not a million miles away. There's a gorge. Do you like gorges?"

"I don't know. What's it like? You grew up here, didn't you?"

"I've never been. You know what it's like. You don't do gorges on your own doorstep. Thank you for last night," he said, suddenly and seriously. Oh God, she thought. "I couldn't sleep, you know what it's like. I just sat there and felt, well. So lonely, actually." Oh *God*. "But you were so lovely. I came to bed, and you opened your arms, and I thought, she wants to hug me, she wants a hug. She wants to look after me. And you held me. It was really nice."

"That's okay," she said, and remembered nothing.

"No, it really meant a lot. And I felt so at *peace*. Peace I haven't felt for . . . well, quite a while. You know what I've been through recently, well, you can guess, you know what it's like. I could have slept like a baby. I didn't actually, ha! I was enjoying it too much, your arms around me, I just kept myself awake. Ha! And you smelled so nice. Quite tired now, actually."

"Well," she said.

"And I thought, she's one in a million, she's really special. A great friend, whatever else happens. Thank you," and he leaned across to kiss her. She wasn't sure if it was meant for the lips or not, she wasn't sure even what she *wanted* this kiss to be, and she was pretty sure he didn't know either, his mouth hovered in front of her face for a bit. Then it made a decision, fell upon the forehead, and she blinked under the earnest pressure of it, and thought, well, that's it then, that's the choice he's made. And she felt oddly relieved and oddly saddened, and she splashed some tomato sauce on the duvet anyway.

"Come on!" he said, and laughed. "We've a whole day ahead of us. It's a holiday!"

They never saw Neil again; they found Marcia in the kitchen, and paid her. "My treat," he said, although she tried to pay half, "no, my treat, you get next time." "You two have a lovely holiday," said Marcia, "nice couple like yourselves." They asked her about the gorge, and she said, yes, it was very beautiful, well worth a visit—no, she hadn't been herself, but the leaflets made it look very nice indeed. But they didn't visit the gorge—next time, he said, if we come back—it was a longer drive than he'd thought, and there was a long drive back ahead of him, he didn't want to spend all his holiday driving. "There's a twelfth century church," he said, "we could pop inside for a bit." So that's what they did, and wandered around for a good twenty minutes—a woman asked if they wanted a guided tour, and they really didn't, but it felt rude to say no. So she bought them a tour for a fiver, he tried to pay, and she said, no, *her* treat, *her* treat. As they stood there, listening to a treatise on medieval pulpitmaking, he tried to hold her hand, and for a while she even let him do so. "That was very nice," he said, when they came out, "I liked that," and he went on to say that religion wasn't really his thing, how anybody could believe in religion in this day and age was beyond him. He walked on, just solving the mysteries of life and death so glibly, and she felt the urge to say she was a devout Christian, to take offence, but she couldn't quite be bothered, and besides, she didn't believe in God. She never had before, and she certainly wouldn't now, she had no reason to believe in God; she had a few Christian friends and after all that had happened she was *deluged* with sympathy cards and maudlin emails and best wishes on the answering machine, for Christ's sake, and all of them assuring her that the pain would pass, the pain *would* pass if only she could give up her troubles to God, she had to put her strength in God. And her husband had said, well, maybe that isn't such a bad idea, and she'd been utterly floored by that, he'd never believed in *anything*, he'd been the one who insisted they get married in a registry office, he'd been the one who'd upset her parents because he said he couldn't go through the whole hypocrisy of pretending to believe when he just, frankly, couldn't. It really pissed her off, this sudden turnabout on his part, the way a tragedy could turn him into someone so patient and caring and sanctimonious; he said they had to find faith in something, otherwise how could they go on, how could they go on?

They walked one end of the town to the other. A stretch of road had been pedestrianized, and now had cobble stones everywhere. "Very olde world," he said, and he pronounced the 'e' on the end of 'olde,' and she supposed that was correct, but it still made him sound a bit of a tit. It began to drizzle, and they took shelter in a WHSmith's. It was a very nice WHSmith's, he said. She bought herself a copy of the Radio Times.

"Do you fancy some lunch?" he said to her at last.

"I've only just had breakfast," she said.

"I know." But it was still raining, so they went into a café anyway. They ordered toasted sandwiches.

"You can talk about your husband if you want."

She thanked him politely, and asked him exactly why she would want to do that.

"I don't mind," he said kindly. "I'll tell you about my girlfriend. If you'd like me to." He breathed in, smiled bravely. "Okay, I'm ready," he said. "Now, this is a bit complicated." And he told her just about the least complicated thing she'd ever heard.

"It's not fair," he said eventually. "She seems so sure. How can she be so sure? Love, it's a complicated thing, isn't it? How do I know that what she feels is the same thing I feel?"

Quite, she said.

"I mean," he went on, "I'd have thought you could only love one person. Or what's it all about? What can it mean otherwise? But now. I can't be so sure. She'd like us to get married. She'd like us to have kids. Can you see me as a father?" He laughed. "I mean, can you?"

She couldn't see why not, lots of people were having kids, there were kids running about all over the place. They had to come from somewhere. "I suppose not," she said.

He smiled at her. Tilted his head. "Why is that, do you think?"

"What?"

"I mean, you know me. What is it about me, what makes you think I couldn't be a father?" He sat a bit closer to her. "Please tell me. I'd really appreciate your insight."

"I don't know," she said. "Maybe you'd make a great father. I bet you would." His face fell a bit. "Yeah," she went on, "I can see you doing it all, the school run, changing nappies, everything. Yeah." By now he looked thoroughly wretched. "I bet you're very fertile, why not?" He perked up at this, supposed he might be.

"But what sort of role model would I be?" he asked her seriously. "I mean, I don't think I'm a bad man. I wouldn't, you know, hurt anyone. But what sort of man would betray . . . I mean, here we are. And what we've done is bad, isn't it? All that stuff in bed. I mean, it was very nice, but really, come on, let's be honest, it's filthy. It's a filthy thing to do. Isn't it?"

"Yes," she said.

He let her pay for the sandwiches, they went out on to the cobbles again. The rain had stopped. They did a bit of window shopping.

"Look," he said. "I'm sorry. This was supposed to be a magical weekend for you. I wanted this to be really magic. And it hasn't been."

She assured him it'd been fine. It certainly beat being at home on a Sunday afternoon.

"And last night should have been magical too. I think . . . I just wanted it too much. It felt like all or nothing. Which is silly, because we're friends, aren't we, you're not going anywhere." He took her hand. "We shouldn't be here, looking in Marks and Spencer. We won't get much chance to do it, we should be shagging, we should be shagging each other's brains out. That would be good."

"Oh, I don't know," she said.

"Please," he said. "Please. Let me try again. Let me finish what I started."

She checked her watch. It was only quarter past three.

They drove back to the hotel. Marcia was surprised to see them, wasn't nearly as welcoming. "Did you leave something behind?" He asked her if they could have their room again. Not for a whole night, just for a few hours. She looked unhappy about this. "I haven't made up the bed yet," she said. He told her that was no problem. She said okay, but she'd need to be paid a full night. He said fine. And she'd need to be paid *now*, if they were just going to take off when they felt like it. Fine, he said, and gave her the money right there and then.

The room was just as they'd left it. The stains of red she'd made on the duvet looked rather lurid. He'd brought his suitcase in from the car, she couldn't see why, and he started to unpack. "For God's sake," she said, and he explained it was just for the toiletries, he had to be clean, she'd want him clean, wouldn't she? And he went to line them all up in the bathroom.

"Let's make magic," he said. He asked if he could undress her, and she said she couldn't really see the point, there was no magic in getting undressed. But he pleaded, he promised it would be fun, so she let him, and it wasn't. "You're beautiful," he said, at last, looking at her naked body. She told him she already knew. "You don't want me to undress you, do you?" she asked, rather sternly, and he said that on balance that wouldn't be necessary.

"Lie on the bed," he told her, and she did. "I'm going to lick you on every inch of your body. I'm going to do it properly this time. You'll see."

"No," she told him. "Enough of that. If you want to fuck me, you fuck me. All right?"

He looked as if she'd broken his favourite toy.

"Listen," she went on. "You want this. Do you hear me? You're the one who wants this. I don't want this. I don't need this. It's you who wants a fuck. In which case, for God's sake, for God's *sake*, just get on and do it."

"You don't want this?" he asked.

"No," she said. "*You* want it. I want to make that very clear." She looked at his penis, and it didn't even have the decency to wilt a little.

"Okay," he said softly. And struggled with a condom wrapper.

"You're not listening," she said. "No fucking condoms. No nothing. Fuck me now, fuck me right this *second*. Or fuck off. Don't you see?" He stared at her. "I don't care. I just don't *care*."

So he fucked her. It was tight, and it hurt, but at least it *felt* like something. And he began to grunt, and she joined in too, one grunt from him, one from her—utterly out of time now, but it was honest, the grunts just came out the way they wanted to.

And from next door, too, the grunts began in earnest.

"I don't believe it," he said, and froze.

But there they were. Louder than theirs. Bolder. And much much happier.

He pulled away—she tried to hold him back, keep him inside, but he had rolled off her now, his face a picture of fury, his penis already dropping and giving up the ghost. "Shut up!" he cried, and banged on the wall.

"Come back to bed," she said.

But he was having none of it. His fists pounded against the homely wallpaper. The goose picture jumped at the impact each time, as if in surprise. "What are you doing?" he screamed. "What's in it for you? Have you even *looked* at each other? She's a tub of lard, he's . . . he's a fucking *dwarf* . . . ! Why are you doing this to us?"

"It's funny," she told him. "Can't you see it's funny?"

And he began to howl a little, as he kept those fists banging uselessly against the wall. Because they didn't care next door, they must have heard him, of *course* they had, but the grunting didn't even pause a beat, on and on it drove, and he was crying now, actually crying, angry tears, every which way. She watched with utter fascination as he at last lost the energy to rail anymore, and sat down on the edge of the bed, sobbing and bawling like a baby.

What it must be like to cry like that, she wondered coolly. She hadn't cried for such a long time. She hadn't even tried for a while. She should, sometime, she decided then and there, she'd give it a bash, see if anything came out.

"She doesn't deserve this," he was saying, "I mean, yeah, she pisses me off, she's such a *child*, I'm so sick of being the adult all the time . . ." And this was so funny, she had to laugh out loud.

He stared at her, surprised, his face wet and red. "Don't you feel any guilt at all?"

"No," she said.

"Jesus," he said. "What's the matter with you?"

"I'm dead inside," she told him. She said it very simply, but the words still sounded gloriously melodramatic, she just had to say it again. "I'm dead inside, that's how they put it," she said. She laughed at that, and his face was such a picture of horror and confusion that she laughed at that too.

They didn't speak for a while. He sobbed a little more, then was still. The grunting next door just went on.

"I'm very tired," he said at last. "I didn't sleep much last night."

"You should get some rest," she said.

He nodded, lay out on the bed. She got up. "Just shut my eyes for a while," he said. "Might as well, the room's paid for." He cuddled up to a pillow. She drew the curtains. "Thank you," he said.

She got dressed. It was still light enough that she could read the Radio Times. She sat on the chair under the TV, read the listings, found out what programmes she'd been missing. There was an old film she quite liked playing on BBC2; she switched on the set, but turned the sound off, followed the last half hour on subtitles.

And a little while after that she climbed into bed next to him. He didn't wake, but moved to her anyway; she opened her arms, and in he came, and she held him. And she even gave him a kiss—just the once, mind, and gently, and on the forehead. And at some point the grunting must have stopped—she didn't notice it anymore, anyway.

## V

He said he'd drop her off at the top of the road. It'd be safer that way, and the rain had stopped, she wouldn't get wet walking home. She said she didn't care. Then he thought, and said, no, he'd drop her outside the house. Why not, he wasn't ashamed. And it was so late at night, surely that'd be okay, unless—and he laughed—her husband was given to staring out of the window at four thirty in the morning. If he was, he'd be very odd! If he was odd like that, no wonder she was having an affair! And she said she'd meant it the first time, drop her where he liked, she really didn't care.

He parked the car, looked at her. "Well," he said. And smiled.

"Well," she said.

"I know that wasn't quite the weekend we'd been looking forward to. But I want you to know, most sincerely. I had a really good time."

She nodded. Fumbled for the door handle.

"We're okay, aren't we?" he said. "We're still friends. We're still going to have those gossips by the third floor lift at lunchtime?"

"Why not?" she said. "I'll see you tomorrow."

"I love you," he said.

And there was nothing to say to that. He broke into a shy grin.

"Well, it's out there now," he said. "That's put my foot in it!"

She pulled at the door handle. And forgot she was still wearing her seat belt. She sighed.

"I didn't know you could love two people at once," he said. "It's a funny thing, this love thing. And I do still love Alice," and it took her a moment to puzzle out who Alice was, "but, you know, if I have to choose between the two of you, I'll go with you. I will. It'll break Alice's heart," and she now just pictured poor Alice, lying on a bed somewhere, glistening with his spit as he licked every inch of her body, wet and sticky and bored out of her tiny fucking mind, "but if that's the way it has to be, then. . . . You don't have to leave your husband," he added helpfully. "You know. I'm not asking for any sacrifice on your part."

"Thanks."

"I'll just fit right in."

"I get it. Thanks."

"You want to go, don't you? Sorry." And he undid her seat belt for her. She pulled it away gratefully. "I just think. What you said. You're a very unhappy person, I think. And that just breaks my heart. Because I know I can make you happy. I can *fill* you with happiness, if you just let me." He opened his arms out for a hug.

She looked at him. She supposed a hug wasn't worth much, not after what she'd given him already. But she was damned if she was going to feel his body around hers again.

He frowned, waiting. "I'll take care of you," he said.

And then, from the trunk, she heard a grunt. She checked his face. No doubt about it, he'd heard it too.

It broke the moment. He lowered his arms. They both looked behind them, even though obviously there'd be nothing to see.

"No," she breathed.

His silly boyish face broke into a beaming smile. "He's all right!" he said. "What a relief! Isn't that a relief?"

"Yes," she said, softly.

"Do you know, I thought he'd died on me. I thought he was back there, you know, already rotting away. I thought I was going to have to slap him straight in the freezer!"

And all she could think of were the babies. The mother hadn't finished giving birth to her babies—there'd been others inside her broken body, needing to be rescued. She had failed them.

"I've changed my mind," she said. "I'd like to look after it."

"What," he said, "the rabbat?"

She had failed them. She should have picked up the mother, she should have checked. She should have picked her up, put her fingers between those flaps of skin, her whole hand if need be. She should have rummaged around, found whatever else was incubating inside, should have pulled them free.

"You said I could," she said. "You said it could be *my* discovery. And

I want it to be. I've got the perfect room to keep it in. It's like a little nursery, it'd be lovely. It'd be happy with me. She'll be happy."

"Yes," he said doubtfully. "I'm sure. But I've got a nice room too. I'm sure we've both got nice rooms."

"You love me," she said. "Give me the rabbit."

There was another grunt.

He licked his lips. She didn't take his eyes off him.

"It is ours," he agreed. "I said it was ours. We've so much to share. But I'm going to be the one who cares for it."

And she could have insisted, maybe. She could have fought him, she could even have offered to hug him, to accept his love, to go on as many weekend shag sessions as he liked. But it was half four in the morning, and she was tired, and the seat belt was off now, wasn't it, and the door was open too—and she got out of the car.

"Don't worry," he said. "I'll take care of everything."

And as she walked up the road, she thought she could hear the grunting from the boot—louder, more desperate. It was calling for her, she knew that, the grunts were for *her*, where are you *going*, and she kept walking, and she didn't look back.

There was a note from her husband waiting for her on the kitchen table. It told her that he loved her and that he hoped she'd had a good weekend and hadn't worked too hard at the conference, and that he'd had to go to bed, he couldn't wait up any longer. It wasn't that long a note, but her husband had appalling handwriting, and she was only halfway through deciphering it when he quietly entered the kitchen.

"Hey," he said softly.

"Hey," she said. "Why aren't you in bed?"

"I was," he said. "But I don't know. I suppose I was waiting for you to get in." He gave her a kiss on the cheek. "How was it?"

"Oh, you know," she said. "I'll tell you tomorrow."

He nodded.

"Go on," she said, "you go back to bed." Please. "I'll be up in a minute, I'll just have a cup of tea, then I'll join you."

"I'll make you some tea, I don't mind."

"It's okay," she told him, firmly but gently, the way she'd been advised, the way they'd both been advised, "I can make tea." And he smiled, and agreed, and they both knew he'd been told not to fuss her, they mustn't fuss each other, and then one day everything would be magically back to normal.

The kettle took a while to boil. She walked into the sitting room, turned the lights on, just looked at it pointlessly. Then she turned the lights off, and closed the door behind her. Then she went into the dining room—well, they called it a dining room, they ate in the kitchen mostly—and she turned the lights on there, she looked at that too. Then she turned the lights off, and closed the door behind her. The kettle still hadn't boiled, so she went upstairs, very quietly. And she opened the door to the nursery. Their useless little nursery. They'd even stripped the wallpaper, just to put up something more colourful and childlike. She turned the lights on, looked at this room as well. They should turn it into a spare bedroom, she thought, be useful for when guests stayed over. Assuming guests would want to stay over anymore. And maybe that boy had been right, maybe loving two people at once would be a bit complicated, maybe it was for the best. And she pulled at a hanging flap of wallpaper, and turned off the lights.

She went downstairs, and drank a cup of tea.

Then she went up the stairs to bed. Her husband was already asleep, just this mound in the darkness. She quickly got undressed—she was getting used to that, she thought, and then it was gone, that really was the last attention she gave that weekend, it was now behind her. She slipped in beside him. He grunted a little, nuzzled against her. And then didn't make another noise, all they had was this companionable silence. She felt warm and safe and utterly unreal.

"Listen," she said, softly. "I don't love you anymore."

He didn't reply. But his breathing became less regular.

"Listen," she said again. "I did love you. Oh, God, I loved you so much. And I wish I loved you now. But I don't. I want to end this, whatever it is we've got. Listen. I want to put it out of its misery."

She wished she could cry. That would be so great, right now. Make the whole thing so much more momentous. But no, dead inside was all she felt.

She had an idea. She turned on the bedside lamp. She wanted to see the expression on her husband's face. And, more importantly, if it made any difference. She studied it carefully for a good few seconds. "That's what I thought," she said at last, then rolled over, and turned out the light.

# CLOWN
## ENVY

Craig Boardman's dad has joined the circus. Craig Boardman told my son all about it in the playground. My son came home in tears, apparently Craig had been boasting about it rather. "I thought you were friends with Craig," I said, and my son sulked, and said, "Not anymore," and I'm not sure who he was most angry with, Craig Boardman, or me, for not understanding why.

I'd only met Craig Boardman's dad once, after I picked up my son from Craig's birthday party. He seemed all right, he worked in the city, he was a bit full of himself, actually. I couldn't imagine why he'd have thrown away a career like that to go and work in a circus. "He's a clown," said my son, as if that explained everything. "The clowns are the best." He asked me whether I would go and work in a circus—preferably as a clown, but it was up to me, whatever suited. I explained I had a job already. I worked in a bank. My son said that wasn't as much fun as working in a circus, and I thought about it for a while, and I said he was probably right.

My wife made us his favourite meal, and I let him play an extra hour on the X-box, but my son refused to be cheered up. I admit, I thought it would soon blow over. Craig Boardman had always seemed like quite a nice kid whenever he'd popped round to play, he always spoke to me politely and ate with his mouth closed; to be honest, he always seemed a rather better catch than my own son; to be honest, taking into account all the sulkings and temper tantrums and refusals to go to bed, there were times I rather envied Craig Boardman's dad. But it didn't blow over. If anything, the situation got worse. My son came home with news that other school friends' parents had all followed

Craig Boardman's dad's lead, and they'd all joined the circus too. Andy Wyman's dad had become a clown, Rachel Pinnocker's dad had become a lion tamer, and in year four Tommy Puce's dad now every night took his life into his own hands and allowed himself to be fired out of a cannon. And their kids had all formed a gang, with Craig Boardman at its head, and they went around the place lording it over the other kids, and bullying those that got in their way. One day my son came home and there were Chinese burns all over his arms, and my wife and I agreed that this had to stop.

I went round to Craig Boardman's dad's house right away. I rang the doorbell. Craig Boardman answered. "Hello, Craig," I said, "I'd like to speak to your father." As I've said, I'd always got on quite well with Craig, he seemed to be a well-brought-up sort of boy, but now he smirked at me insolently before going inside to fetch him. I suppose if you're the son of a clown you don't need to defer to anyone, but I think that's rather a shame. And then Craig Boardman's dad came to the doorstep. He was wearing a white face, and thick painted lips, and he had a red shining plastic nose that flashed every few seconds or so. I presumed he was on his way to work. I told him that my son and his son had had a bit of a falling out, and that I knew boys could be boys, and they'd be friends again soon—but would he speak to Craig about the Chinese burns, because that really wasn't on. And Craig Boardman's dad didn't say a word. His painted lips curved downwards, dramatically, to show me he was sad. He rubbed away mimed tears with his fists. And he indicated I should smell the flower in his buttonhole. I thought it was a peace offering, so I leaned forward as bidden. He squirted water in my face. Then he laughed—but silently, it was a mimed laugh, which seemed all the merrier somehow—and he honked his nose, and he closed the door.

My son didn't seem surprised when I returned home. "He's a clown, Dad," he said, "why would he talk to the likes of you?" And the worst of it was that my wife seemed disappointed in me too, disapproving even. That night in bed she put down her Mills and Boon and fixed me with a serious look. "I don't see why you *can't* join the circus," she said. "It's not as if there's not part time work going as well." My wife, who had always said she'd loved me for me, banker and all. I asked her whether she'd really rather I worked in a circus than in the third most solvent banking conglomerate in Western Europe, and she said, "If you won't do it for your family, at least do it for *yourself*," and I wasn't sure what she meant by that. Our lovemaking seemed pointedly pedestrian, and

I wondered whether my wearing a red plastic nose would have put a bit more life into her. I agreed to go to a circus audition. She smiled at last, made something approaching the right sort of sexual effort. And for my part, I rued the day we had let the council tear down the local library and erect that big top in its place.

I put on my best suit, I went to the circus. There was a line outside. It was composed of nervous middle-aged men all trying to look entertaining, I recognized a lot of them from school Parents' Evenings. We were auditioned in groups of six. The man in charge asked us one by one to explain what we thought we could offer a circus; I assumed he was the ringmaster, but he wasn't wearing a red suit or a top hat, and his T-shirt was stained and he kept picking at it. I told him I wanted to be a clown to impress my son, and he said that, yeah, they got a lot of that.

He led us out into the circus ring. I gazed up at the seats all around, and imagined they were full of paying customers demanding to be amused, and at the thought butterflies started swirling round my stomach most unhelpfully. My feet sank deep into the sawdust, and I looked down, and saw that it was fake and plastic. "Let's see what you can do," the ringmaster said.

First, he had us juggling. I had never juggled before, I didn't think I could. But it was easier than it looked, or maybe I had a natural proclivity for it, I don't know—the three balls were soon dancing through the air, and I knew really that I was the one making it happen, I knew I was catching them and throwing them, but it seemed to me that it was all taking place independently of me, without any effort, the way I keep my heart beating or my lungs heaving without having to think about it, all I was doing was patting the balls on the back in friendly encouragement and sending them on their way. "More balls, more balls!" called the ringmaster, and then I was thrown a fourth ball, then a fifth, a sixth; then he threw in a glass of water, a plastic spoon, a brick—and *still* I could do it, still I could keep them all in the air, in one increasing circle, as if they were all cars on some invisible Ferris wheel and my hands were the fulcrum, no, not so much science, as if it were *magic*. And I dared to believe that I was good at this, and I dared to believe that my son and my wife would be proud of me. I stole a glance at all the other dads. And they were juggling too. And they were juggling a *dozen* balls each, maybe two dozen even, it was hard to see because they were spinning through the air so fast, so much faster than mine, my balls now seemed to me to be meandering through the air as if stunted by arthritis and wheezing for breath. And some of the dads were juggling knives and chainsaws and burning torches, and was that a grenade, was the man next to me really juggling a grenade? They were better than me. They were all better than me. And I lost control, I admit it, I lost confidence, so did the balls, everything came crashing down. The ringmaster looked at me, frowned, didn't say a word, and made a little mark upon his clipboard.

He made us try all sorts of things. Custard pies, collapsing cars, pratfalls—oh, I tell you, I pratted my very hardest, I tried to be the best prat I could be. And at the end of every test he would take out that clipboard, make more marks against it, and at the end of the *final* test he made the biggest marks on his clipboard of all. "Right," he said, looking through the results, and then looking at us, *through* us, as if he could see our very clowning souls. "Right, I've reached my decision. You," and he pointed at me, "yes, you, one pace forward." And I couldn't believe it, and I burned with pride, and I knew I would never go back to the bank again, and I knew this was what I had been born for, after all, to do stunts and japes, and make silly noises, to make people happy, to be *spectacular*. I began to thank him. "You can go home," he said to me. "The rest of you, welcome aboard. Go through that door, you'll find your barracks. You're in the circus now."

I begged the ringmaster to reconsider. And he listened to me, and his face softened, he seemed even quite kindly. But I knew he'd had men beg in front of him before. "It's not your fault," he said. "It's your face. The whole point of comedy is that we can laugh at another's suffering without feeling guilty about it. These other guys, life shits on them, and their faces puff out so amusingly, there's nothing you can do *but* laugh! But you. There's something tragic about you." To illustrate his point he poured water down my trousers and hit me round the head with a frying pan. "You see?" he said. "The way you look now, so humiliated and pathetic, it makes me want to cry." And indeed he wept then, tears rolled down his cheeks, and he asked me to leave.

I got home, and my son was so excited; he was bouncing around the room, singing, "My Daddy's joined the circus, my Daddy's joined the circus!" My wife looked excited too. And I had come up with all sorts of excuses why I hadn't got the job, racism, sexism, flat feet—but when it came to it, I just told them the truth. "I wasn't good enough," I said. And I thought my son would throw one of his tantrums, but he didn't; he looked at me soberly, even touched my shoulder, and said, "That's all right, Dad." And I saw that a certain light had gone from his eyes.

He went to his room. My wife said, "Oh, for Heaven's sake," and put on her coat. I asked her where she was going, but she didn't reply. About an hour later she was back; "There!" she said, rather smugly really, and dropped a sequined dress upon the kitchen table. She'd got herself a job as a trapeze artist, and I must admit I was surprised—my wife had never been what you'd call svelte, not even when we'd first met, and that was years and years ago.

The next Saturday I took my son to see his mother perform at the circus. I hadn't seen a circus show since I was small, and I felt very excited in spite of myself. I bought us some tickets, and some hot dogs, and we took our seats. There wasn't much of an audience, just little patches of sad looking men like me sitting with their kids, and I was disappointed, I thought the circus would have been more popular than this. Then the lights on the ring went up, and on to the fake sawdust bounded every one of our friends and neighbours. Near us, all alone, sat Craig Boardman. He looked rather lost. My son told me he didn't think Craig Boardman's dad had much time for Craig Boardman anymore. I asked my son whether we should invite Craig to sit with us, and my son shrugged, said why not? Craig seemed pleased, and said thank you very politely. I gave him a hot dog, and he ate every last bit of it with his mouth closed.

The ringmaster looked so much more impressive with a hat on his head and a whip in his hand. He brought out the first act. It was the clowns. Craig Boardman's dad was the chief clown, and he was ribticklingly funny. He was also very good when he came back later to lift weights, and he rode a horse standing upright, and he spun plates on sticks, I must admit I began to fall a little in love with Craig Boardman's dad. "Do you see your mother?" I asked, and my son said he did, and pointed—and there she was, at the very top of the tent, climbing on to a swing, squeezed tight into that sequined dress so that all her bits were bulging. We applauded her. She looked so graceful up there, and my heart swelled large and proud. She leaped from the swing, arms stretched out, aiming herself right where Craig Boardman's dad was waiting to catch her, and she missed, and she plummeted to her death fifty feet below.

They said afterwards she wouldn't have felt much, it must have been very quick—though I'm not sure, that fake sawdust was awfully sharp, and it impaled her body in a thousand different places. But at that moment I'm afraid I leaped to my feet. And I cried out, and even to me the cry didn't sound quite human, it was so full of grief, I think, or maybe it was just shock. To think that at one moment my wife had been in the circus, and the next she was lying flat on the ground before us like a squashed jam doughnut. I cried out against the world. I cried so hard. And they turned the lights on me. And everybody began to laugh. The audience, the performers, even my son, even Craig Boardman, even Craig Boardman's dad. Because somehow, in that epiphany of suffering, I had accidentally pulled the right face. A face for comedy, a face everyone could laugh at guilt-free. And I saw the ringmaster, and he was clapping me, and nodding, as if to say, "Fair play, sir, fair play."

That night I made my son his favourite dinner. He helped me, quietly, in the kitchen. I wondered whether he felt ashamed that his mania for the circus had pushed his mother to her death. He said he didn't. He said he felt a certain ennui. He recognized that at some point in any child's life one has to accept the fallibility of one's parents. With me, it was my failure to get a job at the circus, with his mother, it was when she so ineptly made a pig's ear of an elementary trapeze act. "But," he said to me, "with you, at least you tried. But Mum? I'm sorry, but she didn't just miss Craig Boardman's dad, she was *nowhere even near*." He did seem more adult, and I asked him if he was all right, and he said he was, and I think he was lying, but that's the adult thing to do. I was proud of him, but I didn't say. And we sat down to eat.

# ELEMENTARY PROBLEMS OF PHOTOGRAPHY (NUMBER THREE): AN ANALYSIS, AND PROFERRED SOLUTION

A basic problem with early photography was its inability to hold the image of cats. Nicephore Niepce's process of taking a metal plate coated with bitumen and bombarding it with light was quite the discovery, of course, and the further pioneering efforts by Daguerre and Talbot to develop this technique were of huge influence. For the first time in history there really was the sense that a moment in time could be frozen forever, that people and places and events could be preserved accurately. It gave us a glimpse of something godlike, something immortal. We drew a blank with cats, though.

Dogs were all right. There was something so essentially noble and straightforward about a dog, it would have been an offence to the sensibilities had dogs not been photographed. And, although it took a bit of fiddling with the lenses, by the late 1870s it had become increasingly easy to capture the likeness of horses as well. But no one had successfully managed to hold a cat upon film; there were various (unsubstantiated) reports from experimental 'graphers that they had done so (and on the continent, always on the continent!)—only for a little while, and blurred maybe, not a good likeness, though quite definitely feline. But the image never held long enough for anyone to verify these claims, the cats faded away from the pictures within seconds.

Some said it was because the cat had no soul. Others, that it was simply too minor a life form, too low down upon the table of creation for the camera to recognize. And some people—the ones who actually *owned* cats, who knew what they were about, knew their moods and their characters, said that the cats were doing it deliberately. Cats had no interest in their images being preserved on paper via a collusion of light and oil. What was in it for them?

For the sake of simplicity we had long claimed that the photography of cats was impossible, but that didn't mean we thought it was actually, genuinely *impossible*; no one believed that, I think, except perhaps Gerard Pomfrey, but his fustian ideas about the photosciences had long since been discredited. I was certain that the solution was out there, somewhere. It would be a long voyage of discovery for someone. That someone was not going to be me. I don't like cats. I was not prepared to devote my hard-earned photoscopic skills to them.

I still don't know why it was me that Simon Harries contacted. We had both studied at Oxford together, and I remember that back then his views on the inconstancy of calotypes from silver salt solutions were regarded as mildly controversial. But Harries was not the man for controversy, he had neither the charisma nor the gall to carry it off. I had had respect for Harries, I could see there was talent within him, and I think maybe I was the closest he had to a friend—but, still, we were *not* friends, not by any stretch of the definition, and I had neither heard from him nor of him since we'd graduated fifteen years before. I can hardly describe the surprise I felt when I received a telegram from him, let alone my surprise at the contents of that message.

He asked me to visit him at his house in South London that very evening—promptly, at half past eleven. He had something of vital importance to show me. There was no hint in his words that we had had no communication for so long, there was no greeting or attempt at reintroduction, it was as if we had been working side by side in the same laboratory every day. I was half inclined to ignore the thing, but for the urgency of the final sentence. He urged me to come alone, and to tell no one—and I confess, I was intrigued.

I had a light supper, and then caught a hansom cab to Streatham. I hadn't been south of the Thames for a while, and I had forgotten just how much poverty there was to the place. I don't know how man can live in such slum conditions. Still, I was surprised when the cab dropped me off , the driver himself looking eager to get back to the civilizing areas of the city and only too relieved when I told him he had no reason to wait. I had thought that Harries must have found some decent lodgings here, however cheap; but this was not a house, this was a hovel, there wasn't even a doorknocker, I had to beat on the door with my fists. Photography was a science studied by gentlemen; this was not a place where a gentleman could live; what had happened to Harries to bring him so low?

Harries opened the door and showed me in. I would not have recognized him. He had aged. His hair was grey. He had not shaven. His cravat was askew. "What is all this about, Harries?" I asked. I felt I had the right to be a little abrupt.

His eyes wouldn't settle on me, they darted about nervously. "You came alone?"

"As you can see."

"And you have spoken to no one?"

"You try my patience, man."

"Forgive me," he said, and he smiled, and he grasped my hands in his, and shook them briefly, and he began to giggle. "I see so few people nowadays. Oh! but I have done it. I have done it! It is the discovery of the age!"

He lived in one room, I could see, and that a small one; over the floor were papers; over the papers were sheets of acetate, broken or chipped lenses, dyes, gels, scraps of stale food. "I have 'graphed a cat," he whispered to me, eyes shining.

I felt no personal affection for Harries, but I was nonetheless sorry that a man of such potential had gone down such a scientific blind alley. He could see the disappointment on my face; I confess, I did not try to disguise it; he grabbed on to my arm, tight. He said, "I've done it, I tell you!"

"Then let me see," I said.

And then he was smiling again, a crafty little smile, I did not like that smile much. "Oho, not yet! Not yet! Not until midnight! The cats only come out at the witching hour, you'll see, you'll see." And he cleared the debris off the only chair, and invited me to sit down.

A little before twelve, he fetched for me a 'graph. He'd taken a picture of the room. He had taken it from the chair, I think, from the exact place I was sitting. The books were in slightly different positions, maybe, I saw a pile of photoscientific treatises that had since then toppled over. "There's nothing here," I said—"Not yet, not yet," he insisted, "I tell you, midnight!" And I looked hard at the picture, and so did he, and that's how we spent the next few minutes. I felt ridiculous.

The clock struck. Loud, too loud. "Sorry, sorry," said Harries, "I make sure I can never sleep through it. But look, look, on the 'graph!" And I was looking at the 'graph, and of course, I expected to see nothing, and there would be an end to this. I even opened my mouth to say so; I shut it again.

105

For wasn't there something swimming into focus? Wasn't there a blur, and the blur was taking on a more rigid outline, and then a solid shape. "My God," I said, and I apologise, but I was that surprised. Because there, looking out of the picture, indubitably, was a cat. Looking out at me. It looked as shocked as I was. Its eyes were wide in the flash light, its ears were pricked, its fur was standing on edge.

"But it must be a trick," I said. "Simon? Is this not some small child you have dressed up as a cat, or . . . ?"

"I have the proof!" he laughed. "Ha ha, I have *proof*!" And at that he threw aside a few more papers, and lifted from the floor the cat itself. He picked it up by the tail. Its face was set in the exact same expression I saw in the 'graph, its fur still set fast and rigid.

"Dead," I said, uselessly.

"Dead, yes, ha ha, it always kills 'em, don't know why!" said Harries. "Normally they just die, ha ha, and there's nothing to show for it. But this time I set the exposure right! I got the picture! The cat didn't die in vain!"

"And how long have you been doing this?" I asked.

He waved his hand as if it were a matter of utter irrelevance; and, I suppose, to him it was. "There are lots of cats on the streets, sniffing around the waste is a good place to find 'em. Sometimes they claw and bite," and I could see now, yes, there were marks all over his arms, little scars on his cheeks, "but I'm bigger than 'em, ha ha, they're no match for me! I take 'em here, and I 'graph 'em, and I get rid of 'em, and their bodies end up so frozen hard they sink straight to the bottom of the river! But I kept this one, he's my little pet, my little boy. I'm proud of him. He's made me a success, yes, he has, he's made me all proper and worthwhile." And he actually stroked at the dead cat's stiffened fur.

"And what do you want of me?" I asked. And I felt a chill, as if I thought he might want to take a photograph of *me*, he would rob the life from me and set me down on film—but that was silly, no harm had ever come to a human being from being 'graphed, I was not an animal.

"You have a Reputation," said Harries, and he said it like that, with a capital R. "You are a good man. People will listen to you. I charge you to bring my discovery to the world."

"No," I said. I didn't even know I was going to refuse him until I spoke, but the refusal came out immediately, as if all my instincts were revolting against him, as if my intellect knew I wanted no part of this before my mouth did.

"Why not?" he said, and for a second he scrunched his hands into fists and something dark passed over his face—then he relaxed, his face slumped back into the same failed despondency I had known from Oxford. "Why not?" he said again, meek and defeated.

"I am a man of science," I said, "and I duly believe that the purpose of science is to better mankind. And I can see no betterment that comes from the photography of cats, not whether they are alive or dead."

I did not want to leave on such a terse note, and so endeavoured to make some light talk with Harries about his health and the weather, but neither of our hearts were in it, and I soon gave up and took a cab home.

Three weeks later Simon Harries was dead. The police came to my house and asked whether I could help them with their enquiries, and at first I thought they meant I was implicated, and I was fully prepared to get quite angry about the matter. But they assured me that wasn't the case, and made apologies, and spoke to me with such due deference that I fetched my coat and my hat and agreed to go with them.

They took me to Harries' lodgings. In the middle of the room, spread over his papers, was a body, I presumed Harries', covered with a sheet. I recoiled at that, but not at the sight of death, just at the insensitive way in which I'd been allowed to see it.

"Sorry, sir," said the constable on duty. "We've tried to move it, but it weighs a ton, and that's a fact." He showed me a box. He told me it had been left for me, and indeed, it had my name and address written upon the side.

"Would you like me to open this?" I asked, and the policeman said it would be a blessing for 'em if I didn't mind.

I could not imagine why Harries would leave me anything. Inside the box I found his camera, and a dozen or so photographs. The camera was old and outmoded, I dare say he'd never had the funds to purchase a better one; I had no need of it, I had several cameras of my own at home. The photographs were an odd mix; some of them, I assume, had been taken by Harries; some of them, like the portrait of Queen Victoria, no doubt rescued from a newspaper, definitely weren't.

At the bottom of the box I found an envelope. I opened it.

"Can't Stop Them Now," was all it said.

It was an unhelpful note, one of vagueness and imprecision, and unworthy of an Oxford graduate. And I understood why Simon Harries had managed no better than a lower second.

The constable said, "Begging your pardon, would you look at the body, sir? It's got us properly stumped, and you're a man of science and all." I pointed out that my science was photography not medicine, but accepted after further pleading that I was still the best qualified scientist there, and permitted them to present me the corpse.

The sheet was removed. In death Harries looked larger, swollen somehow, as if he'd been the victim of drowning—though his body, naturally enough, was perfectly dry. That he was peculiarly bloated was not the most disturbing thing about him—it was more that his mouth was open, wide open, opened wider than I thought a mouth could stretch.

"For heaven's sake," I said, "give the man some dignity. At least shut the mouth!" And the constable said to me his men had tried to do just that, but the mouth *wouldn't* shut; "The jaws have got stuck somehow, sir." So I had a go. I put on my gloves, and reached out to Harries' face. I saw as I neared it there were fresh scratches upon his cheeks. I pulled on the chin, but it was indeed stiff. For a moment I thought his body had frozen hard like the carcass of the cat he had shown me—but no, I pulled harder, and I could feel some give—I admit, I was none too gentle about it, and at last the hinges of the jaws gave way to my bidding and the mouth snapped tight shut.

"Thanking you, sir," said the constable.

"That's all I can do, I'm afraid," I said. "This death goes beyond the knowledge afforded me by photoscopic theory. I'd say he didn't die easily, though. Poor devil."

Back home I perused the contents of the box once more.

There was nothing new to be gleaned from the enigmatic letter, so I destroyed it. I checked the camera; it had no film. I left it in the kitchen. It was junk, but I thought I might cannibalize it for parts.

I took the photographs up to my study. I sat in my favourite chair, drank a brandy.

Yes, some of them had clearly been taken by Harries. Two of them were of his own lodgings for a start, and I assumed they were failures from his cat experiments. But others seemed to be not of his hand at all, the style was wrong, the composition. There were pictures of empty anonymous streets. There were pictures of famous London landmarks, the one of St Paul's Cathedral at dusk was especially striking. There was a man and a woman outside a church, all dressed up in their best—was it their wedding day? Or was it nothing of the sort?

They looked uncomfortable, was that at the prospect of spending the rest of their lives together, or that someone was aiming a camera at them and stealing the moment and freezing it for his own ends and committing it to film and making it possible that strangers like me could finger at it and paw at it and stare at it without shame? There was Queen Victoria. She didn't seem amused.

I could see nothing to connect the pictures whatsoever. I tried to puzzle it over, but not too seriously; it wasn't my mystery, after all, I didn't have to care. I felt drowsy. I raised a glass to Harries, and toasted him. I meant it respectfully enough, but quite see it may have come out wrong.

I dozed.

And when I woke up, the fire was nearly out, and there was a crick in my neck, and I'd dropped the photographs all over the floor. I looked at the time—and it was on the verge of midnight—and then, soon enough, the grandfather clock downstairs began to chime. But that wasn't what had stirred me, that started *after* I had woken, and it was as if there was a little alarm inside my head and it had gone off, it had made sure I was able to see all the fun. . . .

The top photograph was of Harries' room. And I stared at it. I didn't *want* to stare at it. I didn't want to see a dead cat shimmer into view. But I couldn't take my eyes off it—and yes—soon enough—there it was, the outline, then filling in with more clarity, more depth—there was the cat, sure enough, its 'graph taken at the very point of death. The previous cat had looked merely surprised. This one was angry.

And it wasn't alone.

Because the picture continued to blur, now all around the fringes of it, I could see the blurring ripple beneath my fingers and I all but dropped the photograph, it buzzed to the touch. And there was a sound to it now, a whispering? A hissing. And more cats began to appear.

How many cats had Harries squeezed into his studio? What had he done?

There were a dozen—then there were more—then the picture was *full* of them, a hundred cats, a hundred and one, who could say?—big cats, kittens too, and all spilling out over each other, jostling for space, cramming themselves into every last crevice of space the picture could afford, blotting out the background of the room until all that could be seen was wall to wall cat.

And even though the picture was full, I could see that the 'graph was blurring still, and the hissing was louder now, it was a *seething*—

THE BEST DARK FICTION OF ROBERT SHEARMAN

and there were still more cats being born, but there was no space for them, they were crushing the other cats now, they were bending themselves out of shape too, they were distorting, they were making themselves anew.

And still, still, the cats wouldn't stop. And there was no light to the picture now, it was all just a mass of black, and the black was crying out, I knew that black wasn't a void, it was anything but, it was the weight of all the cats in the world stuffed into an area no more than a few inches square, and still, still the cats wouldn't stop.

And the other pictures.

There were cats piled up as high as St Paul's Cathedral, they were choking up the River Thames. There were cats in the wedding dress, there were cats perched on top of the bridegroom's hat, and pouring out from under his hat, and pouring out from under *him*. There was Queen Victoria, regal, unsmiling, and the cats were prodding at her face, they were prodding at her cheeks, they were forcing a smile out of her whether she liked it or not.

And I knew they were here. That the world was full of ghosts, stuffed together tight, and that we couldn't see. But the camera could see. The camera could see the cats, at least. At least it could only see the cats.

I wanted to throw the photographs from me, get them away as far as I could. But I couldn't move. And I felt something so heavy on my chest—and I knew they were there, all of them, all the cats who had ever died, all of them were sitting on me and crawling over me and trying to find somewhere warm to shelter away from the cold of extinction. I thought I couldn't breathe. I thought I couldn't breathe. Then, then I forced myself to my feet. And, of course, there was nothing pinning me down, of course there was no weight to shift—and, of course, nothing kicked and wailed and howled as it scattered to the floor.

I lit a candle. I went downstairs.

I had to get to the camera. To destroy it? I don't know. To take pictures, lots of pictures, to fill the world with cats, say to everybody, look! look! this is where the dead go!

Film that doesn't show us what is really there, that gives us stories and fantasies instead, what use could that ever be?

And as I went down the stairs I imagined the cats beneath my feet would trip me up, and I held on to the banister rail so tightly. And I imagined my stepping on their tails, my treading down on their backs, the crunch of their bones breaking underfoot, the howls, the mews, the pitiful mews.

I entered the kitchen.

The camera was where I'd left it, on the table.

Wrapped around it—licking it, even?—was a cat. The fattest cat I had ever seen. Greasy too, its fur looked slick and oily and wet.

It bared its teeth at me.

"Get away!" I cried. "Get out of here!"

It wouldn't take its eyes off me. It wouldn't move from the camera.

"Didn't you hear what I said? What do you want? Tell me what you want!" I was ready to bargain with a cat. And I threw the candle at it.

I didn't aim at the cat directly. I think it knew that. I think that's why it didn't even flinch. The candlestick passed harmlessly overhead.

"Get out!" I said, and I mimed throwing something else, although I had nothing left to throw, and of course the cat could see that. But it yawned, it stretched. It gave me a look that I can only describe as reproachful. And then, slowly, in its own time, it slinked away from the camera. It dropped off the table, and for all its bulk landed lightly on its feet.

"You get away!" I said. But it was ignoring me now. I backed away as it trotted towards me, out of the door, out of the room.

I looked for it in the corridor, but it was dark now without the candle. I couldn't see it.

I went to the camera.

I was going to destroy it. But now I picked it up, I felt the urge to take photographs with it. What else is a camera for? No, I was going to destroy it. I was going to smash it down upon the table, now, hard, the glass would shatter, and all the ghosts would be locked away forever somewhere we couldn't see.

And I saw there was film in it. There hadn't been film earlier. I had checked. Who had put the film in?

I hesitated.

I took out the film, and had it developed.

I haven't destroyed the camera.

I've told Cook to keep it in the kitchen. And if the cats get in, and sometimes they do, she is to remove them from the house. But she must be gentle with them. She must give them milk first, and treat them with respect.

I haven't used the camera, either. Though one night I woke up, and I was downstairs, in the kitchen, and I was holding the camera with both hands. And I had never walked in my sleep before. I woke up in time, I went back upstairs, I locked my bedroom door. I keep the door locked every night now.

Maybe I'll destroy the camera anyway. One day. We'll see. I just don't think that would make the cats very happy.

There are African tribes I've heard of, savages really, who don't like the white man taking photographs of them. They fear that it takes their souls. But I worry that the reverse may be true. What if the camera brings a dead soul back? What if every picture confers a little immortality, and the world simply cannot support the weight of all those never-to-be-forgotten memories?

I destroyed the photograph that I had found in the camera. No one else need ever see that. For my part, though, it might as well still exist. For my part, I might as well have framed it, and hung it over my bed. It's not as if I'll ever forget what was in that photograph, not one single detail of it.

The picture was of Simon Harries. And I now know how he died. And I now know why his mouth was open so unnaturally wide, because there was something forcing the bulk of its entire body in. It knew what it was doing, too—the photograph had caught a little jaunty wave of the tail. And I don't think it was the first that had crawled inside Harries' mouth, I think that Harries' bloated body was full of them.

And I remember how I had forced his jaws shut, and the resistance I felt, and I think I must have had that ghost body bitten clean through.

I'll destroy the camera one day. I will. But for now, I treat all cats well, and I sleep with the door locked, and my mouth taped up.

No one can take photographs of babies either. Babies have no souls. But no one wants a picture of a baby.

# GOOD GRIEF

Once in a while, for a joke, they'd talk about what they'd do if the other died. They'd be lying in bed together, dozing, cuddling, they might even just have made love—and it was so warm in there, and death seemed so very far away. Janet would say, "I'm going to get you to scatter my ashes, somewhere really obscure," and he'd ask her how obscure, and she'd laugh, and say, "I don't know, the top of Mount Everest." And David would say, "I'm going to leave you everything in my will, but only on condition you stay the night in a haunted house," and she'd ask where he might find this haunted house, and he'd tell her he'd Google one on the internet—"don't you worry, missie, you're not getting out of it that easily!" She'd tell him that if he died she'd never marry again—and she'd keep his head in a box, or on display on the mantelpiece, to ward off potential suitors. And he told her that he *would* marry again, in unseemly haste that would shock the in-laws, someone young and pretty, and bring her to his wife's own funeral. She kicked him for that. And then they'd doze some more, or cuddle some more—or maybe even make love again, there was plenty of lovemaking to be had back then.

What actually happened, when he found out his wife was dead, was that he went quite numb. He felt sorry for the policewoman who brought him the bad news: she was so upset, she was so young, she probably hadn't done this much before. But only *vaguely* sorry, he wasn't sure how to express himself. And when he thanked her for her time and wished her a nice day he hoped it had come out right.

And it was while numb that he accepted condolences, opened greetings cards telling him "sorry for your loss," received flowers.

That he phoned Janet's parents, first to tell them their daughter was dead, the words slipped out more easily than he expected, too easily— and then on each night thereafter to see how they were, how they were holding up, whether they were doing okay—and he heard their numbness too, the way that the voices became ever softer, their words large and round and bland—and he thought, I'm doing this to them, I'm infecting them with numbness. It was while numbed that he had to take his sister's phone calls, because she'd phone him every night too— "to see how you are, how you're holding up, are you okay"—and she *was* crying, sometimes she'd be unable to speak through the tears, "oh, God, I've lost a sister, I always wanted a proper sister of my own,"—and he felt annoyed at that, that her grief was better than his. Especially when she hadn't even known Janet that well, she had never once given a Christmas present Janet had wanted, Janet had never liked his sister much. He prepared the funeral numbed, was numbed as he organized flowers and arranged a nice buffet for the wake; he was really quite spectacularly numb as he wrote a eulogy to Janet, he wanted to tell the world how he felt now she'd gone forever, but he didn't know how he felt, that was what he was still trying to work out; "I'm in shock," he said, to reassure himself, "it has to be expected, I'm in shock," but it had been *days* now, how long could you be 'in shock' for?

The words of his eulogy did the right things on the page, all sad and regretful, but even as he plucked them out of his brain (from God knows which part) they didn't seem much to do with him, or with Janet, or their seven-year marriage, or their however-many-years-long marriage that they ought to have had. I'm a fraud, he thought. Friends said he shouldn't deliver the eulogy himself, he'd be too upset, let the minister do it. And the minister was a nice old man, and he talked a lot about God, and he had a kind face and kind eyes and a white beard, he was pretty much what David thought God looked like, maybe he *was* God—except David didn't believe in God, and neither had Janet, so wasn't this all a bit pointless? Wasn't it pointless? With her there in the coffin (and the coffin was so expensive, and they were only going to use it the once!), and he couldn't even see Janet inside, it might have been stuffed with old newspaper. And David looked at Janet's parents, and they were crying now, their numbness had broken, they'd snapped right out of it, "why not me?" I'm a fraud, I feel nothing, shout it out, dare you, maybe I never loved her enough to feel, I'm a fraud. The minister read the eulogy, and he got the emphasis wrong, he made all the funny bits too serious, and all the serious bits, the bits about loss and pain and whatever else David had managed to dredge up, all the serious bits just sounded trivial. And David thought, it should have been me after all. And he supposed that meant, I should have been the one who read the eulogy, but now the thought was in his head, he thought, I should have been the one in the car crash. It should have been me. It should have been me.—But not hysterical, not upset. No. Numb.

The collision had been head on. Both drivers were killed. The other woman had been drinking. They told him Janet wouldn't have known anything about it, she'd have died instantly. David supposed that was better, right? To die in ignorance.

She hadn't left a will, and so hadn't put any funny conditions in it. He didn't know where to scatter her ashes. He did it in the park. It wasn't especially obscure, but, so.

At the wake he was told, by a series of well-meaning but irritating people, that he should see the doctor and get himself some sleeping pills. "Why?" So he could sleep, of course! But sleeping really hadn't been a problem, there was so much to do, so much to plan—so many well-meaning people to navigate—that he'd fall asleep the moment his head hit the pillow.

He didn't have nightmares. He didn't have dreams, actually, when he slept he was (ho ho) dead to the world. In fact, David was only ever going to have two more dreams, and only the first he thought of as a nightmare. It happened just a couple of days after the funeral was done and there wasn't anything to plan anymore—and David welcomed it, he'd been expecting *something*, this would be a release—and annoyed too, because it turned out to be entirely the wrong *sort* of nightmare altogether. No dead wife. No car crash. Nothing like grief at all, no grief in which his unconscious state could relax, and kick back, and say, yes, this, *this*, is what I've been waiting for.

This is what he dreamed.

He couldn't close his eyes.

It wasn't even interesting at first, and hardly distressing, and it took him quite a while to work out anything was wrong at all. He was— somewhere, anywhere. He was—standing, sitting, it didn't matter. Nothing was going on. There was nothing to be concerned about. He was just himself, his ordinary self, who else might he be, and he was content, and a little bored perhaps, waiting for the action to start.

It occurred to him that he hadn't blinked for a while. That was just how engaging this dream was—it gave him time to count his blinks.

And now he registered it, of course, he decided he *wanted* to blink. That would feel good. Just a little blink, thank you, he deserved one of those. And he wasn't able to.

This was silly. The brain wasn't sending the right message to the eyes. He sent a message to his brain, from another part of his brain, telling it to pull its socks up. The brain told the eyes to close. To do one of those blink things they were so expert at. David felt the muscles at the sides of his eyes squeeze—just a little, complacently, this wasn't a problem, the eyes knew they could do this (ho ho again) in their sleep. And then, when that didn't work out, the muscles putting a little more effort in, straining.

Nothing. The eyes stared open, resolutely fixed.

David was quite surprised by this. So much so that he raised his eyebrows, and the brows pulled the eyelids ever upwards. David couldn't relax his face from that surprise. He now found he couldn't even lower the eyelids back to where they'd been before, back to where this whole stupid non-blinking problem had started.

"It's all right," he told himself, but it wasn't all right, it was a nightmare, and his eyes were stuck, and he'd forever look like an idiot, some stupid boggle-eyed staring idiot. And where the hell was Janet, shouldn't she be showing up soon, wouldn't dealing with that particular trauma be a bit more *useful*?

Now he thought of blinking, naturally enough, there was nothing he more wanted to do. His body was screaming at him to blink. It was like thinking of an itch, and then in the thought of it needing to scratch—except, no, don't think of itching, keep away from that.

Too late. Because now David was beginning to panic. And panic over such a ridiculous thing—and he felt that itch now, his *eyes* were itching. They were tingling, God, he'd have to scratch them, he'd have to reach up his hand, reach out his nails, and *scratch* them, hard, scratch away that itch, scratch until the eyeballs were shreds.

And he knew the eyelids wouldn't even shut down, the little bits of protection those fragile flaps of skin could offer wouldn't be there. Because the eyelids only moved *upwards* now, didn't they? And at that, oops, he raised them further, he opened his eyes as wide as they would go, and they locked tight into that position. Fixed, bulging, and so very, very ticklish.

David knew he was asleep. And because of that he knew that in real life his eyes must be *closed*. He wanted to wake up, get out of the dream. Before he did something terrible, before the fingernails did their work. But he couldn't. He felt himself hit out at the bed, he was struggling, he was crying out. This other self of his, the one he could detect faintly in the waking world, he was *useless*, wasn't he? If only he could get his eyes opened for *real*, he could shut the ones in his fantasy. But neither of his eyes was willing to help. Staying right where we are, said the dream eyes. So are we, said the ones sleeping in David's bed. And he thought for one merciful moment, it'll be okay, with all this commotion I'll wake Janet, and she'll wake me, she'll look after me, I'll be safe—but, oh—shit—and he could feel he was really screaming out now, no one beside him could have slept through that, but there was no one beside him to hear.

He tried to remember what blinking was supposed to achieve. It was to moisturise the eyeball, wasn't it? Give it a little spray of water. Why would the eye need that? Why would we need to blink so often, did we need that water so very urgently? He thought perhaps we did. He thought perhaps it was essential. And they were *raging* with itches now, his eyes were blazing raw in their sockets—give us some water, we're parched!—and his brain was sending down messages to the fingernails, go to it, lads, scratch away, scratch hard until the eyeballs pop—but (thank God) it seemed the fingernails weren't listening, they stayed right were they were, it seemed no one was taking orders from brain tonight. David's eyes were so large now, so wide open, he could feel the pressure on his forehead. And they were hardening too, all the water was gone, they were tightening up like old mud, and then the cracks would appear, and the cracks would break into bigger fissures, and his eyeballs would *splinter*, wouldn't they, they'd shatter all over his stupid stupefied stupid face.

And he was sweating with fear, and he suspected this was both in the dream and out of it, and maybe that'd be good, all that sweat might run into his eyes and give it the liquid refreshment it needed—except, wait—wouldn't it be very salty—that'd sting, that'd *burn*—and he was screaming different messages at his eyes, no wonder they were getting confused—"Open up!" "Shut down!" and no one was obeying him, someone else was in control, someone else giving instructions to both eyes inner and outer, someone wanted him to *hurt*.

He threw himself out of bed. His eyes snapped open in shock. He fought off the duvet, still wrapped around him, and yes, he had been sweating, the duvet was *drenched*. In his panic he thought that even in real life he wouldn't be able to close his eyes, that he'd be trapped forever looking at this poor empty bedroom that ought to have had two people in it and now only had one—but no, they closed, and again, and again, and again.

He went to the bathroom. Stared in the mirror. Already he was calming down, it was all right, he was all right. He saw reflected back at him not the terrified man of the dream, but someone who was tired, and confused, and so sad, and slumping back into the numbness. But he watched himself blink some thirty or forty times, one blink after the other. Deliberately, enjoying it. Enjoying the sweet sensation of it, and the freedom that he could do as he wished. Enjoying himself, so it seemed, for the first time since Janet had died.

His lips felt a bit thick. He'd probably hurt them when he fell out of bed, maybe he'd bitten them or something. He prodded at them, but they stayed rubbery to the touch. It took him going downstairs and making himself a hot cup of coffee before he got any proper feeling back.

Pretty soon, David realized, people were getting bored with him. This struck him as rather unfair. He wasn't the one who kept on talking about the death, he mentioned it as little as possible. Everyone was sympathetic, but sympathy was so *tiring*.

He'd gone back to work, but the boss soon called him into his office. "I don't think you should be here yet," he said. "I think you should take all the time you need."

"I want to be busy," said David.

"And you can be busy at home, I'm sure. Don't you worry, we can survive without you!" And then the boss looked embarrassed, looked away; people kept doing that.

So by the time the man from British Gas knocked on the door David hadn't seen a living soul for three days. "Suspected gas leak," he said. "I've come to check your meter."

"Oh, all right," said David.

"I'm not disturbing you, then?"

David thought that maybe he was still in his pyjamas, sometimes he didn't get out of his pyjamas all day, it depended on whether he'd remembered to get dressed. He looked down, and saw that he was actually pretty smart today, presentable. "No, no."

"I'll come in then."

David showed the man where the meter was.

"Nice house," said the meter reader.

"Thank you."

"Big."

"Yes."

"You live with someone else, a wife, perhaps, or . . . ?"

"No, no, it's just me."

"Pretty big, just for you on your own."

"Yes," said David. He watched the man take the meter reading. He showed him out.

About half an hour later, the phone rang. David answered it. On the other end he heard someone in tears.

"Hello?" he said. "Hello, who is this? Are you all right?"

"I'm sorry," said the voice. It was a man's voice. He didn't recognize it.

"Who is this?"

"I didn't need to read your meter. I just wanted to see you."

"Hello?" said David. He didn't know why, it just seemed as if the conversation might make more sense started from scratch.

"I'm so sorry for your loss," said the voice. It stuttered in between the sobs. "You must hate me. I'm sorry. It was. My wife, she. She was the one in the car. In the crash."

"Oh," said David. "I don't . . ."

"I'm sorry."

"Yes."

"I just had to . . . oh, shit, can't . . . The words won't. Sorry. See you. See you were okay."

"I'm okay."

"See what I'd done."

"That's okay," said David. "Really."

"Could we meet?"

"What, you mean, come here? I . . ."

And the voice sounded shocked, angry. "To your house? I wouldn't presume. That I should . . . I wouldn't deserve it. No."

"Okay."

"But in a pub? I'm in a phone box. Just down the road from you. There's a pub opposite, do you know it?"

"Well, yes, but . . ."

"The King's Arms."

"Yes, I know."

"I'll be there. Thank you. You've no idea how much this means to me." And the man hung up.

Had David still been in pyjamas, he might not have bothered going out. But all he had to do was put on a pair of shoes, a coat. They're such easy things, shoes and coats.

119

He'd never been inside the pub before, though he passed it most days on his way to work. There wasn't much of an afternoon trade, and the woman behind the bar raised her head to him in dull acknowledgement. The man in the British Gas uniform wasn't crying anymore; he sat on his own, nursing a pint of thick dark beer, and when he saw David he smiled as if recognizing an old friend. He stood up to greet him, and it struck David how short he was, all bullish and tightly squeezed into those blue overalls. "Can I get you a pint?" he said.

"Well, it's a bit early."

"Please, a pint, it's the least I can do."

He bought David a pint, as thick and dark as his own.

"I'm sorry about that stunt with the meter," said the man.

"It's okay."

"Bit of a mad thing to do."

"It's okay." There was a pause. The man wouldn't look at David, stared at his pint instead. David said, "So, what do you really do? You know, for a living?"

"I work for British Gas. I read meters."

"Oh, right. I thought that . . ."

"You thought I was in *disguise*? That I'd, what, rent a costume as a meter reader, and come to your house under false pretences?" And for a moment David thought the man was angry, but he wasn't, he was just appalled at the idea; he laughed at the absurdity of it. "Disguise," he chuckled. "That's a good one. That really would make me mad, wouldn't it? How's the drink?"

"Okay." David sipped at it. It was too hoppy for his taste. He hadn't had beer in years. He and Janet had never bothered with pubs, their perfect evening would be a bottle of nice wine in front of the telly.

"Good. Well, there's more where that came from. I owe you. I don't drink much either. Just so you know. I mean, under the circumstances. Inappropriate. But we couldn't just sit in the pub together without a pint. That'd be gay."

David supposed that it would.

"How are you feeling? How are you holding up?" The man looked him directly in the face, and it was the first time he had. David tried to frame the usual bland reply, but the man continued. "Bet you get a lot of that. I do. Gets pretty annoying, doesn't it?"

"Yes," said David.

"They should mind their own fucking business."

"Yes," said David, with feeling. "They should."

"God knows how I feel," said the man. "I keep crying. In front of strangers. I mean, it's bad enough Tracey's dead. But knowing she took someone with her, that's what makes it hard. You're lucky. You've no idea how lucky. I mean, not that lucky, of course, sorry."

"Well, no," said David.

"D'you bury or cremate her?"

"Oh," said David. "Cremate."

"Tracey didn't want to go with cremate," said the man. "She didn't like getting burned. And besides, she'd say, what if they found a cure? Afterwards we could just dig her up. Couldn't be brought back if she were just ashes. Mind you, I don't suppose they'll ever find a cure for car crashes, but you know, it's what she wanted."

"I never knew what Janet really wanted," said David.

"She drank a lot, Mr Reynolds. I won't tell a lie. I used to ask her to stop. And over the years, I just gave up. And I think, if I hadn't, maybe she'd be alive today. Maybe you'd still have your Janet. Maybe she wouldn't have suffered."

"They say that she died instantly, she wouldn't have felt a thing."

"Yeah, they always say that. But how do they know, eh? I mean, when Janet's head smashed through that sheet of glass. At forty miles an hour. And, what, her skull got pulped. How could they know?"

"Well," said David. "I ought to be going."

"Let me get you another pint."

"I haven't finished this one."

"Tracey didn't drink in the beginning," said the man. "So I wonder. Did I drive her to it? Was it something about me? Because I loved her, you know, I really did. But maybe my love wasn't enough? Or too much? I drove her to suicide, because that's what it was, wasn't it? It's my fault. And murder, I killed your wife, it was down to me."

"Not murder," said David. "If anything, manslaughter."

"Yeah," said the man, "I manslaughtered Janet. I'm sorry." He took a long pull at his beer, and David thought this pause in the conversation might give him a second chance to flee, but no, too late, he was off again. "I'm a bad man. I think I was better with Tracey, you know, in spite of everything, we were a *unit*. Do you know what I mean? Together, we made *sense*."

"I do know what you mean," said David.

"And now I've lost her. And I've lost myself too, because she was the best part of me. I don't have any friends. Can you forgive me?"

"I forgive you," said David.

"Can you find it in your heart to forgive me?"

"I do forgive you," said David.

"I won't ask you to be a friend. I don't deserve your friendship. Just your forgiveness."

"I do, I forgive you," said David.

"Thank you," said the man. "Thank you. I feel. Whew. I feel at peace." He smiled, stuck out his hand. It was big and meaty, at odds with how small his body was. David took it. "I'm Alex," said the man.

"David," said David.

"I know."

The numbness kept returning to his lips, and David didn't know what he should do about that. He'd wake in the morning and feel them with his fingers and they didn't seem to belong to him; he had to smack them together for a couple of minutes just to get some life back into them. When he ate his breakfast cereal the spoon would feel strange in his mouth, the flakes would feel strange, the strangeness made him a bit nauseous. One breakfast they felt so thick and swollen it was as if he'd been anaesthetized at a dentist's. It made him drool. He'd bite his tongue.

David didn't want to go to a doctor, and nearly cancelled the appointment at the last minute. The doctor didn't even want to examine the lips, which was annoying. Was David diabetic? David said that he wasn't. Had he an allergy to shellfish? David assured the doctor he'd been nowhere near a shellfish. Sometimes numb lips, the doctor said, were the first symptoms of migraine headaches, had he had any migraines? No. "Hmm," said the doctor. Then he asked the clincher. He asked if there'd been any trauma in his life recently, any reason he might feel depressed. David admitted his wife had just been killed. "Aha!" said the doctor, and he actually looked pleased. He told David that numb lips were a classic form of stress, of panic attack, of something psychosomatic—he had really nothing to worry about, it'd all come out in the wash when he cheered up. David asked if from now on every single little ailment he ever felt was in some way going to be related to the death of his wife, and the doctor just sort of blinked. "Watch and see if it spreads to other parts of your face," the doctor said. "If it does, I'll put you down for a CAT scan."

One night the numbness of his lips woke David up. He'd been woken by pain before—never by the opposite of it, by pure lack of sensation. He lay there. He ran his tongue over the lips and felt nothing. Smacked them together, nothing.

But no, not nothing.

He felt himself lean forward, just a little—he twitched the lips, he puckered. And there it was. Right next to them. And it was soft and yielding. It was fleshy. It was another pair of lips.

At this he started; he jolted forward in alarm, and thought suddenly that by doing so he'd headbang whoever was kissing him, and he cried out in expectation of the pain. But there wasn't any, and there was no head to collide with—and his own head kept on rocketing forward at great speed and there was nothing there to stop it, until his own spine yanked it back like a seatbelt—and he was breathing fast, panicked—and he slowed that breath down, swallowed, lay his head back upon the pillow. Relaxed. Relaxed. . . . Twitched those lips forward again.

He was kissed for his effort.

It was very gentle, very sweet, and there was just the faint taste of lipstick.

"Janet?" he whispered, and wished he hadn't, because he'd chased her away, the spell was broken.

He spent the next hour or so trying to chase those lips, puckering out at the darkened room to no avail. He must have fallen asleep at some point.

The next morning his lips were numb again, but this time he didn't much try to get the feeling back. So he'd drool during breakfast, so what? And during the day he'd keep prodding at the lips, pressing down on them with his fingers hard—staring at them in the mirror and flexing them slowly. He'd close his eyes and make little moues towards a lover who wasn't there.

He went to bed early that night. "Janet," he said to the darkness. He didn't know how to summon her. He didn't know how to let her know he was ready.

Beneath the sheets his hands balled up into tight fists of frustration.

He dozed, slept in fits and starts. And she came to him at last; he woke and she was *there*, he could feel her, her breath against his mouth, she was so very very close—and he wasn't going to say a word, he'd learned his lesson, he wasn't going to move a muscle. Or not just any muscle, he'd choose the muscle carefully—and he pressed his lips forward. Pressed them on to hers. And he couldn't be sure at first, but there, there was that taste of lipstick, a little bit of something sweet and slippery—and Janet had never been much of one for make-up, but he was glad of it now, just so he could taste something and be sure he wasn't pretending.

He extended his tongue—very slowly, carefully. And it went into a place that was warmer and wetter. Pushed it out as far as it would go—it quivered in the hot breath of his dead lover.

She stayed all night. Sometimes he'd sleep, just for a while—and he'd wake with a start, with the certainty that she'd have crept away, that he'd have lost her once more. But she was always there, that softness, that tickle close to his skin, that body heat, those lips, those lips.

The next morning he found the numbness had spread. It was no longer just his lips, the chin had no feeling, his cheeks felt odd and tingling. He called the doctor for an appointment. This time he *did* cancel at the last minute.

Because he realized she didn't come to him at all—no—she never left—she was always there, she was always just a few delicate millimetres away from his face. He could smell her, and taste, and touch, and *feel*, God, and all it required was concentration and just a little bit of forward momentum. And he went to bed with her. He'd cuddle the pillow and pretend his arms were around her body, and he'd make love to her, and he'd make love to himself.

It took three days of this sort of thing before he began to think that this might be unhealthy. And he determined he had to get out of the house, interact with the living again. Alex had left four messages on the answering machine, asking him to call. So he did.

"I'm glad you came," said Alex. "I wasn't sure you would. But this means that we're friends now, right? We're proper friends."

He'd bought them both a glass of house red. "Because I could tell you weren't really enjoying the beer, I'm not entirely insensitive!" The pub was quiet; nothing but Alex's voice and the occasional burp from the fruit machine. Alex wasn't dressed in uniform now, and he'd lost any authority it might have given him; he just looked like a small sad man with a paunch.

"How are you holding up?" he asked.

"I'm doing okay. I think I'm doing better," said David. "I think I'm adjusting."

"Adjusting. Yeah. Good for you. Yeah, we should all be adjusting, yeah."

Alex finished his drink. David offered to buy him another. There was still time for one more round before they had to get to the cinema.

"No, no," said Alex. "I'm not letting you put your hand in your pocket. All the drinks are on me. I owe you, remember?"

David hadn't been out to see a movie in years. The last time had been with Janet in Marbella. It had been a fantastic holiday, they'd laughed so much. And the weather had been mostly glorious. But the sudden downpour had taken them by surprise, and they had taken refuge in the cinema. They arrived in the middle of an action movie in which Bruce Willis killed lots of people, his wisecracks were dubbed into Spanish. They could just about follow the plot, it wasn't too difficult, and David would whisper to Janet his own suggestions for what an English translation of the dialogue might be, and sometimes they were very funny, and even when they weren't Janet would laugh.

Alex insisted on paying for the tickets. It was for some romcom, David hadn't thought it'd be to Alex's taste. Alex said, "Do you want some popcorn?", and David didn't. "You've got to have popcorn!" said Alex, "my treat!" and bought David a big tub overflowing with the stuff. David picked at it through the trailers, but it didn't taste of anything. "You probably need more salt," said Alan, "here, we'll swap." He gave David his popcorn. But it didn't make any difference, David still couldn't taste a thing.

The movie had lots of jokes, but they weren't necessarily very good jokes. Alex would lean across to David and tell him his own punchlines. He'd lean in very close, and David could smell the hot breath on his face—but for all that, he still wouldn't whisper quietly enough. People kept on glaring at Alex and shushing him. He ignored them.

After the movie Alex suggested they should go off for another drink; David said he was tired; Alex wouldn't hear of it.

The pub was much busier now, and Alex had to shout for David to hear him over the noise. Alex brought to the table an entire bottle of wine, and poured glasses for himself and his friend. It wasn't an especially nice wine, normally it'd have been too acidic for David, he preferred something smooth. But he drank it anyway, and he could barely taste it.

"That stuff you were saying," shouted Alex, "about adjusting. Yeah. I can see the value in it. Because, what do they say? Because life goes on. They do say that, don't they?"

"Cheers," said David.

"It's funny how things work out," shouted Alex. "Because we wouldn't even be friends. If our wives hadn't killed each other. But you're a great friend. I think you're the best friend I've ever had!"

"Thanks," said David.

"It wasn't such a tragedy. If it brought us together."

"No."

"And with no blame on either side! And why should there be? Just a, just an accident of circumstance. My wife killed your wife. But then again, your wife killed my wife, didn't she?"

"Wait a moment," said David.

"I'm just saying. There had to be a car for Tracey to hit. And your wife was the one driving it. And yeah, my wife is a little more to blame than your wife. I don't dispute that. But accident of circumstance, yeah? That day, my wife was the one who happened to be drunk driving. The next day, it might have been *yours* drunk driving. Let's not get too fussed about blame."

"My wife didn't ever go drunk driving," said David.

"No, I know, hey, I'm just saying. What I'm saying is, we're the same. Right? Right!" He clinked his glass against David's, frowned. "No need to get nasty about it."

"Sorry."

"Is this seat taken?" said one girl, and "is it taken?" said her prettier friend. "Do you mind if we join you?" The pub was heaving now, there were no spare tables.

"No, that's fine," said David.

"Fine," said Alex.

The girls' presence seemed to throw Alex off his stride; they chattered together for a minute or so, and then he said, "We went to the cinema."

"Oh . . . yes?" ventured a girl.

"We saw this movie. It wasn't very good."

"It was all right," said David.

"Oh, you say it's all right now, but you were sighing and humphing all the way through it," said Alex.

"Goodness," said a girl. And, "What was it?" said the other.

David told them.

"It hasn't had very good reviews," said the uglier girl to David. "And it's a shame, because I think she was very funny when she was in *Friends*, I just don't know whether she's choosing the right projects, and of course she's getting older now, so maybe she's not getting the offers she once had . . ."

"He is taken, you know," said Alex.

"Sorry?"

"My friend. He is *taken*."

"I didn't mean to . . ."

"Oh, we're not *gay*," sneered Alex. "I bet you think we are. But we were married to *women*. They're dead now. But we still keep them in our hearts, we'll never betray them. We'd do anything for them! Show us some fucking respect, we're fucking mourning!"

By now Alex was on his feet, and the girls were backing into the crowd, and David was dragging his friend out of the pub.

"Get your hands off me, David, I swear to God, I'll fucking *glass* them, what do they think, they think we can't find wives as good as ours?"

"Now calm down," said David. "Come on."

Alex threw him off; David flinched. And Alex looked at him in surprise. "I'd never hurt you," he said. "I'm hurt you think I would."

"All right," said David. "Just breathe."

Alex took a couple of gulps of night air, and began to sob. Dry sobs, they made his little fat body heave with the effort. "I've ruined the evening," he said. "And we were having a brilliant evening. It's the drink. I shouldn't, for her sake, I mean, when you bear in mind. What she. But I've been so down, mate. I miss her. I miss her really bad."

"I know," said David.

"I don't want to be out with *you*. I don't know *you*. I want to be with *her*."

"I understand," said David.

And a look of relief washed over Alex's face, and his eyes lit up, and even his tongue came out for a second, he looked like a little puppy dog so eager to please. "Next time I won't drink. Promise. Just fizzy water. Yeah?" David didn't say anything. Alex's face creased up. "I *need* her," he said. "And you understand."

And his breath was all over David again, and it made him think of Janet, and how close her breath could be, that he wanted to be home with her right now. And he didn't agree to see Alex again, but he nodded, and that was enough.

The trick, David soon realized, was not to think about it too much.

Someone had told him once—it may have been a medical student, someone he met in the university bar—about the way the brain can screen out unwanted objects it doesn't want us to see. The nose is the best example. We all see the nose—he told David, and David thought he was very drunk, and wondered why he was bothering him—we all see the nose *all* the time. It's a big pointy thing sticking straight out the centre of our face, of course we can see it. And if we think about it too much, this permanent obstruction getting in the way of what we want to look at, always there in our peripheral vision, it'd make us feel claustrophobic. It'd drive us nuts. So the brain refuses to acknowledge it. Ignores it, tries to make us look *through* it, makes it seem transparent. David assumed he was a medical student, but he supposed that was just because he was talking about brains and noses and body parts, he supposed he could have been anyone really. And he really wished the student had shut up, he hadn't wanted to think about such things, now he'd been alerted to it he couldn't stop seeing his own nose for days.

And David now had to play the same game with Janet. Because it was obvious to him now—she wasn't just in front of his face, she was *growing herself on to his face*. She was there all the time, always in his peripheral vision, just like a nose—but now there was another nose to contend with, and much more besides. Staring out at her as she stared back at him. He could feel the bristles on his chin flattened against her chin. Her hair tickling his cheeks. Her lipsticked lips. When he breathed, he did so first through his mouth and then through her mouth and then out through the back of her head. Sometimes, when he tried to focus upon any specific object, when he really had to sharpen his eyes and concentrate, he fancied he was having to do so by peering through her forehead, her skull, her very brain. But, like the nose, he tried not to think about it, he *didn't* think about it; like the nose, he found a way of keeping the obstruction in the corner of his eye. Or else, he knew, he really *would* go nuts.

He wondered why she was there. He wondered why he was so special. And then he wondered whether maybe he wasn't special at all—maybe this is what happened to all the poor widowers, maybe they all ended up haunted by a dead wife's face. Maybe they just chose never to talk about it.

Her company made him happy, most of the time. Sometimes the claustrophobia would be too much. Her head right against his head, no room, no space of his own, a wife always there bearing down on him, he couldn't breathe. That's when she would help him. She'd suck in big lungfuls of air, then blow them back into his mouth. She'd give him what he needed. She'd take care of him. She'd breathe for both of them.

It did occur to him that those lungfuls of air she was sucking must have been his air to begin with. But that made him feel a little churlish.

Her mouth would move against his perfectly; when he yawned, she yawned in unison; when he chewed, she chewed; when he forced his mouth into a scowl, a grimace, an artificial grin, just to see, just to test her, yes, she'd do it too. He'd say, "I love you," when he went to sleep at night, and her lips would whisper back the same words to him, in an instant, he didn't even have to wait.

Having her this way was better than nothing.

He didn't like to eat much. He didn't like the way it looked, the concentration he needed to change the way it looked: he had to take his fork and push the food through the back of her head, past her tongue, past her teeth, past her lips, before it could reach his own. Everything he ate seemed now second hand. She'd sucked all the taste out of it all. Sometimes the food was merely stale. Sometimes it seemed like dirt. Like earth.

All he could really taste properly was that lipstick, her lipstick, creamy and gloopy and clamping down on him hard.

One night, as he was brushing his teeth, he felt something wriggling in his mouth. He assumed it was Janet's tongue, it often found its way in there. But out with the gobbet of soil-mint toothpaste he also spat out a worm. It wasn't a very big worm, to be fair, but seeing it there in the sink was still alarming. David stared at it. He gave it a jab with the end of his toothbrush, and it writhed at the touch. "But what are you doing there?" he said. And, "But she was *cremated*!" The worm looked at him, or so David thought, it was frankly rather hard to tell; it twitched, and that might have been a shrug—hey, I'm a worm, what would I know? And then it slid itself down the plughole.

He dreamed of Janet at last. And it was the last dream he ever had, or, at least, the last dream that was truly his.

She was wearing her favourite summer dress, the one she'd wear even when it was cold and raining because she'd say it made her feel better.

"I've been waiting for you," he said, "and for such a long time!" And she kissed him, but as her face leaned in to his she changed direction, she avoided the lips altogether and plumped for the cheek. And what was the good of that, he couldn't taste it at all?

"Should we eat?" she said, and they took their places in the restaurant. It was the same restaurant at which they'd had their first date. Where he'd first dared use the "love" word on her. Where he'd proposed. And it was odd, because they had all been different restaurants.

"How have you been?" she asked. "How have you been holding up?"

"I miss you," he said.

It took a couple of hours for the waiter to take their order, but that didn't matter, and they swapped stories of old adventures together, two lives well led. And after a while David realized he was the only one doing the talking, and Janet was just sitting there, listening, smiling, drinking his memories in, drinking in his happiness.

The food arrived, and it wasn't what David had ordered; he'd thought they were somewhere Italian, but now it was all Chinese. And he didn't expect he'd be able to taste his meal, but it was good, it was so good, that sweet and sour sauce was simply to die for, he cried at how good it was.

They ate their fill. Once in a while David would have to turn his head away, spit out a few worms here and there. And Janet would tut amiably, and say, "David, I thought *I* was the one who's dead!" They'd laugh a lot about that.

It was the same restaurant in their honeymoon hotel. It was the restaurant of every birthday and anniversary. It was the restaurant to which he'd take her to say sorry after they'd had a fight, and where, by accepting the invitation, she was assuring him it was all right, everything was all right, she still loved him.

"I didn't know where to scatter your ashes," he said.

"That's okay."

"I scattered them in the park. I'm sorry."

"But it's a nice park," she said.

"I can't remember," he said. "I keep trying to remember. What the last thing I ever said to you was. Do you know? Can you tell me? Tell me it was something nice. Tell me I said I loved you. Please. I loved you."

It was the restaurant where she'd told him she was pregnant. It was the restaurant to which he'd taken her once she lost the child, because they couldn't face being at home, they didn't want to eat at all.

"Why do you haunt my face?" he asked her. She looked a bit hurt at that.

"You need to move on," said Janet, at last.

"I can't move on."

She paused. "I've moved on."

He took this in.

"Are you breaking up with me?" he asked.

"I'm sorry."

"Is it something I've done?"

"No," she said. "No. It was just. An accident of circumstance. Oh, baby, please. Please don't cry."

"But I love you," he said, and the tears were flowing now, why was he crying now and ruining the date, why now when he'd all those weeks of numbness to get through? "I love you," he said, as if that solved a blind thing, as if that did even the slightest bit of good.

"I know," she said. And she took his hand. And she squeezed it. And she let it go.

It was the restaurant in which he had the dream his dead wife didn't want him anymore.

They talked a bit more after that. Other adventures they'd had, some of them just the same adventures as before. He repeated his anecdotes a little.

"Save me," David said, but it was so quiet he didn't think she heard.

The waiter brought them the bill. "I've got this," said Janet, "it's on me." She took money from her purse, lots of money, and gave the waiter a generous tip. He bowed his thanks.

"Well," she said.

"Well," said David.

"Well," she said, "this has been fun. We should do it again some time."

"Yes," said David, and he knew they wouldn't. And he got up from the table to get her chair, and she thanked him, and let him give her a peck goodbye.

When he woke up he wasn't crying, his face was still dry, he'd wanted to cry, but only in the dream, just the bloody dream. And he thought that he'd lost her, he patted at his face, tried to find some trace of her—and part of him wanted her gone, wanted that freedom, his face back to normal—and another part was terrified she'd kept her promise and had gone for good, and then what would he do, who would he even be? And she was still there—she was still there—she hadn't deserted him—still the numbness—still numb. And he laughed and she laughed in unison and he gulped for air and she gulped too, and he went back to sleep wrapping his arms around himself in a tight hug.

"Look, fizzy water!" said Alex, as he opened the front door, and he laughed, and he waved the bottle about like it was some sort of trophy. He showed David into the house. It was quite a small house; David still felt his own was conspicuously designed for two people, and rattling about there on his own was awkward and embarrassing—but it was hard to believe that Alex had shared this house with his wife, there surely wasn't the space to keep her anywhere. "Nice place, isn't it?" asked Alex, and David agreed. Alex was in a good mood. He seemed very proud of whatever he was concocting in the kitchen, he kept on winking and going back in there to stir it and telling David it'd be a surprise. And, "It's just so nice to have you here, mate," he said. "It's just so nice to have company."

They settled down in the sitting room together for a little while— Alex told David that this stage of the cooking could take care of itself. There wasn't much room, David and Alex sat close side by side on the sofa. "So," said Alex, "how are you holding up?"

"I'm not sure," said David, honestly.

Alex nodded at that, as if it were the wisest thing he had ever heard. "Not still adjusting, then?"

"What?"

"You said you were 'adjusting.'"

"Oh. Yes. Yes, I don't know."

Alex nodded again. "As for me, I took your advice. Knocked the booze on the head. Thanks. Thank you for looking out for me." He waggled the bottle of water again. "Refill?"

"Why not?" said David.

"It's helped me to clear my head a bit. Know where I stand with this whole death thing. The drink, it was keeping me away from those important decisions. But now I know what's going on. What we both need to do."

"Oh?"

"But there's time enough for that," said Alex, as a timer went in the kitchen. "And I think dinner is served!"

"I hope you like this," said Alex, as he brought over to the table a steaming saucepan. "Tracey's the real cook. Well. But I've been practising. Got a book and everything." He tipped on to David's plate a pile of spaghetti bolognaise. "Enjoy!"

Each time David lifted his fork he saw worms wriggle on the end of it. Each time he lifted the fork near his mouth, he at first had to pass it through the back of Janet's skull, and he didn't know why, he thought that as the worms brushed against her brain they *became* her brain somehow, that her brain was unravelling into these flapping tendrils, that in death the brain was finally rotting to these thin white ribbons. In his mouth the brain tasted of soil, and he was used to that, but it was a squirming soil, if he didn't gulp it down quickly it'd try to escape back into Janet's head, and he couldn't have that, you couldn't go home again. So he sucked in those earthworms, and those strands of his dead wife's mind too, he stuffed them in his mouth, he swallowed, swallowed hard so they couldn't come up again and beat a path to freedom, he did it again, the same mechanical exercise, gulping down, trying to gulp all the food away. It took him a minute or two to realize that Alex was looking at him, hard.

"You're not enjoying that, are you?"

"It's fine."

"Fucking typical. Well, then." And Alex got up, and he took David's plate away, and he slammed it into the sink.

David said weakly, "I don't like pasta very much."

"Right," said Alex. "Of course not. You know, I don't think you're putting much effort into this relationship. I'm the one who's doing all the running. Aren't I? I buy the drinks, the cinema tickets, it's me that cooks dinner. You didn't even bring any wine, did you?"

"You told me you weren't drinking."

"Always some excuse with you. Is this what you were like with Janet? Christ. No wonder she drank. No wonder the poor bitch killed herself."

David started to explain that Janet hadn't killed herself. Had she? She'd been happy with him. Wasn't that the case? It'd been an accident, a tragic accident of circumstance.

"Upstairs," said Alex.

"What? No."

"Upstairs, to the bedroom."

"No way."

"Upstairs," said Alex, picking up a knife. "Or I'll fucking *cut* you. I will. I'll cut you, you bastard. Upstairs. Now."

So they went upstairs.

"The problem with you," said Alex. "Is you don't know what love is." And he opened the bedroom door, pushed David inside.

It was like a shrine. The walls were covered with hundreds of photographs, and all of the same woman. Some were posed for, some caught unawares. But either way, whether ready for the camera or not, in each picture she had the same expression, the same smile, and that struck David as odd, how could she always make her face the same, so fixed and unmoving? She wasn't a pretty woman, her head was too round—but she wasn't ugly, had you seen a single picture of her you wouldn't have given her a second glance. But the whole array of these pictures, this presentation of her entire facial repertoire—and she had *one* smile, just *one*—and it made David feel suddenly sick, as if he were looking upon something that wasn't quite human, just something slightly off, something that his brain would have normally have consigned to his peripheral vision. Her nostrils always flared, her eyes so wide and unblinking, and that mouth in each picture contorted into an identical smile, the smile so big and broad and covered with thick gloopy lipstick.

"I've had a bad time," said Alex. "I've had a very bad time. But do you see? Do you see how much I love her?"

"Yes, I see," croaked David through the nausea.

"No, really. Look. *Look.*" And Alex grabbed David's hair, and dragged him to the wall, and forced his face hard against a patch of photos— and all David could think of was what this would do to his invisible wife, he'll squash Janet over all the pictures, he'll squash my wife all over *his* wife, how's that going to look?

Close up, of course, with Tracey's face against his, David couldn't make out any identifying features at all.

"I went to your house," said Alex. "I looked for photos. Just some evidence that you were missing your wife the way I missed mine. But there's nothing, is there? I thought maybe you'd done what I did, put all her things in one room so you could see them better. I *believed* that of you. But you haven't."

"No," said David.

"She gave you all that love. And you gave none back. You can't even *feel* anything now she's dead. Can you? You're a fraud. Aren't you?"

"I'm a fraud," said David.

"Your problem is," repeated Alex, "you don't know what love is. It's not a little thing. It's life and death. You don't give someone your heart one day, make them the centre of your life. Become a unit. And then *adjust* when they die. Well, I'm better than you. I'm not going to adjust. I'll never adjust. You'll see."

And he gave David the knife. David stared down at it, blankly. As ever, numb.

"You've always had such contempt for me," said Alex, gentler somehow. "Right from the start. Do you think I'm that stupid? Do you think I couldn't see? But ask yourself. You kept coming back to me. Why did you do that?"

"I honestly don't know," said David.

"I know," said Alex. "Because you have a job to do." He got on to his knees. "Kill me," he said.

David slowly registered what Alex had said. Looked down at the knife again, then across to Alex, waiting, unafraid, even smiling—smiling like his dead wife in all the pictures about them, it was as if he were trying to parrot her.

"I can't," said David, but his hand was grasping on to that knife, it was getting the feel for it.

"And I can't go on without her. And if you had any fucking balls, you'd feel the same way about your wife. But now. Now. Your wife killed my wife. And now you kill me. It's fitting. It's simple."

And it was simple, David could see that, any fool could see that. The hand was stroking the knife, it *liked* this knife. The brain didn't like it, told the hand to stop, but no one listened to David's brain anymore. He couldn't even feel the blade against his fingers, he was oh so numb.

He bent down to Alex. Lifted the knife, right up to his face, right up to his eyes. And Alex flinched in spite of himself.

"No," David breathed on him, and his breath was hot, but it wasn't his breath, it was hers, it was hers.

"Why not?" said Alex, and he looked like a child, a sad spent little child.

"Because I don't care. I don't care." He dropped the knife to the carpet. Got to his feet. And smiled such a broad smile, and blew him a little kiss. "And I never did."

David left the room, left the house, left Alex weeping on his bedroom floor.

David went home.

He went to every desk drawer, every cupboard. He took from them all the photographs of Janet. He couldn't even remember why he had done that now. He couldn't remember why he wouldn't want to see her face. He looked at that face now. He looked at every single one of those photographs, and studied her face each time. He found her diary, and it wasn't a diary, really, just a notebook of birthdays and doctor's appointments, but nevertheless he read it from cover to cover.

Then he went upstairs to her wardrobe, and pulled out all of Janet's clothes. He didn't smell many, he didn't stroke them—well, maybe one or two. He pulled out her favourite summer dress.

He put all her belongings into a big heap on the sitting room floor. Like a funeral pyre, waiting for a light.

And then he said goodbye to his wife. And he cried. Without sound, but it was real, and it was long, and it hurt.

He hurt. And he grieved. And he let Janet go. He let every trace of her go.

He went to the bathroom mirror to wash his face. He knew now it wouldn't be his face looking back at him. He knew, too, that it wouldn't be his wife's. And he was so tired, so very tired.

He looked at her. He tried to look away. Tried to blink, even—but he wasn't able to blink, he wasn't able to close his eyes, and they opened wide and large and sore.

She wouldn't let him close his eyes. She wanted him to see her at last. She wouldn't let him *not* see.

He felt his eyes harden from lack of moisture. Felt little cracks appear in them. There was no water in his head left, he'd wasted it all, he'd wept it all away. She'd taken Janet's life, and now she was taking his, and she didn't care, she didn't care, she never had, and he *wanted* his eyes to crack, let them fissure, let them pop. But they didn't, they didn't.

"And now," he said, and he smiled, and the smile was big and broad and sticky. "Now, let's have some fun."

# CUSTARD CREAM

She said that she didn't love you anymore, and this time you actually believed her. For once it had the whiff of truth to it—because oh, yes, she'd often say she didn't love you, but you'd always known better; she'd shout it out sometimes, loud so the neighbours could hear—though she didn't care, why should she care about such stuff when she had a strop on?—at the very top of her voice she'd scream that she didn't love you and that she'd never loved you and that she just wished you'd go away. You'd beat a retreat then. Of course you would. You might nip to the pub for a pint or three, wait until she'd simmered down. And by the time you'd come back home, opening the front door very softly and creeping about on tiptoes—yes, you know the drill!—she'd be sobbing in the kitchen, so much easier to reason with, so much more *pliable*—all the venom out of her now, all that's left the tears and snot. And you'd take her hand and squeeze it, but gently this time, you didn't want to hurt her, and she might even squeeze back—but even if she didn't, even if she didn't, it was okay, you'd know it was okay, the shouting had stopped, you'd already won.

But there'd been no shouting this time. "Steve, I don't love you anymore," she said, as calmly as you like, as if she'd been practising, as if she'd been taking lessons, and then she was the one holding *your* hand, giving *your* hand a squeeze, and looking so sympathetic you thought it might make you puke. And it wasn't the quietness that alarmed you, sincere though it made it sound—it was the 'anymore', I don't love you 'anymore', not pretending that she'd never loved you at all, in fact suggesting that there had been love once, accepting the basic fact of her love from the get go, accepting that all those other times she'd wanted you out of her life were just melodramatic freak-outs. But now it was real. This time it was real. It was real. And it was the 'anymore' that clinched it and finally did your marriage in.

But "Why?" you couldn't help but ask. And she said you were useless. You were good for nothing. And there was no blame to it, she wasn't accusing you, and so there was no way you could defend yourself. "Not useless at everything, surely?" you said, and you waggled your eyebrows at her, that would surely make her laugh, it always did, your little jokey attempts at seduction, it was only by joking you'd ever got her into bed. The way you'd pull your kissy face. Now she just stared at the kissy face as if she'd never seen it before, as if it were, what, something horrible like a stroke symptom. She conceded that you weren't useless at everything. She'd been a little unfair. She thought for a moment, and said you were good at getting rid of the spiders.

You actually laughed at that. Just a bit. But she wasn't joking.

And later that evening, staring up at the hotel room ceiling before turning out the light, and replaying the conversation in your head, and trying to work out what you should have said to make it end better, later on, you thought, well, fair enough—fair enough, you *are* good at getting rid of spiders. There's a certain elegance to it even. The way you can sweep them up into a glass, quickly, without fuss, without snapping off any of their legs. Keeping your hand flat over the mouth of the glass so the spider can't escape. Tipping the spider into the toilet bowl and flushing it away. You don't think the spider ever suffered much—it looked only a bit bemused as it bobbed about treading water, then a good yank at the chain and it was sucked down the whirlpool and it was gone forever—and you'd tried to be kinder still, you used to tip the spider out of the window so it could live on in peace in the garden, but Sheila hadn't liked that, she said the spider would find a way back in, the spider had to die—flush it away so there'd not even be a body. Because Sheila was scared of spiders, properly scared, and it was a *real* fear, you know, pretty phobic.

And you hadn't even noticed it when you were courting, maybe she was just braver then, maybe she was keeping it a secret—and as you stood at the altar, the vicar talking, "Do you, Steven Edward Baird," and asking the congregation whether there was any just cause or impediment, not one of your in-laws raised their hands, not one said, "Don't go through with it, mate, she's *mental* for spiders!" Mental for spiders indeed; after you'd used a glass to scoop the spider up she'd throw the glass away so she'd never run the risk of drinking from it, of her lips touching where a spider's body had been—you'd get through a lot of glasses that way, she bought them in bulk cheap at the discount store in town. Because your house certainly did seem to attract a lot of spiders; more than your fair share, surely; every morning, more or less, you'd find one or two of the buggers in the bath or the sink, and there'd be telltale traces of cobwebs in the corners of the rooms and Sheila would just stare at them in dread until you'd get a broom and brush them away—and, oh, Sheila couldn't *sleep* in a room that had a spider in it, there was no telling what a spider might get up to in the dark. Sometimes, you have to admit, that was when you could lose your temper. Sometimes, when it was late at night, and you were tired. Sometimes, but you could hardly be blamed for that.

Especially when the rest of the time you were good, you'd get rid of the spiders for her, you'd be her knight in shining armour. Even if you were her knight for only a couple of minutes each day. Or rather, you *had* been her knight in shining armour; but now she preferred you disposed of them without her knowing, she didn't want to know a thing about it, you had to enter rooms and check them in advance, and *subtly* too, she needed you to check them but needed you to never to acknowledge you were, even mentioning the word 'spider' was enough to set her off itching. It was no good telling her that spiders couldn't hurt her. No good saying they were more scared of her than she was of them—particularly this last, "Well, why do the bastards keep following me around then?" And it really wasn't a clever idea chasing her around with a spider in your hands, just for fun—"look, it's only a little one!"—telling her you were going to put it down her neck. That had been on the honeymoon. She'd hit you with a bottle. You'd needed stitches. It had been so awkward explaining what had happened to that clinic in Marbella.

But since she'd brought it up, you said to her, "Well, if I go, what will you do about the spiders?" And she said that Laura would have to get rid of them—and that was a joke, Laura, your four year old daughter, on her way to becoming an arachnophobe as bad as her mother—and little surprise of that the way Sheila carried on. You'd told Sheila that once, you told Sheila she was going to give Laura a complex, she already refused to sleep with the lights off in case the spiders came to get her—"you're damaging our daughter!"—and you thought Sheila would be so angry, you thought she might hit you, or at least try to hit you, but instead it was worse. It was worse, she just sat down and cried. Oh, she must have recognized the truth of it. And now, as soon as Laura was mentioned, Sheila could tell she'd made a mistake—"It doesn't matter, does it, we'll sort it out," she said, and waved her hand at you dismissively—as if *you* were the one making a fuss about spiders, as if it were *your* insanity, not hers—"Laura and I will cope without you, we'll cope *better* without you."

She told you she didn't love you anymore, and this time she made you believe her. And that's why you straightaway go and pack your suitcase, numb as you are, and embarrassed too—putting in the clothes you thought you'll need, shirts, trousers, socks, what else? Underpants. She tells you there's no rush, in that sympathetic way of hers, but there is a rush, you want to get out of the house as soon as possible, you think the faster you go the more sorry she'll feel for you, the quicker she'll tell you she wants you back. You carry the suitcase out to the car, and you've perhaps packed too much, what did you think you were doing, you're not going on holiday!—and you should have used the new suitcase, the one with the wheels, but it's too late now. And maybe you actually enjoy staggering under the weight of the case, maybe that feels good. You see she's looking out of the window at you, and you pretend you haven't noticed, she actually waves at you, and you don't respond—where's Laura? Couldn't Laura have come to wave you off too? And you suppose there'll be solicitors and things to deal with now, there'll be all sorts of shit to arrange, but there's a part of you that knows too, isn't there, that you'll never see your family again? That this is it? Which is stupid, because you'll probably see them tomorrow, maybe you'll pop back, you can at least swap suitcases. But as you pull off the drive, as you hit the main road, still not looking at Sheila, seeing *through* Sheila, you know this'll be the last glimpse of your wife you'll ever get and it isn't nearly good enough.

You've never needed to look for hotels near your house before, and suddenly they seem to be everywhere. And you wonder why, who would want to holiday in a town like yours? You could stop right away, but you want to drive for a bit, and you put on the radio, and you listen to a song, and you say you won't stop the car, you won't even consider a hotel, not 'til the radio plays a song you like. And after an Elton John and something by a girl group you've never heard of you say that's enough, that's enough, the very next hotel you see. And there's one, and it looks fine, it even has a nice gravel driveway that makes that nice crunching sound when your car drives over it, it'll do.

The girl at reception seems to be too young to be working there. She asks you how long you want to stay. You say you don't know. You say just one night, then you'll see how it goes. She tells you there's a special off-season discount, four nights for the price of three. She doesn't make it sound special, not with that bored voice she's got, she doesn't care whether you take the discount or not. You take it. She gives you a key. It's not like one of those swish electronic keys from that posh hotel you went to with Sheila on that last holiday of yours—and that was a good holiday, remember, you didn't argue once, no one got angry—and when was that anyway, it must have been before Laura, that was years ago—sorry, no, the receptionist is still talking, but it's just about what time dinner is served, and you don't care, you're not hungry and you may never eat again, and you turn the key over in your hand and it's just an ordinary Yale key, old-fashioned, and old-fashioned feels reassuring somehow, and you like the feel of the key's teeth biting into your skin. The receptionist tells you you're in room five, you say that's fine, she tells you it's right down the corridor, and you say fine, and you go right down the corridor to find it.

The room is small. There's no bathroom, just a sink in one corner. A cracked mirror is above it. There's a little TV set on a table, one of those old-fashioned TVs, it's got an aerial on top, it wouldn't surprise you if it were black and white, and now old-fashioned doesn't feel reassuring, it just feels somewhat cheap. The ceiling is polystyrene tiles, the walls are breezeblock. A small square window, it doesn't open. A lamp on each side of the bed, but no tea service, no phone. And the bed is big, and that's good, but it feels hard, and that isn't—hard, and cold, and maybe a little damp, and maybe it's because of that cold, maybe it's because you let a little warm air in when you entered.

You decide you've changed your mind about the four nights for three discount. You'll tell the receptionist in the morning. Provided she hasn't left for school.

You take your clothes off. You wished you'd packed some pyjamas. You shiver. You look at yourself in the cracked mirror and you don't see what looks so bad, not really, you can't see why Sheila wouldn't want you. You even wiggle your eyebrows. You don't bother with the kissy face.

You lock the door, take out the key, put it on the bedside table. You wash. You climb into bed. You lie on your back, think about the day, about your marriage, think about whether if you had a job to get up for in the morning Sheila would still say you were useless. You stare up at the polystyrene ceiling and think right at it, direct all your thinking into it, hard—you count the indentations in it, there are grooves in the polystyrene, random, mostly shallow, it looks like the previous occupants of the room must have thrown things up against it for fun. You wonder whether it'd be fun if you did the same, leave some marks of your own. You think yes, maybe, maybe in the morning. You turn off the light. You pull the covers up. You sleep.

You wake, and it's still dark outside—and normally you'd just close your eyes and go back to sleep, you've made yourself a nice warm patch in the bed, but there's an unfamiliarity about the surroundings that disturbs you, and you remember you're in a hotel room, and remember *why* you're in a hotel room, and something churns inside.

Reach across to the watch on the bedside table. The clock face glares at you. It's a little after three o'clock.

Your stomach churns again, and you realize it's hunger. You should have had something to eat last night after all. You wonder whether they'd do room service—no, not in a little hotel like this, not in the middle of the night. Besides, there's no phone, is there, no phone. Is there a kettle in the room? With sachets of tea and coffee and powdered milk, because sometimes they put a digestive biscuit in there. Sometimes even a custard cream. But there wasn't a kettle in the room. You saw there wasn't when you first came in.

You stare up at the ceiling. And see the bulge.

You don't think about the bulge for a bit, you're still thinking about the existence or non-existence of the kettle and its powdered milk and its potential attendant biscuit possibilities. But you start to focus upon the bulge, try to work out the shape of it. Is it even really there? It's black on black. It's not over your head, it sags down towards your feet. It looks to you like the ceiling is bending inwards somehow, as if a sheet of wallpaper has come free, and is dangling there limp—but no, not quite like that, because the bulge tapers back up to the ceiling again, it's as if the wallpaper instead has an enormous air bubble in it. Hanging over you, wetly, because your eyes have adjusted, you can see now this black is a different black, there's something oily about it—and it's moving ever so slightly, it's rippling. It's peculiar what shadows can do.

And besides, you remember, there is no wallpaper on the ceiling.

You wonder whether maybe there's a kettle after all. Custard creams, you could at least look. And you reach out for the bedside lamp. You blink from the light.

It's important you don't exaggerate what it is you see.

The spider does not fill the entire ceiling. It's not that big. It might fill three quarters of it—and that's because its legs are outstretched at the moment. If it were hunched up properly, the way spiders usually sit, it'd take up no more than two thirds, maybe.

Mind you, you freeze.

The first things you think of gives you flashes of relief. The spider isn't directly above you. It's mostly on the other side of the room. If you sat bolt upright now, you wouldn't even touch it. If you were sitting on the end of the bed, though, you suppose there'd be contact, you suppose the top of your head would be grazing its belly. But you're not doing that. You're not doing that, so that's all right.

(Belly? Abdomen? Is that the right word? Um. Thorax?)

The second thing is—it looks like an ordinary spider. It doesn't have any strange colours on its body. No weird markings. You saw a documentary once, you think, or maybe it was a comic book movie, and it said that the really poisonous spiders had weird colourful markings on them, the nasty foreign ones. This is just a regular black spider— you can see bits of colour on it, certainly, but that's because it's so very big and you're so very close to it, be reasonable—the abdomen (yes, you think, it is abdomen) is fleshier than you might have thought, there are lines of red veins on it. No, this is an ordinary spider, a safe spider, a house spider. Ordinary, of course, in the sense you ignore the fact it's ten-foot long from side to side.

You watch the spider, but it doesn't seem to be doing anything. Maybe, you think, it's asleep. Its body heaves a bit, but that's just regular breathing, isn't it? Or snoring.

You strain to hear. But the spider isn't making a single sound.

You think you're coping with this really very well indeed. Well done. Sheila would probably be panicking.

Your brain tries to send you another message of comfort. It's not over your head, it's not poisonous, Steve, you're fine. You realize that the brain is trying a bit too hard, it's doing its best to stop you from screaming. (Why shouldn't you scream? No, don't scream. Don't scream. The spider. *The spider wouldn't like it*. You won't scream then. Good. Good. Don't scream. Don't scream.)

It must be asleep. It might be asleep.

If spiders sleep.

No, of course they sleep. (But how come they end up in the bath and sink every morning? What have they been doing in the darkness, to get there?)

You could make a run for it.

143

You could make a run for the door, especially if the spider is asleep. The door is on the far corner of the room. You could get out of bed— don't *run* for the door, that might startle it, *tiptoe* to the door. The spider's body isn't blocking the door. There's a leg near it, but still.

You're naked. You've left your clothes on the floor. Near the sink. Near the TV. Near the mirror. Near the spider.

You really wish you'd packed your pyjamas.

It's not that you fear running into a hotel corridor at three in the morning without any clothes on. Maybe you should, but that's not the worry, you think a giant spider might be seen as extenuating circumstances. It's just that—and this might seem an odd thing to realize suddenly, but—you've got skin. And any part of the spider could reach out and touch your skin. And you know right away—you don't want that to happen, not at any cost. You don't want your skin touched. No touching of the skin, please. If you had your pyjamas on, that'd be your armour. You wouldn't mind the spider touching your pyjamas. (Well. You would. But.) But not the skin. Not *you*.

You could make a run for it. If the spider is asleep. (But is it pretending?) You could make a run for the door. But you're not going to.

You don't want the light on. Suddenly, you don't want the light on. The light might wake the spider up. In the light, the spider can't fail to see you. And very carefully, very gently, you stretch your hand out from underneath the bed sheets. You realize you've tucked yourself deep down so that every last bit of you, right up to your eyes, is hidden. You hadn't even known you'd done this. Now this single hand breaks cover, bravely it reaches out across the wide expanse between the safety of the bed and the glare of the bedside lamp—it grasps for the switch—it flicks it off.

Blackness again. And right away, you think maybe you've made a big mistake.

Perhaps the spider will leave. If you go back to sleep, it might be gone by morning.

And it occurs to you—only now—where did it come from? The window is too small, the door is locked. Not up through the sink this time, certainly—it'd have pulled up all the plumbing in the process.

And wide eyed you stare up into the darkness, try to make out the black bulge. Is it still there? You can't be sure. You think you see something move—and then you swivel your head, fast, to your left side, and something in the darkness there shifts as well—and back to the right side, and on the right, the same—you close your eyes tight now, all you can see is the blackness in your head, and here, even here, you can see the faint outlines of shapes, and the shapes are moving, and the shapes are moving towards you.

You open your eyes. In a moment you've grabbed for the light. You think if you brush anything you shouldn't, anything hairy, you'll scream. You don't. Because what you're tracing with your fingers is the wire to the lamp, smooth and plastic, it's really nothing like a spider leg, and you're pulling at it now hard, and the lamp is rocking on its stand, loud and clumsy so the spider can hear, and you've found it, you've found the switch, and you press it.

And the spider has gone.

There's a thrill of relief to that. Just for a moment.

Because—of course—this means it wasn't asleep. (You were right not to make a run for it. You were right not to make a run for it. Well done, you.) It wasn't asleep, and it's moved. It's moved, lightning fast. Where has it moved to?

It's not on the ceiling anymore. It's not on the walls, not to the left or to the right. And that leaves only one place, and you shift in the bed slowly, *very* slowly, because you know you're right, and you don't want to move at all because you don't want to attract attention, but you have to be sure, and—

And three of its legs are now tickling the headboard behind you. And that's not the worst of it, there's another leg, and it's longer than those three legs somehow, it's on the bed itself, it's nestled lazily against the side pillow. The side pillow that's just inches away from the other pillow, the pillow on which you'd buried your head and pressed your cheeks and touched with your eyes and ears and mouth, oh God. Oh God, and you gasp. You can't help it, and a gasp isn't bad in the circumstances—but you're so close to the spider, and the noise causes the spider to flinch. Maybe not even the noise, maybe flinching from the very breath from inside you, God, maybe it feels you've just *spat* on it. You back away, rucking up the sheets as you do so, yanking them free from where they'd been tucked in, damaging your fortress, damaging your cover.

And you're so naked, all your skin.

You pant for breath. You try to be silent. The spider is silent. The spider doesn't make a single sound.

And you wonder whether it can see you. Of course it can see you. It has eight eyes. Bulbous, and dark as oil. And you're reflected in each of them.

You stare at its legs. You force your eyes down to the legs. And you remember how you took such care when you scooped spiders up never to break the legs, because they're so vulnerable, and you wouldn't want the spider to suffer. You never want anyone to suffer, not really. And the legs are now the thickness of bathroom pipes, but the funny thing is they still look vulnerable, you feel that you could still grab hold and snap one off. And at the thought of that, at the thought of the grip that would entail, of the tightness of that grip as you press against the spider, you dry heave. Your body can't help it. And still you stare at the legs—and the hairs that cover them, at this size not so much hairs, more a coat of dark fur—and the fur is quivering, each tip of it standing on edge and dancing within the breeze. Except there is no breeze—the air conditioning is off—there's no air getting in from outside—it feels like there's no air to breathe (oh, you're sharing the same little air with the spider, what's been in its lungs is now inside yours)—so all this quivering, each single hair on the legs flicking back and forth, it's something the spider is doing itself. Does it even know it's doing it? Does it even know that as it's flexing its legs, it's causing all the hairs upon them to thrill? Does it care?

You stare at the legs, because you daren't look up into the eyes again.

And then suddenly, before you realize you'd even decided to do it, you flee. You rush for the door. And as you do you feel something tugging you back, you feel the spider has grabbed you by the leg, and you've no choice, at last you *do* scream, and you jerk away hard—and your leg's caught in the sheets, that's all it is, but it's tipped you off balance, you try to steady yourself but you can't, over you go, over you go, you fall off the bed, and it seems you're falling so slowly, but you hit the floor with a thump. And part of you knows it's all over, your chance of escape over, you've squandered those precious seconds you needed, you should just lie there dazed and give up—but you don't, you *won't*— you kick yourself out of the tangle of bed linen, and you're stumbling up into a run now, head down—and head down is good, because you can hear the spider now, it's behind you, it's chasing, it's back upon the ceiling and skittering across the polystyrene tiles and they make light popping noises as its legs bore grooves into them—it's good that your head is down, because if you were at full height it'd be skimming the underside of the spider's body, and you don't want that, you can't have that, if it touches you you'll *die*. And the room is bigger than you thought, but it's really ever so small, and you're at the door, and your hands are around the knob, and you're pulling at it, and pushing at it, and it won't open—and then you remember it's locked—it's locked and the key is on the bedside table, the bedside table which is now *miles* away, miles from you and the other side of an angry spider. And only now do you dare turn back. And you can see the bedside table. And you can see the key. And you can see the spider coming towards you, and it's not racing, it doesn't need to, but it's still *coming* to you, and it's still so *huge*. And once more you feel the urge to give up. Shall you give up? Just give up. And you can't move anyway, and you wonder whether you're caught in a web. And then you scream again, and the spider flinches too—and you're away, you're away from the door now, you're past the spider, straight back to the bed, you fling yourself upon the mattress and pull the mess of sheets over your head like a naughty little boy who should have been fast asleep hours ago.

The spider stays where it is. Its torso now largely blocking the door altogether. But you don't care. You don't want to try the door again. Not for a long time.

You take hold of the key, but there's nothing you want to do with it. Except turn it over and over in your hand. Tight and hard, you like the bite of the key's teeth, don't you?

You watch the spider. It watches you. It probably watches you.

Some time passes. A long time passes. You think, maybe an hour. You think, maybe lots of hours. Maybe it'll be dawn soon. You don't know what difference dawn will make. But maybe things will be better in the morning. Everything is better in the morning.

But the sun resolutely refuses to rise. It stays night. And the spider stays in its corner of the room. And you stay in yours.

You wonder why this is happening.

Is it your fault? For all the spiders you've killed. Is this some sort of revenge? You tried so hard to be merciful. You were never cruel. You were never, ever cruel. And had it been up to you, you'd have never hurt anyone. It was Sheila's doing. It was Sheila. You were only following orders.

"I'm sorry," you say out loud. And your voice sounds cracked, and you're not sure whether that's fear, or that you've not spoken for so long, or maybe it's genuine remorse. Yes. That'd be the one, let's go with that.

The spider says nothing to this. Naturally. But it repositions itself on the wall, adjusts its legs. As if better to hear what you might have to say. As if to get comfy for your story.

But you have no follow up. You try to think of one, but you can't.

"That's it," you say.

And that too is the moment when the bulb on the bedside lamp blows.

For a second when you're plunged into darkness you think that something much worse has happened—that this is death—that the heart that has been pounding away inside your chest all this while has finally given up the ghost and called it quits—that the spider has taken offence at your ridiculous apology and leaped halfway across the room in an instant and bitten your head off. And then you're reacting, faster than you could imagine; all the adrenalin that has been coursing through your body hits the motherlode, and you're throwing yourself across the bed, to the other side, to the other lamp—because you mustn't let that spider hide itself in the black. And the light snaps on, and you blink, and the spider's eyes are inches away from yours. And in those few seconds it *did* leap across the room, it did come for you, and a moment later it'd have been on your face, in your hair, it'd have wrapped itself around your body, who knows?—and the two of you are so close now, and as it quivers you can feel the motion against your own skin. And it stares at you, as if to say, "Well, what now?", and even this near it is still silent, you think you'd be able to hear something but still there's nothing, and you think you could bear it if only it made the slightest sound.

Then—sound; but it doesn't come from the spider; it comes from *behind* it. And it's so hard to tear your gaze away from the spider's now, but you force yourself, you look *through* it, and watch as a beetle crawls up the breezeblock wall. It meanders, unhurried, unbothered.

It's the size of your chest, and there was a time maybe when finding an enormous insect on your bedroom wall might have alarmed you. But now you want to call out to it—run away! Fast! Get back to where you came from! (Under the bed? Are there more bugs lurking under your bed?—and even though you're face to face with a ten-foot spider, you find yourself shrinking away from the edge towards it.) The beetle is an idiot. The beetle is a moron. The beetle is cheerfully strolling past a spider, and it's not even trying to go in a straight line, it positively *lingers*, doesn't it know what danger it's in? And for a moment the spider too can hardly seem to believe the stupidity of its prey, it almost considers letting the thing go—and then it turns from you, it's skittering up the wall after it, and for the first time you can appreciate how fast the spider is, it can turn its body about in an instant, it can manipulate its eight legs with grace and skill that is frankly beautiful.

And the spider appears to squat over the beetle, and even now the beetle doesn't seem alarmed, if anything it's somewhat bemused to find something impeding its journey. Its struggles are of confusion, not fear—and then the spider draws out its fangs, and they're wrong, they look *wrong*—they're white, they're white like enamel, they look like giant human teeth, a brilliant bright white sliding out of its black veined body. And the spider hesitates just for an instant, and you could swear it's for your benefit, it's looking at you, there you are reflected once more in all its oily eyes—what is it, a warning? What, showing off? "Look what I can do!"—and then the fangs speed downwards, and the force of them is terrifying, and the teeth pierce right through the carapace shell of the beetle, and there's a blunt crack, and you can hear the punctured beetle *groan*—and you can't help but hug your fleshy naked body, and you realize the pyjamas wouldn't have worked as armour after all. And the beetle is shuddering now, its stupid eyes bulging out, and it seems to fatten and swell, as if it's being pumped full of something, soon it isn't just the eyes that start to bulge. And its hard shell seems to be covered with grease. Is it a spider that injects its victims with venom? Or is that wasps? Or snakes? The beetle is still whimpering, but now the spider caresses it with a single leg. And it could be just to hold its food in place, because moment by moment as you watch the beetle seems to be becoming less a solid and more a liquidy gloop—but there's also something calming about it, as if the spider is trying to ease its distress. As if to say, I know you're my dinner, and I know that's pretty harsh, and I know what's going on inside your dissolving body is hardly welcome to you. But I don't want to be cruel about it. I don't want to be cruel. And part of the shattered carapace comes off altogether, and drifts to the floor like a feather.

And when the spider starts to feed, at last it makes a sound. And you've heard it before. Sometimes you and Sheila would take little Laura out to a cafe. Laura liked to have fizzy drinks with lots of ice in, and suck them up through a straw. But it was always the straw that appealed most to her, not the lemonade or the Fanta or the Coke—she liked slurping noisily at the ice cubes. Other people in the cafe would glare at you all; you would tell Laura off—"Stop that, it's disgusting!" Because it truly was, the greed of it, the unashamed demonstration she wanted to make that she was enjoying her drink and everyone should know, the way she'd smack her lips each time she swilled up another melting shard of ice. Sheila never even seemed to hear it. Or she'd say, "Leave her alone, she's having fun," or, "She's not doing any harm." And she'd look at you, and you knew what that look meant, this is *my* daughter, not yours; until you pay your way, until you find some *use* in this family, you don't get any rights. And Laura would grin at you, she'd actually grin, because she could do whatever she bloody liked, because she had more authority than you, and you'd feel such rage towards her then that you could feel your fist itching, and you'd think, not again, and you'd think, why do they keep pushing me to this, and you'd think, not Laura, she's just a kid, if you're going to be angry, direct it at the mother. And you'd dig your fingernails into your hands, and that calmed you down a bit, you liked the feel of them biting at your skin, the little hurt—and Sheila would smile so blandly as if she didn't know what she was putting you through, and Laura would just carry on, and she'd blow down her straw hard so that the dregs of her drink would bubble and froth.

You watch the spider as it feeds, as it slurps. And your stomach starts to rumble. You can barely believe it. Revolted as you are, seeing the spider eat is making you hungry.

The spider doesn't notice at first. But now the rumbling has started, it won't stop. Your stomach crying out for some little food, whatever it may be.

The spider pauses. It seems uncertain. Then it slowly crawls down the wall towards you. You flinch—and the spider seems to shake, no, not that now, no more of that. And you see that hanging from its mandibles is a piece of beetle.

You can't be sure what that means. Not until it drops the piece of meat beside you, and turns back to its own dinner.

The chunk of liquefying insect inks a stain on the white sheets. And the spider resumes its sucking—then stops when it sees you haven't touched your meal.

It comes up to you. What is it? Angry? Impatient?

You prod the goo with your finger. It's sticky, and surprisingly warm.

The spider seems to wait as you put a little glob of it in your mouth.

It doesn't seem to mind when you choke on it, when you bring it straight up again. Sheila would have minded. Sheila would have been very offended. But the spider is fine. It even looks pleased. It flexes its mandibles at you in encouragement. It's giving you the kissy face.

That said, the spider won't leave until you've taken another bite.

This time it stays down. You try not to think of the food in your mouth as beetle. It's like thick gravy. You don't think of that. You think of custard creams. You think of custard creams, and how all the salty goo is just the custardy filling in the middle. And all the hard bits, you give no thought to what they might really be, they're just little crumbs of biscuit. You swallow down the custard creams, warm custard creams, meaty custard creams, and your stomach growls with approval.

The spider's back at its own meal now. The beetle is a husk. And as the spider sucks away one remaining surprised eye pops inwards, and that's the last trace that the feast had ever been a living creature.

When you get up off the bed, the spider doesn't mind.

You walk to the door, quietly, carefully. You've been playing with the key in your hand for so long now it feels odd to put it in the lock, for a moment you feel a little lost without its teeth sharp against your skin. You turn the key. It doesn't move, it's stiff, and you start to panic—and you shoot a look back at the spider, and it's watching your antics quite cheerfully now, you're pals, you can do what you like. So you take a deep breath, force the panic back down. You put the key in again, try it calmly, calmly. This time the tumblers move, the door gives.

And you suppose you could leave just like that.

The spider is surprised. So are you. But it looks up perfectly amiably as you approach it. And even now, you think you are maybe saying goodbye. And you're wondering why you're wanting to do that, and the brain, your poor brain that has tried so hard to keep you safe and sane, it's sending you frantic warning messages—you're free, Steve, you're free, get out now, get out now whilst you can . . . !

You don't want to touch the spider. You don't want any contact with that creature. You can cope with the small ones, you always could. Catch them in a glass, flush them down the toilet. But the big ones, you've discovered, they can really make your flesh crawl.

You don't want to touch the spider. But still. You punch it in the eye.

It squawks. You didn't know a spider can squawk. It feels good to make a spider squawk.

It feels good that it's making a noise at last. You hate being given the silent treatment. You always told Sheila that. She could shout at you all she wanted, but what drove you mad was when she sulked.

You punch it again, harder this time, harder now you know the eye isn't hard like glass. It grazes your knuckles, but that feels *good*, doesn't it, it always feels good. You punch it—no, not an it, it's a her, you punch her, you don't want to hurt her, but she's had this coming. And on the third punch something gives way, something breaks inside, there's that nice crunching sound like car wheels over gravel. And there's wetness, and the smell of something bad, and what's sprayed against your skin is thin and brown like weak tea.

The spider falls off the wall. And you want to give her a kick for good measure, you even swing back your foot to do so. But you really don't want to touch those hairy legs, there's something about them even in your rage that just revolts you.

You walk back to the door, and every instinct is telling you not to look back, don't look back, you've had your revenge, given her little punishment—now get out, get out whilst you have the chance. But you do look back, and you half expect the spider to be springing out at you, enraged. And do you know, you'd have so much more respect for her if she did? But they never do. She's still in the corner of the room, her surviving eyes streaming with tears, and looking all oh-so confused, but-what-did-I-do, Steve? Oh, how you hate all those but-what-did-I-do's, and you resist the impulse to go right back and give her one more slap. Her squawking now sounds less like pain, it's disappointment, it's betrayal. Or so you think, but how are you supposed to know? How do you know what a spider looks like when it's confused, what are you meant to be now, some sort of spider expert? It's not your fault.

But, "I'm sorry," you say anyway, and the spider reacts the same way Sheila always does, she ignores you, she doesn't even dare acknowledge you, and if only they'd acknowledge you, can't they see you're just wanting to make things better? It's not nice to be ignored. And you know you won't ever hurt them again, you won't, you promise yourself you won't. You've never wanted to hurt anything in the first place, you're the one who'd even scoop up bugs gently so their legs stay on.

It's not your fault.

You open the door.

You've escaped.

You take one step out.

There are spiders everywhere. On the walls, and crawling over the ceiling. So many of them they're stepping over each other, they're knocking each other off and on to the floor. Further down you can see a mass of them blocking the corridor, that there are hundreds of spiders all jammed fast, as if they all got stuck trying to go through a revolving door at the same time, legs and abdomens and eyes all higgledy-piggledy with no room to budge, legs and eyes and sharp white fangs.

And you feel a certain relief. Because whatever has happened, this looks apocalyptic. This has nothing to do with you.

It's not your fault.

You think of Sheila. And you know how badly she needs rescuing. She can't survive in a world like this. And you feel something cold and fresh in your head—*Good.* But Laura too, you think, your own daughter, what about Laura, how will she . . . *Good*, it says again. Good, good, good.

You know what? You know what? You just don't love them *anymore.*

You step back into the bedroom.

The spider looks at you balefully. She's still crying out the ruins of her shattered eye.

And then she does something that Sheila always did. She forgives you.

She extends a leg, seems to beckon. She forgives you. She wants you back.

You return to the bed. You wipe away the brown gunk off your chest, a little self-consciously. You did the same with Sheila's blood once, that time you went too far. "Sorry," you say again, and by God, you mean it. You'll never hurt anyone again.

She wraps a leg around you, and your skin revolts to the touch of a spider, and at the same time it delights at the warmth of her fur. You're cold, you're so cold. And hungry.

She fetches you your dinner. And you settle down to eat.

# COLD
## SNAP

### i

There hadn't been a specific moment when Ben had stopped believing in Santa Claus. One Christmas he'd thought that a fat man in red travelling the world in a sleigh was credible—the next, he hadn't. There'd been no trauma that had disillusioned him. Indeed, it had been a good year, that year; his parents were still smiling back then, every day there were so many smiles. "Listen," said his Daddy, sitting him on his knee, holding him there steady, "listen, it's okay for you not believing in Santa, okay? But just don't go spoiling it for anybody else. Let your friends hang on to Santa as long as they can. Once he's gone, he's gone forever." Ben hadn't thought of it that way before, that he'd never get that innocence back, and it gave him a little pang, and for one awful moment he thought he might even cry—but it was all right, Daddy wasn't cross with him, Daddy was holding him on his knee, Daddy was holding him safe. "Is it a deal, old chap?" And Ben liked it when Daddy called him 'old chap', and he assured him, cub's honour, he'd keep his scepticism to himself.

Not that the existence or non-existence of Santa Claus was the sort of topic that was often discussed in the school playground. It was all talk about football and techno battle rangers and whether breathing in close to girls would give you spots. Actually, Ben's belief in Santa Claus had outlived his belief in God. He could more easily conceive of a man who'd spend his time giving presents to strangers whilst being flown about by reindeer, than he could a being who'd get stuck up on a cross to save those strangers' sins. The inconvenience to Santa Claus alone must have been immense, and his generosity overwhelming. But Jesus? There had to be limits.

So, yes, I suppose it's true—seeing Jesus Christ there, in his bedroom that Christmas Eve, his body cast into strange shadow by the dazzling white of the snow falling outside the window, holding in his hand not a sack of toys but, I don't know, a cross maybe, a cross on the road to Calvary—yes, I suppose *that* would have been the greater shock. But seeing Santa Claus there was still quite surprising.

"Hello, Ben," said Santa Claus. "Did I wake you?"

"Yes," said Ben.

"Oh, good," said Santa.

Ben knew it was Santa right away. He was the perfect synthesis of all the Santas he had ever seen, on Christmas cards, on TV cartoons, on Coca Cola bottles. "Some children sleep very soundly," Santa went on. "You wouldn't believe how hard it can be sometimes, to wake up a child that just doesn't *want* to be woken. It's the hardest part of the job."

"Really?" asked Ben.

Santa thought about it for a moment. "No, not really," he said. "Flying around the world in one night, that's from the North Pole to the South and back, and zigzagging to all the countries in between, it's not a straight line, you know—now, that's hard. To be honest, waking children hardly compares. To be honest, waking children is comparatively a cinch. But, you know." He smiled at Ben. "I'm glad you were easy to wake, just the same."

"Are you real?" said Ben.

"Yes," said Santa.

"Okay."

"Do you want to touch me? You can touch me if you want."

"Okay."

"I'll come closer," said Santa, and shifted his bulk towards the bed so that it wobbled in a very real way, and Ben could see that Santa was real perfectly well now, and he didn't need to touch him, actually, he had proof enough. But, "Go on, touch that," said Santa, and Ben thought it'd be rude not to, so as Santa offered him his hand, he brushed one of the fingers, just for a second, "no, harder than that, if you want to know if I'm *real*," and Ben grasped it, actually grasped it, the finger as fat as a sausage.

"There we go," said Santa. "There, you see." And this close Ben could see that Santa really was very fat, and very red, and very bearded, and his eyes were twinkling.

"Your finger's very cold," said Ben.

"The snow's coming down thick out there," said Santa. "Cold enough to freeze your blood. Do you have anything to eat?"

Ben thought, tried to remember what his Daddy and Mum used to leave out for Santa back when he'd believed. "We've got some mince pies downstairs."

"I mean, anything warm?"

"I could put one in the microwave."

Santa considered this. "Okay," he said.

So they went down to the kitchen, the little boy in blue pyjamas, the fat man in red following politely behind. "Try and walk where I walk," said Ben, "walk to the edge of the stairs, they creak in the middle."

"Okay," said Santa, but he was so fat, and his feet were so big, that try as he might he couldn't avoid the creaks altogether. And Ben winced, thinking that at any moment his Daddy might be woken up. In the kitchen Ben turned on the lights, and saw that Santa's beard was not all that white, that was just the snow, Santa's beard looked very grey, and very old.

"I'll get you a mince pie," said Ben, and opened the cupboard, and took out a box of Mr Kipling's own.

"Something warm," said Santa. "Can I have a soup?" And he pointed into the cupboard, and at all the tins of soup. "I'm not allowed to cook things, not with a flame, not without Daddy," said Ben. "It's okay," said Santa, "I'll do it, I'm old enough." And he took from the cupboard the first three tins his hand could claw—pea and ham, and minestrone, and chicken noodle, he all but ripped off the lids with the can opener at such ferocious speed, and poured the contents into one saucepan. He put the saucepan on the gas ring, lit it. Santa stood over the meal as it cooked, and Ben could see that Santa was drooling a little, there was spit running out of Santa's mouth and mixing with the melting snow in his beard, "I'm so hungry," said Santa, and winked, almost apologetically—and even though the soup couldn't be warm enough yet, he hadn't let it stand for long enough, "that'll have to do," he said, and took a large wooden spoon from the shelf just beside the spice rack, the spice rack Daddy never even bothered to use, Mum had used spices but not Daddy, Daddy's cooking was much simpler—and stuck the spoon into the pan, and scooped up the mix of soups, and ate.

"Would you like to sit down?" asked Ben. He'd even put out a place mat. Santa waved the invitation away, stood over the cooker, and shovelled lukewarm soup into his face. He didn't come up for breath for a good five minutes. "Thanks," he said, and smiled at Ben, and wiped bits of noodle and green pea from his beard with the back of his hand, "yeah, I'll have that mince pie now." And he took one, and popped it into his mouth whole.

Ben wrinkled his nose. "If you're Santa—and you are," he added hastily, he really didn't want to go through all that weird finger touching again, "then why have I never seen you before?"

"I only visit when it snows. London hasn't had a white Christmas in years."

"Oh," said Ben. An intelligent boy, he wondered why, whether this was to do with needing the right reindeer conditions, something like that. Instead he said, "Do I get a present, then?"

"What?"

"A present. I mean, that's why you're here, right?"

"Right," said Santa. "It's waiting for you, right now, under the tree. Shall we go and look?" And Santa grinned soup-spattered teeth, and led Ben into the sitting room, as if it were *his* sitting room, as if this had been *his* house all along. Ben recognized the tree that he and his father had bought and decorated together a couple of weeks ago—but it looked a bit taller now, as if it were standing up straight, as if it were a soldier on parade saluting the arrival of its commanding officer. And the fairy lights were on, and they were *flashing*, and what's more they were flashing different colours, and Ben had been quite sure they hadn't done that before. And underneath the tree, in front of all the other presents, in front of all the *ordinary* presents, was the one from Santa. The wrapping paper couldn't disguise what it was.

"How did you know?" breathed Ben.

"It's what you want, isn't it? It's what you most want."

"Yes," said Ben.

"I got your letter," said Santa, and chuckled. "And you've been a particularly good boy this year."

"I didn't write a letter," said Ben. "I don't believe in you anymore."

Santa frowned at that. "I certainly got a letter," he said, a little huffily. "I don't come to homes where I'm not invited. What do you think I am?"

"Sorry," said Ben, and Santa smiled, and opened his arms for a hug. And Ben didn't really want to hug Santa, but he thought he better had, he didn't want Santa to be hurt, and the present was just what he wanted, the second thing he most wanted in all the world. Ben couldn't

THE BEST DARK FICTION OF ROBERT SHEARMAN

get his arms around Santa, they barely stretched around the midriff, and there was a peculiar smell to Santa's coat, something animal, something Ben thought probably was reindeer.

"Can I open my present now?" said Ben.

"Just a formality to get out of the way first," said Santa. And suddenly in one of his hands was a piece of old parchment, so long it unrolled down to his knees, and in the other a pen. "Proof of receipt," he said, "sign on the dotted line." And Ben signed, and then went to the present, and now that he got to it he saw that even the wrapping paper was flashing and changing colour, and he looked at Santa in wonder. Santa laughed. "Boys like you don't care about fancy paper," he said, "it's the present underneath that counts. Rip it open, Ben, rip it apart!" And Ben laughed at that, he couldn't help himself, and he tore into the wrapping paper, and found that there was still more wrapping paper beneath, flashing away. Santa laughed too, "Deeper than that! Come on, Ben, chop chop!" And Ben tore deeper. "I love this bit," said Santa, "really, this is the best bit, seeing all the kids' faces light up when they get their toys. I always make sure I stay for this." And Ben touched spokes, and chains, and handlebars, and tires, and soon enough all the wrapping paper lay upon the carpet, flashing more feebly now, like a dying animal, and then it flashed no more, and then it was dead. And Ben marvelled at his shiny new bicycle.

"It's got eight gears," said Santa, helpfully. "It's one of the good ones. Brand new, too, I never deal in second hand goods. And stabilizers, you know, until you get your balance."

"Keep away from him," said Daddy, standing in the doorway.

He was holding a knife, and Ben's first thought was that meant Daddy must have been to the kitchen to fetch it, and he'd have seen all the mess caused by the soup, he hadn't had a chance to clean it up yet—he was in so much trouble.

"Well, now," said Santa.

"Keep away from him," said Daddy again.

"I'm nowhere near him," said Santa, perfectly reasonably. "He's by the tree."

"Don't sign the contract, Ben, whatever you do."

"Put the knife down, Davey," said Santa.

"No."

"Davey, come on, put the knife down. You're scaring the boy." And at that Ben realized that yes, he *was* scared, he hadn't had time to think of it 'til now. His Daddy didn't look like his Daddy, so wild-eyed, shaking. And his name was David, although his friends called him Dave, and his Mum used to call him Day—not all the time, just when she was really happy, I love you, big Day, she'd say, and kiss him—but not for a while now, not a long while, most of the time she called him Dave. No one ever called him Davey.

Daddy licked his lips.

"We both know that you're not going to use the knife," said Santa.

"You have no idea what I can do," said Daddy.

"I know precisely what you can do," said Santa. "I've got you on my list, remember? I've *got you on my list*." Santa walked towards Daddy. "Keep back," said Daddy. "No," said Santa. "I'm warning you," said Daddy, but he was the one backing out of the way. "Go on then," said Santa, opening his arms out wide, just as he had to Ben earlier, as if he wanted a hug. "Go on. Stick me with your knife. It's not a very big knife. And I have so much fat to cut through, so much flesh, centuries of it. Go on, see if you can slice deep enough to hurt me." "Keep back," said Daddy, but Santa didn't.

"Go on," said Santa, "if that's what you want Ben to see. If that's what you want him to remember." Daddy gave a noise that might have been a sob, and Santa took the knife, and it vanished into a big red pocket. "You silly boy," Santa said, "you silly boy." Ben thought that Santa must be very cross, and thought that Daddy thought so too, because he flinched when Santa raised his hand to him—but then Santa smiled, and ruffled Daddy's hair affectionately.

"Don't sign the contract," said Daddy weakly.

"Don't worry about Ben's contract, just you worry about yours," said Santa. And at that Daddy went pale.

"No," he said. "Please." And Santa just smiled, not without sympathy. "Can't you . . . ?" and Daddy licked his lips once more. "Can't you just go next door? Can't you go somewhere else instead?"

"I could," said Santa. "But I came here, didn't I?" And Daddy made a little gulp like a hiccup, and Santa said, "Now, now, none of that. You'll scare Ben. Don't scare Ben."

"I've got a bike," said Ben.

"So I see," said Daddy.

"It's good, isn't it?"

"It's good," said Daddy.

"It *is* good, actually," said Santa. "Eight gears, stabilizers. Not just any old rubbish."

"Please," said Daddy softly.

"No," said Santa, and that was that. "You'd better get your clothes on," he added. "Both of you."

"Ben doesn't have to come," said Daddy.

"You're not going to leave him alone in the house, surely? Not on Christmas Eve. Not when anyone could get in."

"No," said Daddy, dully. "You're right."

"It'll be an adventure for him."

Ben liked the sound of that. "Please, Daddy, can I have an adventure?"

"Of course," Santa said. "And you can bring your bike."

"Can I, Daddy? Can I bring my bike?"

"Leave the bicycle here, Ben," said Daddy. "You don't want to take the bike."

"I do," said Ben.

"He does," said Santa.

"It's slippery out there."

"It's got stabilizers," said Santa.

"Stabilizers," said Ben.

"Please, Ben," said Daddy.

"Let him take it," said Santa. "Let him get to ride it with you. Share his bike with his Daddy. Give him that pleasure at least."

Daddy said, "All right."

Ben said, "Hurray!"

Daddy said, "You'd better go and dress up warm, though. Go and put on your warmest clothes."

"The very warmest," Santa said to both of them. "It's so cold out there, it'll freeze your blood." And he clapped his hands together. "No time to waste, come on. Chop chop!"

## ii

The weather reports said there was going to be a cold snap. No one was prepared. Industry would be affected, said the news, public transport would be at a standstill. Daddy told Ben that for school the next morning he'd have to wear his very warmest clothes. He'd have to put on his thickest sweater and his thickest gloves, and wear the stripy scarf. Ben didn't like the scarf, it made his neck itch, but Daddy didn't care. "You're not going down with any bug, not on my watch," he said. "Your Mum'll kill me." Ben laughed at the thought, and said Mum wouldn't kill him. "Yes, she would," said Daddy.

Ben made it to school and back again through the cold snap quite intact, the scratchy stripy scarf had beaten off all the germs. Daddy was pleased. "There you go, old chap. You're okay. You're safe."

And that evening Ben stood with his Daddy by the window, watching from the street lamps how the rain seemed to be slowing down, how it had begun to drift lazily in the wind, as if in no particular hurry to hit the ground.

"It's snowing!" said Ben.

"Yes," said Daddy.

"I love snow," said Ben.

"Yes," said Daddy. "Still. It won't settle."

But it did settle. The next morning there was a thin blanket of white over everything. Daddy made Ben wear his scarf to school all the more tightly. "Still. It won't last," said Daddy. But it did last.

Ben didn't know why the adults didn't like the snow. It was like rain, but *fun* rain. They seemed almost frightened of it—the weather forecaster kept giving updates about snow conditions with due gravity, and Daddy listened with gravity too, unsmiling, tense. Ben didn't get it. Snow was all over Christmas cards, it was in every Christmas song (well, the good ones, not the religious ones), it was Christmas. Pictures of Santa Claus everywhere, beaming out at him, standing knee deep in the white stuff. "Do you think we'll have a white Christmas?" Ben asked. "I shouldn't have thought so," said Daddy, "it's weeks off, I'm sure it'll have blown over by then. Don't you worry." Ben wasn't worried. "I'm dreaming of a white Christmas," he sung. It was the only line of the song he knew. "I've got the video somewhere," said Daddy. "*White Christmas*. Would you like to watch it with me?" "Okay." "This weekend?" "Okay." So that Saturday they watched *White Christmas* together; they cuddled up close on the sofa, Ben liked to do that when they watched telly, in case there were scary bits. There were no scary bits in *White Christmas*. "Daddy, the song wasn't in it," said Ben, at the end. "No," said Daddy. And then, "I'm sorry," as if he'd let his son down.

And still the snow fell.

"Can we have a little chat, old chap?" asked Daddy one evening. And he looked serious, even a bit stern, and Ben felt a little scared. "Up here on my knee," said Daddy, and Ben felt better, he knew up on the knee meant it was going to be all right.

"I know Christmas is going to be a little odd this year," said Daddy. "Different."

"I know," said Ben.

"But I just want you to know. That we'll have a good Christmas. Don't you worry. Don't you worry about that."

"Okay," said Ben.

"Do you believe me?"

"Yes," said Ben.

"The way to look at it," said Daddy. "Is that you'll get two Christmases this year. One with me, one with Mum."

"Yes."

"Double the fun!"

"We don't have to. We could still have one together."

"I'm sorry, old chap."

"We could talk to Mum about it."

"I'm sorry, old chap, I don't think so."

"Okay."

"But whatever you want, goes. Whatever else. This will be the *best* Christmas ever. I promise you. Hey. Hey, look at me. Hey, Ben. Do I ever break my promise?"

"I don't know."

"Have I ever broken my promise?"

"No."

"I do my best. I do my best, you know."

"Can we have Christmas dinner?" asked Ben.

"Of course we'll have Christmas dinner!"

"I mean, properly. With turkey. And gravy. And those little sausages."

"Absolutely we will."

"The way Mum makes it."

"I'll make the very best Christmas dinner I can. You can help me if you want. Turkey and chipolata sausages, roast potatoes. Stuffing, you like stuffing, don't you?"

"And can we have a Christmas tree?"

Daddy gave him a hug. "There's no way," he said, "that a son of mine isn't going to have the best Christmas tree there is." And he hugged his son tight, so tight. "Just as soon as the snow eases off, we'll go and get one. You can help me if you want. You can help, would you like that?"

But the snow didn't ease off. Still the snow fell.

"Daddy," said Ben that weekend, "are we going to get a Christmas tree soon? Because all my friends have trees." "Yes, Ben." "And Mum's got one, she's got her tree." "I said yes! . . . Yes, Ben. Sorry. Yes. We'll go and get a tree. We'll go this afternoon." So they drove into the town centre in the car. "Look at the speed these people are driving," said

Daddy, "they're maniacs. In these conditions!" Ben could feel the car slide a little on the road. He thought it was fun. "You're okay, you're safe," said Daddy, and Ben knew he was. They bought a Christmas tree from a man selling them on the pavement outside that cinema that had closed. "Not much left," the man said, "the best ones are gone." It's true, there wasn't much to pick from; on one or two the needles had half fallen off, and yet the man was still charging thirty-five quid. "That's scandalous," said Daddy, and the man just shrugged. "I like this one!" said Ben. "Can we have this one?" The tree was a bit on the stumpy side, and at the top the stem split into two on either side, it looked as if it had a pair of mutant ears. "Look at the ears, Daddy!" laughed Ben. "I'm sure we can find you a better tree than that one, old chap," said Daddy, "what would your mother say?" "No, I want Big Ears!" said Ben. "Forty-five quid," said the man, "you've got yourself a bargain there," and he even helped Daddy lug it out to the car, he took one ear and Daddy took the other, "thank you," he said with a big grin as he pocketed the cash, "and merry Christmas!"

The tree wouldn't stand up straight in the living room, it lolled to the right like a drunkard. "What we need to do," said Daddy thoughtfully, "is put all the decorations on the left, to weigh it down a bit." Ben asked whether they could do the decorations today, and Daddy said of course they could, no time like the present! Where were the decorations kept? Where did Mummy put them? And Ben said he thought Mum might keep them in a cupboard under the stairs. So Daddy went and had a look in the cupboard, he pulled all sorts of things out. "No luck, old chap," he said, "any other ideas?" Ben thought maybe the tinsel and the fairy lights and the balls were all in the spare bedroom, then, in one of the cupboards there, and Daddy asked him if he knew which cupboard might be most likely, but Ben didn't. "Okay," said Daddy. He emptied the contents of each cupboard on to the bed, putting them all back in again neatly before opening another one—it was quite a good system, but after an hour or so he tired of it, and just stuck back everything into any cupboard any which way. "She wouldn't have taken the decorations with her, would she?" asked Daddy. Ben didn't know. Daddy went on, "I mean, what would be the point? She has, though. She bloody has." Daddy tried phoning her; she was out; he didn't leave a message. Daddy fumed for a bit, "I can't believe she'd do that," he said. "To me, yes, okay. But not to her own *son*." He phoned her again, and this time left a message that was very terse. "Let's have some dinner, old chap," said Daddy to Ben, "there's nothing for it." Ben asked whether they were going to decorate the tree, and Daddy looked a bit helpless, and said they'd have to buy some more decorations first—no, they couldn't go out today, they'd already been out the once—no, look, it was snowing, look at all the snow. Ben ate fish fingers and chips; Daddy had pea and ham soup, he always had soup, he said it was the least bother. Mum phoned back. Daddy listened to what she had to say. "Oh. Right. But we've . . . Right. No, I'll go and check. Right. Sorry. Thanks for . . . thanks for calling back." The decorations were in the cupboard under the stairs after all, Ben had been right first time; they were all kept within a box for an old vacuum cleaner. They decorated the tree, they got out all the tinsel and the fairy lights and the balls. They put a star on the tip of one of the ears, and an angel on the other. Ben loved it. "Sorry, Ben," said Daddy.

Still, the snow fell. Ben's school closed a few days early. "Lucky you!" said Daddy. "I still have to make it into work!" Ben was disappointed, though. There wasn't much work to be done at school this close to the holidays, and now he'd never find out how that advent calendar would turn out, that had been getting quite exciting.

The Saturday before Christmas Daddy took Ben back out into the snow. "Christmas shopping!" he said. "It'll be fun!" The snow was falling thick now; each day, it seemed to Ben, a mass of adults outside the window were doing their best to wreck the snow, driving over it and walking on it and turning it to mush—but each night the snow fell again, and by morning had brought back the blanket, unbroken, pure. Ben knew he was as much to blame, though—he loved crunching his footprints into the snow, crunch, crunch. Knowing that within an hour of his doing so fresh flakes would cover up any trace he had ever been there.

"I want you to get a really nice present for your mother," Daddy said, and gave to Ben more money than he had ever seen. "Can you hold on to that?" Ben could. Ben had no idea what to get Mum, so Daddy and Ben looked around the department stores together.

"What are *you* going to get Mum?" asked Ben.

"Oh," said Daddy. "Well. We've agreed not to buy each other any presents this year."

"Oh," said Ben. "Okay."

"It's just easier that way."

"Okay."

"We agreed," chuckled Daddy, "that this way we'd have more money to spend on you, old chap! So you come out of this rather well! It's all for you!" And then, "Ben, I'm sorry, what is it, what's wrong?" And Ben said he didn't want the extra presents, he didn't want any of this to be his *fault*. And Daddy hugged him right there, he stooped down and hugged him, and assured him that none of this was anything to do with him. It was adult stuff, just silly adult stuff. "The truth is," he said, "the reason Mummy and Daddy aren't buying each other presents . . . is that we just don't like each other very much at the moment." And in spite of himself, Ben brightened at that.

Ben bought his Mum a couple of gift baskets of bubble bath from the Body Shop.

On the bottom level of the department store, on the concourse between a Poundstretcher and a British Home Stores, there was a Santa's Grotto. Surrounding the grotto was a little garden, decorated with fake snow, and tinsel.

"Would you like to see Santa, Ben?" There was quite a long queue, and an unsmiling woman in a booth was selling tickets.

"No."

"Oh. Are you sure?"

"I don't believe in Santa Claus. I didn't believe in him last year either." Ben put his head to one side, and considered. "I probably did the year before."

"What a funny little chap you are."

"Don't you remember? You told me. You told me not to tell anyone, in case I spoiled the fun."

"That's true," said Daddy idly, "we mustn't spoil anyone's fun. Shall we go home then?"

"Okay."

"Okay."

The snow was falling in thick clumps. Ben laughed at the sight of it. "Come on, Ben," said Daddy. "Let's get to the car."

"No, Daddy," said Ben. "Look!"

And he tilted his head back. He opened his mouth, and stuck out his tongue. And the snow rained on him, it rained all over his face—and some of the flakes too, they landed on his tongue. He turned to Daddy. Eyes gleaming. "You try it!"

Daddy nearly said no, he so nearly did. But he too put back his head, the tongue came out, he pulled a funny face. "Gurr," he said. Ben giggled.

"What does it taste like?" said Ben.

"I don't know. Water. It doesn't taste of anything."

"No," said Ben. "You're not trying hard enough." He caught a few more flakes, and then smacked his lips appreciatively. "Delicious!"

"Delicious!" said Daddy. "Apple pie!"

"Chocolate cake!"

"Ice cream!"

"Um. Peanuts!"

"Old socks!"

Ben laughed aloud at this one. And they stood there in the car park, as the Christmas shoppers fought their way around them, catching snow on their tongues, and Daddy laughed too. They were both laughing. Ben found Daddy's hand, just as Daddy was reaching for his.

"It's going to be a white Christmas, isn't it?" said Ben.

"Yes," said Daddy. "Oh God." He squeezed Ben's hand a little tighter.

The next day was a Sunday, so that meant Ben got to spend it with his Mum. Some Sundays Richard was there too, some Sundays he wasn't. This Sunday Richard was there. "Come on," said Mum. "We're going Christmas shopping, it'll be fun!"

Ben had given up asking his mother why she preferred Richard to Daddy. "It's not as simple as that," she'd said. "But why, Mummy?" "It's not something I want to talk about." "Mummy, why?" And then she'd told him that she didn't want to be called Mummy anymore, he was too old for Mummy now, surely? He wasn't a baby. She'd rather be called Mum, from now on, Mum. And that had surprised Ben, and he tried to call her Mum ever afterwards. Even if sometimes he forgot.

Richard had a son, but Ben had never met him. He was a few years older. Richard wasn't going to spend Christmas Day with his son either.

"I want you to buy something for your Dad," said Mummy. And she gave Ben some money, and he thought it was at least as much as Daddy had given for her present, and he was pleased.

"What shall I get him?" asked Ben.

"That's up to you, isn't it?"

Ben was dressed in his warm clothes, thick sweater, thick gloves, stripy scarf. Mum wore a faded fake fur coat Daddy had bought her years ago. As they walked in the town centre snow settled on their hair. "You look like abominable snowmen!" joked Richard. Ben said he was the abominable snowman, but Mum was the abominable snowwoman, and Richard loved that, "Good one, sport. Lisa's an abominable snowwoman, all right!" Ben didn't like the way Richard called his Mum Lisa, so easy, as if he somehow owned the name. He called Lisa an abominable snowwoman on and off throughout the day, and Lisa always laughed, long after the time it had stopped being funny.

They shopped together for another couple of hours or so. Mum said, "Richard's got a treat for you, Ben!" And Richard laughed, and said it was only a little thing. He'd bought Ben a ticket for Santa's Grotto. Would Ben like to go to Santa's Grotto? He'd queued all this time to buy a ticket from the unsmiling woman at the booth, and now all Ben had to do was join another queue to see Santa. Would Ben like to see Santa? In Santa's Grotto?

"No, thank you," said Ben.

"Oh," said Richard. "I have already bought the ticket, though."

"Come on," said Mum. "You'd like to see Santa, wouldn't you?"

"I don't believe in Santa."

"Don't believe in Santa? But he's in that grotto over there!" Richard joked.

"You're going to see Santa," said Mum. "Richard's spent all that money."

"It's only a little thing," said Richard, "only seven pounds fifty."

"Seven pounds fifty! And you didn't even say thank you!"

"I did say thank you," said Ben.

Mum marched Ben out of Richard's earshot—but not so far, Ben thought, that Richard couldn't hear if he really wanted to. "Now, listen, mister," she said. "I've had enough of this. Sulking all day in front of Richard, when he's trying, can't you see how hard he's trying? Okay, you don't like him. Tough. Because I do like him. In fact, I love him. So you'd better bloody well get used to him. Because he's not going anywhere, not if I can help it." And then she marched him back to where Richard was smiling, still smiling. "What do you say, sport?" he said, holding out the ticket. "Want to see Santa after all?"

The queue to see Santa lasted a good forty-five minutes, and Ben suspected his mother regretted making such a fuss he did so because she'd clearly lost patience after waiting only ten. "What is Santa doing to them in there?" she muttered. Richard joked, "Well, they're certainly getting their seven pounds fifty's worth!" At last an elf took Ben away; Mum and Richard waved as he went.

Santa Claus was too young, and he wore padded clothes and a stuck-on beard. "Ho ho ho!" he said.

"Hi," said Ben.

"Want to sit on my knee?"

Ben shrugged, and did. He perched there a little precariously, and Santa wasn't allowed to hold him fast the way his Daddy could.

"What do you want for Christmas?" asked Santa.

"Nothing."

"Come on. You must want something. What's your favourite toy?"

Ben shrugged again.

"Do you want an action figure?"

"No."

"A computer game?"

"No."

"An—I don't know—what do you call them, one of those Lego things? Come on, kid, help me out here."

Ben couldn't get what he really wanted, and certainly not from a man in a shopping centre. He'd tried asking Jesus for it, and he hadn't believed in Jesus for years, but he'd asked him anyway. "If you fix this," he'd said, "if you can just make them love each other again, I'll believe in you. I'll go right on believing in you." But Jesus hadn't listened. Not even when he'd offered the deal. "If you make them love each other," and Ben had hesitated over this, then just—hell with it—gone straight ahead and said it, "they don't even have to love me. They don't have to love me. It's okay. I'll be okay." But Jesus hadn't done a thing, he didn't exist, and nor did Santa Claus, it was all such rubbish, it was shit.

"A bike?" said Santa Claus. Now a little desperate. "How about a bike?"

And actually, a bike didn't sound so bad. "Yeah, go on then, a bike."

"Great," said Santa. "Merry Christmas!" And gave him a present from his sack, something small and square and in shiny paper that very definitely wasn't a bike. When Ben came out of the grotto, his Mum and Richard were talking closely, and giggling. "Oh, there you are," said Mum. "That was quick!"

It was agreed that Ben would spend the night at his Mum's; now school was finished, he could be simply dropped back to Daddy's later the next day. Christmas Day with his father, Boxing Day with his mother and Richard, then New Year's Eve with his mother and Richard, New Year's Day with his Daddy. That was the plan, it was a good plan, everyone was happy with that. "Let's get home," said Mum, meaning *her* home, although her house still didn't feel like home to Ben, it had the wrong smell, it had the smell of *visiting* all over it. Richard settled down in front of the television, Mum made herself and Richard a cup of tea. "What would you like to do?" she asked Ben.

Ben didn't know.

"How about writing a letter to Santa? It's not too late to reach the Pole, not if we get it to the post box quick!"

Ben said he didn't believe in Santa anymore.

"I used to help you to write letters to Santa. Do you remember? Every Christmas?" He did remember, actually, but he wasn't going to admit to it. She looked at him, for a moment she looked almost afraid of him—a very adult sort of afraid, the afraid that comes when you simply don't know what to say anymore. "I love you, Ben. You know that, don't you?"

"Yes."

"I love you very much."

"Yes."

"All right then."

"Okay."

"I'll fix you some dinner. All right. Something nice and warm. And then we're going to sit down, just the two of us, and write a letter to Santa."

"Oh, Mum . . ."

"Just the two of us, no Richard, all right?"

"But, Mum . . ."

"No buts. What would you like Santa to bring you?"

"A bike," said Ben.

"All right then," she said. "A bike, that's what we'll say."

They had dinner that evening, all three of them, and Richard made jokes, and then they watched television, like a family. And Ben was pleased his Mum forgot all about the letter to Santa Claus, though he supposed he wouldn't have minded writing one with her really, not if it made her happy.

And still—the snow fell.

### iii

Only a few months after they were married, David and Lisa Noakes bought themselves a small house in South London. It was ideally situated. It was just a street away from an underground station, they could be in the city within half an hour. There were lots of local shops nearby, even a little supermarket on the corner. And in walking distance there was a school. "That might be handy," said David, "you know, just in case you still want to have any kids." David was still a little shy of marriage, he still couldn't quite believe Lisa had agreed to become his wife in the first place. "Of course I still want kids!" laughed Lisa. "Silly!" And she kissed him, and he hugged her, and they put a down payment on the mortgage, and that was that.

It was a few years, however, before David and Lisa got around to having that kid. And by then the house wasn't as ideally situated as it had been. The little supermarket had closed down, but nothing had come along to replace it. And Lisa didn't like the other local shops, they were either too expensive, or she got funny looks in there, she said, after one funny look she refused to step inside one particular newsagent's for years. However convenient the underground station, it was also very noisy, and it seemed to attract drunken youths at weekends, they gathered around it at all times of night shouting and flinging bottles. Lisa wondered whether they shouldn't move. "At least there's the school," said David. Lisa agreed; but it wasn't an especially *good* school. And David said yes, they really ought to give young Ben the best start in life they could. But they didn't move.

Or, at least, David and Ben didn't.

Step outside David and Ben's semi-detached, and you'd see: cars, all piled up high on the kerbs. The offending newsagent's. A unisex hairdressing salon. A skip, placed down the road months ago, it now seemed to be a permanent fixture. An off licence. Houses crammed tight together in both directions, as far as the eye could see.

What you wouldn't normally see would be a forest. Surrounding the house entirely, as if this thing of bricks and glass were some strange alien imposition upon a landscape so wild that all the trees looked animal, somehow: angry and untamed; the branches jutting out at any angles they wanted to, no matter how sharp, no matter how impossible; the very bark bulged. There was no checking these trees, they were the kings here—and yet they seemed to defer to *something*, because they still shied away from a natural path, and flanked it on both sides. A winding path that stretched on into the distance.

Ben, bundled up in his warmest sweater and warmest gloves and stripy scarf, was surprised to see the forest there. But Santa wasn't surprised, this was clearly what he'd been expecting. And the look on Daddy's face wasn't surprise either. He looked tense, a little resigned maybe, but there was nothing there to suggest he hadn't been expecting this as much as Santa. So Ben decided not to be surprised either.

"Come on, Ben," said Santa. "Let's get these stabilizers on your bike. Just until you get your balance!" They clipped right on. "All right, you're set to go!"

"Are you still sure you want to ride the bike, Ben?" asked Daddy.

"Would you push me, Daddy?"

". . . Of course I will."

"You don't need to push him," said Santa. "He's got stabilizers."

"I'll push my son's bike if he wants me to."

"No, it's okay, Daddy. I forgot, the stabilizers will take care of it."

"Oh. Are you sure?"

"I'm sure. This is fun. Look at me! I'm riding a bike!"

"Are we walking far?" Daddy asked Santa.

Santa shrugged. Maybe he was being unhelpful. Maybe he just didn't know.

And off they set, crunching the snow down the path the trees had left them. The two men, and the little boy on his bike, sometimes racing ahead excitedly, sometimes ringing them. "Try to walk where I walk," Santa told Daddy.

"Why, is the ground slippery?"

"No. But let's not leave more footprints than we have to. Let's not spoil the *beauty* of this." And it was easy for Daddy to do that, Santa's footprints were so big. Daddy looked behind from time to time, and soon he couldn't see the house, only that single pair of footprints, and the thin grooves where Ben's tires had cut into the snow. And as the snow fell more heavily, he soon couldn't even see those. All around them was the snow, now a blinding white, Daddy and Ben had to shield their eyes from the glare. Santa put on a pair of sunglasses. "Here," he said, and handed Daddy and Ben sunglasses too.

Neither Daddy nor Santa spoke for another hour. On they both trudged, faces grim—except once in a while Santa would catch Ben's eye, and give him a friendly wink. As if to say, this is only a game! Don't let on! And Ben would wink back, when he was sure his Daddy couldn't see. The snow continued to fall, but there was no wind to disturb the silence. "Please," said Daddy at last. He said it so softly, but it broke right through that silence—and Ben and Santa both stopped, turned to look at him.

"Please," he said again.

"No," said Santa. Not unkindly. But firm.

"But I'm all he's got."

"He's got his mother."

"His mother and I . . . it's difficult . . . we might sort things out one day, I don't . . ." Santa watched Daddy sympathetically. Ben looked away, suddenly embarrassed. "I've tried so hard to hold on to him," said Daddy.

"I know," said Santa.

"How do you know?"

"I can tell."

"Daddy, it's okay," said Ben.

"I've tried so hard," said Daddy.

"I know, Daddy."

"I know. I can tell. We can both tell, can't we, Ben?"

"I'm not going a step further," said Daddy.

"Now, come on," said Santa. "None of that. Chop chop!"

"Daddy, don't," said Ben. Don't what? Spoil the fun for the rest of us?

"Why the bloody hell did you write him a letter, Ben?" said Daddy. He wasn't shouting, not really, but it still seemed awfully loud in the still of that forest. "He wouldn't have come if you hadn't written."

"I didn't write to him."

From his pocket Santa took a letter. He handed it to Ben's Daddy. Daddy recognized the handwriting, and it wasn't Ben's. And he slumped, it seemed he suddenly got very tired. He handed the letter back to Santa.

"Okay," said Daddy.

"We can walk on?" asked Santa.

"Okay," said Daddy.

And on they walked.

Soon Ben couldn't ride his bike through the ever thickening snow, he had to push it. "Walk where I walk," said Daddy. "Why?" "You know. What he said. The beauty of it all. Let's keep the beauty of it all." Ben tilted his head back at one point. "Look, Daddy!" he said, and caught the snowflakes on his tongue. "You do it too."

Daddy stopped. Daddy caught snowflakes on his tongue too. Santa stopped too, but he didn't try to force the pace, he looked indulgent, smiled at them both, he looked like Santa on a Christmas card.

"Delicious!" said Ben.

"What do you taste?"

"Chocolate cake," said Ben.

"Marzipan," said Daddy.

"Apple pie!"

"I can fix that for you," said Santa. And he did, with just one snap of his fingers. "There," he said. And the snow that melted in their mouths tasted of pies, of cakes, of hot fudge, all sweet and creamy. "No," said Daddy, gently. "This is our moment. This is *ours*." And Santa nodded, a little ashamed, and the snow went back to tasting of bland water. Daddy and Ben held hands and drank the snowflakes until they could drink no more. Then, with just a glance shared, they both agreed to walk on—Daddy's feet dwarfed in Santa's footprints, Ben's dwarfed in his Daddy's.

"Not much further now," said Santa, kindly.

The sleigh was a bit rusted. It had seen better days. So too had the reindeer. They huddled together for warmth. On seeing their master return, the fitter of the pack tried to stand to attention. "No, no, at ease, boys," and the reindeer relaxed into their harnesses gratefully.

"Well, then," said Santa to Daddy, awkwardly.

"Well," said Daddy.

There was quiet for a few seconds. "You needn't look at me like that," said Santa. "I gave you a good toy, didn't I? I only ever give the best toys."

"I don't remember what it was."

"It was probably a bike. I give a lot of bikes."

"No, it wasn't a bike."

"Let's just say it was a bike," said Santa.

Daddy thought about that. "Okay," he said.

"I remember your little face lighting up when you got it," said Santa. "That's always the best bit. Watching the faces light up." And Ben was surprised to see that Santa was crying.

Daddy gave Ben a hug. "I tried very hard," he said. "I tried my hardest."

And Ben now knew he should have been pleading for his father. But he'd been too busy riding his bike, spinning about, cutting those grooves into the snow. He'd been too busy for *months*, going to school, eating his fish fingers, pretending it was all okay, that it was all going to be okay. And it was now too late for him to plead. "Will I see my Daddy again?" Ben asked Santa.

Santa looked genuinely surprised that he'd asked. "Oh," he said. "Maybe. But never like this. Never again like this."

One more hug. "That's nice," said Santa Claus. "Strip."

Daddy had put on all his warmest clothes—two layers!—so it took him a while. He made a pile on the ground, sweaters, shirt, vest, then shoes, then trousers, underpants. He remembered the sunglasses, actually snorted in amusement he'd done so, put them on the pile, squinting at the bright white. The last clothes he took off were his socks; he could now delay it no longer, and Daddy winced as his bare feet now sank deep into the snow.

Ben wasn't sure he'd seen his father naked before. He looked so fragile. Daddy clapped his arms around his sides to keep warm, but soon stopped, there wasn't any point. He stood there, shivering, his balls fluffed up with hairs standing on end, his willy shrunk to a cork. He looked so *young*. Ben had never thought of his Daddy being young before.

"It won't take long, I promise," said Santa.

And sure enough, the feet were already hooves, better protection against the cold, and Ben could see Daddy sigh gratefully for that. The hide stole over his body, thick and strong, not strong enough, maybe, not in this weather, it could freeze your blood—but warmer than his man skin, that was a comfort at any rate. He pitched forwards when his hands became hooves as well; his head bowed down beneath antler weight.

"That's it," said Santa. "There you are. You're beautiful. You're beautiful." He smiled at Ben. "Isn't he beautiful?" And Ben couldn't deny it.

Santa turned to the other reindeer. "This is your new brother!" he said. They were too weary to do much more than shrug their heads, non-committal. "You all try so hard for me," he said. "For me, you fly the skies. You're the best." He stroked their heads, one by one. He reached one near the back. "And you, you're so very tired, aren't you? Such a long journey. So many long journeys. But you've always tried so hard." The reindeer turned its human eyes to Santa, and nuzzled his hand. Santa laughed. "Thank you. Thank you. I love you." And so tenderly, he caressed its head. And broke its neck.

In that silence the snap of bone sounded louder than it probably was. It had been such a gentle twist, really, and so quick, the reindeer wouldn't have felt a thing. But it couldn't have been that gentle—one of the bones had ripped through the skin ("rip it open, rip it apart!"), Ben could see it jutting out, sharp and white. The harness kept the reindeer in place, slumped in death as it was; when Santa released it, the body fell to the ground. The snow that caught it was so soft.

Santa harnessed his new reindeer into place.

"I'll give you the bike back," said Ben.

Santa stopped.

"I want my Daddy," said Ben.

He hoped he sounded bold and defiant. He hoped he wasn't crying. Santa stroked his beard.

"So, what's the deal here?" he said. "You give me the bike back, I give you back your father? And we're quits? Fair exchange, no robbery?"

"Yes," said Ben.

"And what, I give the bike to some other kid instead?"

"Yes," said Ben.

"Interesting," said Santa.

He went to the bicycle. Looked it over thoughtfully. Ran his finger critically over the frame.

"But see, here's the problem," said Santa. "It's been *used*. Hasn't it?"

"Yes," said Ben.

"You've been riding it in the snow. Your choice. Remember, your choice."

"Yes," Ben breathed.

"I only give the best toys. Nothing second hand."

"I know," said Ben.

"Well then," said Santa Claus. And gave him a grin that was meant to be reassuring. Ben saw that the teeth were somehow still stained green with pea and ham soup.

Santa got into his sleigh. "You'll be all right," he said. "Your mother loves you very much. It moved me, how much. And I'll be seeing you again. Whenever there's a white Christmas." He gave the reins a single flick. "Yee-hah, git!" he said. "On, Donner and Blitzen! Come on, chop chop!" And off he flew into the night sky, so fast that Ben's eyes couldn't follow him.

# iv

And this is how the story could end. With a little boy lost. By his side a used bicycle, and a dead reindeer whose blood was now staining the white snow red. But things are rarely that simple.

Ben wheeled his bike home. It didn't take long. The forest was gone; there was the underground station, though. There were no youths outside it now, the trains didn't run on Christmas Day. He had to cross the road, and looked left, then right, then left again, just as his Daddy had taught him. He took the bicycle indoors. He went to bed.

The next morning Ben went down to the kitchen. His Daddy was sitting there, eating a bowl of cornflakes. Ben yelped, gave him a hug. "Not now, Ben, I'm having breakfast. Pull up a chair, you have your breakfast too." Ben poured himself some cornflakes. They ate together. "After breakfast, we can open our presents," said Daddy. "Yeah!" said Ben, "happy Christmas!" "Happy Christmas," said Daddy.

In the hallway Daddy saw Ben's new bike, propped up against the front door. It had dripped melted snow on to the carpet. Daddy looked at Ben, then tutted, just the once. Then without a word he picked up the bicycle and carried it to the back door, put it out into the garden.

Christmas Day was fine. Really, fine. The presents were fine. Ben opened his presents, taking them from beneath the lopsided tree with the ears. He'd got lots of toys, and a book about boats. ("You like boats, don't you?" said Daddy. "Yes," said Ben.) Daddy liked his present from Ben, a range of male toiletries from the Body Shop. "Thanks." Ben wanted to tell him that Mum had bought it for him mostly, it was Mum he should thank, but he knew somehow it wouldn't be the right thing to say. "I'll go and make dinner," said Daddy at last. "Can I help?" "No," said Daddy, "play with your toys, read about boats." The dinner was fine. The gravy was more solid than liquid, and the turkey was too dry. But the stuffing and the chipolata sausages were great. "They're the best bits anyway," said Daddy, and Ben readily agreed. After dinner, they watched television, they watched *Doctor Who* and then *Eastenders*. Ben cuddled up to his father. "Not too close, Ben, you're being too clingy," said Daddy. So Ben got off the sofa, and played with his toys a bit more, read a bit more of his boat book. "Time for bed," said Daddy.

Daddy tucked Ben in to bed. "I promised you the best Christmas ever," he said.

"Yes."

"That wasn't it."

"No."

"But it was okay, wasn't it?"

"It was okay."

On Boxing Day Mum came to pick up Ben bright and early. "Merry Christmas!" she said when Ben opened the front door to her, and gave him a huge hug. "Dave, I know we'd agreed I'd bring him back tomorrow morning, but would the afternoon . . ." "That's fine," Dave interrupted.

Richard didn't come to the front door, he was waiting in the car. He never came to the door. "Merry Christmas!" he said to Ben. He was wearing a Santa hat, he looked like a cretin. Ben opened lots of presents, he got lots of toys. Richard had bought him a present too. "I hope you like this, sport," he'd said, and looked really rather nervous as Ben unwrapped it. Ben had already decided not to like it, but it was actually pretty good—it wasn't his *best* toy, but it was definitely in the top five, it was good. They all had Christmas dinner, and that was lovely—"Delicious!" said Ben—and they all pulled crackers—Daddy had forgotten the crackers!—and they all put on paper hats, even Richard put on a paper hat, he put it over the top of his Santa hat, and he looked even more like a cretin than before, but it still made Ben laugh. They all played some board games. Ben won the first two, Richard won one—"I'm catching up with you now!" he joked, and picked up the dice, "fancy another?" "I'm rubbish at games," said Mum, "I just don't have the right sort of brain! I never win *anything*!" And Richard kissed her, and Ben didn't mind much.

On New Year's Eve, Richard was wearing the Santa hat again. Ben wondered if he'd ever taken it off. Mum let Ben stay up 'til midnight, and have a sip of champagne. "But don't tell your father," she said, "your father will kill me," and Ben promised. They sang Auld Lang Syne, and did the arm crossing thing, even though Richard got it wrong, Ben thought he got it wrong deliberately, but it was a bit funny. "Happy New Year, darling," said Richard to Lisa. "Can't be worse than the old one," Lisa replied.

The snow stopped falling. The snow melted.

Ben had bad dreams. And one night in February, as he lay in bed, he suddenly got it into his head that he was all alone in the house. His Daddy wasn't there anymore. Anybody could come into his bedroom and get him, and Daddy wouldn't be there to stop them. He got up. He listened at his father's door for any reassuring sounds of snoring. He couldn't hear anything. He began to cry, but as quietly as he could—and then he went downstairs, walking only at the sides to avoid the creaks. All so that he wouldn't wake Daddy, he mustn't wake Daddy, and it was ridiculous, because Daddy wasn't there to be woken, was he? He wanted to scream out his name. But he was terrified to hear his own voice that loud in the dark, he was terrified that his Daddy wouldn't answer. The door to Daddy's study was shut. Ben pushed it open.

His Daddy sat by the computer, completely naked. Ben didn't think he'd ever seen his Daddy naked before, he wasn't sure.

177

It took a moment for Daddy to realize his son was standing there, and then his face flushed. "Ben! Can't you knock?"

"I can't sleep . . ."

"Go to bed!"

"I can't sleep!"

"Go to bed, I'll be upstairs in a moment! Go to bed this instant!"

And Ben ran back to his room. By the time Daddy joined him, he'd found time to put some trousers on. Daddy was still a bit angry, but he'd calmed down. "You can't just go opening doors," he said. "It's just not on, is it? What's the matter?"

"I can't sleep," said Ben. "I'm frightened."

Daddy sighed. "Well, think of something happy."

"I can't."

"Of course you can. Don't be ridiculous."

Ben nodded. "Okay, I'll try."

"Good boy."

"Daddy, on Christmas Eve . . ." And it was hard to tell in the darkened room, but Daddy seemed to stiffen at that. "I'm sorry," said Ben. "I'm sorry about . . . I'm sorry."

Daddy didn't say anything for a long while. And Ben wanted to go on. He wanted to say he'd betrayed his father, that was why he'd lost him. And he wanted him back. And he wished Daddy would call him 'old chap' again; he did it once in a while, but only without thinking, and then Daddy would look guilty as if he'd been caught in a lie.

But Ben had said too much as it was, he knew it, far too much. Daddy said at last, "Go to sleep." And so Ben did.

It was wholly a coincidence that only two weeks later Daddy told Ben he had something serious to discuss with him. He sat stern behind the kitchen table, and Ben wished he'd invite him on to his knee, he could take anything he said if it were knee-given. "You like Uncle Richard, don't you?" Daddy and Mummy had been talking, and it seemed only fair that Mummy got to live with Ben for a while. Instead, even. And the schools were better in Mummy's area, it was more practical. So.

Ben was confused, he couldn't work out who'd betrayed whom anymore. "You still love me, don't you?" asked Ben. "Of course I love you, you're my son," said Daddy. And he could have left it like that, but he didn't, he *didn't*, he said, "But I just can't reach you anymore."

Ben still visited his Dad most Sundays. One day Daddy said, "I've found a girlfriend. Her name's Rachel." Ben asked if he had to meet Rachel, and Daddy looked a bit awkward, and said not yet, Rachel didn't like children very much. And Ben was glad. "But I've got a picture of her on the computer, would you like to see?" Daddy was posing with his arms around a woman, and they were both smiling, but it seemed to Ben Daddy was smiling too wide, the way he smiled whenever he saw Mum on the doorstep. Rachel looked very young. Daddy looked old. Ben had never thought of his Daddy being old before.

"Let's get those stabilizers off!" laughed Richard. "You're not a baby anymore!" He took Ben to the park, and there they practised balancing on the bike. "It's all a question of not wobbling," said Richard. Richard held the back of his saddle for a while, and then it took Ben a few seconds to realize he'd let go, that Ben was riding the bike, he was doing it all by himself. "Yeah!" said Ben. "Yeah, you did it!" said Richard. Richard said he'd taught his own son to ride a bike a few years ago; Ben had met him now, but he didn't have anything to say to him, Justin was fourteen, what was there to say to someone so old? "We did it!" said Richard. "Didn't we? Give me a hug." So Ben did. "You'll be able to ride that bike everywhere now!" said Richard. Ben agreed. But he didn't ride the bike much after that, it'd been more fun with the stabilizers.

Richard and his Mum never got around to marrying. Which meant it was much smoother altogether when Richard dumped her for someone else. Ben listened to his Mum cry over the phone at his university halls. "I've tried so hard, Ben," she said. "But he just didn't try at all." "He just didn't love you enough," said Ben. He played with the phone wires. He hated these phone calls with his mother, he never knew what to say. "You'll find someone else," Ben went on, "you deserve someone better, Lisa." "I don't want anyone else," said Lisa. "Okay." "I want Richard, don't I?" "Okay. Well, then." "You're a good boy, Ben." "Okay. I've got to get off the phone soon, there's a queue." "I wish you would call me Mum."

Ben invited his father to his graduation ceremony, but he wasn't able to make it. Four years later, when he married Sophie, he invited him to the wedding. Daddy did make that one. But Ben didn't put him up on top table with his mother, he put him on table twelve with some of the minor guests. If his father were offended, he didn't show it. After the reception, before Daddy drove home alone, he found Ben. He shook Ben by the hand. "Well done," he said. "Thanks for coming," said Ben.

Right from the beginning Ben and Sophie had discussed children. "I don't want any," said Sophie. "Nor do I," said Ben. "I'm not sure what I'd say to one!" Sophie laughed, and agreed—better to get a cat instead. When Sophie turned forty, she told Ben she was leaving him. She'd found someone else, someone she thought she could mother babies for. "It's not you," she said, "it's my biological clock ticking." Ben had thought for some time that maybe the cats weren't enough, that maybe cracking out a baby or two wouldn't be such a bad idea after all. But he really hadn't wanted to pressure Sophie with his doubts, he'd kept them to himself. He told her at last how he felt. She looked torn, genuinely torn. "But I've already found a new boyfriend and everything," she said, and left.

He and his father sent Christmas cards to each other, and on Christmas Day itself Ben would always phone. One year he forgot to send the card, and apologized for that during the annual call. "Oh, don't worry," said Daddy, "I don't like Christmas cards anyway!" Ben laughed; nor did he; they agreed they were a waste of money; they never bothered sending any to one another ever again. Pretty soon after that the phone calls dried up as well. "I love you, Dad," said Ben, quite unexpectedly that last year. There was a baffled silence on the other end, and then Daddy said, "And I love you too." But still, the phone calls dried up.

His mother died first, and Ben thought that was wrong, it should have been his Dad, it should have been the other way round. He knew it was a cruel thing to think, but that didn't stop it from being just what he felt.

The weather reports said there was going to be a cold snap. But Ben was prepared. The snow began to fall, and the experts said it wouldn't settle, but it did settle; then they said it wouldn't last, and it did. People began to talk about the possibility of a white Christmas. London hadn't had a white Christmas in over forty years. Probably global warming was to blame.

Christmas Eve. When Ben looked out of his window, he saw the usual view, a building site and Budgen's. If he opened the front door, he saw a forest. He went to the kitchen. He took out some mince pies. He took out some soup, too. Then he went to the living room, sat on the sofa, and waited for midnight.

Midnight came, and midnight went. Ben got bored. He turned on his television. *White Christmas* was playing. A part of the TV schedules for a hundred years, and still going strong. Ben couldn't concentrate on it, switched it off. He let himself doze for a bit. He found he could doze quite easily, now he had no one to talk to.

One in the morning. Then two.

Ben sighed heavily.

He put on all his warmest clothes. Sweater, gloves. Not a scarf, though. Scarves made his neck get scratchy, and he'd long ago realized the joy of being an adult is that no one can make you wear scarves if you don't want to.

He went out into the cold. He walked through those animal trees, down that winding path, crunching through the snow. Half a mile along he realized he'd forgotten to bring sunglasses, he'd forgotten how bright the white was. He considered going back to fetch them. Then, "Oh sod it," he said out loud, and marched onwards.

Eventually he found Santa Claus. Santa was leaning, winded, against a tree. "I've been waiting for ages," said Ben.

"Yes. Sorry. I'm a bit . . . oof . . . I'm a bit out of puff." Santa Claus looked old and cold. "It's so hard to keep going, Ben," he said. "They don't believe anymore. They don't believe in *anything*."

"Come on," said Ben. "Rest on me." And he took Santa by the arm, and gratefully Santa leaned into him. And together they hobbled onwards down the path, back the way Santa had come.

They didn't talk for all those hours. Except for just the once. When Ben asked, "How much further?" and Santa replied, "I don't know. I've never known." And then added, as an afterthought, and it didn't seem connected at all, "I tried so hard. I tried so hard."

At last they reached the sleigh and the reindeer.

"Well, then," said Santa.

"Well."

And then nothing. "Oh, for God's sake," said Ben impatiently. And he began to strip.

He made a pile of clothes on the forest floor. He took off his socks last, and his feet burned against the ice. He liked that. He wanted them to burn.

"And now you," he said to Santa.

For a moment Santa looked surprised. And then there was the flutter of a smile, gone in an instant; it might have been nothing more than a grimace against the falling snow. Santa took off his big red coat, his great black boots. He took off his beard. The beard was fake, it had always been fake.

And there both men stood shivering in the snow. Ben looked Santa over, and Santa gave an apologetic smile, acknowledging the poor figure he cut. He wasn't fat anymore. He looked as if he hadn't been fed in weeks. Ben could see Santa's ribs pushing underneath his skin, and that in the cold the ribs were turning blue.

Ben put on Santa's suit. He put on the beard.

Santa licked his lips. "Are you going to break my neck?" he asked. But Ben told him to get dressed. Into all the warmest clothes Ben had, Santa was too thin for them, they hung baggy, he looked as if he were drowning in them.

"Go home," said Ben. "There's mince pies waiting. And hot soup. Go home, into the warm." And the man who had been Santa Claus nodded, and without saying another word, turned and went.

Ben inspected his reindeer. One of them nuzzled at his hand, turned to him with those all too human eyes. And Ben didn't know for sure, but he *believed*. That his father had been with Santa all the time. That he'd once betrayed him, but now he'd won him back. That they'd been lost, both of them—but were now found.

And the snow continued to fall.

# PANG

When he came home from work he found her sitting at the kitchen table. Smiling sadly, she tapped the chair next to her and indicated he should sit down. So he did.

"We need to talk," she said, and, of course, he knew straight away something was wrong. They didn't ever need to talk, they never *needed* to talk. If one of them ever wanted to say something, it was easy, they'd just come out and say it, it didn't need to be prefaced by anything, it didn't need an *announcement*. One talking, one listening, that was the way it worked, and then back into that companionable silence they both enjoyed.

"It's my heart," she said. "It's been giving me, I don't know. Pangs."

"Pangs?"

"Pangs, yes. I think that's the best way to describe it."

He didn't know what to say. He knew something was probably expected of him, but God only knew what. One of her hands, the one that wasn't gripping a mug of cold and forgotten coffee, lay on the table. She didn't seem to be inviting him to touch it or hold it or do anything in particular to it, but he could reach it without it looking contrived, so he did so. He gave it a sympathetic squeeze. It was cool with sweat.

"There," he said. And "There," he said again. And then, in what he hoped sounded helpful, "Well, it's something we'll sort out. Isn't it? We'll just have to jolly well sort it out. Take care of you. You're not going anywhere!"

"Darling . . ."

"You'll have to take it easy. We'll go on a holiday, somewhere restful, wherever you like. I've got holiday due, I expect, in August, can you hold on 'til then? And I can do more work round the house, get you off your feet a bit . . ."

"Darling, I've been to the doctor's."

"And that's a start too. Yes, good."

"They've done lots of tests. And I'm fine. Really, fine. There's nothing physically wrong with me whatsoever."

"But that's. Well. That's great. Well!" And he gave the hand another squeeze.

And that sad smile she'd been wearing throughout the whole wretched conversation got a little sadder. "But I've still got the pangs," she said. "It can only mean one thing, I think. I think I don't love you anymore."

Absurdly he didn't know what to do with her hand any longer. It seemed ridiculous he was still holding it. He shouldn't be, surely, not like this, not now? He didn't want to let go, though, just like that, it might make her think he was being angry, or cruel, or wanting an argument. But he knew he couldn't cling on to the hand indefinitely, she'd be the one to take it away if he left it too long, and he didn't want that extra rejection. He came to a decision. He gave it another squeeze, as friendly as anything, and then swung his own hand upwards, very deliberately, to scratch his nose.

And there was silence. Just that sad smile from her, and the nose scratching from him, working at an itch that hadn't even been there in the first place.

"Is it something I've . . . ?" And she was shaking her head. "Or something I've not . . . ?" And still the head shook. "Well, what?"

"I don't know," she said. "Maybe love, it just stops sometimes. Do you think? It just stops."

"Maybe it hasn't really stopped," he said. "I mean, if it were just a pang, a pang doesn't sound so bad."

She frowned, gave it a little thought. "No, I'm pretty sure it's stopped."

"But you can't, one day, after fifteen years . . ."

"Seventeen years."

"Seventeen. Good God, is it really?"

"Oh yes."

"Seventeen. God. Well. Even more reason."

"You must feel the same way," she said. "Just a little. Don't tell me I'm not the only one."

And he wanted to help her. He'd always tried to agree with her, to like the same films she'd liked, to enjoy the same food. He'd always thought if it mattered so much to her that he shared her opinion, he'd do his level best to accommodate. But he couldn't now. Not this time. And he wished he hadn't let go of her hand so easily, because it began to dawn on him that he might never get the chance to hold it again.

"I've got something for you," she said. "I want you to take this back." For a moment he thought she meant the wedding ring, and said so, and she told him no, it was a *beautiful* ring, they'd chosen it together, and it symbolized seventeen years, seventeen wonderful years, she'd always treasure it. He felt a little better for that. And then she plonked a Tupperware box down on the table.

He peeled off the plastic lid.

"Do you recognize it?" she said gently. And no, he didn't, of course he didn't, he'd given it to her all those years ago.

He wasn't sure if he was meant to inspect it, but she gave him a nod of encouragement, and so he prodded it gingerly with his finger.

"Seems in pretty good nick," he said.

"Oh yes," she said. "I've taken good care of it. Do you know, I've not so much as looked at another man all the time we've been together. No, that's in good working order, that's as new."

"Well done," he said gruffly.

"Thank you."

"I don't want it back. You can keep it."

"Oh, darling, you say that now. But you might need it again." She looked a bit embarrassed, then said, "And there's no rush, but at some point I'm really going to need mine . . ."

"Oh yes."

"In your own time. There's no rush."

There wasn't much to say after all that. They waited out the time it took her taxi to arrive with conversation as polite as it was artificial; he wished they could simply have retreated into those happy silences they were used to, but now even that seemed too intimate. And then the doorbell rang, she let him carry her luggage out to the car—she'd hidden it, already sorted and packed, in the spare room, so that he wouldn't see the evidence of her leaving him before she'd had a chance to explain, and later that night as he lay in a bed which seemed much too big and much too still, he wondered whether that had been a kindly or a cruel thing for her to have done. And then, promising she'd be in touch, and exhorting him to take care of himself, she got up on her tiptoes to peck him on the forehead, as if all this time he'd been not so much a husband as an infant, got into the cab, gave him a wave, and was driven away.

He didn't expect to sleep that night. He surprised himself and drifted off fairly easily, and, yes, he had nightmares, but they were only the nightmares he *usually* had, ones about aging and unpopularity and ugliness and spiders and his mother and pressures of work, nothing at all about being abandoned by his wife. When the next morning he lay in bed on his own he felt so perfectly normal that he even thought maybe everything was all right, that he didn't *care*. And then it occurred to him that this was his first day waking up into a world in which no one loved him, and he felt something very like a pang himself.

He got up, shaved, washed, dressed, went downstairs to pour himself a bowl of cereal. He'd forgotten about the Tupperware box sitting on the kitchen table, and seeing it there, lid off, its grisly contents exposed, made him lose his appetite. He didn't want to look at it, he'd put it in a drawer somewhere, eat his Corn Flakes and have done with it. But something about that little pang he'd felt made him think he should give it a closer look, and reluctantly he poked at it with his finger once more.

And to be fair, it wasn't *especially* grisly. He just wasn't comfortable having body organs lying around the breakfast things, he was squeamish like that. His heart lay, fat and gleaming, in a pool of thinly pinking water. He put his nose to it, gave it a cautious sniff: he didn't quite know why, because he had no idea what hearts ought to smell like, and all he could detect was something slightly stale and coppery. He felt a thrill of alarm, but when he raised his head and sniffed again, he realized that it was even stronger away from the heart—the kitchen always smelt a bit funny, there was something wrong with the fridge. No, as far as he could see, his heart was fine. He probably should have kept the lid on overnight, though, as a couple of moths were floating inside the tub, drowned in the bloodied water. He fished them out, wondered why they'd been attracted to the heart in the first place, did hearts glow in the dark? He decided that, in his lunch hour, he'd pop over to the library and find a book about biology and see.

His wife had always been a woman of firm resolve. Once she'd made a judgment—whether it was on shellfish, that b&b in Wolverhampton, or the decline of the Conservative party—it was not to be altered. So he certainly didn't expect that she'd have changed her mind, that when he came back from work that evening she'd be cooking dinner in the kitchen, all forgiven, all forgotten, and his heart safely stowed somewhere away from his view. But as the day wore on, he began to allow himself a little hope, that her natural stubbornness would weigh against throwing over so many years of marriage, and by the time he put the key in the front door he almost had believed that all would be well. But it wasn't. And the heart was still, unarguably, implacably, *there*, the only living thing in the house waiting for him to come home. He peered at it, and it beat a little harder at his presence, like a dog wagging its tail at the arrival of its master. Three more moths were floating at its side; he fished them out, binned them, and went upstairs to get changed.

That was the Tuesday. She didn't come home on the Wednesday either, nor on the Thursday. By the Friday he'd stopped expecting anything at all, but there it was, a little neon flash on the telephone, he'd no reason to believe it was her, but it was—one click, and there was her voice, playing on the answering machine. His heart gave a little flip of excitement. (He heard it splash back down in its plastic box.) He called the number she'd left him straight away.

"Where are you?" he asked.

"Oh, don't ask, darling," she said, "I'd rather not tell you. I need a little space to sort out how I feel."

He realized that all hope was not lost, then. She might still come back to him. "So, all's not lost. You might still come back to me . . ."

"No, darling," she said firmly, "no." And he thought, she's just saying that, she can't know. But this time he kept it to himself. "How are you, darling? I've been worried about you."

"Oh," he said. "Thank you. But I'm fine."

"Are you sure?"

"Yes," he said. "Really."

"It's okay," she said, after a pause, "not to be fine, you know. It really is. You've always been so big and strong for me, you've been wonderful like that. You don't have to be strong anymore. Have you cried yet? You can cry if you want."

"No," he said, irritated. "Why, have you cried?"

"Oh yes," she said. "Buckets." He felt ridiculous, as if this were some sort of contest. "But then, I've been crying for *ages*, darling."

"Right," he said. "So. Anyway."

"Anyway. I wanted to ask if it would be all right if I called around tomorrow."

"Of course. You don't have to ask. I mean, this is your house."

"No, I *do* have to ask. I really do. I just want to pick up a few odds and ends, you know. Can you have my heart ready?"

He'd decided he had to be the one who hung up first, but somehow she still got her goodbye in ahead of his. He stood by the phone for a while, then realized he hadn't yet taken off his coat, hadn't closed the front door even. "Right," he said, as he did so, "right," he said, as he changed out of his work clothes into something slightly more casual, "right, best get to it, then. Best jolly well get to it." And he began to look for his wife's heart.

Realistically, there were only a few places it could be: the cupboards in the spare bedroom, the hatch under the stairs, a small chest of drawers in the room he'd privately felt it rather pretentious they called the study. His wife was not so sentimental that all the keepsakes and knickknacks she kept should clutter up the house—some married couples, of course, kept their hearts on the mantelpiece beside the wedding photos, but she'd found such public displays of affection in rather poor taste. "What is it they're trying to prove?" she'd ask her husband after a dinner with friends, "if you truly love someone you don't need to put it on *display*," and now they were safely at home away from prying eyes she'd lean forward and give him a little kiss on the lips. He worked methodically through all the likely cubby-holes, but no heart was to be found. It had to be *somewhere*; he wouldn't have thrown it out, surely; it couldn't have been given to Oxfam, what would they want it for? And instead, pouring from these hidden pockets around the house, all the little remnants of his marriage. The Valentines cards he had given her. Long expired passports they had acquired for a single holiday in Tenerife they hadn't enjoyed and never repeated. Their wedding certificate. And before he knew it he was crying, at last he was crying, but it wasn't what you're thinking, really it wasn't—these were tears of *frustration*, of course they were, where was this bloody heart, why the bloody hell wasn't the bloody thing where it was supposed to be? Emptying out old shoeboxes, spilling junk to the floor, but nothing beating, nothing alive. And as he sobbed he allowed himself to resent his wife, just a little bit—sod her, *sod* her, why was she disrupting his life like this, why was he looking for something she'd so freely given him only to demand it back again, you can't do that with presents, it wasn't *right*. He hadn't asked for her bloody heart in the first place; she'd been the one who'd pursued him, she'd done all the pursuing, she'd chased him and hunted him down and told herself that he was to be hers, and she always got what she wanted.

A sudden pain in his chest. It only lasted a couple of seconds, maybe not even that. But it took him a full minute to get his breath back, to rise to his feet, step over the debris of the past, and make his way down to the kitchen.

He looked at his heart. It was still beating, of course—if anything, it seemed to be beating rather faster, which was reassuring perhaps. He idly picked out the fresh moths it had acquired, and thought to go. But as he looked more carefully he made out little pinpricks of white, spotted all over. Had they been there before? He couldn't be certain. He remembered his heart being a perfect sea of rich pink, but he had to admit that when he'd looked at it, his mind had always been on other things. Maybe it had always been a bit . . . well . . . *speckled*. He fetched the book he'd borrowed from the library, wondered again why diagrams on the page never look remotely like the real thing when it's sitting in a Tupperware box. Yes, see, the line of spots started at the tricuspid valve, then spread up to the . . . right atrium. He flicked through the book but could find no mention of white spots at all; he supposed he could have looked the white spots up in the index, if only he could have guessed what on earth to call them. So he looked up both Tricuspid Valve and Atrium (Right) in the index instead, but had no joy there either. He put the book away. Rather nervously, fearing another spasm, he pressed down on a cluster of spots gently—then harder, then harder still. Nothing.

He could take it to a doctor, he supposed. Sit in a waiting room for a couple of hours, only to find out that the white spots were perfectly normal. And, by doing so, show the whole world that his wife didn't feel it was a heart worth keeping anymore. Most likely the pain was because he hadn't stopped to eat before he'd gone hunting through the cupboards upstairs; now that he was in the kitchen he realized he was ragingly hungry. He rinsed his bloodied hands under the tap, opened a tin of baked beans, and tried to work out what he should do next. And as he filled his stomach, and began to feel so much better, the answer became clear.

The next morning he got up early, and was standing outside the butcher's when the shop opened. "I want a heart," he told the girl behind the counter, "as close to a human's as you've got, a thirty-nine year old woman having pangs." When he reached home, and opened it up on the kitchen table, he wondered whether the girl might have looked a little harder. He compared it to his own, side by side, and even allowing for the growing proliferation of white specks across its surface, his was clearly in better nick. For a start, this pig heart was unashamedly *blue*. It had its pink bits, to be sure, but only as little islands in these vast oceans of discolouration. It was the wrong size as well, just a little too small, and had bits sticking out its side which he was quite sure shouldn't be there in the first place; after he'd trimmed off some of the weirder looking crags, the heart looked even more pathetic. He considered nipping back to the butcher's, getting a second heart—maybe he could bolt it on to the side, somehow, give the whole thing a bit more body—but even in his rising panic he realized that wouldn't fool anybody. The greatest problem, though, was the heart's texture. His own, beating away softly in the tub, fairly gleamed; this pig heart looked as dry as death. He rooted through the cupboards, trying to find something he could glaze it with to give it some extra sheen; with great care he painted the pig heart with vinegar using the back of a soup spoon. Most of the vinegar ran off the sides, but enough of it got between the cracks that after a little while the whole thing fairly sparkled. Of course, it now stank. He tried to mask that by spraying it with old perfume he found on his wife's dressing table, and that was so strong he was forced to paint the whole organ with a new coat of vinegar to try to take the edge off.

The doorbell rang.

"Hello, how are you?" she said, and there was a smile of practised cheer as if they'd just been introduced at a party. He asked her if she'd like a coffee. "No, no, I won't stay, I'll just pick up the . . . is this it? . . . thanks." And she dropped the bagged heart into her handbag, without bothering to look at it or sniff at it. He was relieved, of course, but also a little hurt.

"We need to talk," he said, and hated the very words.

"I know. I know. We do need to talk. And I'd hoped we'd talk today, but something popped up, I have to go and . . . But soon. I'll call you. Well. Thanks for this," she said, tapping the handbag, "thanks for looking after it," and she blushed, realizing what she'd said.

"Are you giving it to someone else? Is there someone else?"

"No. God. No. It's not been a week . . ."

"I'm seeing someone else," he said.

"You are?"

"Yes."

"It's not been a week."

"You don't mind, surely?"

"No. No, I don't mind. God. Well, good for you. Well. What's her name?"

"Gillian," he said, without hesitation. He was pleased by that, because he'd no idea he had a single word left in his head before it popped out of his mouth like that. It could just as easily have been anything, it could have been 'pipecleaner,' or, or 'sandpit.'

"Well," she said, and smiled again, but it was a different smile this time. "As I say, thanks. As I say, I'll call soon." She left her keys on the table, and the spare keys, and the back-up set. She wasn't coming back.

He closed the door behind her as gently as possible—it somehow seemed all the crueller that way. And he heard a clatter in the kitchen, and, hurrying back, saw that his heart was on the floor, writhing about in some distress. At least this time there'd been no pain, and he supposed that was an improvement; it had clearly spasmed so hard that it had flipped out of the Tupperware box altogether. Having spent hours hacking away and polishing the pig's heart he no longer felt quite so squeamish handling his own. He picked it up, blew the dirt off, turned it over, and promptly dropped it on the floor again in surprise.

The underside of the heart wasn't so much covered with spots as welts. Studded into the pink tissue, a couple were the size of ten pence coins. They looked like bones growing there—could they have even been bones? he didn't know—he ran his finger along the surface of one of these white blobs, pushed hard, and he thought that maybe it yielded a little under the pressure. He set the heart back in the box, looked at it thoughtfully. Then he decided to turn it back over, because it looked slightly healthier that way up. And then he decided to put the lid back on, put a blanket over it, and shut it away in the cupboard where they kept the best china, because it looked a *lot* healthier that way.

His first weekend as a single man was pleasant. He watched television programmes he'd never have watched with his wife, and realized that although they were no better than the ones they'd watched together, they were now, at least, *his*. There was an unmistakeable thrill to be in charge of the remote control, and when he tired of what he was watching, he'd flip through all the channels as fast as he could—by Sunday night he'd got pretty speedy. He ordered in fast food on the Saturday, and enjoyed it so much, he ordered the same thing for the Sunday. "Yes, it's me again," he told the delivery man as he handed him his pizza, but he couldn't be sure whether it was the same chap or not inside his motorcycle helmet. And he tried not to think of his heart. And he tried to think instead of Gillian.

Gillian worked in the Human Resources department, which meant that her entire job was a complete mystery to him. He didn't know why his brain had come up with her name, but he supposed it might just know something he didn't. Back at work on Monday, he looked at all the women in his open plan office. They were a pretty unprepossessing bunch, but at least Gillian wasn't married, and was probably a bit younger than most. In her early thirties, he guessed, maybe even in her twenties—it's so hard to tell girls' ages when they get that overweight. When she went outside for a cigarette break he followed her.

"Hello," he said. "I thought I'd like to get to know you better."

She blew smoke out of the side of her mouth, said nothing.

"I mean," he soldiered on gamely, "only if you'd like that too. I wondered if you'd like a drink some time. If you'd like that too."

"You mean on a date?"

"Oh," he said, as if surprised by the very concept, "I meant a drink. But, yes, it could be a date, yes."

She looked him up and down. He felt irritated. He knew he was past his best, but at least he'd had a best, he didn't look like a beached whale in a skirt. "Aren't you married?" she asked.

"Yes. No. Well, sort of. A bit."

She shrugged to shut him up. "I don't really care either way." So why did you ask, then? "You like Italian?" Yes, he liked Italian. So she gave him the name of a restaurant in town. "See you there at eight thirty." She took a final puff on her cigarette, crushed it under heel, and waddled back to work.

After he'd scrubbed and brushed and deodorized, and tried to recall other preliminaries he should perform before a date, he opened up the cupboard, took out the tub, fished out the moths that had impossibly got inside, and gave his heart an examination. At first he assumed that he was looking at the underside, it was so covered with those bony welts, but then he realized that all the little spots had clustered and hardened all over. He weighed it in his hands, and guessed it must be a good three, maybe four pounds heavier since he'd last held it. He put it down, thinking hard. He checked his watch. There was plenty of time—he'd got dressed and ready to leave a good two hours early, as usual. Then he came to a decision, and went to fetch the knife.

He worked on the bigger of the blotches first. He considered that so much damage had been done there already, he could hardly make it much worse. He hoped the nodule wasn't too deep, but as he inserted the blade into the gap between pink and white and pushed carefully at an angle, it met resistance. He pushed deeper still, and just as he thought he didn't dare push any further, that sticking knives into his heart may not after all be the wisest course of action, he felt the bony substance at last giving. It prised out with a slight sucking sound; at first he was a bit too timid about yanking the thing out once he'd got purchase, and it sank back into the tissue with a plop, but he'd now seen what needed to be done and that all it took was a bit of gusto. He freed the pebble, put it into a saucer; where it had been cutting into the heart most deeply there was a bit of gristle attached, a bit of blood, but all in all it was a remarkably clean excision for a beginner. Mind you, there was now a hole in his heart, but it wasn't a *hole*, not really, it was just a little pockmark.

By the time he was attacking the seventh lump he was almost enjoying himself—he got a little careless and knifed through some living tissue, and that gave him a pang of discomfort. He staunched the bleeding as best he could, then put a sticky plaster over the cut. He held the heart up to the light, appraised it dispassionately. Not too bad at all. Of course, there were lots of bone bits left, like rivets, but they seemed too small to worry about for now. He felt around the rim of one of the holes he'd created, and it had been so numb during the surgery itself he was surprised to feel that it itched to his touch. A furious itch, and he couldn't help himself, he had to scratch away at the crater, scratch deep and for all he was worth, and the more he scratched, the greater the itch, it felt so *good* and yet it was *burning*, he wasn't scratching now he was tearing, and he literally had to pull his hand away from it with the other to stop. Under his fingernails now were fine shreds of pink, he'd got spots of blood upon his cuff. He checked his watch again. There was still time to change his shirt— thank goodness for that!

She was waiting for him. Black nail varnish, a nicely patterned top, her skirt a little shorter. "Hi," she said, and let him kiss her cheek. There was a bottle of white wine in front of her, and she'd already drunk about half of it.

"Sorry I'm late," he said, although he wasn't late nor sorry.

They talked as they waited for their food to arrive. They didn't watch the same TV shows. He hadn't even heard of her music. She seized upon the garlic bread when it arrived. "I love garlic bread!" she positively enthused, "do you love garlic bread?" He said he did, and she smiled; it was the first thing they'd found in common. She pushed an entire piece into her mouth, and it barely touched the sides. "It's very wide, my mouth," she told him, and grinned. He wondered what her heart was like. Wide and plump and rubbery, like a trampoline.

And as they ate it turned out they had still more things they could agree on. The people she hated at work were, by and large, the same people he suspected hated him. He'd never liked Denise from Marketing. "No, she's a bitch," Gillian agreed, devouring a tiramisu and draining the second bottle of house white.

"Things have gone rather well," he said. "Do you think? I mean, this could happen again."

"Sure," she agreed. "Why not?"

"I mean, we could be friends. *Really* friends."

"Sure," she said, and shrugged.

"I have something for you," he said. He reached into his bag, and offered her his heart.

"Oh," she said. "Now look. This is just a date. Isn't it? I mean."

"You don't have to take it now," he said. "I was just saying. You know, if in the future, you *wanted* my heart. For any reason."

"Sure," she said. "Wow." She tried to pour herself another wine, realized the bottle was empty, and accepted his glass when he pushed it towards her.

"I'll get the bill," he said. "This is on me."

Outside it was starting to rain. "Better get a taxi," said Gillian. "Too pissed to drive."

"I'll get you one," he said. "You stay here, in the dry. I'll get one." He stood on the pavement for a full three minutes waving his arms like a windmill. And he thought, this is nice, I'm being protective of her, she'll think this is nice.

He held the door open for her, as she told the driver where she lived. "Thanks," he said. "This has been nice."

She looked at him in surprise. "Aren't you coming with me?"

"Sure," he heard himself say.

Inside she lit a cigarette. The driver told her there was no smoking in the cab. "It's all right," she said. "I'll open a window." He told her there was no smoking at all. "If you don't like it, then chuck me out." The driver said nothing, and drove on. "Don't give him a tip," she said loudly, and blew smoke in the direction of the window when she remembered to do so. "Can I see that heart again?" she then asked unexpectedly.

He gave it to her. She peered at it curiously, holding it close to her face, ash dropping on to it. "Looks like a Swiss cheese," she said. "And what are all these knobbly bits?"

"It's not much of a heart," he admitted. "I just need someone to take care of it. It needs taking care of, you see."

"I've never been given a heart before," she said. "Not by anyone." She kissed him in the ear. He wondered whether she'd been aiming for somewhere better and had missed, but now she was there she coated the inside of it with her tongue. "Did you like that?" she asked him. He told her it was very nice.

In spite of what Gillian had told him, he gave a generous tip. The taxi driver glared at him and drove off. Gillian staggered into her house. "Denise!" she called. "Denise!"

"Who's Denise?"

"My flatmate. You know Denise. Good, she's in bed. I told her to make herself scarce. Come on. Do you want a drink?"

He told her he didn't need another. She fetched a bottle anyway. She sat him down on the sofa, then stuck her tongue once more in his ear. He tried to tilt his head so that she could work her way to his mouth, pretty soon she got the general idea. And before long they were all tongues and teeth—well, to be fair, most of the teeth were hers, and he thought at least two of the tongues—and he was trying to remember how you breathed during kisses like this, it was through the nose, that was it, and she didn't taste like his wife whatsoever.

"Come on," she said, and all but pulled him to his feet.

On top of her duvet were half a dozen stuffed toys. He felt a twinge of affection for Gillian; here she was, all hard-drinking and hard-smoking, but deep down she was still just a little girl who slept with teddy bears. He felt he'd caught the real person unawares, seen beneath the brassy exterior something small and sweet she liked to keep hidden. Then he remembered that she'd obviously planned on bringing him back here, so always knew he'd see her toys, and didn't know what to think any longer. "Listen," she said, as she swept a Snoopy in World War One goggles on to the floor, "I should say. I'm not going to give you *my* heart."

"Of course not," he said. "That's okay."

"I mean, I *can't*. You see? When I was fourteen I sent it to Robbie Williams. I was a really big fan of his."

"He must get a lot of hearts."

"Yeah. I had such a crush. Thing is, I'd really like it back now. I've written to him lots of times, put in stamped addressed envelopes, he wouldn't have to pay the postage. But nothing."

"He must get a lot of post."

"Sometimes I think," she said, and she was thinking, she was tilting her head to one side as if to egg her brain on, and it looked odd to see her think whilst quite so drunk, "I think that we give away our hearts too easily. You know? We're all in such a hurry to get out there and fall in love as soon as we possibly can. And maybe we're missing out, that maybe our hearts would feel so much better if we just kept them inside our chests. I mean, what does Robbie Williams want with my heart anyway?"

"He must," he said again, "get a lot of hearts."

"It's the reason I smoke," said Gillian. "And why I eat so much. I keep thinking, if I keep *damaging* my heart, he's not going to want to hang on to it so much, is he? He's going to want to post it back, just to get rid of the thing. But I wanted you to know," she said, and kissed him again, "if you think I'm holding back. If you think I'm not putting myself into it completely. That's the reason why."

And they had sex. He didn't especially feel she was holding back, but now she'd put the doubt in his head he couldn't not let it nag at him. And at the moment of climax, he thought, so that's adultery. That's it. I'm an adulterer.

"Ssh," she said. "What was that?"

He strained to hear. And yes, there it was again. A sort of scream, not too loud, but eerie, inhuman. And after that, an all too human one.

"Christ, what now?" muttered Gillian, and went to see. He followed her.

"What the fuck is *that*?" Denise from Marketing was standing in the sitting room, pointing at his heart. It was shrieking in what could only be pain, high-pitched and plaintive. And it was glowing so brightly, with a fierce white light that lit the whole room—he saw moths dancing about in the spotlight beam. He had to get close, and shield his eyes, to take a closer look. The bone had spread again, and the remaining patches of pink were straining against it, bulging, livid.

"I don't need this," said Denise from Marketing. "I've got fucking work in the morning. I don't need to be woken up by someone's fucking heart."

"Sorry, Denise," said Gillian.

"Hello, Denise," he said, and wished that he was wearing some clothes.

"I want you out of my flat," said Denise from Marketing. "Both of you," she added, indicating the still wailing heart.

The rain hadn't yet eased off, but he didn't think Denise from Marketing would let him wait for a cab. As he walked the darkened streets, lit only by the heart's unearthly glow, its occasional cries sounded particularly loud, and passers-by would cross the road to avoid him. It was as he was getting into a taxi that his heart, which had behaved itself for ten minutes and done more dramatic than hushed quivering, let out a shriek so agonized and despairing that the driver took off without him. He slipped off his coat, wrapped it round the tortured muscle—at first just to muffle the sound of its screams, but as he held it close to his chest, the chest from which it should never have been ripped, he believed it was more to give it as much warmth as he could. The heavens opened; his clothes stuck sodden to his skin. And all he'd say is "ssh" and "it's all right" and "nearly there," and give little noises he hoped were comforting.

By the time he reached home, and opened out his bundle on to the kitchen table, the heart had almost completely ossified. There was one small streak of pink tissue, trying its utmost in spite of all to do its job and pump blood and oxygen around his body. "It's all right," he said softly, "you don't have to try so hard. It's all right, I'll stay with you, I'm jolly well staying with you." Within an hour it was dead.

"I'm sorry," he said, and meant it. "I'm sorry," although he really couldn't see what else he could have done. "Sorry," but it hadn't been his bloody responsibility, had it? He left it, no longer gleaming, just a bony off-white, even the moths weren't interested anymore. He decided what to do with it in the morning. He slept particularly well that night.

The next day at work a nervous Gillian approached his cubicle.

"I'm sorry about what happened," she said. "But I want you to know I really like you, and I'd love to try again . . ."

"I think," he said, coolly, looking up from his work for the first time, "I can do a bit better, don't you?"

And so he could. He soon realized that the worst a woman could do was to say no—and it's true that some *did* say no, but a lot didn't, and fewer said no the more said yes. He didn't give a toss if they were married; if they broke their husbands' hearts, that was their lookout. He lost a bit of weight. He got himself a little stud earring—and, truth be told, it did make him look a bit stupid, but not very stupid, and, more importantly, not stupid *enough*. "We shouldn't go back to mine," said Denise from Marketing. "Why?" he smirked, and so they did, and as they were humping away he liked to imagine the crying he heard in the room next door was something to do with him.

Three months later his wife came back. She was waiting for him on the doorstep when he got in from work.

"You could have phoned," he said.

"You told me I could come around whenever I liked."

"Not bloody likely. Anyone could be here." He opened the door. "You can come in for a bit."

"Good news," she said. "My pangs have stopped."

"Great news," he said, and lit a cigarette. "What's that got to do with me?"

"I made a terrible mistake," she said. "Or maybe it wasn't a mistake. Maybe I *had* to go away for a while. Just to realize that I love you, that I only love you. Maybe I had to put myself through that, put us both through that, just so I'd know for sure. Do you think?"

He just stared and smoked.

"All right," she said. "I admit, I did find someone else. He didn't treat me right. I tried to give him my heart, but it wouldn't do anything, wouldn't beat for him at all, it just lay there like a dead weight. And he said it smelt funny." She fetched it from her bag, held it out for him to take.

"It does smell funny," he said.

"I know."

She continued to hold it out. He continued not to take it. At last she put it down on the table, between them, as a compromise.

"I've nowhere to go," she said.

"There's the spare room. You can have it for one night. Just one night."

She nodded. Waited for him to say something else. When he didn't, she nodded once more, then went upstairs.

He opened a bottle of wine. After he'd finished his second glass, he supposed he ought to see how she was getting on. Whether she wanted some dinner, he suddenly thought, maybe she was hungry. And he was surprised to feel some concern, where had that come from?

He went into the spare room. She'd been through the cupboards, there was debris all over the bed. From an empty shoebox she'd found his heart. She was holding it in one palm—he'd forgotten how, in death, it had grown so small and wizened.

"Put that back," he said. "That isn't yours anymore."

"Look," she said softly. "Look." And she began to stroke it. She blew on it gently.

"It's not yours," he said, uselessly.

And as he watched, the rock cracked. Pink tissue broke through the stone and bone. "Look," she said again. It was struggling, and then it managed a beat, and once it had managed one, it seemed all too happy to beat again. "Look," she said, and kissed it. The last of the rock crumbled away at her touch. "I love you," she said. "Look. I love you. Look how much." And she offered his heart out to him, as good to new.

Dazedly he reached for it. She smiled, nodded. He took hold of it. Looked at it, as it swelled with new life. And then he dug his fingernails in, dug them in deep, dug 'til it bled. "No," she said. And began squeezing hard, so that one of the ventricles bulged then burst. "No, stop!" And ripped it apart, tearing at it, pulling off gobbets of it, showering them on to the spare room carpet.

"I told you," he said. "It isn't yours. You gave it back."

And his wife began to cry. He looked away in disgust.

"One night only," he said, "and then you find somewhere else to stay." He wiped his hands on his shirt, then left, closing the door behind him.

"I'll get you back," she said softly. "It'll take time, but I'll get you." And she looked down at the bloody chunks strewn all over the floor. And saw that, in spite of all the damage that he'd inflicted on it—all the damage they'd both done—the shattered heart still, stubbornly, beat.

# BLUE CRAYON,
# YELLOW CRAYON

Andrew Kaplan was coming home, at last, and it'd be for a *real* holiday, not like that time last August when the company called him back to work after only four days' leave, they'd guaranteed he wouldn't be needed in until January 5th, that would very nearly give him two weeks. "Great," his wife had said, when he'd phoned her and told her the good news, and Andrew asked whether his daughter would be excited too, and his wife assured him that she would be. The flight from Boston was packed with British people who'd be getting to see their families, and there was a revelry in the air, nothing too outspoken, nothing drunken or boisterous, they were respectable denizens of middle management—but there were polite smiles everywhere, everyone seemed to be sporting a smile, and the stewardesses were wearing tinsel on their name badges, it all seemed very festive.

The aeroplane took off half an hour late, but Andrew wasn't too worried, he knew that nine times out of ten any delay is made good in transit. But when the pilot came over the intercom and apologized once again that they were going to have to circle Heathrow for the fourth time—"The runways are all full, everyone wants to get back for Christmas!"—Andrew began to worry about his connecting flight from London to Edinburgh. By the time all the passengers had filed off the plane and made their way to baggage claim, no one was smiling anymore. Andrew was almost resigned to the idea that he'd missed the connection, but then he dazedly realized that his suitcase was the first on to the conveyor belt—and that never happened!—and if he *ran* he might just make it to the check-in desk on time; and so that's what he did, he *ran*, and his case was heavy, laden down with so many special presents for his family, but he didn't let that stop him—he raced down the travelator from terminal three to terminal two, apologizing as he pushed other passengers to one side—and it was going to be okay, if he kept up this pace he was going to make it with *minutes* to spare, and he burst into the departures hall and looked up at the monitors for his flight details—and there they were, it hadn't taken off yet!—and there was a word in red right beside it, and the word was 'cancelled.'

And for a moment he felt quite relieved, because it meant he had no reason to run anymore, and he'd done his best, hadn't he? And for another moment he was quite angry. And then he just didn't feel anything very much, he was just so tired.

No more flights to Scotland tonight. Sorry. Yes, the inconvenience is highly regrettable. There will, of course, be compensation, and somewhere for Mr Kaplan to rest until service resumed in the morning. But Andrew didn't want an airport hotel, or, God knows, did they just mean some sort of darkened lounge he could sit in?—it's all he had thought about on the flight over, that after three months away he was going *home*. He remembered what his wife had said, one of those last times he'd managed to get through to her on the phone—"We've never been apart so long before." He'd asked her whether his daughter was looking forward to Christmas, and his wife had said, "Of course she is, she's five years old, Christmas is all she thinks about!" And she'd explained that they had already decorated the tree together, and sent out the cards, and been carol singing—all the things they'd always done as a family, and this time he'd been away for them, and she didn't press that point, she didn't try to make him feel guilty—but then, she didn't need to. And Andrew stood in the airport terminal and fumed; by rights he should be flying home right now, by rights he should be somewhere in the air over Birmingham. "I need to get back," he said to the woman behind the counter, "I need to get back tonight, whatever it takes." It was Christmas Eve tomorrow, he needed to know that when his daughter woke up on Christmas Eve her father would be there ready for her.

He was told there was a last train to Edinburgh, leaving from King's Cross station within the hour. He joined the queue for a taxi, then pleaded with the people in front to let him go first, then paid them all ten pounds each. The taxi fare cost him fifty quid, but by this stage of the proceedings Andrew didn't care about money anymore—on the radio there was playing a non-stop medley of Christmas hits, and Andrew wasn't in the mood for them, and the driver seemed quite put out when Andrew told him to turn them off. Andrew apologized with a healthy tip that used up all his spare cash. Andrew tried to call his wife to tell her he'd be late home, but his mobile phone was confused, it was still hunting for a signal from an American network provider. He asked the taxi driver whether he could use his phone. The taxi driver refused.

He bought a ticket with his credit card. The train was already filling up. He dragged his suitcase down the platform, and carriage after carriage he couldn't spot an empty seat. He was starting to despair—and there, at the very last compartment, there were seats galore, the train was almost deserted. He couldn't see why, he looked for a sign that said it was a different class, or required special reservation, but no, nothing. He climbed aboard, heaved his case into the empty luggage rack, plopped himself down wearily into a seat. He had a whole table to himself. He smiled at the people around him—"Pretty lucky!" he said, but they didn't reply. There were a couple of businessmen sitting together, a young mother with a girl, an elderly mother reading a magazine, a middle-aged man who was asleep. Andrew decided to take his cue from this last passenger; he closed his eyes, and by the time the train pulled out of the station Andrew was snoring gently.

"Bang!"

And Andrew was awake, and there was the little girl, and she was leaning over his table as if she owned it, and she was pointing a gun at him, except it wasn't a gun, it was two fingers, with a third wiggling underneath as a trigger. "Bang! Bang! Bang!"

Andrew wasn't sure whether to respond or not. With his own daughter he tried to play along as much as possible, no matter what strange pretending game she flung at him, that was what a daddy was supposed to do. But this wasn't his daughter, and he didn't know whether he should encourage her, frankly he didn't know whether he should be talking to her at all. So he sort of half went for it; he clutched at his chest, he said, "Ugh!" quietly, as if he'd been shot, as if he were dying, but it was all a bit pathetic, and even as he did it, Andrew could feel himself blushing red with embarrassment.

The little girl didn't seem to mind. She looked delighted by this unexpected piece of playacting. "Bang! Bang!" she went, she shot him twice more for good measure, and Andrew didn't know what he was supposed to do this time, he was already dead, wasn't he? And she laughed out loud, and then, with a scream, turned and ran down the aisle to the other end of the carriage. She didn't shoot at any of the other passengers, and Andrew didn't know how he felt about that, whether he was annoyed or just a little bit proud.

He looked towards the girl's mother, but she didn't appear even to have noticed, she was staring dully out of the window. He looked around the rest of the carriage, with a rueful smile—kids!—but no one caught his eye. The old woman was still reading her magazine; the businessmen had run out of things to say, and were looking away from each other; the middle-aged man was still asleep.

Andrew rather envied him, because here came the girl again, running back down the aisle, whooping. Andrew wondered how anyone could sleep through a racket like that.

His head felt muzzy, he knew he was teetering upon the edge of sleep, and if only he could fall in the right direction he'd be dozing soundly all the way home. Why wouldn't the girl shut up, why wouldn't she just sit down and shut up—he'd never let *his* daughter run riot on a train, especially not when it was late at night, especially not when there was a passenger onboard who was clearly fighting jetlag—and he felt a resentment for the mother who was *still* not doing a thing to help, *still* just looking out of the bloody window, really!—and he tried to force the resentment down, because he knew if he let it the resentment would keep him awake, it'd growl away at his innards, he'd be unable to relax. And here came the girl again—

"Ssh!" he said, and glared at her, and put his finger to his lips. And she stopped dead, and looked surprised, and a little hurt maybe that her one playfellow, the one person who had given her a damn, had turned against her. Her bottom lip trembled. She began to cry.

"No, no," said Andrew, "ssh!" And he put his finger to his lips again, but this time with a smiley face, see, all smiles, he wasn't cross with her, not really. But it was no good. The tears were in full flow now, the girl let out a misery that was profound and was sincere, and was very, very loud, she began to scream the place down. He hadn't realized you could scream tears out like that.

Andrew panicked a bit, looked quickly at the other passengers. But no one seemed to mind. The woman didn't raise her eyes from her magazine. The businessmen turned their heads in the child's direction, but with supreme indifference—and then quickly turned away again, as if annoyed that the pair of them had been caught looking at the exact same thing.

And the mother said, very soft, but stern, "Come and sit down." And for a moment Andrew stupidly thought she might mean him. But the girl sulkily turned, and went back to her seat. "Get out your colouring book. Play with your crayons." The little girl was still crying, angry little sobs, but she did what she was told. And all the while the mother didn't so much as glance at her, her attention still upon the window and whatever she could make out from the darkness.

The little girl took out her crayons. She looked down at her colouring book. Grim, not a hint of a smile. The crying had almost dribbled to a halt, there was just the odd little moan punctuated with sudden sniffs. Andrew watched her, carefully; the little girl didn't seem to notice he was spying on her, but then, then, in one instant she turned her head towards Andrew, right at him—and what was that in her smile? Rage? Triumph? Something adult anyway, something almost sneering, and it made Andrew feel small and ashamed.

And then she was at work with her crayons. She wasn't colouring anything in, she was *attacking* the book, stabbing down hard with the bright blue stick, slashing at the page. And now, in her left hand, she produced a yellow crayon, and she was stabbing down with that too, she was showing no mercy, the crying had stopped, she was instead giving grunts of effort as she stabbed as hard as she could. And Andrew realized only he could see this, her mother took no interest whatsoever, and Andrew thought he should alert her, because this was wrong, something was terribly wrong—and as the child spattered blue and yellow cuts deep into the paper she looked at him again and he could see there was spit bubbling out of her mouth, was it even foam? And Andrew opened his mouth to say something, he didn't know what, but before he got the chance—

—the woman had turned from the window. She didn't look angry, or annoyed, or frustrated—that was the oddness of it—her face looked perfectly composed and neutral. "Enough," she said, calmly, and stood up, and she was pulling the little girl up too, by the shoulders, and up into her arms. And the little girl began to scream again, and this time it was a scream of fear, she knew she was in trouble now—and the mother didn't care, she was into the aisle, and carrying the girl up to the other end of the carriage, the girl struggling and kicking and lashing out, and yet for all that still holding on tight to her crayons and her colouring book. And the mother and child were gone.

The sudden silence was a shock. Andrew closed his eyes right away, to see if he could find that drowsiness again, but the silence rang right round his head.

He looked out of the window. It was black out there, just black. He couldn't see a thing, not a single house, or a tree; it was as if someone had painted over the windows, and there was a glossy shine to the black that began to give Andrew a headache.

Presently the woman came back, and sat down in her seat. Andrew was pleased to see the noisy little girl wasn't with her.

He closed his eyes again. A couple of minutes later, when he opened them, he saw that one of the businessmen had fallen asleep. He closed his eyes once more; when he opened them, a few minutes after, he saw that the second businessman had succumbed too, and his head was lolling against his partner's, and they seemed huddled together for warmth and protection. It almost made Andrew laugh out loud—and he decided that he'd like to take a picture of them with his phone, and send it to his wife. She would find it funny, and she could show it to their daughter too! He took out the phone, but it still hadn't found a signal.

Next time he closed his eyes he wanted to see whether he could make the old woman fall asleep too. But she didn't, she remained forever glued so sourly to her magazine. Never mind.

The mother was staring out at the blackness of the night.

He wondered where the little girl had got to.

The mother then took a thermos flask out of her bag, and poured herself a cup of tea. She sipped at it, turned back to the window.

Andrew closed his eyes one last time, tried to fall asleep. The train rocked from side to side as it sped down the tracks, it made him feel like a baby, it made him feel drowsy. But all the while he listened out for the return of the little girl, he knew the little girl would be back soon, must be, he was tense with anticipation of the noise she would make.

He refused to open his eyes for a good ten minutes. He kept himself busy by reciting, silently, and in strict chronological order, the captains of the English cricket team since Len Hutton. When he reached the present day, he opened up—and looked—and the girl *still* hadn't returned. The mother had put away her tea now, the old woman was still reading, the businessmen and the middle-aged man all still asleep.

Where was she?

He got to his feet. No one looked up. He walked down the aisle to the end of the compartment. The electronic door trundled open for him with a hiss.

The girl wasn't to be seen. He tried the far door, but it was locked, this was the end of the train. A sign said the toilet was vacant, and Andrew knew that little girls aren't always very scrupulous about locks. He hesitated, then knocked gently upon the door. "Are you all right?" he called.

There was no answer, and that annoyed him, she must have been in there for twenty minutes now, twenty at the very least, time for him to recite the English cricket team and back again! And he realized he needed the toilet anyway, he hadn't been since halfway over the Atlantic Ocean, and so when he knocked again it wasn't just as an interfering busybody, but as a man who had waited long and patiently for the lavatory and was now claiming his due right to pee.

He pushed upon the door, very tentatively, and it swung open, and he peeked his head around the door, fully prepared to make protestations of surprise when he saw the little girl inside—but there was no one there—and he supposed that was a good thing, he hadn't really wanted the embarrassment of a girl with her undies round her ankles—but where was she then? Where had she got to? And the answer crept over him, and any urine that had been nestling in his bowels froze to ice and was never going to come out now, not ever. . . .

. . . The mother had thrown her overboard. She must have thrown her overboard.

She had had enough of her tantrums, and had picked her up, and marched her down the aisle, and to the window, and chucked her out. And he could imagine the little girl's screams being cut off as she was sucked into the night, and how her body would have fallen down the side of the speeding train, as if she were flying, as if she were a witch, a little witch who'd lost her broomstick, falling until her head smashed against the track.

And then the mother had calmly returned to her seat. And all the while since had been staring out into the blackness. The blackness into which she had tossed her child.

No.

That couldn't be it.

Think.

He had had his eyes closed. And what had happened, surely— yes—was that the girl had walked past him to the *other* end of the compartment—tiptoed past, probably, unusually quietly, but girls were peculiar things, weren't they, maybe she was playing some sort of game?—she was now no doubt terrorizing another compartment altogether. And the mother? The mother who had just sat in her seat the whole time (half an hour more like, really) whilst her daughter ran amok somewhere without supervision? That made her a bad parent, perhaps, but he could live with that, he wasn't the best parent in the world either, was he, was he? She could be a bad parent, that still made more sense than that she was a murderer.

He sighed with relief, and only then realized he'd been holding his breath. And he closed the toilet door; he couldn't do anything especially useful in there, but he splashed some lukewarm water on to his face, he wiped it off with a paper towel. It was better than nothing, better that than he'd had a wasted journey.

And with full confidence he walked back down the aisle to his seat at the other end of the compartment. And he was going to sit down, he really was, and that would have been the end of the matter—but there was just a moment's hesitation, the need to satisfy some stupid lingering doubt—or maybe it was something to do with velocity, he was already on a trajectory to the next compartment, why stop short, why not walk straight on and look?

The electronic door wouldn't open for him. He tugged at it. It wouldn't budge.

It wasn't *locked*, nothing like that, what would be the point? But it was jammed, very definitely jammed, and there was probably nothing suspicious in that, no cause for alarm, it wasn't as if his compartment had been deliberately segregated from the rest of the train (why on earth did that pop into his head?). But he pulled at the door with all his might, he grunted with the effort. Until he became convinced that all the passengers behind him were watching, and laughing. And then he stopped, and he turned about, and of course no one was watching, no one even cared.

He stood there, bit his lip. Tried to work out what to do.

The girl was small, maybe she was hiding somewhere in the carriage? (Silently, for over half an hour?) He walked down the aisle again, and he looked this way and that, he looked underneath the tables and upon all the rows of seats. And he thought, has she got off? Could she simply have got off? The train hadn't stopped at any stations yet, it was two hours' journey until York—but maybe they had *reached* York; he hadn't thought he'd fallen asleep when he'd closed his eyes before, but maybe he had without realizing it, he was jetlagged to tiny bits, maybe they'd passed a *dozen* stations and he hadn't even noticed, maybe the train had stopped and the little girl had got off—late at night—on her own—and her mother had stayed onboard and waved her goodbye—for some reason—and—

"Excuse me," he said softly to the old woman with the magazine, "has the train stopped anywhere yet?"

The old woman looked up, at last, and stared at him, and she didn't reply—and it didn't seem to Andrew that she was being rude, there was utter blankness in that expression, maybe she didn't understand English? (Although the magazine was in English, wasn't it?) She continued to stare, she wouldn't look away.

And he said, "What happened to the little girl?" And at that her mouth began to open, very slowly, it was almost as if he could hear the creak of those old lips parting, and muscles that had lain dormant for so long began to grind as they were forced into action—and suddenly Andrew didn't want to see what would happen next—he didn't want to see that mouth open—he didn't want to see what might be inside—and he whipped his head away from her, he backed off, he fought down a sudden swell of panic and breathed and breathed again and felt his heart steady. He looked back at the old woman, he forced himself to, and she was once more staring intently at her magazine, it was as if he'd never approached her in the first place.

He saw that her eyes weren't moving, she wasn't *reading* anything, it was all staring, just stares. He walked past her and turned around to look at the pages, and saw that across the centrefold was a picture of a young woman, a model, prettier than the old woman could ever have been. He wondered if she'd been gazing upon this one picture for the entire journey. He wondered why.

He went back to the end of the carriage. He pulled down the window, and took a deep breath of fresh air, and felt better.

And he could see that it was possible, look. See how the window opened nice and wide? A little girl could squeeze through there, no problem. He himself could squeeze through, probably, if he hunched his shoulders a bit. That was all it would take, and then he'd be with the girl, they'd both be off this train and the wretched journey would be over. And the blackness was *perfect*, he could see the beauty of it now, this close up, his face so close it was *grazing* it. So shiny, new even—and the little girl hadn't suffered, he could see that now, she had just flown away into the dark and would never have hit the ground, the wind so fast and carrying her off safely. And he knew then that he would do it too. He would do it. He would do it. He would step out into the blackness. He would do it. He would never see his wife or daughter again, but then, was he ever going to have seen them anyway, what, really? Because he couldn't believe that, he couldn't picture that, the three of them together, around a Christmas tree, laughing, hugging, it was beyond imagining, it seemed so fake—and there was nothing fake about the blackness, that was the only truth, why not accept it? He would do it. And the wife and daughter might be sad, for a bit, he wondered if they would. But they'd never find his body, it'd be lost within the black.—And he wondered whether his luggage at least would make it home, he had Christmas presents for his family, he'd like them to have something nice to open on the big day.

He stepped forward. He felt something hard under his foot. He toyed with it for a moment, rolled it under his sole, then frowned, wondering what it was. He lifted the foot to see.

There were two crayons. One blue, one yellow.

He picked them up. He looked at them for a while.

When he walked back into the compartment the lights seemed dimmer somehow. As if the darkness had seeped in from somewhere, or was it just because he was tired? Because he was so tired. And the old woman was asleep now, her head slumped awkwardly, uncomfortably, and she'd dropped her magazine on the floor—and Andrew thought he should pick it up for her, but he never wanted to go near her again, and as he passed her down the aisle he pressed his body hard against the opposite row of seats.

Everyone was asleep. Except the mother, who was no longer looking out of the window, she was looking at *him*. And smiling.

"Ssh," she said, and she put her finger to her lips. "Let's not wake them."

"No," said Andrew.

She tapped at the seat next to her. "Come and sit down," she said. And Andrew did.

The woman took out her flask and poured herself a tea. She asked whether Andrew would like one. He thanked her, said no. And she nodded at that, as if that was what she'd been expecting, and smiled, and sipped at her tea, and looked back out of the window again, as if her audience with Andrew was at an end.

Andrew felt he should leave her, get up, return to his own seat. But he felt so heavy.

He was still holding the crayons, bunched together tight in his fist.

"Excuse me," he said, and the woman looked at him. "Excuse me," he said again, and held the crayons out to her.

He wondered what she'd do. Whether the woman would look shocked. Or remorseful. Whether she'd get violent, or cry, or confess. But her face didn't change at all, it was most disappointing.

"Is that some sort of Christmas present for me?" she said.

"Yes," said Andrew. "No. I mean. For your daughter."

"Do you have a daughter?"

"Yes."

"Then why don't you give your presents to her?" And her eyes twinkled, because she was teasing him—was she teasing him?

"No," he said. "I mean. You don't, I. I thought. I think your daughter may have dropped them."

She took them from him then, looked at them hard, studied them even. "I don't think these can be my daughter's," she concluded finally, and handed them back.

"Why not?"

"Because I don't have a daughter."

*Anymore*, thought Andrew—he dared her to say it, *anymore*. "Oh," he said.

The woman smiled. And went back to the window.

"No," said Andrew. "I mean. Hey."

She looked back.

"You don't have . . . ?"—and he so much wanted to ask directly, he'd seen her with her, hadn't he, the whole carriage had—although he knew that if he woke them up they would all deny it, he knew that with sudden cold certainty, if they even talked to him, if they even acknowledged him at all. He wanted to say, but I saw you with the girl, the girl you got rid of, what did you do to her? And instead he said, "You don't have a daughter? Well, have, have you ever wanted one?"

The woman raised her eyebrows at that, amused, and Andrew blushed.

"I don't have anyone," she said. And she held his gaze this time, daring him to contradict her—but, no, it wasn't that, she wasn't daring him at all, she spoke with the confidence of utter truth, she knew he wouldn't contradict her, why would he try?

"I'm sorry," said Andrew. "So, you've no one to spend Christmas with?"

"No."

"I'm sorry." And he felt an urge to invite her home, she could stay with his family, she could be his family, he felt it rise up inside him, if he had been breathing more freely then it might even have popped out.

She stared out at the night. He stared at it too. And it seemed to him they were hurtling through a void, they were nowhere at all, nowhere, that the tracks would end and the train would fall into the void deeper and deeper and they would be lost, it seemed to him this may have already happened.

"Are you seeing your family for Christmas?" she asked.

And he told her.

He told her of the presents he had for them in his suitcase. For his daughter he had some dolls bought specially in Boston, all of them famous figures from the American Revolution, she wouldn't find them anywhere else! And for his wife he'd picked up some perfume at duty free. But now these gifts felt a bit paltry. What would his daughter want with a figurine of Paul Revere? But little girls were so good at playing games, weren't they, he had seen her have hours of fun with a cardboard box, she had pretended it was a car, and a dinosaur, and a spaceship, and she'd said to Andrew, play with me, *pretend* with me—but Andrew wasn't very good at pretending, when his daughter shot him with her fingers and Andrew fell over he always tried a bit too hard and he was sure she was embarrassed by his efforts; she had taken that cardboard box, pretended it was a time machine, and a zoo, and a *father*, he'd come home once and she'd got a box and was pretending it was *him*. He didn't know what to do with his own daughter, and each time she'd grown, and aged, and changed. And what would his wife want with perfume? But he had a better present for them, something he couldn't wrap, should he tell? He'd be coming home for good. For good. No, not this time, but soon, very soon. Because for the last year and a half he'd been doing these trips to the States, and his wife had said to him, you're missing out on your daughter's childhood! and he had said, but it's my *job*, I have to go where they tell me, do you think I have any choice? But now he was coming home for good, by April he'd be back in Britain, they said some time in the spring, it'd be May at the latest. He'd be home, and his wife had said, you're not only running out on her childhood, you're running out on *me*—and she wouldn't be able to say that anymore. She wouldn't be able to complain about a bloody thing. And when he told them both, and he'd tell them on Christmas morning, he'd keep it as a proper present, how happy they would be! Because his wife was wrong, he wasn't trying to avoid her, that was ridiculous, he loved her, he was pretty sure he loved her, being at home with her again would take some adjustment but it would be worth it.

He was scared. Of course he was scared. He couldn't remember his wife's name. How odd. The jetlag. His own wife's name, and he was fairly certain she'd had one. He couldn't remember his daughter's name. He wondered whether he might have written them down somewhere, maybe they were on his mobile phone, along with the names of his bosses and his secretarial staff and all his clients, but no—no—he'd call them now, he'd ask—but there was still no signal, the phone said it couldn't find a network provider. And he was scared, because he knew when he got home there would be *that* conversation, because *that* conversation always happened when he got back, sooner or later. And when he'd tried calling his wife recently she'd been so curt with him, she sounded so very far away—and when he told her he'd be home for Christmas for a whole two weeks she sounded almost sarcastic—"Great," she'd said—that was all—"Great." And she never let his daughter come to the phone anymore, she was too busy being asleep in bed or playing with cardboard boxes or being dead. And he knew then. Oh God, he knew then. His wife didn't love him. Not anymore. She had once. Not anymore.

And his daughter. His daughter, his daughter was dead. She was dead. And his wife hadn't even told him! She hadn't told him, because he was in Boston, what good would it do? She hadn't told him because she was angry with him, she'd had a daughter, and she'd slipped through his fingers, she'd got lost in the blackness of the night. Though, to be fair, maybe she had told him, didn't he remember that time—wasn't there a phone call—wasn't there a conversation, and a lot of tears, and he'd had to go to a meeting, they were waiting for him, he wasn't going to listen to this shit, "Bastard!" she'd said, she'd screamed her tears out, he hadn't realized you could *scream* tears out like that, "now, now," he'd said, "I'll be home for Christmas, we can talk about it properly then." "Great," she'd said. Oh God. Oh God. He'd had a daughter, and she was lost, and he was lost too.

The woman who had never been a mother and had never had a daughter took his hand. She smiled. She asked if he would like that cup of tea now. He said yes.

"Wipe away your tears," she said.

"Yes."

She poured him a cup. It was steaming hot. It tasted bitter.

"You get some sleep," she said. "Don't you worry. I'll wake you when you get home."

"Yes. Thank you. Yes."

He settled back in his seat. It felt so soft suddenly, and it was peaceful, there wasn't a sound. And the train rocked from side to side as it sped down the void, it made him feel like a baby, it made him feel drowsy.

"Can I keep the presents?" she asked. He didn't know what she meant for a moment. "The crayons?" He gave them to her. She put them in her pocket. She smiled again, took his hand again, squeezed it. She let him sleep.


It wasn't the woman who woke him up. It was a station guard, shaking his shoulder gently. "Come on, mate, end of the line," he said. There was no one else in the compartment, and the lights were on full. "Come on, some of us have Christmas to get home to!"

Andrew fetched his luggage from the rack. It felt lighter than he remembered. He stepped out on to the platform. Edinburgh was icy, and wet, and right, and home, and he breathed the air in, and felt awake.

He caught a taxi. The taxi driver was playing a medley of Christmas songs. Andrew didn't mind.

He couldn't find his keys. He hammered at the front door. "Let me in!" he cried. And then, to take the desperation out of his voice, "Let me in, it's Santa Claus!"

And his wife opened up. There she was. Oh, there she was.

"Do you love me?" he said, and he could see that she did, her eyes shone with it, he hadn't realized how very obvious love could look. "I love you," he told her, "I love you," and decided not to add that he couldn't remember her name.

"Where is our daughter?" he said. "Is she all right? Is she alive?"

He didn't wait for an answer, he ran up the stairs, ran to the bedroom. His daughter was in bed, and stirred at his noise. "Daddy?" she said. She rubbed at her eyes. "Daddy? Is it really you?"

"Yes," he said, "yes, darling, I'm home, I'm home, and I'm never leaving again!" He wouldn't leave, sod the job, sod Boston, he'd found something he thought had been lost, he wouldn't let go. And she was better than he remembered, she'd reached the age at last where he would never feel uncomfortable with her, or anxious, she was perfect, she was *shiny*, what luck.

He pulled her out of bed, right by the shoulders, held her, hugged her, and he kissed her head and he kissed her hair. And he knew her name, it was all right. She smelled to him of earth, and mud, and dead leaves, but it was all right. He rocked her in his arms. And after a while he stopped, but the rocking just kept on going, and he didn't know what it was.

# FAVOURITE

The first surprise was that my younger brother phoned me at all. The second was what he had to say.

"Mum's dead," he told me, and burst into tears.

"Now calm down," I said. "Are you all right?"

"Of course I'm not all right! Mum's dead, and I'm never going to see her again. I had all these chances to see her, so many chances, and they're all wasted now, I used them up."

"Okay," I said. I took the phone to the armchair, settled down. I could see this conversation lasting quite a while. "Okay," I said again, once I'd got myself comfortable, "how did all this happen? Tell me about it."

"The leukaemia," he said. "The leukaemia's finally got her."

"I didn't know she had leukaemia," I said.

"Yeah, well, there's lots that you didn't know. I suppose I just didn't want to tell you. I suppose you've had it easier." From anyone else that might have sounded like a rebuke, but not my baby brother. He was just telling the truth.

"It all sounds pretty horrible," I said sympathetically. "Leukaemia's a rotten way to go, I expect. So it wasn't a shock, or anything, was it? I expect, at the end, you must have felt a bit of relief."

"Well, yeah," he admitted, "but that's not the point, is it?"

I supposed not, and he began crying again.

"When did all this happen?" I asked.

"Last Thursday."

"Thursday? Mum's been dead the best part of a week, and you wait until now to tell me . . ."

"I've been feeling very down," he said. And although I couldn't see him, I knew he'd be sticking out his bottom lip, just like he always did as a kid. You'd tell him off, he'd know he was in the wrong, and out would pop that lip, right on cue.

"It doesn't matter," I said, although it did, and I couldn't help but feel a little hurt. "I just would like to think you could turn to me if you needed me. I'm here for you, sweetie. I love you."

"I know," he said. "I know you are." The bottom lip was still out, I could all but hear it on the end of the phone, quivering. "Oh, Connie," he said. "I'm never going to see Mum again. I'm *never* going to see my own *mother . . . again.*"

There was a lot more talk like this, but eventually he hung up—he was calling long distance, he said, and it was peak rate, and he'd forgotten he'd been the one who'd phoned. He thanked me again for listening, it had helped him a lot. I didn't think I had helped him, actually, he sounded just as upset as before, but I didn't like to argue. Before he went he threw me one last tidbit. "It's not fair," he said. "That's what gets me. I'm the youngest. You and Anthony, you had bags more time to spend with her than I did. It's just not *fair.*" And there was no answer to that.

After he'd gone I paced around the house for a bit, and then decided I really ought to call Anthony. I couldn't remember the phone number, and had forgotten where I'd written it down, so it was nearly an hour before I dialled the number and heard his voice.

"Hello?" Anthony said.

"Hello, Anthony," I said, feeling strangely formal. "It's Connie." And added, unnecessarily, I hope, "Your sister."

"Oh, hello, Connie," said Anthony.

Anthony was my elder brother. I spoke to him even less frequently than I did my younger. The last time would have been the previous Christmas. First we'd stopped doing presents, then we'd stopped the visits and the cards. The phone calls were the only thing we had left, a few awkward minutes grabbed some time between the Queen's Speech and the turkey.

"I just heard from Kevin," I said, quickly, as if eager to explain why I was breaking protocol and phoning him when there were no decorations up. "He said Mum's dead."

"Yes, I know," said Anthony. "He called."

"Oh," I said. "When was that?"

"Let me think," he said, and did. "Thursday."

I felt put out by that, and couldn't help but give a disappointed "Oh." And then a "he's only just phoned me," which sounded a bit pathetic and needy.

"We're brothers," he said. "Brothers are closer, aren't they?" And I thought, no, not really. You've never much liked Kevin, he was eight years younger than you and when we were kids that was too much of a gap, at best he'd been an irrelevance, at worst something you could be cruel to. I was quite certain Anthony didn't like Kevin. And I'd been pretty sure Kevin didn't like Anthony either.

"How did he sound to you?" I asked.

"How did he sound to *you*?"

"Well," I said, "he was pretty upset."

"Oh, for God's sake," said Anthony, "he was unbearable with me. Crying down the phone. He just has to get a grip. Did he cry for you?"

I slipped right back into the role I'd played when we were children, lying for Kevin, trying to protect him. "Not very much."

"I bet he did," said Anthony. "I bet he cried during the whole call. He has to get a grip. I mean, what is he now, twenty-eight? He has to get himself some sort of job, some sort of life, he can't be the baby forever. I said to him he should pull himself together, find a job, stop being so irresponsible."

"You didn't say all that to him on Thursday, did you?" I asked. "I mean, Mum had just died and everything . . ."

"Yeah, maybe I went a bit too far. But I'm right, Connie, you know I am. He was always Mum's favourite, right from the start she spoiled him. I think he'll be better off without her, stand on his own two feet. And no, I didn't say *that* to him on Thursday," as I began to interrupt, "I'm not totally insensitive." He thought for a bit. "All this grief," he said, "it's so ridiculous. All this wailing and gnashing of teeth. I shan't be that way when Mum goes, I tell you. I'll show a little more dignity."

I asked him what he meant.

"I've been through so much worse already," he reminded me. "It's nothing to lose a parent, you *expect* that. But my wife died, and she was so young, and *that's* difficult."

I'd bumped into Anthony's wife by accident out shopping only a few months ago. We'd had a coffee and a chat. She'd told me that getting away from Anthony was the best thing she'd ever done. "He means well," she'd said, "but, God, he's bitter." Of course, I hadn't told Anthony I'd seen her. It wouldn't be right.

"How's work?" I asked, changing the subject.

"It's all right," he said shortly, meaning it probably wasn't. Anthony worked as a beautician and hair stylist—and, in fact, wasn't gay, and resented the idea people thought he must be. He carried that resentment into work every day, his wife had told me, which is why all the women's faces he worked on always came out the other end looking so grumpy. As I say, bitter.

The change of conversation, the attempt at ordinary pleasantries, was a signal to both of us that this phone call had outlived its usefulness. Before I hung up, I told him what Kevin had said about it not being fair. "Well," said Anthony. "It isn't, is it?"

The next day after work I drove over to my parents' house. I'd been the only one of their children not to have moved far away, but I still didn't visit as often as I should have. I rang the bell, and Dad answered the door.

"Hi, Dad," I said. "How are you?"

"Oh, I'm fine," he said, and gave me a kiss. He let me in, took my coat, asked me how work was going.

"I heard about Mum," I said. "Kevin phoned me."

"Oh dear. Was he very upset?"

"He was a bit."

"Did he cry a lot?"

"Yes."

"Oh dear." Dad bit his lip. He'd never really known what to do about Kevin—he'd been Mum's favourite, not his. "Well, I suppose that's to be expected."

"Is Mum around?"

"Yes, of course," said Dad. "She's in the kitchen. I think she's making gingerbread men."

When I went into the kitchen, Mum looked happy enough. She was covered in flour, and wearing her favourite apron, one that Kevin had given her for Christmas a few years back. "Hello, sweetie," she said. "I'm making gingerbread men!"

"Yes, Dad told me."

"I think this lot are going to come out rather well." Mum only made gingerbread men when she was trying to avoid thinking about other things. The times we were going through our school exams, the time when Anthony was in hospital to have his tonsils out, that horrible month when she found out Dad was having an affair and for a while we all thought the marriage might be over . . . we'd all been drowning in gingerbread men back then.

"I heard about you and Kevin," I said.

She stopped dead in mid-bustle. Smoothed down her apron. "Yes," she said quietly, "I thought you must have."

"Leukaemia."

She nodded. "Very unpleasant. Is he all right? No, don't tell me. I'm better off not knowing."

There was quiet for a while. She managed a smile, but it was a little guilty, I think. Then clucked her tongue, said to herself, "Well, that's that over," and got back to her baking. I watched her for a bit.

"It must be hard for you," I said eventually. "Kevin was always your favourite, wasn't he?" It was meant to be sympathetic, not be an accusation of anything, but it all came out wrong.

"Your father and I didn't have favourites."

"Not Dad, maybe. But you did." I remembered the little story she'd once told us. How she'd always wanted a boy, more than anything in the world. But she'd got it a bit wrong with Anthony, he was her first child, she was awkward, maybe tried too hard. She knew she'd do better with her next one, but that had been a girl, me. So she'd given it another go, and out had popped another boy, her perfect boy, this time he was just right. And as we watched she'd lifted him in the air, because Kevin was still very young, and given him a kiss.

"God, did I tell you that? God, that's awful. I was joking, Connie. Sweetie, it was a joke." But it wasn't. And Anthony had known it, and I had known it, and by God, Kevin had certainly known it. "Poor Kevin," she said.

"He'll be all right."

She nodded briefly, went back to the oven.

"It just seems so cruel," I said suddenly, and my voice may have been a bit too loud. "The whole lot of it."

"Is there anyone special in your life yet?" she asked me. "Some man? You'd be so pretty if you tidied yourself up more. Put on a face, did something with your hair." But I didn't want to talk about that.

She gave me a gingerbread man, still warm from the oven. I bit off its head. It was too sweet, she'd put too much sugar in, she always put in too much sugar. "Nice?" she asked, and I nodded. "I wish you could take some of these to Kevin," she said with a sigh. "I know how much he loves them. They're his favourites."

I said nothing. Ate the rest of its body, torso and feet, just to be polite.

"Will you be going to my funeral?" she asked me. "Will you see Kevin there?"

"I doubt it," I said. "I doubt he'll even invite me. Why should he?"

But, in fact, Kevin did invite me. I was quite taken aback. But I checked at work, found out if I did some early shifts I could take the day off without eating up my holiday time, I was happy with that. When I got to the church I looked around for Anthony, but couldn't see him anywhere. With a little buzz of pride I realized that Kevin had invited me and not his elder brother, that I was favoured after all. It put me in a good mood for the whole service.

Mum had never been a religious person, and nor, I thought, had Kevin. But he stood up at the lectern and read some very nice verses surprisingly well. They were all about death and life and eternal love. I doubt he got the proper meaning across, but they certainly sounded very sad and moving. I told him so afterwards, and he thanked me for coming.

"It's a pretty good turn-out," he said. I looked around, but didn't recognize anybody. Friends of his, I supposed, or a part of my mother's life she'd shared with him not me.

"How are you holding up?" I asked. He nodded solemnly, as if this were an answer. He looked weak and vulnerable, but then he always looked weak and vulnerable. Right from the start he was the sort of person who invited you to protect him or to persecute him. Mum and I had protected—just about everybody else had gone the other way.

I remembered the way he was bullied at school; he'd always be coming home with a grazed knee, or his lunch money stolen, always crying. I'd decided to do something about it. One day I'd waited for the most regular of the bullies, laid into him with my fists, secured from him not only the money returned with interest but the promise he'd never bother my brother again. Kevin had been furious. From now on, he'd told me, crying, always crying, his life would be a living hell, the kid who needed his *sister* to protect him. "It'll be humiliating," he'd said. "I hate you."

Now we stood together, and I didn't know what to say to him, and he didn't know what to say to me. And I smiled kindly and took his hand and squeezed it, and he nodded solemnly once more, doing the whole orphan thing. Being so brave. And I felt a flash of Anthony's impatience, for God's sake, you're twenty-eight years old, and watched with disgust as he began to cry. "It'll be okay, sweetie," I said.

Mum's body was in an open coffin. She'd been made up and looked pretty, if a little exhausted. I suppose that's what the leukaemia does to you, it must really wear you out. She certainly looked older and feebler than the Mum I knew. I said you could see it had been a struggle for her, she was at peace now. And Kevin said he knew it was best for her, it was selfish to wish she was still alive, but he couldn't help it, he was selfish.

The body was cremated, and Kevin was told he'd be given an urn of her ashes. "Would you like some of them?" he asked me kindly. I thanked him, of course, but told him the ashes should be his.

"Have you seen her recently?" Kevin asked me in a hush. "I mean, is she all right?"

He shouldn't have asked, and he knew it. What could I say? "Mum's dead, Kevin," I told him. "They're putting her in an urn."

It was maybe a year and a half after that that Mum died for Anthony. There'd been a cyst, apparently, and everyone had assumed it had just been a trivial thing. But the cyst had grown and ripened and spread and felled Mum dead in her tracks. Thank God it had all been a lot quicker than the leukaemia. I sent Anthony a letter of condolence, and his thank you reply was very stiff and cool—but since everything Anthony ever wrote to me was stiff and cool, I read nothing untoward in that. And then, a few months later, he phoned me up and said he was unexpectedly in the area—could he buy me lunch?

There was a little Spanish place he said was his favourite, we could have tapas. And it struck me that only Anthony could have favourite restaurants for a part of the country he never visited. I made an effort before going to see him, washed my hair, put on make-up. I knew he wouldn't mean to, but he'd sit there critically and judge me, it was his job. I arrived and he was already there, drinking a glass of wine. He was immaculate, of course; he looked sleek and groomed and shiny, and I thought he'd probably plucked his eyebrows.

We automatically shook hands, then realized we were related to each other, and kissed cheeks.

"You look well," I said.

"So do you," he replied smoothly. And frowned. "But if I could give just a little advice . . . ?"

"If you want."

"Clear and simple is a good choice, keep it natural. But you can overdo simplicity, you know. You could stand to wear a little more make-up."

"I am wearing a little make-up. Look."

"I'm just saying. There's a pretty face under there, it just needs bringing out."

"Look. I've got lipstick on, and some mascara too. Look."

"All right. I'm just saying. It's just that the boyish look suits some, and not others. And you could stand to look a little more feminine."

We ordered some tapas. He spoke to the waiter as if he knew him.

"I'm sorry about Mum," I said. "How are you holding up?"

He thought about this, finished chewing, then plucked an olive stone from his mouth. "It's been very odd," he said. "I actually cried. Do you know, I actually cried." He shook his head, in some amusement. "It's true. I'd wake up, tears would be coming out of my eyes. Streaming. Most peculiar." He popped another olive into his mouth.

"Only to be expected," I said. "Mum being dead and everything."

"Why is it expected, do you think?" And he bored those eyes on to me. Yes, the eyebrows were plucked, I'm sure of it.

"I don't know," I floundered. "You'll never see her again."

"Oh, no, that's not it," he replied, and I felt put in my place. "I'm always prepared for that. Every time I'd see Mum or Dad, I'd always say goodbye to them as if for the last time."

"Right," I said.

"Because you just don't know, do you? What's around the corner. That comes of having a wife who's died so tragically. Even the two of us, when we say goodbye after lunch, I'll say it as if it's for the last time. Just to be sure."

"Right," I said.

"No, all the crying was something more *psychological* than that. More profound, from within me. You know, when I reached my eighteenth birthday, I thought, that's it, I'm an adult now. Things will change, I'll feel different. I'll *be* different. But I wasn't different at all. And then, when I got married. Now it'll happen, I said to myself, walking up the aisle. I took Nicola to the Algarve, and for the whole honeymoon I waited in vain for adulthood to kick in. With Mum's death, I think maybe I'm finally there. I feel, at last, that I'm a man."

I was going to say "Right" again, but stopped myself. I watched as he deliberately skewered another olive on to a stick, aiming exactly for the very centre.

"And my work's improved," he said. "I think there's a new maturity to it. Everybody says so. Well, most people anyway. The ones who count. They say that within my celebration of life there is now a recognition of death. It's very fulfilling. I mean," he went on, twisting that stick into the olive, twisting it on ever further, "there's still room for development. I'm interested to see what will happen to me when Dad dies. But, you know, I'm happy now," and he *did* look happy, actually, and that was a good thing, I supposed, "there's no rush, I can wait."

"You should call Kevin," I said. "Have you called Kevin? Now you've both lost Mum. It's something you should talk about."

"I must do that," he agreed.

"And we should keep in touch. You know. More than we do."

"We must."

He smiled at me indulgently then. "That's the thing about you," he said. "You always want to put people *right*. Make sure we're just a happy family."

"Oh," I said. "Do you think so?"

"You're just like Mum. You look a lot like her, you know. Or you could do. If you just took a bit of care, wore a bit of make-up, did a bit of work to your hair."

"Yes, you said."

"I could help you make more of yourself. I'd be glad to. Free of charge, of course. Well, save materials. Free labour."

And all I could think of was Mum lying there in that coffin, all made up to look pretty before they'd burned her, her hair neater than it had ever been in life, her cheeks pink and lips red to hide the pallor—because she must have been pale, mustn't she, underneath? And it was silly to care because it wasn't as if she were *my* Mum, not exactly. And I couldn't tell Anthony, because it wasn't exactly his Mum either.

"Thanks," I said. "I'm fine."

"I know you are, sweetie," he said. "I was just saying."

I offered to pay for the meal; it seemed only fair, since he was the one who was mourning. And he insisted we go dutch. We kissed on the cheeks as brother and sister would do, and then somehow ended up shaking hands anyway, that all went wrong somehow. And he said goodbye to me as if it were the last time he'd ever see me, and I wondered if it might be.

Mum and Dad died for each other at exactly the same time. There was a car crash. The policeman told me they wouldn't have felt anything.

I tried phoning Mum, because I knew she'd be upset. And when there was no answer I began to get worried. A few hours later she called me from a phone box. "It's a bit embarrassing," she said. "But obviously your father and I can't live together any more. Can I stay with you for a bit?" I picked her up in the car, and she flung her arms around me. "Oh God," she said. "It was horrible. Our heads passing through the windscreen like that. I don't care what that policeman said, it really hurt." She reached out and took my hand tightly; I couldn't steer the car properly when she did that, so I pulled over to the curb—I didn't want her dying in a car crash twice the same night. "You're the only one left, Connie," she said. "You're the only one left."

I don't have a big house, but it has a spare bedroom, and I'd naturally assumed it could easily accommodate any visitors should the need arise. But in all the years I'd lived there the need never had arisen, not even once. It was full of boxes: old school books, clothes I hadn't worn since I was a girl, dolls. I did my best to stick everything into the back of the wardrobes. "Thank you, sweetie," said Mum. "Oh, thank God for you, thank God for you." She took my face in her hands gently, stroked my cheeks. "I'm going to need more wardrobe space," she said.

For the next few days she didn't do very much. I'd go off to work in the morning, and by then she'd already be up, watching television, spread out on the sofa in her nightie. When I'd come home she'd still be there, watching repeats of soaps she'd already seen earlier that day. Sometimes she'd perk up and ask if she could help with anything—tidying up, making dinner. Then she'd cry with frustration when the vacuum cleaner wasn't the same model she was used to, or when the cutlery wasn't in the drawer she'd expected.

"Your father was a wonderful man," she'd tell me from time to time. "There never was a man more kind, more gentle, more tender."

Of course, I went to see Dad. It was no surprise he didn't want to know how Mum was getting on, I knew how awkward that would be. "I've found someone else," he said. "I'm happy." I didn't tell Mum, but she found out anyway. "That shit," she said, and began to sob. "He was just waiting for me to die. He couldn't keep his hands to himself even when I was alive."

It seemed churlish to mind Mum staying with me. She did her best. She tried to keep out of my way, not make any mess. And the insomnia wasn't her fault, and certainly she could hardly have crept around the sitting room any more quietly. But it was knowing she was there at all. I'd lie in bed at three in the morning, seething as I heard her tiptoe down the stairs, open cupboard doors in the kitchen so gently. Cry to herself in such a quiet selfless little sob.

One night I got up to confront her. She was in the kitchen making gingerbread men. There was flour everywhere, flour that I knew she'd have cleared up before morning. She started at me guiltily.

"I didn't disturb you, sweetie," she said. "I didn't, did I?"

"No," I answered truthfully. "What are you doing?"

I helped her to cut the little gingerbread figures, I put a smile on every one. "What do you think happens when we die?" she asked me suddenly.

"I don't know, Mum," I sighed.

"I mean, when you die to *everyone*. When there's no one around any more who knows who you are. No one who remembers you. Do you think we just vanish forever? I think we do. I think we must do. If there's not even a *memory* of who you were, what choice do you have?"

"I don't know."

"Oh, Connie," she said, and stroked my face with floury fingers. "Oh, sweetie. Who's going to remember you? How many people can you die for, when no one knows who you are? Oh, sweetie, what ever will become of you?"

One day I came home from work to find a man sitting with Mum on the sofa. He was in his early thirties, wore glasses. She told me she thought he was reasonably good looking, and I could do much worse than let him take me on a date. I didn't know what to do. I apologized to the man, and he said it was all right—in fact, he *was* rather lonely, and he wasn't doing anything that night; my mother had showed him a photograph of me when I was a little girl, and he appreciated I had aged in the mean time, but I was certainly his type. So he was up for the date if I was. He told me his name was Mike, and he shook my hand—then, as an afterthought, he kissed me on the cheek as well. I took Mum to one side and asked her where she'd found him, and she said it was the supermarket. For a moment I thought she meant she'd *bought* him there and I was confused, but Mum laughed and said, "No, sweetie, he's a greengrocer there. He was serving behind the counter. Seriously, sweetie," she whispered, confidentially, "he's a catch. You can never have too much fruit."

Mike waited as Mum took me to the bathroom, did my make-up, fluffed my hair. "You look so pretty," she cooed.

We went to a local restaurant. Mike didn't buy one of the expensive wines, but the one up from the one up from the house red. It was quite nice. I realized that life selling fruit in a supermarket was more interesting than I'd have imagined, and he had many funny anecdotes to tell me. I tried gamely with anecdotes of my own, and he was a gentleman and laughed at the end of each one. Then he took me home and shyly said he hoped we could do it all again some time soon. And I said okay, and gave him my phone number. Then Mum said, no, no, what's the point in that? "Don't spare my blushes!" she laughed. "I think you should go to bed together right now! Life is fleeting, and you never know when it'll be over. Just grab every chance you've got."

We made love, and it hurt a bit, but not as much as I was expecting. Mike said sorry, and I could see he really meant it, so I told him it didn't matter. I thought he might then have gone home, but he didn't. We lay there together for a while, not really knowing what to say. "Your Mum's nice," Mike ventured at last. I told him I was going to the toilet, and he said okay. And I asked if he wanted anything, a drink or anything, anything to eat, but he said he was okay.

Downstairs my Mum was making gingerbread men. She was very excited.

"I think he's lovely," she said. "He reminds me of your father. So kind, so gentle, so tender. But it's up to you, sweetie. What do you think?"

She went to the cupboard I used to keep my baked beans in, and took from it a plate. She plonked a gingerbread man on to it. "Here," she said. "Fresh from the oven."

I bit its head off. "You've been using salt again, Mum," I said.

"Have I?"

"Yes. It looks the same as sugar, but really, it's not."

But I ate the rest of the body, just to be polite. And I cried.

"Ssh," said Mum, and took me in her arms. "It's okay, Mummy's here. Mummy's here." And at that I couldn't help it, I cried all the louder. "You were always my favourite," she told me. "You were, baby. Sweet sweet baby. All the others have gone, but you stuck by me. I love you. And I'm never going to leave you, not ever."

I thanked her, said good night.

Mike was upstairs, no doubt waiting for me to come back to him. And Mum was downstairs, committing unspeakable acts in the kitchen. So there was nowhere for me but the garden. It was cold and I couldn't stop shivering. And I delivered up a prayer, of sorts, my first since I was a child. For anyone who might care to listen.

Oh God, I don't know how I'll react. How I'll mourn, whether I'll cry, whether I'll go numb. Whether it will be a passing fleeting moment, and then all will seem as it was. You can't know until it happens to you. But please, God, please. Let me know what it feels like. To find out how I'll be when my mother dies.

# ONE MORE
# BLOODY MIRACLE
## AFTER ANOTHER

My daughter Laura is pregnant. I wouldn't mind, but she's only two years old. Her little girl stomach is distended with the weight of her baby inside; she only started to walk nine months ago, and now she's having to prop herself up clinging to the walls, otherwise that big bulge in her tummy will topple her over. My wife is so happy about it. She's over the moon. She'd always wanted a child, she told me that clearly on our very first date—I'd asked what she was interested in, expecting her to come out with a hobby or her favourite TV programme, and she said just one thing—"Breeding." And now she gets to have a grandchild too, and she's already knitting it socks and booties. "I'm going to be a nanna," she says, "I'll be the best nanna in the world. It's a blessing." I'm not so sure. I wonder whether a family can be just a little too blessed.

My wife had loved being pregnant. She would show off about it to all her friends, and wear clothes that emphasized her swelling bump. And she was fascinated by the way her body would change daily; I'd come home from work sometimes and she'd be waiting for me, standing in the hallway, naked, all the better to show the latest instances of her metamorphosis, she'd point out the darkening of the areolas around her nipple, or the way her belly button had pushed out. And she'd delight in her glow; "Look, darling," she'd say, "I'm glowing, can you see how much I'm glowing?" Laura hasn't got the vocabulary to express herself properly yet, but it's clear she's not enjoying her pregnancy quite so much. She sighs as she heaves her bulk around her little playroom, sometimes she's in tears. My wife tries to be supportive, and is full of good advice about what to expect in the third trimester, and ways Laura can best nurture the foetus—but for all her good intentions, she often gets impatient with her. "You don't know how lucky you are!" she snaps at her. "Why, all around the world now there are women just *begging* to conceive, they're trying all sorts of unnatural methods with frozen sperm and sieves. And here you are, and it's fallen into your lap. And look at how you glow!" Sometimes my wife gets so angry with Laura she won't speak to her for days. Once I even saw her slap her. It wasn't too hard, though, and it was only across the face—she wouldn't do anything that might hurt that little baby within.

We didn't realize Laura was pregnant for a while. Try as hard as we can, we're not expert parents, and when at first our little daughter ballooned in weight we just thought we were feeding her too much. It wasn't until the morning sickness took hold of her that my wife recognized the symptoms; she had been taken exactly the same way, her daily vomiting both loud and copious, and how she'd gloried in it, her face rising up from that toilet bowl at me all full of smiles, "Darling, you're going to be a Daddy!" Laura would wake up each morning and have to toddle to the bathroom and throw up, and her mother would be there, pulling her hair back so it wouldn't get caught in the effluence, and stroking that hair, and telling her that she was going to be all right, and telling her how lucky she was. I'd suggested we take Laura to a doctor, but my wife was dead set against that— this was an unusual thing, we both knew that, and they'd want to run lots of lab tests on Laura like a lab rat, they'd take her away from us. "And this is *our* miracle," said my wife, "this is all *ours*." We hid Laura away. It wasn't as if it were that hard. Laura attended playgroup on Thursday mornings, and we merely cancelled that, my wife thought the other little girls there would be jealous. And it wasn't as if anyone ever visited, it wasn't as if we had many friends left, most of them had got bored with us when my wife had been expecting.

I suppose one of the first things I wondered about was who the father might be. After all, it wasn't as if Laura had much of a social life, I couldn't see there could be that many contenders. And I asked myself some searching questions, but I was pretty sure it wasn't me; I was able to reassure my wife on that score. Certainly, I loved Laura; I hadn't felt quite as involved with the whole pregnancy thing as my wife had been, truth to tell I'd been a little ambivalent. But when I saw my daughter for the first time—in that hospital bed—all bald and squalling—oh, I felt such a sudden rush of love for her, and I just wanted to pick her up in my arms, and the nurse gave her to me to hold, and I was terrified I'd break her, fragile little thing like that, and the nurse laughed and said she was stronger than she looked. And I'd held her tight then, and I've held her tight since, whenever that rush of love came over me I'd lift her out of her cot and give her the biggest cuddle—had I made her pregnant doing that? Had my love been too much? My wife thought it was unlikely, but I couldn't help worrying about it. The only alternative I could see was that it might have happened at the playgroup. There was a woman in charge of the playgroup, and all the assistants at the playgroup were women too, and only mothers ever collected their children from the playgroup, fathers were too busy—really, it was wall to wall women at the Shillingthorpe Nursery, I can assure you. But some of the toddlers left in care were boys, and I was a boy myself once, I know what naughty tricks boys can get up to. And I went along to the nursery one morning. I stood outside and watched them secretly through the window. None of the little boys seemed sexually boisterous, but I suppose you never can tell. I wondered whether Laura had led them on a bit, had she been flirty, had she flaunted herself, had she been a bit of a tramp?

But my wife had another, better explanation. "It'll be a virgin birth," she said. "You know, like that one in the Bible." And it was funny, because she'd never been a religious person before, we'd got married at a registry office at her suggestion. And there was that time my mother came over, and all she'd done was ask whether we were going to get Laura christened, and the way my wife had shouted at her, had told her to mind her own business, it had reduced my mother to tears, and I'm quite sure Mummy meant no harm. "No, I'm not having it," my wife said when I asked her to forgive my mother, "it's too late for her now, she had a child once and she's had her chance, she's not going to ruin my baby the way she ruined hers." But now my wife would study the Bible, looking for some way to make sense of this unexpected blessing bestowed upon us. "It stands to reason," she told me. "The first virgin birth was out of the stomach of a grown woman, in the sequel God would want to make it harder."

And one of the great joys of my wife's pregnancy had been choosing Laura's name together. We'd lie side by side in bed, and try different ones out for size, and we'd laugh at them all, we'd laugh so much back then. "Mary Marshall, Moira Marshall, Mattie Marshall." And we chose Laura in the end, because Laura was the name of my wife's late mother, and my wife's mother had died very young and my wife had never known her well but she was certain she'd have loved my wife very much, and she wanted her mother to be commemorated somehow because she thought it'd have meant the world to her. And because it was the name of the very prettiest of my ex-girlfriends. Though I didn't share that information with my wife. And, no, we didn't christen her, but how proud I was when we signed her name on the birth certificate, that name somehow made her real, it turned her into a person. And I had hoped that now there was a new baby in our lives we could do the same thing; we'd lie in bed, we'd say names, we'd laugh. But my wife wasn't having any of it. "He already has a name," she told me. "He's Jesus." And that did solemnify the mood somewhat, it was hard to laugh in bed when you knew that the messiah was growing inside your infant daughter's belly in the room just across the hall.

I wouldn't want to give you the impression that my wife wasn't kind to Laura, because she was, quite often; and she's the one who had to spend all day with her, after all, I got to go to the office, I got some escape from it. And Laura does moan too much. The way she complains about her cramps, you'd think no one had ever been pregnant before! You'd think her own mother herself hadn't been pregnant, and she'd had the cramps too, she was bent double with them, but she'd smiled through them, she'd welcomed them with open arms. But I feel sometimes that my wife doesn't talk to Laura very much, she just talks to the foetus inside her—and even when she addresses Laura by name, tells her to clean her teeth or pick up her toys, it's the bump she's looking at. And me too—I still pick her up, I still hold her in my arms, but I feel I'm faking it, I no longer quite get that rush of love, I try to, I look for it, but it's just out of reach. I hold Laura in my arms, and I can feel her little heart beating, but now I think, is it *her* heart? Or is it Jesus's? And it troubles me. Laura cries so much, and my wife feels no sympathy, she tells her she should be grateful to be the vessel of the Living Lord. And I don't know, I think there might be a less spiritual reason for this pregnancy, but I admit it, I can't feel much sympathy either. Because she's my little girl, and she's hurting, and I wouldn't want her hurting for the whole wide world—but deep down I wonder whether she might have brought this on herself, that she might just be a cheap slapper.

The cramps were so bad this morning. Laura came to our room, and she was crawling along the floor, it was as if she'd regressed all the way back to a one year old. And there was blood. I insisted we take her to the hospital, and at first my wife refused, but I could tell she was scared, and I was able to convince her to do the right thing. And the doctor inspected Laura. He took X-rays. And even then I wondered whether we'd got the symptoms wrong, that Laura wasn't pregnant, that our daughter was merely a fat kid who threw up. But no, he was amazed; he said he'd never seen anything like it; "Mr and Mrs Marshall, your little girl is with child." "Yes, yes," snapped my wife, "but what of the baby, is He all right, is He going to be okay?" The doctor smiled through his medical bemusement. "Everything's all right," he assured us, "the baby's fine. You're going to have a healthy granddaughter."

My wife didn't say much in the car, and Laura didn't either, she could tell her mother was cross. I tried to be cheerful. I said that maybe it'd be okay, or maybe the doctor had made a mistake. Until my wife retorted, "It's not going to be okay, Jesus wouldn't come back as a *girl*, would He? That's just ridiculous." So I said nothing for a bit. I then said, that maybe if the baby wasn't Jesus, we could all have some fun thinking up another name for it instead? But my wife said she didn't care, and Laura was still being quiet, and I had to admit I couldn't think of anything appropriate.

But when we got home there was a message on the answering machine. It was the doctor. And he sounded excited, and that wasn't a surprise, he'd sounded excited from the start, he hadn't had the time to get fed up with the pregnancy like we had. I nearly turned the message off, but my wife stopped me. And the doctor said they'd examined the X-rays of the foetus. And it was incredible. It was incredible, there were no words for it, it was incredible. Because she was pregnant. Not Laura—well, yes, Laura, but not just Laura—the foetus, the foetus inside her. The foetus was pregnant. Inside that little lump of life growing inside our daughter was another living lump littler still, not even a lump, no more than a speck, but it was thriving, and it was getting bigger, and it was human. And the doctor said he couldn't tell the gender of the speck for sure, but he thought it might have a penis. A new baby. A new miracle. And my wife standing there listening to the news, and tears rolling down her cheeks—and my daughter, feeling at her stomach involuntarily, tears streaming too—and I thought I knew why they were both crying, there was despair on my daughter's face, and I looked at my wife's, expecting only to see relief and awe, but no, no, that was despair, I think she had a new despair of her very own.— And I have to be honest, I felt a bit emotional as well.

Laura's still cramping badly, but we've given her painkillers, and we've closed the bedroom door so we can't hear her. And my wife and I are alone. And my wife has put on perfume, and she never wears perfume, not now. She's come to me, and she's smiling again, and I see the smile is made of lipstick. The smile is meant to be seductive, or maybe it's trying to be happy, or maybe it's just trying to look shy and awkward, and shy and awkward is its best bet. "I love you," she says. "I love you." And she kisses me, and we haven't kissed for a long time, and I'm a bit taken aback, I don't think of her as anything other than a mother anymore. "We've still got it, baby, haven't we?" comes the whisper in my ear. "We've still got it?" And she asks me to make love to her. "Fill me with your baby juice, we can be special too, can't we, we can be special too, tell me we can be special." How she glows. And it seems wrong, that we're competing with our own daughter like this, but my wife wants a baby of her own, and whatever she wants, that's what I try to give. And I do my best. I really do. I strain inside her and try to think baby thoughts, I try to will something new to life. But I keep thinking of my grandchild on her way, and of my great-grandchild too, and all the descendants that may be following after, and I'm sad to say, I can't help it, I droop a little, I droop, I feel so very old.

# FEATHERWEIGHT

He thought at first that she was dead. And that was terrible, of course—but what shocked him most was how dispassionate that made him feel. There was no anguish, no horror, he should be crying but clearly no tears were fighting to get out—and instead all there was this almost sick fascination. He'd never seen a corpse before. His mother had asked if he'd wanted to see his grandfather, all laid out for the funeral, and he was only twelve, and he really really didn't—and his father said that was okay, it was probably best Harry remembered Grandad the way he had been, funny and full of life, better not to spoil the memory—and Harry had quickly agreed, yes, that was the reason—but it wasn't that at all, it was a bloody dead body, and he worried that if he got too close it might wake up and say hello.

And now here there was a corpse, and it was less than three feet away, in the passenger seat behind him. And it was his *wife*, for God's sake, someone he knew so well—or, at least, better than anyone else in the world could, he could say that at least. And her head was twisted oddly, he'd never seen her quite at that angle before and she looked like someone he'd never really known at all, he'd never seen her face in a profile where her nose looked quite that enormous. And there was all the blood, of course. He wondered whether the tears were starting to come after all, he could sense a pricking at his eyes, and he thought it'd be such a *relief* if he could feel grief or shock or hysteria or something... when she swivelled that neck a little towards him, and out from a mouth thick with that blood came "Hello."

He was so astonished that for a moment he didn't reply, just goggled at her. She frowned.

"There's a funny taste in my mouth," she said.

"The blood," he suggested.

"What's that, darling?"

"There's a lot of blood," he said.

"Oh," she said. "Yes, that would make sense. Oh dear. I don't feel I'm in any pain, though. Are you in any pain?"

"No," he said. "I don't think so. I haven't tried to . . . move much, I . . ." He struggled for words. "I didn't get round to trying, actually. Actually, I thought you were dead."

"And I can't see very well either," she said.

"Oh," he said.

She blinked. Then blinked again. "No, won't go away. It's all very red."

"That'll be the blood," he said. "Again."

"Oh yes," she said. "Of course, the blood." She thought for a moment. "I'd wipe my eyes, but I can't seem to move my arms at all. I have still got arms, haven't I, darling?"

"I think so. I can see the right one, in any case."

"That's good. I do wonder, shouldn't I be a little more scared than this?"

"I was trying to work that out too. Why I wasn't more scared. Especially when I thought you were dead."

"Right . . . ?"

"And I concluded. That it was probably the shock."

"That could be it." She nodded, and that enormous nose nodded too, and so did the twisted neck, there they were, all nodding, it looked grotesque—"Still. All that blood! I must look a sight!"

She did, but he didn't care, Harry was just so relieved she was all right after all, and he didn't want to tell her that her little spate of nodding seemed to have left her head somewhat back to front. She yawned. "Well," she said. "I think I might take a little nap."

He wasn't sure that was a good idea, he thought that he should probably persuade her to stay awake. But she yawned again, and look!—she was perfectly all right, wasn't she, there was no pain, there was a lot of *blood*, yes, but no pain. "Just a little nap," she said. "I'll be with you again in a bit." She frowned. "Could you scratch my back for me, darling? It's itchy."

"I can't move."

"Oh, right. Okay. It's itchy, though. I'm allergic to feathers."

"To what, darling?"

"To feathers," she said. "The feathers are tickling me." And she nodded off.

His first plan had been to take her back to Venice. Venice had been where they'd honeymooned. And he thought that would be so romantic, one year on exactly, to return to Venice for their first anniversary. They could do everything they had before—hold hands in St Mark's Square, hold hands on board the vaporetti, toast each other with champagne in one of those restaurants by the Rialto. He was excited by the idea, and he was going to keep it a secret from Esther, surprise her on the day with plane tickets—but he *never* kept secrets from Esther, they told each other everything, it would just have seemed weird. And thank God he had told her, as it turned out. Because she said that although it was a lovely idea, and yes, it *was* very romantic, she didn't want to go back to Venice at all. Truth to tell, she'd found it a bit smelly, and very crowded, and *very* expensive; they'd done it once, why not see somewhere else? He felt a little hurt at first—hadn't she enjoyed the honeymoon then? She'd never said she hadn't at the time—and she reassured him, she'd *adored* the honeymoon. But not because of Venice, because of him, she'd adore any holiday anywhere, so long as he was part of the package. He liked that. She had a knack for saying the right thing, smoothing everything over.

Indeed, in one year of marriage they'd never yet had an argument. He sometimes wondered whether this were some kind of a record. He wanted to ask all his other married friends, how often do you argue, do you even argue at all?—just to see whether what he'd got with Esther was something really special. But he never did, he didn't want to rub anyone's noses in how happy he was, and besides, he didn't have the sorts of friends he could be that personal with. He didn't need to, he had Esther. Both he and Esther had developed a way in which they'd avoid confrontation—if a conversation was taking a wrong turning, Esther would usually send it on a detour without any apparent effort. Yes, he could find her irritating at times, and he was certain then that she must find him irritating too—and they could both give the odd warning growl if either were tired or stressed—but they'd never had anything close to a full blown row. That was something to be proud of. He called her his little diplomat! He said that she should be employed by the UN, she'd soon sort out all these conflicts they heard about on the news! And she'd laugh, and say that he clearly hadn't seen what she was like in the shop, she could really snap at some of those customers sometimes—she was only perfect around *him*. And he'd seen evidence of that, hadn't he? For example—on their wedding morning, when he wanted to see her, and all the bridesmaids were telling him not to go into the bedroom, *don't*, Harry, she's in a filthy temper!—but he went in anyway, and there she was in her dress, she was so beautiful, and she just beamed at him, and kissed him, and told him that she loved him, oh, how she loved him. She wasn't angry. She wasn't ever going to be angry with him. And that night they'd flown off to Venice, and they'd had a wonderful time.

So, not Venice then. (Maybe some other year. She nodded at that, said, "Maybe.") Where else should they spend their anniversary then? Esther suggested Scotland. Harry didn't much like the sound of that, it didn't sound particularly romantic, especially not compared to Venice. But she managed to persuade him. How about a holiday where they properly *explored* somewhere? Just took the car, and *drove*—a different hotel each night, free and easy, and whenever they wanted they could stop off at a little pub, or go for a ramble on the moors, or pop into a stately home? It'd be an adventure. The Watkins family had put their footprints in Italy, she said, and now they could leave them all over the Highlands! That did sound rather fun. He didn't want it to be *too* free and easy, mind you, they might end up with nowhere to stay for the night—but he did a lot of homework, booked them into seven different places in seven different parts of Scotland. The most they'd ever have to drive between them was eighty miles, he was sure they could manage that, and he showed her an itinerary he'd marked out on his atlas. She kissed him and told him how clever he was.

And especially for the holiday he decided to buy a satnav. He'd always rather fancied one, but couldn't justify it before—he knew his drive into work so well he could have done it with his eyes closed. He tried out the gadget, he put in the postcode of his office, and let it direct him there. It wasn't the route he'd have chosen, he was quite certain it was better to avoid the ring road altogether, but he loved that satnav voice, so gentle and yet so authoritative. "You have reached your destination," it'd say, and they'd chosen a funny way of getting there, but yes, they certainly had—and all told to him in a voice good enough to be off the telly. The first day of the holiday he set in the postcode to their first Scottish hotel; he packed the car with the suitcases; Esther sat in beside him on the passenger seat, smiled, and said, "Let's go." "The Watkinses are going to leave their footprints all over the Highlands!" he announced, and laughed. "Happy anniversary," said Esther. "I love you."

On the fourth day they stayed at their fourth stately home of the holiday a little too long, maybe; it was in the middle of nowhere, and their next hotel was also in the middle of nowhere, but it was in a completely different middle of nowhere. It was already getting dark, and there weren't many streetlights on those empty roads. Esther got a little drowsy, and said she was going to take a nap. And the satnav man hadn't said anything for a good fifteen minutes, so Harry knew he *must* be going in the right direction, and maybe Esther sleeping was making him a little drowsy too—but suddenly he realized that the smoothness of the road beneath him had gone, this was grass and field and *bushes*, for God's sake, and they were going down, and it was quite steep, and he kept thinking that they had to stop soon surely, he hadn't realized they were so high up in the first place!—and there were now branches whipping past the windows, and actual trees, and the car wasn't slowing down at all, and it only dawned on him then that they might really be in trouble. He had time to say "Esther," because stupidly he thought she might want to be awake to see all this, and then the mass of branches got denser still, and then there was sound, and he hadn't thought there'd been sound before, but suddenly there was an awful lot of it. He was flung forward towards the steering wheel, and then the seatbelt flung him right back where he had come from—and that was when he heard a snap, but he wasn't sure if it came from him, or from Esther, or just from the branches outside. And it was dark, but not yet dark enough that he couldn't see Esther still hadn't woken up, and that there was all that blood.

The front of the car had buckled. The satnav said, "Turn around when possible." Still clinging on to the crushed dashboard. Just the once, then it gave up the ghost.

He couldn't feel his legs. They were trapped under the dashboard. He hoped that was the reason. He tried to open the door, pushed against it hard, and the pain of the attempt nearly made him pass out. The door had been staved in. It was wrecked. He thought about the seatbelt. The pain that reaching it would cause. Later. He'd do that later. Getting out the mobile phone from his inside jacket pocket— not even the coat pocket, he'd have to bend his arm and get into the coat first and *then* into the jacket. . . . Later, later. Once the pain had stopped. Please, God, then.

Harry wished they'd gone to Venice. He was sure Venice had its own dangers. He supposed tourists were always drowning themselves in gondola-related accidents. But there were no roads to drive off in Venice.

He was woken by the sound of tapping at the window.

It wasn't so much the tapping that startled him. He'd assumed they'd be rescued sooner or later—it was true, they hadn't come off a main road, but someone would drive along it sooner or later, wouldn't they? It was on the *satnav route*, for God's sake.

What startled him was the realization he'd been asleep in the first place. The last thing he remembered was his misgivings about letting Esther nod off. And some valiant decision he'd made that whatever happened *he* wouldn't nod off, he'd watch over her, stand guard over her—*sit* guard over her, he'd protect her as best he could. As best he could when he himself couldn't move, when he hadn't yet dared worry about what might damage might have been done to him. What if he'd broken his legs? (What if he'd broken his spine?) And as soon as these thoughts swam into his head, he batted them out again—or at least buried them beneath the guilt (some valiant effort to protect Esther that had been, falling asleep like that!) and the relief that someone was there and he wouldn't need to feel guilt much longer. Someone was out there, tapping away at the window.

"Hey!" he called out. "Yes, we're in here! Yes, we're all right!" Though he didn't really know about that last bit.

It was now pitch black. He couldn't see Esther at all. He couldn't see whether she was even breathing. "It's all right, darling," he told her. "They've found us. We're safe now." Not thinking about that strange twisted neck she'd had, not about spines.

Another tattoo against the glass—tap, tap, tap. And he strained his head in the direction of the window, and it hurt, and he thought he heard something pop. But there was no one to be seen. Just a mass of branches, and the overwhelming night. Clearly the tapping was at the passenger window behind him.

It then occurred to him, in a flash of warm fear, that it was so dark that maybe their rescuer couldn't see in. That for all his tapping he might think the car was empty. That he might just give up tapping altogether, and disappear into the blackness. "We're in here!" he called out, louder. "We can't move! Don't go! Don't go!"

He knew immediately that he shouldn't have said don't go, have tempted fate like that. Because that's when the tapping stopped. "No!"

he shouted. "Come back!" But there was no more; he heard something that might have been a giggle, and that was it.

Maybe there hadn't been tapping at all. Maybe it was just the branches in the wind.

Maybe he was sleeping through the whole thing.

No, he decided forcefully, and he even said it out loud, "No." There had been a rhythm to the tapping; it had been someone trying to get his attention. And he wasn't asleep, he was in too much pain for that. His neck still screamed at him because of the strain of turning to the window. He chose to disregard the giggling.

The window tapper had gone to get help. He'd found the car, and couldn't do anything by himself. And quite right too, this tapper wasn't a doctor, was he? He could now picture who this tapper was, some sort of farmer probably, a Scottish farmer out walking his dog—and good for him, he wasn't trying to be heroic, he was going to call the *experts* in, if he'd tried to pull them out of the car without knowing what he was about he might have done more harm than good. Especially if there *was* something wrong with the spine (forget about the spine). Good for you, farmer, thought Harry, you very sensible Scotsman, you. Before too long there'd be an ambulance, and stretchers, and safety. If Harry closed his eyes now, and blocked out the pain—he could do it, it was just a matter of not *thinking* about it—if he went back to sleep, he wouldn't have to wait so long for them to arrive.

So he closed his eyes, and drifted away. And dreamed about farmers. And why farmers would giggle so shrilly like that.

The next time he opened his eyes there was sunlight. And Esther was awake, and staring straight at him.

He flinched at that. And then winced at his flinching, it sent a tremor of pain right through him. He was glad to see she was alive, of course. And conscious was a bonus. He hadn't just hadn't expected the full ugly reality of it.

He could now see her neck properly. And that in its contorted position all the wrinkles had all bunched up tight against each other, thick and wormy; it looked a little as if she were wearing an Elizabethan ruff. And there was blood, so much of it. It had dried now. He supposed that was a good sign, that the flow had been staunched somehow, that it wasn't still pumping out all over the Mini Metro. The dried blood cracked around the mouth and chin as she spoke.

"Good morning," she said.

"Good morning," he replied, and then automatically, ridiculously, "did you sleep well?"

She smirked at this, treated it as a deliberate joke. "Well, I'm sure the hotel would have been nicer."

"Yes," he said. And then, still being ridiculous, "I think we *nearly* got there, though. The satnav said we were about three miles off."

She didn't smirk this time. "I'm hungry," she said.

"We'll get out of this soon," he said.

"All right."

"Are you in pain?" he asked.

"No," she said. "Just the itching. The itching is horrible. You know."

"Yes," he said, although he didn't. "I'm in a fair amount of pain," he added, almost as an afterthought. "I don't think I can move."

"Not much point bothering with that hotel now," said Esther. "I say we move right on to the next, put it down as a bad lot."

He smiled. "Yes, all right."

"And I don't think we'll be doing a stately home today. Not like this. Besides, I think I've had my fill of stately homes. They're just houses, aren't they, with better furniture in? I don't care about any of that. I don't need better furniture, so long as I have you. Our own house, as simple as it might be, does me fine, darling. With you in it, darling."

"Yes," he said. "Darling, you do know we've been in a car crash. Don't you?" (And that you're covered in blood.)

"Of course I do," she said, and she sounded a bit testy. "I'm itchy, aren't I? I'm itching all over. The feathers." And then she smiled at him, a confrontation neatly avoided. Everything smoothed over. "You couldn't scratch my back, could you, darling? Really, the itching is *terrible*."

"No," he reminded her. "I can't move, can I?"

"Oh yes," she said.

"And I'm in pain."

"You said," she snapped, and she stuck out her bottom lip in something of a sulk. He wished she hadn't, it distorted her face all the more.

"I'm really sorry about all this," he said. "Driving us off the road. Getting us into all this. Ruining the holiday."

"Oh, darling," she said, and the lip was back in, and the sulk was gone. "I'm sure it wasn't your fault."

"I don't know what happened."

"I'm sure the holiday isn't ruined."

Harry laughed. "Well, it's not going too well! The car's a write-off!" He didn't like laughing. He stopped. "I'll get you out of this. I promise." He decided he wouldn't tell Esther about the rescue attempt, just in case it wasn't real, he couldn't entirely be sure what had actually happened back there in the pitch black. But he couldn't keep anything from Esther, it'd have been wrong, it'd have felt wrong. "Help is on its way. I saw a farmer last night. He went to get an ambulance."

If the Scottish farmer *were* real, then he wouldn't ever need to bend his arm to reach his mobile phone. The thought of his mobile phone suddenly made him sick with fear. His arm would snap. His arm would snap right off.

"A farmer?" she asked.

"A Scottish farmer," he said. "With a dog," he added.

"Oh."

They didn't say anything for a while. He smiled at her, she smiled at him. He felt a little embarrassed doing this after a minute or two—which was absurd, she was his wife, he shouldn't feel awkward around his wife. After a little while her eyes wandered away, began looking through him, behind him, for something which might be more interesting—and he was stung by that, just a little, as if he'd been dismissed somehow. And he was just about to turn his head away from her anyway, no matter how much it hurt, when he saw her suddenly shudder.

"The itch," she said. "Oh God!" And she tried to rub herself against the back of the seat, but she couldn't really do it, she could barely move. The most she could do was spasm a bit. Like a broken puppet trying to jerk itself into life—she looked pathetic, he actually wanted to laugh at the sight of her writhing there, he nearly did, and yet he felt such a pang of sympathy for her, his heart went out to her at that moment like no other. On her face was such childlike despair, *help me*, it said. And then: "Can't you scratch my fucking back?" she screamed. "What fucking use are you?"

He didn't think he'd ever heard her swear before. Not serious swears. Not 'fucking.' No. No, he hadn't. 'Frigging' a few times. That was it. Oh dear. Oh dear.

She breathed heavily, glaring at him. "Sorry," she said at last. But she didn't seem sorry. And then she closed her eyes.

And at last he could turn from her, without guilt, he *hadn't* looked away, he hadn't given up on her, in spite of everything he was still watching over her. And then he saw what Esther had been looking at behind his shoulder all that time.

Oddly enough, it wasn't the wings that caught his attention at first. Because you'd have thought the wings were the strangest thing. But no, it was the face, just the face. So round, so *perfectly* round, no, like a sphere, the head a complete sphere. You could have cut off that head and played football with it. And there was no blemish to the face, it was like this had come straight from the factory, newly minted, and every other face you had ever seen was like a crude copy of it, some cheap hack knock-off. The eyes were bright and large and very very deep, the nose a cute little pug. The cheeks were full and fat and fleshy, all puffed out.

But then Harry's eyes, of course, *were* drawn to the wings. There was only so long he could deny they were there. Large and white and jutting out of the shoulder blades. They gave occasional little flaps, as the perfect child bobbed about idly outside the car window. Creamy pale skin, a shock of bright yellow hair, and a bright yellow halo hovering above it—there was nothing to keep it there, it tilted independently of the head, sometimes at a rather rakish angle—it looked like someone had hammered a dinner tray into the skull with invisible nails. Little toes. Little fingers. Babies' fingers. And (because, yes, Harry did steal a look) there was nothing between the legs at all, the child's genitals had been smoothed out like it was a naked Action Man toy.

The little child smiled amiably at him. Then raised a knuckle. And tapped three times against the glass.

"What are you?"—which Harry knew was a pointless question, it was pretty bloody obvious what it was—and even the cherub rolled his eyes at that, but then smiled back as if to say, just kidding, no offence, no hard feelings.

The child seemed to imitate Harry's expressions, maybe he was sending him up a little—he'd put his head to one side like he did, he'd frown just the same, blink in astonishment, the whole parade. When Harry put his face close to the window it hurt, but he did it anyway—and the child put its head as close as it could too. There was just a sheet of glass between them. They could have puckered up, they could almost have kissed had they wanted! And at one point it seemed to Harry the child *did* pucker up those lips, but no, it was just taking in a breath, like a sigh, a hiss. "Can you understand me? Can you hear what I'm saying?" The child blinked in astonishment again, fluttered its wings a bit. "Can you get help?" And what did he expect, that it'd find a phone box and ring the emergency services, that it'd fly into the nearest police station? "Are you here to watch over us?"

And then the cherub opened its mouth. And it wasn't a sigh, it *was* a hiss. Hot breath stained the glass; Harry recoiled from it. And the teeth were so sharp, and there were so many, how could so many teeth fit into such a small mouth? And hiding such a dainty tongue too, just a little tongue, a *baby's* tongue. The child attacked the window, it gnawed on the glass with its fangs. Desperately, hungrily, the wings now flapping wild. It couldn't break through. It glared, those bright eyes now blazing with fury, and the hissing became seething, and then it was gone—with a screech it had flown away.

There was a scratch left streaked across the pane.

Harry sat back, hard, his heart thumping. It didn't hurt to do so. There was pain, but it was something distant now, his body had other things to worry about. And whilst it was still confused, before it could catch up—and before he could change his mind—he was lifting his arm, he was bending it, and *twisting it back on itself* (and it didn't snap, not at all), he was going for his coat, pulling at the zip, pulling it down hard, he was reaching inside the coat, reaching inside the jacket inside the coat, reaching inside the pocket inside the jacket inside the—and he had it, his fingers were brushing it, his fingers were gripping it, the phone, the mobile phone.

By the time he pulled it out his body had woken up to what he was trying to do. Oh no, it said, not allowed, and told him off with a flush of hot agony—but he was having none of that, not now. The phone was turned off. Of course it was. He stabbed at the pin number, got it right second time. "Come on, come on," he said. The phone gave a merry little tune as it lit up. He just hoped there was enough battery power.

There was enough battery power. What it didn't have was any network coverage. Not this far out in the Highlands! Not in one of the many middles of nowhere that Scotland seemed to offer. The signal bar was down to zero.

"No," he insisted, "no." And the body really didn't want him to do this, it was telling him it was a *very* bad idea, but Harry began to wave the phone about, trying to pick up any signal he could. By the time a bar showed, he was raising the phone above his head, and he was crying.

He stabbed at 999. The phone was too far away for him to hear whether there was any response. "Hello!" he shouted. "There's been a car crash! We've crashed the car. Help us! We're in . . . I don't know where we are. We're in Scotland. Scotland! Find us! Help!" And his arm was shaking with the pain, and he couldn't hold on any longer, and he dropped it, it clattered behind his seat to the floor. And at last he allowed himself a scream as he lowered his arm, and that scream felt good.

The scream didn't wake Esther. That was a good thing. At least she was sleeping soundly.

For a few minutes he let himself believe his message had been heard. That he'd held on to a signal for long enough. That the police had taken notice if he had. That they'd be able to track his position from the few seconds he'd given them. And then he just cried again, because really, why the hell shouldn't he?

He was interrupted by a voice. "Turn around when possible." His heart thumped again, and then he realized it was the satnav. It was that nice man from the satnav, the one who spoke well enough for telly. The display had lit up, and there was some attempt at finding a road, but they weren't on a road, were they? And Satnav was confused, poor thing, it couldn't work out what on earth was going on. "Turn around when possible," the satnav suggested again.

Harry had to laugh, really. He spoke to the satnav. It made him feel better to speak to someone. "I thought I'd heard the last of you!"

And then the satnav said, "Daddy."

And nothing else. Not for a while.

For the rest of the day he didn't see anything else of the child. He didn't see much else of Esther either; once in a while she seemed to surface from a sleep, and he'd ask her if she were all right. And sometimes she'd glare at him, and sometimes she'd smile kindly, and most often she wouldn't seem to know who he was at all. And he'd doze fitfully. At one point he jerked bolt upright in the night when he thought he heard tapping against the window—"No, go away!"—but he decided this time it really was the wind, because it soon stopped. Yes, the wind. Or the branches. Or a Scottish farmer this time, who can tell? Who can tell?

In the morning he woke to find, once again, Esther was looking straight at him. She was smiling. This was one of her smiling times.

"Good morning!" she said.

"Good morning," he replied. "How are you feeling?"

"I feel hungry," she said.

"I'm sure," he said. "We haven't eaten in ages."

She nodded at that.

Harry said, "The last time would have been at that stately home. You know, we had the cream tea. You gave me one of your scones."

She nodded at that.

Harry said, "I bet you regret that now. Eh? Giving me one of your scones!"

She nodded at that. Grinned.

"The itching's stopped," she declared. "Do you know, there was a time back there that I really thought it might drive me *mad*. Really, utterly loop the loop. But it's stopped now. Everything's okay."

"That's nice," he said. "I'm going to get you out of here, I promise."

"I don't care about that anymore," she said. "I'm very comfortable, thanks." She grinned again. He saw how puffed her cheeks were. He supposed her face had been bruised; he supposed there was a lot of dried blood in the mouth, distorting her features like that. "In fact," she said, "I feel as light as a feather."

"You're feeling all right?"

She nodded at that.

"Can you open the door?" he asked. She looked at him stupidly. "The door on your side. Can you open it? I can't open mine."

She shrugged, turned a little to the left, pulled at the handle. The door swung open. The air outside was cold and delicious.

"Can you go and get help?" he asked. She turned back to him, frowned. "I can't move," he said. "I can't get out. Can you get out?"

"Why would I want to do that?" she asked.

He didn't know what to say. She tilted her head to one side, waiting for an answer.

"Because you're hungry," he said.

She considered this. Then tutted. "I'm sure I'll find something in here," she said. "If I put my mind to it." And she reached for the door, reached right outside for it, then slammed it shut. And as she did so, Harry saw how his wife's back bulged. That there was a lump underneath her blouse, and it was moving, it *rippled*. And he saw where some of it had pushed a hole through the blouse, and he saw white, he saw feathers.

"Still a bit of growing to do, but the itching has stopped," she said. "But don't you worry about me, *I'll* be fine." She grinned again, and there were lots of teeth, there were too many teeth, weren't there? And then she yawned, and then she went back to sleep.

She didn't stir, not for hours. Not until the child came back. "Daddy," said the satnav, and it wasn't a child's voice, it was still the cultured man, calm and collected, as if he were about to navigate Harry over a roundabout. And there was the cherub!—all smiles, all teeth, his temper tantrum forgotten, bobbing about the window, even waving at Harry as if greeting an old friend. And, indeed, he'd brought friends with him, a whole party of them! Lots of little cherubs, it was impossible to tell how many, they would keep on bobbing so!—a dozen, maybe two dozen, who knows? And each of them had the same perfect face, the same spherical head, the same halos listing off the same gleaming hair. Tapping at the window for play, beating on the roof, beating at the door—laughing, *mostly* laughing, they wanted to get in but this was a game, they liked a challenge! Mostly laughing, though there was the odd shriek of frustration, the odd hiss, lots more scratches on the glass. One little cherub did something very bad-tempered with the radio aerial. Another little cherub punched an identical brother in the face in a dispute over the rear view mirror. They scampered all over the car, but there was no way in. It all reminded Harry of monkeys at a safari park. He'd never taken Esther to a safari park. He never would now. "Daddy Daddy," said the satnav. "Daddy Daddy," it kept on saying, emotionless, even cold—and the little children danced merrily outside.

"Oh, aren't they beautiful!" cooed Esther. She reached for the door. "Shall we let them in?"

"Please," said Harry. "Please. Don't."

"No. All right." And she closed her eyes again. "Just leaves more for me," she said.

For the first few days he was very hungry. Then one day he found he wasn't hungry at all. He doubted that was a good thing.

He understood that the cherubs were hungry too. Most of them had flown away, they'd decided that they weren't going to get into this particular sardine tin—but there were always one or two about, tapping away, ever more forlorn. Once in a while a cherub would turn to Harry, and pull its most innocent face, eyes all wide and Disney-dewed, it'd look so *sad*. It'd beg, it'd rub its naked belly with its baby fingers, and it'd cry. "Daddy," the satnav would say at such moments. But however winning their performance, the cherubs still looked fat and oily, and their puffy cheeks were glowing.

Harry supposed they probably were starving to death. But not before he would.

One day Harry woke up to find Esther was on top of him. "Good morning," she said to him, brightly. It should have been agony she was there, but she was as light as air, as light as a feather.

Her face was so very close to his, it was her hot breath that had roused him. Now unfurled, the wings stretched the breadth of the entire car. Her halo was grazing the roof. The wings twitched a little as she smiled down at him and bared her teeth.

"I love you," she said.

"I know you do."

"I want you to know that."

"I do know it."

"Do you love me too?"

"Yes," he said.

And she brought that head towards his—that now spherical head, he could still recognize Esther in the features, but this was probably Esther as a child, as a darling baby girl—she brought down that head, and he couldn't move from it, she could do whatever she wanted. She opened her mouth. She kissed the tip of his nose.

She sighed. "I'm so sorry, darling," she said.

"I'm sorry too."

"All the things we could have done together," she said. "All the places we could have been. Where would we have gone, darling?"

"I was thinking of Venice," said Harry. "We'd probably have gone back there one day."

"Yes," said Esther doubtfully.

"And we never saw Paris. Paris is lovely. We could have gone up the Eiffel Tower. And that's just Europe. We could have gone to America too."

"I didn't need to go anywhere," Esther told him. "You know that, don't you? I'd have been just as happy at home, so long as you were there with me."

"I know," he said.

"There's so much I wanted to share with you," she said. "My whole life. My whole life. When I was working at the shop, if anything funny happened during the day, I'd store it up to tell you. I'd just think, I can share that now. Share it with my *hubby*. And we've been robbed. We were given one year. Just one year. And I wanted *forever*."

"Safari parks," remembered Harry.

"What?"

"We never did a safari park either."

"I love you," she said.

"I know," he said.

Her eyes watered, they were all wide and Disney-dewed. "I want you to remember me the right way," she said. "Not covered with blood. Not mangled in a car crash. Remember me the way I was. Funny, I hope. Full of life. I don't want you to spoil the memory."

"Yes."

"I want you to move on. Live your life without me. Have the courage to do that."

"Yes. You're going to kill me, aren't you?"

She didn't deny it. "All the things we could have done together. All the children we could have had." And she gestured towards the single cherub now bobbing weakly against the window. "All the children."

"Our children," said Harry.

"Heaven is *filled* with our unborn children," said Esther. "Yours and mine. Yours and mine. Darling. Didn't you know that?" And her wings quivered at the thought.

She bent her head towards him again—but not yet, still not yet, another kiss, that's all, a loving kiss. "It won't be so bad," she said. "I promise. It itches at first, it itches like hell. But it stops. And then you'll be as light as air. As light as feathers."

She folded her wings with a tight snap. "I'm still getting used to that," she smiled. And she climbed off him, and sprawled back in her seat. The neck twisted, the limbs every which way—really, so ungainly. And she went to sleep. She'd taken to sleeping with her eyes open. Harry really wished she wouldn't, it gave him the creeps.

Another set of tappings at the window. Harry looked around in irritation. There was the last cherub. Mewling at him, rubbing his belly. Harry liked to think it was the same cherub that he'd first seen, that it had been loyal to him somehow. But of course, there was really no way to tell. Tapping again, begging. So hungry. "Daddy," said the satnav. "My son," said Harry. "Daddy." "My son."

Harry wound down the window a little way. And immediately the little boy got excited, started scrabbling through the gap with his fingers. "Just a minute," said Harry, and he laughed even—and he gave the handle another turn, and the effort made him wince with the pain, but what was that, he was used to that. "Easy does it," he said to the hungry child. "Easy does it." And he stuck his hand out of the car.

The first instinct of his baby son was not to bite, it was to nuzzle. It rubbed its face against Harry's hand, and it even purred, it was something like a purr. It was a good five seconds at least before it sank its fangs into flesh.

And then Harry had his hand around its throat. The cherub gave a little gulp of surprise. "Daddy?" asked the satnav. It blinked with astonishment, just as it had echoed Harry's own expressions when they'd first met, and Harry thought, I taught him that, *I taught my little boy.* And he squeezed hard. The fat little cheeks bulged even fatter, it looked as if the whole head was now a balloon about to pop. And then he pulled that little child to him as fast as he could—banging his head against the glass, thump, thump, *thump*, and the pain in his arm was appalling, but that was good, he *liked* the pain, he wanted it—thump one more time, and there was a crack, something broke, and the satnav said "Daddy," so calm, so matter-of-fact—and then never spoke again.

He wound the window down further. He pulled in his broken baby boy.

He discovered that its entire back was covered with the same feathers that made up the wings. So for the next half hour he had to pluck it.

The first bite was the hardest. Then it all got a lot easier.

"Darling," he said to Esther, but she wouldn't wake up. "Darling, I've got dinner for you." He hated the way she slept with her eyes open, just staring out sightless like that. And it wasn't her face anymore, it was the face of a cherub, of their dead son. "Please, you must eat this," he said, and put a little of the creamy white meat between her lips; it just fell out on to her chin. "Please," he said again, and this time it worked, it stayed in, she didn't wake up, but it stayed in, she was eating, that was the main thing.

He kissed her then, on the lips. And he tasted what would have been. And yes, they would have gone to a safari park, and no, they wouldn't have gone back to Venice, she'd have talked him out of it, but yes, America would have been all right. And yes, they would have had rows, real rows, once in a while, but that would have been okay, the marriage would have survived, it would all have been okay. And yes, children, yes.

When he pulled his lips from hers she'd been given her old face back. He was so relieved he felt like crying. Then he realized he already was.

The meat had revived him. Raw as it was, it was the best he had ever tasted. He could do anything. Nothing could stop him now.

He forced his legs free from under the dashboard, it hurt a lot. And then he undid his seatbelt, and that hurt too. He climbed his way to Esther's door, he had to climb over Esther, "sorry, darling," he said, as he accidentally kicked her head. He opened the door. He fell outside. He took in breaths of air.

"I'm not leaving you," he said to Esther. "I can see the life we're going to have together." And yes, the head was on a bit funny, but he could live with that. And she had wings, but he could pluck them. He could pluck them as he had his son's.

He probably had some broken bones, he'd have to find out. So he shouldn't have been able to pick up his wife in his arms. But her wings helped, she was so light.

And it was carrying Esther that he made his way up the embankment, up through the bushes and brambles, up towards the road. And it was easy, it was as if he were floating—he was with the woman he loved, and he always would be, he'd never let her go, and she was so light, she was as light as feathers, she was as light as air.

# Jason Zerrillo is an Annoying Prick

They'd all agreed, being with Jesus had been a right old laugh. He could get a bit holier-than-thou sometimes, obviously, but not with them, not with the Gang, just with the plebs, just with the ones Jesus sometimes referred to privately as 'Mr and Mrs Ordinary.' With the Gang he was different, he would clown around; sometimes, in the middle of one of those sermons of his, with him sounding so earnest and solemn, he'd catch their attention, and he'd pull a face or cross his eyes or stick out his tongue for a split second, as if to say, God-get-me-out-of-here! Or Can't-wait-'til-we-can-sink-a-few-beers. And at the beginning, before he got famous, the hours had been good too—it had been so *easy*, a little spot of preaching in the afternoon, then the rest of the day could be theirs. They could go fishing, they'd get tickets for a gladiator game maybe, they'd just kick around the synagogue eyeing up the girls, not doing much. Jesus wearing that big lazy grin of his—Jesus always took his work seriously, yeah, but he took his *play* seriously too, and there were nights he'd go to taverns and order these enormous jars of water, just plain tap water, then turn them into wine—and *fortified* wine too, these babies were forty percent proof, and then the Gang would carry the jars back to Jesus' place and then they'd lounge about and get pissed. And some nights, when he was in the right mood, or when they'd got him pissed enough most likely, they might get him to perform some miracles too. One night he turned Simon Peter into a goat. God, they'd laughed at that. God, even Simon Peter had seen the funny side eventually.

They all agreed, it had been such bloody fun, and it didn't much matter whether they *believed* too much, Jesus didn't ask them to justify their faith. He'd just say, go with the flow, don't embarrass me in public, you're my apostles now—and that was fair enough. Some of the stuff he came out with was nonsense, even Jesus knew that. The night after he'd said that 'meek shall inherit the earth' bit he'd laughed like a drain, he'd rolled his eyes with them afterwards when they went out on the lash and said he'd never live that one down.

It was hard to pinpoint the exact moment when it all just stopped being fun. But the Gang agreed, it was around the time Jason Zerrillo had appeared upon the scene. And it may not strictly have been Zerrillo's fault, but that didn't matter, no one liked Zerrillo, Zerrillo was an out and out tit.

He hadn't even seemed much of a problem at first. "I've got a surprise for you tonight!" said Jesus, "I want you to meet someone!" All the apostles had planned a quiet night in, a bit of manna, some fatted calves, an awful lot of wine. "This is Jason Zerrillo!" said Jesus. "And he's a mime artist!" And that made sense of his appearance, at least: he looked so peculiar with his painted white face, his white gloves, his top hat, his mouth a dab of black lipstick pulled into a knot. And Jason Zerrillo showed them what he could do—he walked against the wind, he pretended he was trapped in a box and kept patting against the invisible glass looking for a way out. "That's great," said Bartholomew, "yeah, that's a riot. Now, who wants a bevvy?" "No, no," said Jesus, "tonight we're going to have a bit of *culture*, Jason's got lots more, he's going to *perform* for us." And the Gang sort of shrugged, and they supposed that was all right, there wasn't a lot of culture in their lives, the closest they got was when Jude got really paralytic and started lighting his own farts. Jason did his whole repertoire for them: he pulled an imaginary rope, he walked up and down imaginary stairs, fought imaginary duels with imaginary rival mime artists. He watered and sniffed at imaginary flowers; he plucked one of the flowers out of the imaginary earth, then with a show of exaggerated bashfulness, eyes downcast, finger in mouth, presented it to Jesus. Jesus was entranced. "He's really very good, isn't he?" he said. "When I first saw him there in the crowd I thought he was having a fit, or needed exorcizing from demons. But he's actually quite a talent."

The show lasted nearly four hours. The apostles all agreed privately that the mime was very skilled, but that his act needed some judicious editing. "And I didn't buy that mute thing for a moment," added James, son of Zebedee. "I bet he could really talk if he wanted to."

The next night Jason Zerrillo was back again at their digs, waiting for them. "We going out on the tiles tonight, boss?" Simon the Zealot asked Jesus. "No," said Jesus, "I want to see some more mime." Simon said, "But we didn't go drinking last night either, I'm gasping!" And Jason Zerrillo smirked. He pulled his face into an uncanny imitation of Simon's, his eyes blubbing, bottom lip stuck out in a sulky pout, and he played an invisible violin. Jesus laughed. "You prick," raged Simon, "you want a knuckle sandwich?" And Simon advanced on the mime artist, but Jesus held up his hand. "Lo," said Jesus, "no branch can bear fruit by itself, it must remain in the vine. Neither can you bear fruit unless you remain in me." Simon the Zealot looked perplexed. "And what the hell's that supposed to mean?" he asked. But Jesus wouldn't say.

And from then on, wherever Jesus went, the mime was sure to follow. Every day that Jesus would cast some evil spirits into swine, say, or he'd heal lepers, or raise men from the dead, there too would be Jason Zerrillo. And before long he'd learned to mime *alongside* Jesus; so there he'd be, the son of God, performing these great miracles, and next to him for all to see was this white-faced clown, acting out the same scenes in exaggerated dumb show. The mime got quite as much applause as Jesus himself, but Jesus didn't care. "This is my true and trusted servant," he'd say, as he took his curtain call, "and I am well proud of him." And of an evening, when the apostles wanted to relax, now they'd have to sit through a replay of all the day's greatest hits, Jason Zerrillo fine tuning the adventures of the day and turning them into little comic episodes of thrills and hijinks without benefit of speech or props. His presentation of the parable of the Prodigal Son was quite masterly, and Jesus laughed, and shed a tear, and said that this was high art indeed, look, it worked on so *many* different levels.

The Gang met in secret. They all agreed they couldn't take it anymore. Someone would have to tell Jesus—they'd go on strike, either the mime went or they did. But there was no telling Jesus anything anymore. He wasn't the funny silly jokey preacher they'd once loved with the lazy smile and the wandering hands—he had fire in his eyes now, and his parables had become darker and more apocalyptic, and he'd sometimes lose his temper for no reason at all, there had been that time he'd knocked over all the tables in the temple, what on earth had that been all about? The only time Jesus seemed happy now, the only time they ever saw him smile, it was when he was watching his pet dance about and gurn and juggle invisible balls—Jesus would giggle until the tears rolled down his cheeks, Jesus wept. They knew that if they forced Jesus to choose, he wouldn't choose them. They had to take matters into their own hands.

And then there was that awful supper. Andrew had suggested they all go out for a meal, it was about time they had an evening out—and Jesus had agreed, much to their surprise, but of course he'd insisted he take his favourite toy with him. The mime bounced about and pulled faces, but for once Jesus wasn't amused, he just glowered into his food, nothing could cheer him up. At last he said, "One of you will betray me." And the apostles didn't know where to look—they'd *all* betrayed him, really, hadn't they? But it was for his own good, and he'd see that one day, it was an *intervention*, Jesus would feel so much his old self when he'd been cured of his mime artist addiction. They'd all drawn lots: Judas had been the one to go to the Romans, he'd shopped Jason Zerrillo, said he'd been calling himself King of the Jews or some such nonsense. Judas was given thirty pieces of silver; he told the rest of the Gang that that was nice, they could buy Jesus a nice present with it, that'd make him feel better, something fun, maybe a gift token, he could get whatever he wanted.

The Romans came with swords. And there was some confusion— it was dark—everyone was drunk—Jason Zerrillo was skulking in the shadows pretending to be a camel passing through the eye of a needle of all things. And the Romans got the wrong guy. That's what happened. They got the wrong guy, and when the apostles tried to explain the next day there were so many forms to fill in, so much red tape to wade through, really, they couldn't even begin to make sense of it.

Jesus was crucified. They nailed him to a cross at Golgotha. And the skies blackened with thunder, and Jesus cried out to the Lord. And the apostles stood by, awkward, guilty, God, was there egg on their faces! And in front of the cross, Jason Zerrillo danced about, his arms stuck out at right angles like a scarecrow, wincing at an imaginary crown of thorns, miming what it would feel like to have a spear stuck right into your side. And Jesus looked down on him, and said, "Not now. Really. Not now." And died.

The next day the Gang met up for coffee. They could barely look each other in the face for shame. "I don't think," said Matthew heavily, "there's going to be any way we can put this right." "All we can do," said James, son of Alphaeus, "is carry on his work. Do what he'd have wanted us to do. Whatever it takes." "Whatever it takes," they solemnly agreed, and they all shook hands, and they left the cafe, and went out to preach across the world, and never saw each other again.

The first apostle to be martyred was James, son of Zebedee. He was put to death by sword. And as he died, he looked up and he saw Jason Zerrillo there, contorting his white face into a comical display of agony, look how careless I've been, what's this sword doing sticking into my body? Andrew refused to be crucified in the same manner Jesus had been, he said he was unworthy, and so was killed in Patras with his legs splayed; in Rome, Simon Peter pleaded the same thing, and was nailed upon his cross upside down. And Jason Zerrillo was there for both of them, for Simon Peter he did a handstand. Bartholomew died in Armenia, Thomas in India, Jude the Farter died in Beirut—and in their final moments, as they reached out to Heaven and glory, out of the corners of their eyes there they'd spy Jason Zerrillo, imitating their deaths in dumb show. Was it mockery, or was it mercy of a kind? They couldn't be sure.

The last surviving apostle was John. John had never liked Jason Zerrillo either, but had held his tongue, he'd never spoken out against him. That said, in truth, he'd never spoken up for him either.

Ninety-four years old, living in exile in Patmos, he was hardly surprised when there was a knock at the door. He let Jason Zerrillo in. "I know why you're here," he said.

Jason Zerrillo said nothing.

"All my friends have died. I know that. They died bravely. They died for something greater than themselves. But that was never part of the deal, was it? That we had to die?"

Jason Zerrillo said nothing.

"I'll be dead soon," said John. "I have lived for longer than I should have, and seen things I would rather have not seen. Such terrible things. And then we'll all be dead, all the Gang, we will all be the same. Dead forever, and what difference does it make whether I died fixed to a cross or in a warm bed?"

Jason Zerrillo said nothing.

"I am not afraid to die," said John. "And when I do, when I see my friends, if they think they have anything to blame me for, I'll answer them. And when I see Jesus, if he blames me—then I'll know."

And Jason Zerrillo said nothing.

"I'm not afraid to die," insisted John. "If dying is such a great thing, what are you still doing clowning about? With your fucking white face and your fucking white gloves?"

Jason Zerrillo said nothing, because Jason Zerrillo never said anything, Jason Zerrillo was a mime.

"I am," said John—he whispered it—"I am afraid to die."

And Jason Zerrillo smiled with all his teeth, and left.

And John sat down and tried hard not to die. But it seemed to him that was like trying to escape from an invisible box, trying to walk against the wind.

# GRANNY'S GRINNING

Sarah didn't want the zombie, and she didn't know anyone else who did. Apart from Graham, of course, but he was only four, he wanted *everything*; his Christmas list to Santa had run to so many sheets of paper that Daddy had said that Santa would need to take out a second mortgage on his igloo to get that lot, and everyone had laughed, even though Graham didn't know what an igloo was, and Sarah was pretty sure that Santa didn't live in an igloo anyway. Sarah had tried to point out to her little brother why the zombies were rubbish. "Look," she said, showing him the picture in the catalogue, "there's nothing to a zombie. They're just the same as us. Except the skin is a bit greener, maybe. And the eyes have whitened a bit." But Graham said that zombies were cool because zombies ate people when they were hungry, and when Sarah scoffed Graham burst into tears like always, and Mummy told Sarah to leave Graham alone, he was allowed to like zombies if he wanted to. Sarah thought that if it was all about eating people, she'd rather have a the vampire: they sucked your blood for a start, which was so much neater somehow than just chomping down on someone's flesh—and Sharon Weekes said that she'd tried out a friend's vampire, and it was great, it wasn't just the obvious stuff like the teeth growing, but your lips swelled up, they got redder and richer and plump, and if you closed your eyes and rubbed them together it felt just the same as if a boy were kissing you. As if Sharon Weekes would know, Sharon Weekes was covered in spots, and no boy had ever kissed her, if you even so much as touched Sharon her face would explode—but you know, whatever, the rubbing lips thing still sounded great. Sarah hadn't written down on her Christmas list like Graham had done, she'd simply told Santa that she'd like the vampire, please. Just the vampire, not the mummy, or the werewolf, or the demon. And definitely not the zombie.

Even before Granny had decided to stay, Sarah knew that this Christmas was going to be different. Mummy and Daddy said that if she and Graham wanted such expensive toys, then they'd have to put up with just one present this year. Once upon a time they'd have had tons of presents, and the carpet beneath the Christmas tree would have been strewn with brightly wrapped parcels of different shapes and sizes, it'd have taken hours to open the lot. But that was before Daddy left his job because he wanted to "go it alone," before the credit crunch, before those late night arguments in the kitchen that Sarah wasn't supposed to hear. Graham groused a little about only getting one present, but Daddy said something about a second mortgage, and this time he didn't mention igloos, and this time nobody laughed. Usually the kitchen arguments were about money, but one night they were about Granny, and Sarah actually bothered to listen. "I thought she was staying with Sonia!" said Mummy. Sonia was Daddy's sister, and she had a sad smile, and ever since Uncle Jim had left her for someone less ugly she had lived alone. "She says she's fallen out with Sonia," said Daddy, "she's coming to spend Christmas with us instead." "Oh, for Christ's sake, *for Christ's sake*," said Mummy, and there was a banging of drawers. "Come on," said Daddy, "she's my Mummy, what was I supposed to say?" And then he added, "It might even work in our favour," and Mummy had said it better bloody well should, and then Sarah couldn't hear anymore, perhaps because they'd shut the kitchen door, perhaps because Mummy was crying again.

Most Christmases they'd spend on their own, just Sarah with Mummy and Daddy and Graham. And on Boxing Day they'd get into the car and drive down the motorway to see Granny and Granddad. Granny looked a little like Daddy, but older and slightly more feminine. And Granddad smelled of cigarettes even though he'd given up before Sarah was born. Granny and Granddad would give out presents, and Sarah and Graham would say thank you no matter what they got. And they'd have another Christmas meal, just like the day before, except this time the turkey would be drier, and there'd be brussels sprouts rather than sausages. There wouldn't be a Boxing Day like that again. Partly because on the way home last year Mummy had said she could never spend another Christmas like that, and it had taken all of Daddy's best efforts to calm her down in the Little Chef—but mostly, Sarah supposed, because Granddad was dead. That was bound to make a difference. They'd all been to the funeral, Sarah hadn't even missed school because it was during the summer holidays, and Graham had made a nuisance of himself during the service asking if Granddad was a ghost now and going to come back from the grave. And during the whole thing Granny had sat there on the pew, all by herself, she didn't want anyone sitting next to her, not even Aunt Sonia, and Aunt Sonia was her favourite. And she'd cried, tears were streaming down her face, and Sarah had never seen Granny like that before, her face was always set fast like granite, and now with all the tears it had become soft and fat and pulpy and just a little frightening.

Four days before Christmas Daddy brought home a tree. "One of Santa's elves coming through!" he laughed, as he lugged it into the sitting room. It was enormous, and Graham and Sarah loved it, its upper branches scraped against the ceiling, they couldn't have put the fairy on the top like usual, she'd have broken her spine. Graham and Sarah began to cover it with balls and tinsel and electric lights, and Mummy said, "How much did that cost? I thought the point was to be a bit more economical this year," and Daddy said he knew what he was doing, he knew how to play the situation. They were going to give Granny the best Christmas she'd ever had! And he asked everyone to listen carefully, and then told them that this was a very important Christmas, it was the first Granny would have without Granddad. And she was likely to be a bit sad, and maybe a bit grumpy, but they'd all have to make allowances. It was to be *her* Christmas this year, whatever she wanted, it was all about making Granny happy, Granny would get the biggest slice of turkey, Granny got to choose which James Bond film to watch in the afternoon, the one on BBC1 or the one on ITV. Could he count on Graham and Sarah for that? Could he count on them to play along? And they both said yes, and Daddy was so pleased, they were so good he'd put their presents under the tree right away. He fetched two parcels, the same size, the same shape, flat boxes, one wrapped in blue paper and the other in pink. "Now, no peeking until the big day!" he laughed, but Graham couldn't help it, he kept turning his present over and over, and shaking it, and wondering what was inside, was it a demon, was it a zombie? And Sarah had to get on with decorating the tree all by herself, but that was all right, Graham hadn't been much use, she did a better job with him out of the way.

And that was just the start of the work! The next few days were frantic! Mummy insisted that Granny come into a house as spotless and tidy as could be, that this time she wouldn't be able to find a thing wrong with it. And she made Sarah and Graham clean even the rooms that Granny wouldn't be seeing in the first place! It was all for Granny, that's what they were told, all for Granny—and if Graham sulked about that (and he did a little), Daddy said that one day someone close to *him* would die, and then *he* could have a special Christmas where everyone would run around after *him*, and Graham cheered up at that. On Christmas Eve Daddy said he was very proud of his children, and that he had a treat for them both. Early the next morning he'd be picking Granny up from her home in the country—it was a four and a half hour journey there and back, and that they'd been *so* good they were allowed to come along for the trip! Graham got very excited, and shouted a lot. And Mummy said that it was okay to take Graham, but she needed Sarah at home, there was still work for Sarah to do. And Sarah wasn't stupid, the idea of a long drive to Granny's didn't sound much like fun to her, but it had been offered as a treat, and it hurt her to be denied a treat. Daddy glared at Mummy, and Mummy glared right back, and for a thrilling moment Sarah thought they might have an argument—but they only *ever* did that in the kitchen, they still believed the kids didn't know—and then Daddy relaxed, and then laughed, and ruffled Graham's hair, and said it'd be a treat for the boys then, just the boys, and laughed once more. So that was all right.

First thing Christmas morning, still hours before sunrise, Daddy and Graham set off to fetch Granny. Graham was so sleepy he forgot to be excited. "Goodbye then!" said Daddy cheerily; "Goodbye," said Mummy, and then suddenly pulled him into a tight hug. "It'll all be all right," said Daddy. "Of course it will," said Mummy, "off you go!" She waved them off, and then turned to Sarah, who was waving along beside her. Mummy said, "We've only got a few hours to make everything perfect," and Sarah nodded, and went to the cupboard for the vacuum cleaner. "No, no," said Mummy, "to make *you* perfect. My perfect little girl." And Mummy took Sarah by the hand, and smiled at her kindly, and led her to her own bedroom. "We're going to make you such a pretty girl," said Mummy, "they'll all see how pretty you can be. You'll like that, won't you? You can wear your nice dress. You'd like your new dress. Won't you?" Sarah didn't like her new dress, it was hard to romp about playing a vampire in it, it was hard to play at *anything* in it, but Mummy was insistent. "And we'll give you some nice jewellery," she said. "This is a necklace of mine. It's pretty. It's gold. Do you like it? My Mummy gave it to me. Just as I'm now giving it to you. Do you remember my Mummy? Do you remember the Other Granny?"

Sarah didn't, but said that she did, and Mummy smiled. "She had some earrings too, shall we try you out with those? Shall we see what that's like?" And the earrings were much heavier than the plain studs Sarah was used to, they stretched her lobes out like chewing gum, they seemed to Sarah to stretch out her entire face. "Isn't that pretty?" said Mummy, and when Sarah said they hurt a bit, Mummy said she'd get used to it. Then Mummy took Sarah by the chin, and gave her a dab of lipstick—and Sarah never wore make-up, not like the girls who sat on the back row of the school bus, not even like Sharon Weekes, Mummy had always said it made them cheap. Sarah reminded her of this, and Mummy didn't reply, and so Sarah then asked if this was all for Granny, and Mummy said, "Yes, it's all for Granny," and then corrected herself, "it's for *all* of them, let's remind them what a pretty girl you are, what a pretty woman you could grow up to be. Always remember that you could have been a pretty woman." And then she wanted to give Sarah some nail varnish, nothing too much, nothing too red, just something clear and sparkling. But Sarah had had enough, she looked in the mirror and she didn't recognize the person looking back at her, she looked so much older, and greasy, and plastic, she looked just like Mummy. And tears were in her eyes, and she looked behind her reflection at Mummy's reflection, and there were tears in Mummy's eyes too—and Mummy said she was sorry, and took off the earrings, and wiped away the lipstick with a tissue. "I'm sorry," she said again, and said that Sarah needn't dress up if she didn't want to, it was her Christmas too, not just Granny's. And Sarah felt bad, and although she didn't much like the necklace she asked if she could keep it on, she lied and said it made her look pretty—and Mummy beamed a smile so wide, and gave her a hug, and said of course she could wear the necklace, anything for her darling, anything she wanted.

The first thing Granny said was, "I haven't brought you any presents, so don't expect any." "Come on in," said Daddy, laughing, "and make yourself at home!", and Granny sniffed as if she found that prospect particularly unappealing. "Hello, Mrs. Forbes," said Mummy. "Hello, Granny," said Sarah, and she felt the most extraordinary urge to curtsey. Graham trailed behind, unusually quiet, obviously quelled by a greater force than his own. "Can I get you some tea, Mrs. Forbes?" said Mummy. "We've got you all sorts, Earl Grey, Lapsang Souchong, Ceylon . . ." "I'd like some tea, not an interrogation," said Granny. She went into the lounge, and when she sat down in Daddy's armchair she sent all the scatter cushions tumbling, she didn't notice how carefully they'd been arranged and plumped. "Do you like the tree, Mummy?" Daddy asked, and Granny studied it briefly, and said it was too big, and she hoped he'd bought it on discount. Daddy started to say something about how the tree was just to keep the children happy, as if it were really their fault, but then Mummy arrived with the tea; Granny took her cup, sipped at it, and winced. "Would you like your presents, Mummy? We've got you presents." And at the mention of presents, Graham perked up: "Presents!" he said, "presents!" "Not your presents yet, old chap," laughed Daddy amiably, "Granny first, remember?" And Granny sighed and said she had no interest in presents, she could see nothing to celebrate—but she didn't want to spoil anyone else's fun, obviously, and so if they had presents to give her now would be as good a time to put up with them as any. Daddy had bought a few gifts, and labelled a couple from Sarah and Graham. It turned out that they'd bought Granny some perfume, "your favourite, isn't it?" asked Daddy, and "with their very own pocket money too!" "What use have I got in perfume now that Arthur's dead?" said Granny curtly. And tilted her face forwards so that Sarah and Graham could kiss it, by way of a thank you.

Graham was delighted with his werewolf suit. "Werewolf!" he shouted, and waving the box above his head tore around the sitting room in excitement. "And if you settle down, old chap," laughed Daddy, "you can try it on for size!" They took the cellophane off the box, removed the lid, and took out the instructions for use. The recommended age was ten and above, but as Daddy said, it was just a recommendation, and besides, there were plenty of adults there to supervise. There was a furry werewolf mask, furry werewolf slippers, and an entire furry werewolf body suit. Granny looked disapproving. "In my day, little boys didn't want to be werewolves," she said. "They wanted to be soldiers and train drivers." Graham put the mask over his face, and almost immediately they could all see how the fur seemed to grow in response—not only outwards, what would be the fun in that?, but inwards too, each tiny hair follicle burying itself deep within Graham's face, so you could really believe that all this fur had naturally come out of a little boy. With a crack the jaw elongated too, into something like a snout—it wasn't a full wolf's snout, of course not, this was only a toy, and you could see that the red raw gums inside that slavering mouth were a bit too rubbery to be real, but it was still effective enough for Granny to be impressed. "Goodness," she said. But that was nothing. When Daddy fastened the buckle around the suit, straight away Graham's entire body contorted in a manner that could only be described as feral. The spine snapped and popped as Graham grew bigger, and then it twisted and curved over, as if in protest that a creature on four legs should be supporting itself on two—the now warped spine bulged angrily under the fur. Graham gave a yelp. "Doesn't that hurt?" said Mummy, and Daddy said no, these toys were all the rage, all the kids loved them. Graham tried out his new body. He threw himself around the room, snarling in almost pantomime fashion, he got so carried away whipping his tail about he nearly knocked over the coffee table—and it didn't matter, everyone was laughing at the fun, even Sarah, even Granny. "He's a proper little beast, isn't he!" Granny said. "And you see, it's also educational," Daddy leapt in, "because Graham will learn so much more about animals this way, I bet this sends him straight to the library." Mummy said, "I wonder if he'll howl at the moon!" and Daddy said, "Well, of course he'll howl at the moon," and Granny said, "All wolves howl at the moon, even I know that," and Mummy looked crestfallen. "Silly Mummy," growled Graham.

From the first rip of the pink wrapping paper Sarah could see that she hadn't been given a vampire suit. But she hoped it wasn't a zombie, even when she could see the sickly green of the mask, the bloated liver spots, the word "Zombie!" far too proudly emblazoned upon the box. She thought it must be a mistake. And was about to say something, but when she looked up at her parents she saw they were beaming at her, encouraging, urging her on, urging her to open the lid, urging her to become one of the undead. So she smiled back, and she remembered not to make a fuss, that it was Granny's day—and hoped they'd kept the receipt so she could swap it for a vampire later. Daddy asked if he could give her a hand, and Sarah said she could manage, but he was helping her already, he'd already got out the zombie mask, he was already enveloping her whole face within it. He helped her with the zombie slippers, thick slabs of feet with overgrown toenails and peeling skin. He helped her with the suit, snapped the buckle. Sarah felt cold all around her, as if she'd just been dipped into a swimming pool—but it was dry inside this pool, as dry as dust, and the cold dry dust was inside her. And the surprise of it made her want to retch, but she caught herself, she swallowed it down, though there was no saliva in that swallow. Her face slumped, and bulged out a bit, like a huge spot just ready to be burst—and she felt heavier, like a sack, sodden—but sodden with what, there was no water, was there, no wetness at all, so what could she be sodden with? "Turn around!" said Daddy, and laughed, and she heard him with dead ears, and so she turned around, she lurched, the feet wouldn't let her walk properly, the body felt weighed down in all the wrong areas. Daddy laughed again, they all laughed at that, and Sarah tried to laugh too. She stuck out her arms in comic zombie fashion. "Grr," she said. Daddy's face was shining, Mummy looked just a little afraid. Granny was staring, she couldn't take her eyes off her. "Incredible," she breathed. And then she smiled, no, it wasn't a smile, she *grinned*. "Incredible." Graham had got bored watching, and had gone back to doing whatever it was that werewolves do around Christmas trees.

"And after all that excitement, roast turkey, with all the trimmings!" said Mummy. Sarah's stomach growled, though she hadn't known she was hungry. "Come on, children, toys away." "I think Sarah should wear her suit to dinner," said Granny. "I agree," said Daddy, "she's only just put it on." "All right," said Mummy. "Have it your own way. But not you, Graham. I don't want a werewolf at the dining table. I want my little boy." "That's not fair!" screamed Graham. "But werewolves don't have good table manners, darling," said Mummy. "You'll get turkey everywhere." So Graham began to cry, and it came out as a particularly plaintive howl, and he wouldn't take his werewolf off, he *wouldn't*, he wanted to live in his werewolf forever, and Mummy gave him a slap, just a little one, and it only made him howl all the more. "For God's sake, does it matter?" said Daddy, "let him be a werewolf if he wants to." "Fine," said Mummy, "they can be monsters then, let's *all* be monsters!" And then she smiled to show everyone she was happy really, she only sounded angry, really she was happy. Mummy scraped Graham's Christmas dinner into a bowl, and set it on to the floor. "Try and be careful, darling," she said, "remember how hard we worked to get this carpet clean? You'll sit at the table, won't you, Sarah? I don't know much about zombies, do zombies eat at the table?" "Sarah's sitting next to me," said Granny, and she grinned again, and her whole face lit up, she really had quite a nice face after all. And everyone cheered up at that, and it was a happy dinner, even though Granny didn't think the turkey was the best cut, and that the vegetables had been overcooked. Sarah coated her turkey with gravy, and with cranberry sauce, she even crushed then smeared peas into it just to give the meat a bit more juice—it was light and buttery, she knew, it looked so good on the fork, but no sooner had it passed her lips than the food seemed stale and ashen. "Would you pull my cracker, Sarah?" asked Granny brightly, and Sarah didn't want to, it was hard enough to grip the cutlery with those flaking hands. "Come on, Sarah," laughed Daddy, and so Sarah put down her knife and fork, and fumbled for the end of Granny's cracker, and hoped that when she pulled nothing terrible would happen—she'd got it into her head that her arm was hanging by a thread, just one firm yank and it'd come off. But it didn't—bang! went the cracker, Granny had won, she liked that, and she read out the joke, and everyone said they found it funny, and she even put on her paper hat. "I feel like the belle of the ball!" she said. "Dear me, I *am* enjoying myself!"

After dinner Granny and Sarah settled down on the sofa to watch the Bond movie. Mummy said she'd do the washing up, and she needed to clean the carpet too, she might be quite a while. And Daddy volunteered to help her, he said he'd seen this Bond already. Graham wanted to pee, so they'd let him out into the garden. So it was just Granny and Sarah sitting there, just the two of them, together. "I miss Arthur," Granny said during the title sequence. "Sonia tells me I need to get over it, but what does Sonia know about love?" Sarah had nothing to say to that. Sitting on the sofa was hard for her, she was top heavy and lolled to one side. She found though that she was able to reach for the buckle on her suit. She played with it, but her fingers were too thick, she couldn't get purchase. The first time Bond snogged a woman Granny reached for Sarah's hand. Sarah couldn't be sure whether it was Granny's hand or her own that felt so leathery. "Do you know how I met Arthur?" asked Granny. Sitting in her slumped position, Sarah could feel something metal jab into her, and realized it must be the necklace that Mummy had given her. It was buried somewhere underneath all this dead male flesh. "Arthur was already married. Did you know that? Does it shock you? But I just looked at him, and said to myself, I'm having that." And there was a funny smell too, thought Sarah, and she supposed that probably *was* her.

James Bond got himself into some scrapes, and then got out of them again using quips and extreme violence. Granny hadn't let go of Sarah's hand. "You know what love is? It's being prepared to let go of who you are. To change yourself entirely. Just for someone else's pleasure." The necklace was really rather sharp, but Sarah didn't mind, it felt *real*, and she tried to shift her body so it would cut into her all the more. Perhaps it would cut through the layers of skin on top of it, perhaps it would come poking out, and show that Sarah was hiding underneath! "Before I met him, Arthur was a husband. And a father. For me, he became a nothing. A nothing." With her free hand Sarah tried at the buckle again, this time there was a panic to it, she dug in her nails but only succeeded in tearing a couple off altogether. And she knew what that smell was, Sarah had thought it had been rotting, but it wasn't, it was old cigarette smoke. Daddy came in from the kitchen. "You two lovebirds getting along?" he said. And maybe even winked. James Bond made a joke about re-entry, and at that Granny gripped Sarah's hand so tightly that she thought it'd leave an imprint for sure. "I usually get what I want," Granny breathed. Sarah stole a look out of the window. In the frosted garden Graham had clubbed down a bird, and was now playing with its body. He'd throw it up into the air and catch it between his teeth. But he looked undecided too, as if he were wondering whether eating it might be taking things too far.

Graham had tired of the werewolf suit before his bedtime. He'd undone the belt all by himself, and left the suit in a pile on the floor. "I want a vampire!" he said. "Or a zombie!" Mummy and Daddy told him that maybe he could have another monster next Christmas, or on his birthday maybe. That wasn't good enough, and it wasn't until they suggested there might be discounted monsters in the January sales that he cheered up. He could be patient, he was a big boy. After he'd gone to bed, Granny said she wanted to turn in as well—it had been such a long day. "And thank you," she said, and looked at Sarah. "It's remarkable." Daddy said that she'd now understand why he'd asked for all those photographs; to get the resemblance just right there had been lots of special modifications, it hadn't been cheap, but he hoped it was a nice present? "The best I've ever had," said Granny. "And here's a little something for both of you." And she took out a cheque, scribbled a few zeroes on to it, and handed it over. She hoped this might see them through the recession. "And Merry Christmas!" she said gaily.

Granny stripped naked, and got into her nightie—but not so fast that Sarah wasn't able to take a good look at the full reality of her. She didn't think Granny's skin was very much different to the one she was wearing, the same lumps and bumps and peculiar crevasses, the same scratch marks and mottled specks. Hers was just slightly fresher. And as if Granny could read Sarah's mind, she told her to be a good boy and sit at the dressing table. "Just a little touch up," she said. "Nothing effeminate about it. Just to make you a little more you." She smeared a little rouge on to the cheeks, a dash of lipstick, mascara. "Can't do much with the eyeballs," Granny mused, "but I'll never know in the dark." And the preparations weren't just for Sarah. Granny sprayed behind both her ears from her new perfume bottle. "Just for you, darling," she said. "Your beautiful little gift." Sarah gestured towards the door, and Granny looked puzzled, then brightened. "Yes, you go and take a

267

tinkle. I'll be waiting, my sweet." But Sarah had nothing to tinkle, had she, didn't Granny realize there was no liquid inside her, didn't she realize she was composed of dust? Sarah lurched past the toilet, and downstairs to the sitting room where her parents were watching the repeat of the Queen's speech. They started when she came in. Both looked a little guilty. Sarah tried to find the words she wanted, and then how to say them at all, her tongue lay cold in her mouth. "Why me?" she managed finally.

Daddy said, "I loved him. He was a good man, he was a kind man." Mummy looked away altogether. Daddy went on, "You do see why it couldn't have been Graham, don't you? Why it had to be you?" And had Sarah been a werewolf like her brother, she might at that moment have torn out their throats, or clubbed them down with her paws. But she was a dead man, and a dead man who'd been good and kind. So she nodded briefly, then shuffled her way slowly back upstairs.

"Hold me," said Granny. Sarah didn't know how to, didn't know where to put her arms or her legs. She tried her best, but it was all such a tangle. Granny and Sarah lay side by side for a long time in the dark. Sarah tried to feel the necklace under her skin, but she couldn't, it had gone. That little symbol of whatever femininity she'd had was gone. She wondered if Granny was asleep. But then Granny said, "If only it were real. But it's not real. You're not real." She stroked Sarah's face. "Oh, my love," she whispered. "Oh, my poor dead love."

And something between Sarah's legs twitched. Something that had long rotted came to life, and slowly, weakly, struggled to attention. You're not real, Granny was still saying, and now she was crying, and Sarah thought of how Granny had looked that day at the funeral, her face all soggy and out of shape, and she felt a stab of pity for her—and that was *it*, the pity was the jolt it needed, there was something liquid in this body after all. "You're not real," Granny said. "I am real," he said, and he leaned across, and kissed her on the lips. And the lips beneath his weren't dry, they were plump, they were moist, and now he was chewing at her face, and she was chewing right back, like they wanted to eat each other, like they were so hungry they could just eat each other alive. Sharon Weekes was wrong, it was a stray thought that flashed through his mind, Sharon Weekes didn't know the half of it. This is what it's like, this is like kissing, this is like kissing a boy.

# ALICE THROUGH
## THE PLASTIC SHEET

Alan and Alice liked Barbara and Eric. Barbara and Eric were good neighbours. Barbara and Eric were quiet. Barbara and Eric never threw parties—or, at least, not *proper* parties, not the sort of parties with music and loud noise; they'd had a dinner party once, and Alan and Alice knew that because they'd been invited beforehand, inviting them had been such a good neighbourly thing for Barbara and Eric to do. And Alan and Alice had thanked Barbara and Eric, and said that it was a very nice gesture, but they wouldn't accept, all the same—they gave some polite reason or other, probably something about needing a babysitter for Bobby (although Bobby was a good boy, he didn't need a babysitter). But the real reason they didn't go was that they *didn't* know Barbara and Eric. They liked them, they liked them perfectly fine. They were good neighbours. But they didn't want them to be *friends*. As good neighbours, they worked. Good neighbours was good.

Barbara and Eric had a dog, but it was a quiet dog, it was just as quiet as Alan and Alice's own. They had two children, but they were grown-up children, and the three times a year the grown-up children visited Barbara and Eric (Christmas, both parents' birthdays) they did so without fuss or upheaval. Some weekends Alan would see Eric, out clearing leaves from the front garden, out mowing the lawn, and Alan might be out tending to his own lawn, and the two of them would recognize the mild coincidence of that, Eric might raise a hand in simple greeting over the fence and Alan would do the same in return; for her part, Alice might smile at Barbara in the supermarket. And when Barbara put the house up for sale, Alan and Alice didn't know why—"Hello!" said Alice cheerily one day when she saw Barbara at the checkout queue, "So, where are you off to then?" And Barbara had told her that Eric was dead, Eric had had a heart attack, Eric was *dead*— months ago now, and she couldn't bear the loneliness any longer, she worried quite honestly that the loneliness would drive her mad. And she'd broken down in tears right there in front of Alice. Shrill, with lots of noise, it wasn't like Barbara at all. And Alice said she was sorry, she offered Barbara her condolences, she offered Barbara her handkerchief, she said she and Alan had had no idea, "how dreadful!" and "we had no idea!" And later she told Alan she'd felt a bit embarrassed, how *could* they have had no idea? How could all that death and suffering being going on not thirty feet away without their knowing? She supposed they hadn't been especially good neighbours after all.

"We're going to miss them," said Alice, as the family gathered around—Alice, Alan, little Bobby, even the dog got in on the act—and peered through the curtains to watch the removal men take the last pieces of Barbara's life away.

"I suppose we will," said Alan. And let the curtains twitch back.

"They're never going to sell it like that," said Alan one night at dinner. Alan worked in sales, he was an expert on sales. He was pretty much Head of Sales really, or would have been had Old Man Ellis not nominally still been in charge, but Alan was pretty much *de facto* Head of Sales, even Ellis had said so, pretty much everyone accepted that. "The first rule of sales," said Alan, "is you have to let the consumers know you've something to sell in the first place. There's no point in being coy about it."

There was a "For Sale" sign stuck into the lawn of the house they all still thought of as Barbara and Eric's, but, as Alan said, it wasn't well displayed. It was positioned right beside the largest of the trees so it was permanently obscured by shadow; from the road you could barely see it at all. "It'll never sell," said Alan, and sliced into his potatoes with an air of smug finality—and it did the trick, this was certainly where the conversation ended, neither Alice nor Bobby nor the dog showed any inclination to contradict him.

Later that evening, Alan was giving Bobby a game of Super Champion Golf Masters IV on the Xbox, and Bobby was playing as Tiger Woods and Alan was playing as Jack Nicklaus but frankly would rather have played as Tiger Woods, but Bobby had been a good boy and had done his homework promptly and done the washing-up without being asked and was in consequence allowed first pick—and as all this was going on, Bobby said he had an idea. Alan said, well, champ, I'm all ears. And Bobby suggested that maybe he and his Daddy could move the "For Sale" sign away from the tree and into a more prominent position. That would help everybody, wouldn't it? Though he didn't use the word 'prominent.' And Alan thought about it as he made Jack Nicklaus putt, and then said that they really shouldn't bother; after all, wasn't it quite nice that they didn't have any neighbours, wasn't it nice that it was all so quiet? Wouldn't it be nice if no one moved in ever, couldn't it be their little secret? And Bobby shrugged, and said okay, and made par. Bobby was really a very kind and considerate child; Alan had been warned by his friends at work that children could start getting snippy when they got older, and Alan was watching out for it, but here was Bobby eight years old already and there was no sign of it so far. Bobby would say that playing golf with his father on the Xbox was the best part of his day, and Alan would like that, sometimes Alan was touched. What did his friends at work know anyway? Maybe Bobby would always be like this. Right then Alan decided he liked Bobby as a person, not just as a son but a Person in his own right—one day, when he was older, he looked forward to sharing a pint with him in a pub, men together, he'd be so much better company than his friends at work, he didn't like his friends much. He looked forward to playing golf with Bobby for real.

Anyway, Alan was wrong. The house was sold within the week.

The van arrived early in the morning, before Alan went to work, and stout uniformed men began unloading boxes and furniture on to the next door lawn. When Alan returned home nine hours later they were still at it; and Alice was *still* watching it all from behind the curtains. "You haven't been here all day, have you?" asked Alan, and Alice said, "Of course not!" and looked a bit cross. "Alan," she said, "there's so much *stuff*, how do they have so much stuff? How are they going to fit it all in the house?" "I'm hungry," said Bobby, and he sounded unusually plaintive—and the dog began to yip for food as well—"It's all right, champ," said Alan, "let's go and see what's in the fridge, shall we?"

After supper Alan went back to join Alice at the window. "They'll have to stop soon," said Alice. "It's getting dark. You can't go moving stuff in the dark. That makes no sense, does it? You won't be able to see what the stuff is."

Now the removal men were offloading from the van a green Chesterfield sofa. It was large and heavy, and the men struggled with it in the summer evening clamminess. At last it was out, and down—

and joined three other sofas on the lawn, just as big and cumbersome, all in different colours—one was black, one was burgundy, one was a beige so lurid it could hardly be called beige at all. All four of them were still covered in their protective plastic sheets, not a single sofa had ever been used.

"It's all been brand new," said Alice. "All the televisions, the washing machines, the hi-fi system. All still in their packaging. Isn't that peculiar?"

"I expect so," said Alan, "if you like. And what of our new neighbours themselves? What do they look like?"

"I haven't seen them yet," said Alice. "I keep on looking, but there's been no sign. I might," she admitted ruefully, "have missed them," and she turned to Alan for the first time since he'd come home, her eyes so full of apology as if she'd let him down somehow. Then she started, she realized she'd taken her eyes off the game, and back whirled her head towards the chink of opened curtain.

"Maybe," said Alice suddenly, "I should go over there."

"Why?"

"Maybe," Alice said, "I should take them a cup of sugar."

"What for?"

"It'd be the neighbourly thing to do."

"They probably have sugar," said Alan. "They have four sofas and, look, three widescreen TVs. Look."

"I'll take them some sugar," said Alice, and she tore herself away from the window, and hurried to the kitchen. Alan followed her. She poured the sugar into a cup—not one of the best cups—she wasn't offering them the cup to keep, the cup was merely a receptacle for the sugar, she wanted the cup back—but she didn't want any awkwardness, if the cup were to be accidentally sacrificed in the spirit of good neighbourliness then it was going to be a cup she didn't like all that much. And then, now appropriately armed, she went outside and up the driveway to the next door house. Alan watched her from the window. He was surprised to see that in the little time it had taken Alice to fetch the sugar that the removal van had gone; the lawn was bare; the garden was deserted; night had fallen. Alan saw Alice knock at the door. He saw Alice pause, then knock harder. He saw her bite her lip and chew it, it was what she always did when she couldn't make up her mind. Then she set the cup down gently, carefully, upon the welcome mat; she stood up, waited expectantly, as if that very act alone might have attracted the neighbours' attention.

"Can we play golf, Daddy?"

"Isn't it a bit late?"

"Please, Daddy."

"All right. Just for a little while."

"Can I be Tiger Woods again?"

At last Alice came home. "They weren't in," she said.

"So I gathered."

"I waited a bit, though."

"So I gathered."

She frowned. "Who are you tonight, Alan?"

"I'm Jack Nicklaus," said Alan.

"And I'm Tiger Woods," said Bobby.

Alice drifted back to the window. She gave a little cry of surprise that caused Alan to miss his stroke. "What?" he said.

"The cup," she said. "It's gone."

"Right," said Alan.

"They must have been in after all," said Alice. "How very rude. I wonder," she went on, and she pressed her hands hard against the window, as if she could force her way through it, be that tiny bit nearer, "I wonder what they're *like*."

Alan said, "I just wonder why you care."

They said no more about it, and when they went to bed Alice undressed silently, and went to sleep without saying good night. Alan wondered whether she was in a mood or not—but it was so hard to tell, she was usually pretty quiet in the bedroom, it had never been a place for noise or chat.

Theirs had never been a relationship based upon romance. Not even at the start, not oven on that first date. And for the first few years this had nagged at Alan a little, he suspected he was doing something wrong, missing out on something nice all his friends at work got. So he would take to giving Alice boxes of chocolates, sending her the odd bouquet of flowers every now and again. And Alice would eat the chocolates, and she'd put the flowers in a vase, and she'd do both readily enough, but never with any especial gratitude; indeed, sometimes she'd give him a look, *that* look, as if to say, "what do I want these for?" So he stopped.

Alan hadn't wanted a date anyway, not after Sandra, not after what Sandra had done to him and (he supposed) what he had done to her. But Tony had said to him one day, "You could do with a girlfriend, feller," and Alan respected Tony, Tony was very senior in sales, at that time Tony was pretty much the *de facto* head. Alan thought at first this was typical Tony banter, and Alan laughed along, but Tony assured him he was being very serious. "It shows stability of character, feller," he said. "It shows us you're somebody we can rely upon." And he recommended Alan try someone he knew, he recommended Alice, and so Alan gave Alice a call, and Alice suggested they meet for dinner that very Friday. Alan could come and pick her up, early would be best, there was an Italian restaurant she liked around the corner, close enough that if the date wasn't working to either of their advantages they could skip dessert and she could be back home without wasting the entire evening.

Alan dressed up for the date. He took a second set of clothes with him to the office, and at five o'clock got changed in the toilet. Alice had dressed up too; when she opened the door to him Alan noticed right away how immaculate her make-up was, nothing too much, nothing garish or extreme—and it took him a few long seconds to recover and look through the shininess and see the woman underneath. She looked him up and down. She nodded. She gave him a polite smile, and he gave one back, just as polite. He told her his name was Alan. She nodded again, fetched her coat.

As they were walking down the street to the restaurant, Alice suddenly stopped. It caught Alan up short, right in the middle of some smart observation he'd been making about the weather.

"Have you forgotten something?" he asked.

"Yes. No. Oh," she said, "oh." And looked him up and down again, and chewed at her lip. She looked quite distressed for a moment, and Alan felt a sudden desire to protect her, to assure her that everything would be okay. "Please don't take this the wrong way," she said.

"No, no . . ."

"But. Your tie."

"My tie?"

"It's just wrong. It doesn't go with that jacket at all."

"Oh," he said. And then, somewhat lamely, "It's my best tie."

"Would you mind?" she asked. "I'm sorry. Would you mind if? We went back? I have ties. I have a better tie for you."

"Oh. Well. If you'd prefer."

"I would."

"If it means that much to you."

"It does."

"All right then." And they turned around and walked back to the house. Alan resumed his weather remark from where he'd left off, but he soon stopped, his heart really wasn't in it.

"You wait down here," Alice said. "Make yourself at home. I won't be a moment." And she went upstairs. Alan looked around the sitting room. It was pretty. The wallpaper was a woman's wallpaper, but quite nice. Everything was clean and ordered and well vacuumed, and there was the smell of recent polish, and Alan thought to himself that he could get used to that.

"Here," said Alice. And she was smiling, and it was proper smiling this time, there was a warmth to it. "Try this one." She held out to him a tie, quite formally, draped over her arm. It was pure black. Alan put it on, taking off his own tie with stripes. Alice gave him an inspection.

"Yes," she said. "Yes. Oh. Oh. Just wait," and then she went back upstairs. This time she came down with a jacket, and a shirt, and some shoes. "Try these," she said, "these will go with the tie." And she was smiling all over now, her face was one big beaming smile, and Alan couldn't help but beam back, and he did as he was told.

"Why do you have all these clothes?" he asked, and she stopped smiling, and gave a sort of shrug.

She didn't smile again for the rest of the evening. The moment had been lost. He had lasagne, she fettuccini. The lasagne took longer to cook than the fettuccini, and that kept her waiting, and he felt a bit guilty. She didn't respond to his conversation; his small talk was too small, he realized, and he longed suddenly for Sandra with whom he could have talked about *anything*, even if there sometimes had been shouting and swearing included, and though the restaurant was quite busy and the tables squashed too close together Alan felt desperately lonely. He didn't expect Alice would want dessert. She did. She ordered tiramisu. Alan was so surprised that he ordered tiramisu as well, even though he didn't like tiramisu.

And when she had devoured the tiramisu, after she had consumed it deliberately and precisely, Alice laid down her dessert spoon and examined Alan quite intently. She chewed her lip. "I cannot decide," she said, at last. "Whether we're going to be friends or not. I can't work you out."

And Alan said something about how he hoped they'd be friends, and she laughed at that, shook her head.

He paid for the meal; she let him. He walked her home, and neither of them said a word. He pretended they were both enjoying the still of the night. "You'd better come in," she said. He supposed this was so he could retrieve his own clothes. But as soon as the front door was closed behind them she tore into him, she ripped off his tie, his jacket, began to unbutton his shirt. Then she grabbed at the trousers, and Alan suddenly thought, the trousers are *mine*, she's at last touching something that's *me*.

And he knew then that she would look after him. That she'd make sure he looked good for the office and wore the right things, that she cared, she actually *cared* about him, that somebody out in the whole wide world was prepared to do that. She proposed to him on their fourth date, and he could see no reason to refuse. He asked Tony to be his best man, and Tony said yes, and although asking Tony was a good career move it wasn't just that, Alan genuinely felt quite grateful his boss had played matchmaker. It was during the best man speech that Tony announced Alan's promotion. Alan and Alice had a son called Bobby, and the way he was conceived wasn't especially romantic either, but Alan admired the way Alice took all those vitamins and boosters to facilitate the chances of pregnancy once she'd decided it was time they had a baby. And they all moved to a bigger house, and the neighbours were nice and quiet and elderly. And Bobby was bought a dog when he was deemed old enough to take care of it. And the sex between Alan and Alice swiftly became more sober, more manageable, and ultimately more for special occasions, and that was a good thing, a Good Thing, and Alan only very rarely thought of Sandra at all. And Tony, Tony was long dead, Tony had died years ago, Alan took his job and the power that went with it, Alan very rarely now thought of Tony either.

---

By the time Alan got home from work he was already in a bad mood. Sales were down, and that of course was nonsense; there were more and more people in the world, and people needed more and more Stuff, and Stuff just happened to be what they were selling. Impressing upon his workers the logic of this had exhausted him. As *de facto* head, he felt responsible for their incompetence.

"They're having a party," said Alice, the moment he closed the door.

"Who's having a party?"

"The neighbours. Housewarming, I bet. And they didn't invite us."

Alan began to reply to that, but Alice shushed him. She raised a finger for silence. "Listen," she mouthed. So he did. And yes, he supposed it was true, he could hear the beat of distant music.

"Why would they invite us? They don't know us."

"That's right, Alan, take their side. All I know is . . . that what they're doing is *invasive*. I feel *invaded*. How long's this music going on for? What if we can't sleep?"

"It isn't very loud," said Alan.

"What if Bobby can't sleep?"

"I'll be able to sleep," said Bobby, cheerfully.

"It's like an *invasion*," said Alice. "And I think you should go over there, and ask them to turn it down."

"It's still early," said Alan. "If the music is still playing later. Then. Then we'll see."

The family ate their dinner in silence. Silence, except for the bass thumping from next door. Alice deliberately didn't mention it, but Alan was annoyed to hear she was right, it *was* getting louder, and it *was* invasive. There was a snatch of something familiar about the music, but he couldn't place it, the melody was smothered by the thump. Alan tried to talk, he hoped that some dinner conversation would drown out the neighbours, or at the very least distract him a bit. He would have liked to have told his family about his day, about the slump in sales, but he knew they wouldn't be interested. "What did you learn at school today, Bobby?" he asked at last—"Give me one fact you learned," and Bobby promptly gave him the date for the Battle of Naseby. There wasn't much to add to that. "Hey, good boy," said Alan, relieved to see the dog slouch past the open doorway, "hey, come here, come here, boy." The dog trotted closer, but when he saw that Alan had no intention of feeding him anything, turned right round and trotted away again.

"I bet the music will be off by nine o'clock," said Alan. "That's the watershed. Everyone knows that."

Bobby did the washing-up, and so as a treat was allowed to be Tiger Woods 'til bedtime. Alan enjoyed concentrating on golf for a while; he almost persuaded himself he couldn't hear the beat of music getting louder and thicker and uglier, couldn't hear the pointed sighs of despair from his wife.

"It's gone nine o'clock," Alice said at last. "You said they'd have stopped by now."

"I said they might have."

"Bobby has to go to bed. Bobby, will you need ear plugs?"

"I don't need ear plugs," said Bobby. "I'm fine. I kind of like it. Night, Mummy. Night, Daddy."

Alan and Alice watched television for a while.

"There's a child here trying to sleep!" Alice suddenly cried, and she didn't even wait for a commercial break. "That's what I don't understand! How they can just ignore that!"

"They don't know we've got a child," said Alan.

"They didn't bother to ask. It's gone ten o'clock."

"I know."

"Next, it'll be eleven. Eleven!"

"Yes, I know."

The music never stopped. There was never a pause when one song ended, and another waited to begin. Alan idly wondered how they managed to do that. Was it just lots of little songs mashed into one unending paste, or were his neighbours simply playing the longest song in the world?

At last Alan and Alice went to bed. Alice used the bathroom first. Alan got undressed in the bedroom. At first he thought the music was quieter in the bedroom, and that was good, that was a relief. But then he realized it wasn't quieter, it was just different—and this different, if anything, was louder. He heard Alice spit out her toothpaste, and she really spat, she really went for it. They swapped positions, bedroom out, bathroom in, and he brushed his teeth as well. He thought he saw the mirror reverberate to the sound of the beat, but he had to really stare at it to check, and he wasn't sure whether it was just the effect of his head moving as he breathed. He got into bed beside Alice. She had her eyes screwed up tight, not wanting to look at him, not wanting to let in the world. He turned off the light.

As soon as the red neon of the clock radio turned midnight, that very second, Alice said, "That's enough."

"Yes."

"You have to do something now."

"All right." Alan turned on the bedside lamp. He put on his dressing gown, his slippers.

"Tell me what you're going to say to them," said Alice.

"Um. Please turn the music down?"

"Ask them to turn the music *off*."

"I will."

"Down isn't good enough."

"All right."

"And be firm."

"Yes." He went towards the door.

"You can't go out like that," she said. "Not in your pyjamas."

"But I've just been woken up . . ."

"It sends entirely the wrong message," said Alice. "It robs you of any authority. You should look smart, formal even. Wait. Wait." She got up, looked through the wardrobe. She handed him a jacket, a freshly ironed shirt. "This will do," she said. She smiled as he put the clothes on, she was enjoying this. "Now, go. And whilst you're there, get me my cup back."

He stepped outside into the night. The air was still so clammy, but there was a welcome breeze to it, and Alan closed his eyes and drank it in and *enjoyed* it; he wished he was still wearing his pyjamas, he'd have loved to have felt it properly against his skin. He could feel the sweat already beginning to pool behind the layers of his suit, and rebelliously he loosened his tie—

And listened. Because he could now hear what the music was, and it wasn't aggressive, it posed no threat, it was charming, charming. And he felt the urge to go back inside, go and fetch Alice—yes, and Bobby too, wake him up, wake him and the dog, bring them all out for this. How much we take it for granted, thought Alan, when it plays on every television ad, when it's pumped into every department store, when it's allowed to define just one little month of the year, when it sells *stuff*— you get sick of it, or you screen it out—but now, *here*, in the middle of a July heat wave, how incongruous it sounds, how *nostalgic*. Memories of days long ago, when he was a child, when his mother was still alive, when his father still talked to him—and he felt his eyes pricking with happy tears, he should rush inside, get his family whilst the music lasted, this was a treat. But he didn't go back inside. He didn't want his family there. He didn't want them, and the thought of that surprised him, and hurt him a bit, and somehow made him lighter too. And he stood on his porch, and listened, and basked in the little breeze he could feel, basked in the sound of 'Hark the Herald Angels Sing' as it segued seamlessly into 'Santa Claus is Coming to Town.'

But he knew Alice would be watching him. She'd be watching from behind the curtains. Watching and waiting. So he set his face into the proper authoritative pose, he straightened his tie again. And he marched down the garden path, out on to the pavement, through the next door gate, into strangers' territory.

There was no light visible from the house. All the curtains were closed. It looked as if everyone had gone to bed—no, more than that, it looked as if the house were deserted, as if it had been long ago abandoned and no one had lived in there for years and no one ever would again. It looked like a dead place. And he nearly turned back—not out of fear, Good God, no—but because it was ridiculous to think that such music could be coming out of a house like that. But it was, it was.

The mat in front of the house said 'Welcome' upon it. Alan stood to one side of it; he didn't want to be accused of accepting even the smallest part of their hospitality. He knocked on the door—gently, very gently, because he didn't want to wake the household up. Then he realized how stupid that was; he lifted the knocker high, he let it swing.

He knocked like this for a little while. There was no answer. He felt like an idiot, knocking away, in the middle of the night, dressed like he was going to a business seminar, and no one paying him any attention. He stooped down to the letterbox, lifted the flap, called through. He felt a cold draft from it—they must have had their air conditioning on. "Hello?" he called. "Hello? Is there anyone there?" He hated how weak and anxious his voice sounded. "Hello? Could you turn the music down a little? Hello?" You idiot.

He tried knocking again. He then tried knocking whilst calling through the letterbox at the same time. "Please!" he cried. "I've got a family and they can't sleep! Really, you're being a little selfish! And, and. And if you don't quieten down, I'll . . ."

Alan had no idea how to finish that sentence, so it was just as well that at that very moment the music switched off. The sudden silence was numbing. He blinked in it.

"Oh," he said. "Well, thank you. Thank you, that's very kind! Sorry to be a nuisance, we don't want to be . . . But it was past midnight and I . . . Well. Well, welcome to the neighbourhood!"

With that he eased the letterbox back into position, gently teasing it closed with his fingers so it wouldn't make any unwelcome sound. And he left their porch, walked up their driveway. He turned around, and the house was still so dark, and the curtains still drawn—and he doubted anyone could see him, but nevertheless he gave a friendly neighbourly wave.

The sound that burst out of that house a few seconds later almost knocked him off his feet. It couldn't have been loud enough to have done that—not really—that was silly—but the sudden blast of it frightened him, and he did stagger, he did, he nearly toppled to the ground. It took his brain a few precious moments to realize it was just music, maybe music ten times louder than before—and a few moments longer to identify the song as 'Auld Lang Syne.' But in even that little time he was overcome with an almost primal terror, that this was the roar of a monster, that this was the roar of *death*, that he should run from this inhuman scream wrenched so *impossibly* out of the perfect silence, that he should run away fast whilst he still could. And he very nearly did; he suddenly knew with absolute cold certainty how very small and useless he was before that wall of noise, and how very quickly the night had become very dark indeed, he could be lost within that pitch darkness, and within the battle cry the pitch was shrieking out, he *knew* that he'd drown in that noise and be lost forever. . . .

And instead he found a rage within him he'd long forgotten, or never even guessed he had.

He stood his ground.

"Should auld acquaintance be forgot, and never"—"You *fucks*!" he screamed at the music. "You selfish *fucks*! I've got work in the morning! And a wife, and a son, and a dog—we've all got work in the morning!"

And up on the first floor he saw a curtain twitch—a little chink of light, then gone.

"I see you!" he raged. "I see you up there! Do you think I can't see you?" He picked up a loose piece of crazy paving, he ran towards the house, towards that noise, he hurled it up at the window. It struck. For a moment he thought he'd broken the glass, terrified he had—then he *hoped* he had, hoped he'd smashed the whole fucking pane in—and was disappointed when the paving bounced back harmlessly.

"I'm coming to get you!" Alan screamed.

"We'll take a cup of kindness yet, for the sake of auld lang syne . . . !"

He raced out of their garden and into his own. He scrabbled at the door of his garage. He pulled out a metal stepladder, it clanked in his grasp. He felt his jacket rip under the strain, but that was too bad, *fuck* Alice for making him wear a jacket in the first place. For a terrible moment as he lugged the ladder out into the darkness he thought the song might have stopped, and he didn't want that, then what would he do?—but no, it was back on for another bout, 'Auld Lang Syne' was ringing in another new year, just so loud, just so selfish, just so fucking festive. He dragged the ladder out of his garden, first pulling on one side then on the other, it looked as if the two of them were dancing together to the music.

And now he was leaning the ladder against their house—no, *slamming* it against the house, and up he went, the metal rungs creaking under his weight—"I'm coming to get you!" he shouted again, but perhaps less confidently than before, and he knew his rage was still powering him on, but maybe it was starting to ebb away, who knows, just a little? And he looked down once, and he wished he hadn't, because the night was so black now, everything was so *black*, and he couldn't see the ground below. But still he climbed, "I'm coming to get you," but almost softly now, like it was a secret, and suddenly there were no more rungs to climb, he was at the top, and—look! happy coincidence!—he was right by the window. And there was no light behind, the curtain was closed tight. "Hey!" He banged upon the glass. "Hey! Open up! Open up!" And this close to the music he thought it was buffeting him, that the force might knock him from the ladder, but he was strong, he was holding firm—nothing could stop him now, and any terror he might be feeling in his gut, that was just a *private* terror no one could see, right? Right? "Open up! One last chance!" And he banged again—

And the curtains opened.

And the music stopped.

Later on, he would doubt what he saw in that room. He would suspect that he'd misunderstood it at some fundamental level. Alice would ask him about what had happened that night, and he'd lie, he'd just say he never got a glimpse inside the house at all. That the neighbours had resolutely refused to show themselves, that he still had no idea who their enemies were. It was so much easier that way. He almost began to believe it himself.

The curtains pulled back all the way, they opened wide and he was blinded for a moment in the light of the room. So maybe that's why he couldn't see who had opened them, because someone had to have, surely, they couldn't open themselves? But there was no one in the room—no one—Alan thought there was at first—he gasped when he saw those figures, they looked so human—so lifelike—but . . .

But they were dummies. Dummies, the sort you'd get in clothes shops, modelling the latest fashions. There was a child wearing sports gear, and he was lying on his back, his body splayed out over cardboard boxes. The child looked dead in that position, or wounded, that wasn't a natural way for a body to lie—so why then was he smiling so widely? There was a man, and he was in a business suit (and, Alan noted, not a suit as good as his, this dummy didn't have someone like Alice to dress him, quite clearly!)—and he was almost standing, propped in the corner of the room, head swivelled towards the window, almost facing Alan but not quite, almost grinning at Alan, almost grinning *because* of Alan, but not really, not quite. And the third figure—the closest figure—oh—she was naked, and Alan felt such guilt suddenly, here he was staring at her, like she wasn't a woman at all, just an object, a slab of meat—but wait, she *was* just an object, just a dummy, what was the problem? And her breasts were perfect symmetrical mounds, and they looked quite inhuman, so why did Alan want to look anyway?— and her legs were long and smooth and had no trace of hair on them, the (frankly) pretty face locked into a smile too, but it was a cautious smile, a demure smile—it made her look so innocent, as if she needed protecting—or, wait, did it just make her look stupid? She was bending over, her arse in the air, one hand dangling towards the floor as if in a painful yoga position—and now it looked to Alan as if the man in the corner was *inspecting* that arse, as if he were examining it critically, and his grin was because he had that job, who wouldn't grin if their job was arse-examiner?—and the little boy in the sports clothes was rolling around on the floor laughing at the fun of it. And all three of them wore Santa hats, little red Santa hats, as if they weren't just part of some Christmas revelry but were Christmas decorations them very selves.

And that's when the dog began to bark, and it was loud, and it was fierce, and it was the fury of a dog defending its territory and its family from attack—and in a moment the curtains pulled back shut, impossibly fast—and Alan was lost again in the darkness, and suddenly the stepladder was falling one way and he felt himself falling another. "I'm going to die," he thought, quite clearly, "I'm falling back into the black," and down he crashed, and he wondered whether death would hurt. And he wasn't bothered, and he wondered *why* he wasn't bothered, and his brain said to him, "God, Alan, just how depressed *are* you?" but he put that out of his head quickly, he always put it from his head, he had no time for depression, and besides, he didn't want that to be his final thought as he died. But he wasn't dead—that fact now dawned on him—he hadn't fallen that far after all—and he was lying in the little flowerbed that only so recently Barbara and Eric had worked at hard to make look pretty.

There was still barking, but it was definitely inside, so he was safe— but what if the beast burst through the door? And he hadn't got time to pick up the stepladder, they could *keep* the stepladder—he stumbled to his feet, ran from the garden, so fast that it wasn't until he reached his own bedroom he realized how bruised he must be and how much those bruises hurt.

"You got them to turn down the music," said Alice, in the dark. She sounded snug and cosy beneath the duvet. "Well done."

"Yes," said Alan. "But I think I woke up their dog."

That night Alan dreamed of the woman dummy. He couldn't help it. He dreamed of her breasts, and decided quite formally that they were a lot firmer than Alice's—from what he could remember of Alice's breasts, that is. The dummy's were too perfect to be human, too round, too sculpted—but inhuman was better than nothing, surely. He dreamed that there *had* been hair on that too smooth plastic skin, something soft there after all. He dreamed that the dummy was smiling at him.

And the next morning Alan woke up, and was surprised at how refreshed he felt. He was in a good mood. A cloud had lifted—he'd known the cloud would just go away if he didn't think about it, and now he could be happy again, couldn't he?—he couldn't even remember why he'd been unhappy in the first place. He thought of the breasts and he smiled—and he looked across at the still sleeping Alice and he smiled at her too, oh, bless. He felt he could face the day with equanimity. And next door was quiet, no music, no barking, everything back to normal.

He went to his car. The stepladder was propped against the garage door. The neighbours had brought it back. That was kind of them. The neighbours had brought it back. The neighbours had been around and brought it back. All smiles, how kind of them, all smiles and breasts. The neighbours had been around, they had left that still dead house, they had stolen into his garden in the night, they had come on to his property, they could have come up to his very front door, they could have been leaving their footprints all over his welcome mat, they could have been wiping their plastic hands all over his door knocker. How kind. The neighbours—they'd been around—in the dark, whilst he slept, whilst his family slept, whilst they slept and would never have known. They'd brought the stepladder back. He could have it back. He could use the stepladder again. He was welcome. He was welcome. He could come over with his stepladder, and climb up, and look through their windows whenever he wanted. He was welcome.

Alan felt a pain in his chest, and had to sit down to catch his breath.

At work, sales continued to slump. Alan called a meeting for his staff. He told them to buck their ideas up. That everyone was counting on them. That he was trying his best to be harsh but fair, everyone could see him being harsh but fair, right? Some of them smiled, and promised Alan that they would indeed buck up, and a couple of them even seemed convincing.

At home Alice would tell him that the barking was at its loudest in the afternoons. It'd start a little after lunchtime usually, and would continue throughout the day. The worst of it was that Bobby's dog was incensed by it. He'd run around the house, yipping back in pointless fury. Alice said she could cope with one dog barking, maybe, at a pinch. But to have two in stereo was beyond her.

The dog next door would settle down each evening. That was when the music came on. It was always Christmas music, but you could only ever tell which song it was by standing out in the front garden. That way you heard not only the beat, but could get the full benefit of the sleigh bells, the choir, the dulcet tones of Bing Crosby, the odd comical parp from Rudolf the Reindeer's shiny red nose.

They tried calling the police. The police took down their details. Said they'd drive by and see for themselves.

One evening the neighbours played 'O Little Town of Bethlehem' seventy-four times straight times in succession. Bing Crosby sang it. Bing sounded angry. Bing hated them and wanted them to suffer. When the song eventually segued into 'Once in Royal David's City,' Alan and Alice felt so relieved they almost cried.

And in the day time, Alice would tell Alan, when Bobby came home from school, as he did his homework and his chores, he'd be humming Christmas carols under his breath. She asked him to stop. She screamed at him to shut the hell up.

At work, Alan was forced to call an emergency meeting. He had to use that word in the memo, 'emergency.' He told his sales force to work harder. He begged them. Or else he'd be obliged to take punitive measures. He had to use that phrase in the follow-up memo, 'punitive measures.' One or two openly laughed at him.

Alice said she'd called the police again, and that they'd just said the same thing as before. So Alan called them. He explained the situation very calmly. The police took down his details. Said they'd drive by. Said they'd see for themselves.

The neighbours were at last unpacking their belongings. Their front lawn was littered with cardboard boxes, sheets of plastic wrapping. The breeze would blow them over the fence. And each morning Alan would leave for work, and walk through a flurry of Styrofoam and polystyrene balls.

The dog continued to bark. Bobby's dog stopped. Bobby's dog couldn't take it anymore. He'd hide in the kitchen when the barking started, and he'd whimper. He'd piss on the floor in fear. He'd throw up.

Alice told Alan that he had to speak to the neighbours again. To go over there, knock on their door, demand an answer. He suggested they should do it together, that as a family they would more represent a united front. Bobby asked if he could come too, Bobby got very excited, and his parents said no, and Bobby got disappointed and a little cross. Alan and Alice walked to the neighbours' house. The music playing was 'O Little Town of Bethlehem' again, but it wasn't Bing this time, it was some other version, so that was good, that was all right. The welcome mat read "Welcome—Welcome to our Home Sweet Home!" Neither Alan nor Alice wanted to tread on it. They stood in the porch and knocked and called through the letterbox. There was no reply. "We're not giving in," Alice told Alan, and he agreed. "We're not going home until we've got this straightened out."

But some hours later they had to.

The police told them they should stop phoning them. What they were doing, they said, was harassment. Not only to the neighbours, but to the police receptionist. Their neighbours were fine, good people; they shouldn't hate them just because they were different. "But different in what way?" asked Alan, and he wasn't angry, and he clearly wasn't shouting, so he didn't think he deserved the subsequent warning. "Just different."

Alan and Alice tried knocking on the doors of other people in the street. Neighbours they'd never said hello to, not in all those years. But no one was ever in.

One evening Alan came home to find Bobby was in the front garden. He was playing in all the bubble wrap. "Look, Daddy," he said, "I can make it go pop!" He was jumping on it, rolling around in it, setting off a thousand tiny explosions. He was laughing so much. Alan told him to get away from it, get inside the house. It wasn't theirs, it was rubbish, get away. Bobby looked so hurt—but couldn't he play in it, couldn't he and Daddy play in it together? "It's not safe," said Alan. "You stupid boy, you idiot. It isn't *clean*."

And Bobby still looked hurt. His mouth hung down in a sad little pout. But then the pout became a scowl. His face contorted. It actually contorted. And slowly, Bobby raised his hand, he raised a single finger. He held it out defiantly at his father.

That night Bobby wasn't allowed to play golf on the Xbox.

Alan and Alice slept wearing ear plugs. But Alan thought he could still hear the music. He couldn't be sure. Whether the thumping was the bass beat, or his own heart.

And he dreamed about the mannequin next door with her fake plastic body and tits, and her fake plastic smile. "Oh, Barbara," he grunted one night, as he took her from behind, bending over like that, arse pointing up to the heavens, just asking for it. He liked to call her Barbara. With his heart thumping away like the drums of 'Winter Wonderland.'

Bobby still played in the garden. Alan would watch him from the window, catching pieces of polystyrene on his tongue like snow. He'd knock on the glass, try to get him to stop, but Bobby couldn't hear, or wouldn't hear, and he looked so happy, like an eight year old on Christmas morning. Tilting back his head, mouth wide open, the white specks of packaging floating down on to his face. Spitting them out, or swallowing them down, whichever way the fancy took him.

Alice worked out that the barking next door stopped if no one made a sound. So they tried not to provoke the dog, they trod gently, tried not to walk on floorboard creaks, they kept the television on mute. They talked in whispers, if they talked at all.

"Do you fancy a game of golf, champ?" whispered Alan to Bobby one evening. "We haven't played golf in ages." And Bobby shrugged. "You can be Tiger Woods if you like," said Alan. And so they played golf together, one last time, and Bobby didn't try very hard, and still won anyway. "We can play real golf one day, if you like," said Alan. "Real golf, not just this fake version, the real one in the fresh air. We can go and have a pint together in a pub. We can be friends."

At work, Old Man Ellis summoned Alan to a meeting. It was just the two of them, in that airless little office. Ellis told Alan that if he couldn't handle his staff, he'd find someone who could.

One night Alan came home with a good idea. The idea had been buzzing around his head all afternoon, it had kept him happy. "Let's give them a taste of their own medicine!" he cried, and he didn't even bother to whisper, let's see what they make of *that*! And he and Alice got together all their favourite CDs, and they played them in the hi-fi, and turned the volume up as far as it would go. Alice played her Abba, Alan his Pink Floyd. And next door went crazy—the dog began barking like nobody's business, the retaliatory Christmas music was deafening. But it didn't matter, it was *fun*, Alan and Alice rocking out to 'Voulez-Vous' and 'Comfortably Numb.' Even Bobby joined in, and

Bobby was grinning, and Alan hadn't seen Bobby smile for such a long time, and his heart melted, it did. "Can I play some music too?" asked Bobby, and Alan laughed, and said, "Sure!" And Bobby played something his parents didn't recognize, and it had a few too many swear words in it for either to approve—but they were all jumping up and down to it, and Alan said, "I'm not sure you can dance to it, Bobby, but it's got a good beat!" And for some reason they all found that simply hilarious. At last, of course, they had to give up; they had no more music to play; they were exhausted. And it hadn't done any good, Bing Crosby was screaming out apoplectic rage, and their own dog was a quivering wreck of piss and sick. But as they got into bed that night, Alice said to Alan, "Did you recognize it? That was *our* song. Do you remember? That was the song we used to play, back when we first met." And Alan didn't think they'd ever had a song, they'd never been that romantic, had they? But she kissed him, and it was on the lips—it was very brief, but it was sweet—and then turned over and went to sleep. Alan lay there in the dark and wondered which song she had been referring to. Probably one of the ones by Abba.

The next morning, beneath the sea of cardboard and plastic and bubble wrap crap, Alan saw that there were now holes in the lawn. Craters even. It was like a battlefield. And he supposed that last night the neighbours had let the dog out. And that afternoon, at work, he sacked three of his team force. He called an emergency meeting, and sacked them at random. One of them even cried. "But I've got a family," she said. "Tough," said Alan. "We've all got fucking families."

Alice phoned Alan at work. She never did that. "Are you coming home soon?" she asked.

"What's the matter?"

"It's the dog. He's very ill."

"Well, he's always a bit ill, isn't he?"

"This is different. Oh God, he got out of the house. I don't know how, but he escaped, and he's just crawled his way back and . . . Come home soon."

Alan explained he was really very busy, and that he didn't know much about dogs, and there was nothing he could do to help. But he still left work early, he drove back as quickly as he could.

By now Bobby was home from school. He was crying. "Oh, Sparky," he said. "Sparky, please don't die." And all at once he was an eight year old again, Alan's special little boy, and he loved him so much, and he pulled him into a hug. And Bobby clung to him, and sobbed all over his suit. "Please, Daddy, don't let Sparky die."

"I won't," said Alan. "I won't. What did the vet say? You have called the vet?" And both Alice and Bobby looked at him blankly. Alan felt cross. "Well, why not?"

"Look at him," said Alice.

The dog was doing its best to stand on all fours, but the paws kept sliding beneath him. At first Alan thought it was simple weakness—but no, it was odder than that, the paws themselves looked so shiny and slippery, they couldn't get purchase on the kitchen tiles. The dog was trying hard not to look at anyone, it almost seemed to be frowning with human irritation—I know how to stand, don't worry, I'll puzzle it out in a moment. Around him lay clumps of fur, big handfuls of it. There was a pool of liquid that looked a bit like cream but smelled much worse.

Then the dog sneezed—a peculiar little squeak like a broken toy, and it almost made Alan laugh. And it was too much for the dog, its legs shot out from underneath him, his belly slumped to the floor in one big hilarious pratfall. And the dog opened its mouth, as if to give some punchline to the gag, and instead retched out a little more of that cream.

"They did this to him," said Alice. "They poisoned him."

"We can't know that."

"Fuckers," said Bobby. "Dirty shitty little fuckers, they did this. Pesky nasty motherfucks." And he glared at his parents, and that eight year old innocence was lost again, and Alan thought it was probably lost for good.

"Hey, boy," said Alan, bending down towards the dog. "Hey, champ. How are you doing? Don't you worry, champ, everything will be fine." And the dog's eyes bulged wide, in utter confusion, and it retched again. But this time there was no mere trickle of cream. It *poured* out, thick and fast, as if some hose inside had just been turned on. No wonder the eyes bulged—there was more liquid here than there was room inside the dog's body, surely!—it was as if each and every one of his innards had been diluted into one same sticky mulch and were now being pumped out of him on to the floor, coming out now in waves, lapping against the dog's head and getting stuck in the remaining scraps of fur, lapping against the open eyes that stared on beadily in vague disinterest, the contents of his entire body swimming lazily past him and his not even showing the inclination to care. There was a pinkish quality to the cream now, and Alan thought that might be the blood—but the creamy beige flattened the pink out, it became a beige so lurid it was hardly beige at all. And oh God, it wasn't even liquid, not really, it was like a syrup, soft and smooth, and the dog was now quivering in it, seemed to be supported by it and floating upon it, this syrup so thick you could stand a dessert spoon up in it. Clean, and pure, and hard like plastic.

The dog gave one last shudder, as if trying to shake out the last of its body's contents; a few last drops out, all done? Good.

"Sparky," said Bobby.

"Now, we have to be brave," said Alan.

"Fuckers," said Bobby.

"Now, now."

"Yes," said Alice. "Fuckers."

Alan opened his mouth. He wasn't sure why, to say something, what? Something conciliatory possibly, or just some sort of eulogy for a dead pet, something suitably touching for the circumstances. His family looked at him expectantly. "What," he asked, "do you want to do?"

"Revenge," said Bobby. "We'll get revenge. We'll poison *them*, we'll poison *their* dog. We'll . . . we'll put shit through their letterbox."

"Right," said Alan, "right, or we could . . ."

Alice looked at him. Stared at him, in fact. "What, Alan?" she said, and it was so soft, that was the dangerous thing. "Well? Well, tell us. What can we do?"

He tried to think of an answer to that. She waited. Give her her due, she waited. Then she tutted with exasperation, and stormed out of the room.

Alan and Bobby watched the dog for a little while. Even now the fur was still falling from its body, each hair a rat deserting a ship that had already sank. Alan thought he should close the dog's eyes, if only for Bobby's sake, but he didn't. Instead, "Come on," he said, awkwardly, reaching out to put his arm around his son, then thinking better of it. "Come on, let's leave poor old Sparky in peace." They left the kitchen, and Alan left the door behind them.

Alice was waiting for them both in the sitting room. "Here," she said.

She handed Alan a little cellophane bag, the same she'd use to pack his lunch for work and Bobby's lunch for school. Inside nestled what looked like three sausages, small and thin, with knobbles on—and they were three turds, Alice's turds, and they looked so dainty, they looked like polite little lady turds.

"Oh God," said Alan.

And Bobby grinned at that, a wolfish grin that showed his teeth. "Yeah, all right!" he said, and left the room. He returned a minute or two later, still all smiles, his dog was dead but everything was okay now because they had a plan. And he was carrying his own offering in his bare hands, proud, like a hunter, like a child who had now proved himself a man—look upon the fruits of my labours!—and it was a big greasy hot dog of a turd, and Alan realized that Bobby was really no longer just a little boy.

"You expect me to put these through their letterbox, just like that?"

"Not at all," said Alice. "We need to tell them why. We need them to know we know." She went to her desk, found an envelope, a nice big padded one. She wrote on it in bold felt tip: DOG KILLERS. She took her bag of chipolatas dangling from Alan's still outstretched hand, dropped it inside; Bobby dropped his inside as well.

"Now we're just waiting for your contribution," said Alice.

"Don't you think we've got enough?"

"This is a present from the entire family."

So Alan went to the toilet. He took the envelope with him. He thought of his wife and son outside the door waiting for him. It was too much pressure. He couldn't perform like that. He strained and strained, he honestly tried. But nothing popped out. He opened the envelope, looked at the turds inside for moral support, at the pioneering turds that would be forebears to his own turds. It did no good.

He flushed away an empty bowl.

"All done?" asked Alice as he emerged.

"Yes," he lied.

And his family nodded at him grimly. "Then," said Bobby, "it's time."

The neighbours' house was actually quiet when he stepped outside. It was too early for the Christmas music, and the dog was taking a break from barking. It was peaceful, and Alan almost believed this was a joke, that nothing really had happened, that Barbara and Eric still lived there, and all was well. He wondered if he were being watched as he walked up the driveway. By *them*, his enemies—and by *them*, his family—both sides watching his progress secretly from behind curtains. He tried to hold the envelope as nonchalantly as possible, as if it wasn't the sole reason for his paying a visit, as if, with his pet dog dead, he now wanted to take his pet envelope for walkies instead.

The sun was already setting as Alan reached the front door, and that was peculiar.

For once he didn't want to attract attention. One simple delivery, and he was done. Gently, very gently, he pushed open the flap of the letterbox. He bent down to it, he peered through into the house—but there was nothing to see, it was dark. Pitch dark, and Alan got the sudden thought that it was from inside the house that the night was leaking. He felt a slight draft from it. He shivered, looked back. The light was almost gone already, get it over with. He measured the envelope against the letterbox, and it was a perfect fit, the right size exactly, and he balanced it there, began to feed it in.

And then from the other end he felt a tug.

At first he thought he'd just hit an obstruction, he prepared to adjust the angle so he could push it through more easily—but then he felt it again, a definite *tug*—there was something waiting behind that door, and it'd taken hold of the envelope, it was pulling it in.

Instinctively Alan pulled back, and he didn't know why—he wanted this delivered, didn't he? But from inside the house he heard a growl, something thwarted, something angry, and he knew then he mustn't let this envelope go inside that house, he mustn't let any part of his wife or his son go in there, not even the worst part of them, not even their shit. And he pulled back harder, and the growler was *shocked* by that, at the sheer nerve of it, there was a gnashing of teeth too, Alan was sure of it. And he set his feet upon the welcome mat to try to get a better grip, and he looked down at it, and that was a mistake, because there was nothing now on the welcome mat, no wording at all—and more than that, there was really nothing there, it was smooth and soft and oh so slippery, and Alan couldn't stop himself, Alan fell backwards, Alan let go.

The envelope was snatched away; the letterbox slammed shut; the jaws of the house, they slammed shut. And Alan cried out in frustration and fear, and suddenly realized how very dark the night was.

When he got home, Alice was in the bedroom waiting for him. She was wearing her underwear. She never showed that. He could see her breasts peeking out, saying hello. "But where's Bobby?" he asked.

"Bobby went to bed hours ago," said Alice. "Hey. You did it. You big, bad, bold man. You've been husband to me, and father to our boy. You've protected your family, you've kept us safe."

And for only the second time since he'd known her, she tore into him. She ripped off his tie, his jacket, her hands were all over him, her lips too. "I want you so much," she said, "I *love* you so much," and she pulled him down on to the bed—"Oh, okay," said Alan—and, oh God, she was everywhere, how was she doing that, when she only had two hands, and she was in him and now he was in her and that last bit was pretty unexpected—"I love you!" she shouted, and he wanted her to hush, Bobby would hear, the neighbours would hear—and it was all so silent out there, there was no music at all, and Alan could picture them maybe as a family sitting around the contents of the envelope soberly, "Well, I guess we learned our lesson,"—and Alan wished the music was back, just a bit of it, just to give him a bit of rhythm, it had been a long time since he'd done anything like this. "I love you," cried Alice, "Alan, why did we ever stop? Why did we ever stop loving each other?" And Alan didn't know.

Alan was woken by Alice with a kiss.

"I have to go to work," he said.

"Couldn't you just stay here with me?"

"Not really," he said.

"Okay."

There was still no sound from next door, and Alan supposed that was a good thing.

Alan phoned Alice from work. He never did that.

It was late morning, he wanted to hear her voice.

"I love you," he said.

"That's nice," she replied. "Will you be home at the usual time?"

"I think so. I hope so."

"Good."

He phoned her again later in the afternoon, but this time there was no answer.

When he got home at last he was surprised to see the dog was waiting for him.

The fur had fallen out, every last hair of it. But the dog didn't seem too distressed by this. His face was etched into one big doggy grin, tongue lolling out. He waddled towards Alan on those shiny smooth paws of his.

"Hey," he said. "Hey. Good dog. Good boy."

He stroked at his off-beige skin, and it was a little sticky to the touch.

Bobby was playing on his Xbox.

"Hello, champ," said Alan. "What about Sparky, then? Sparky pulled through!"

Bobby didn't look up; he was too absorbed in his game. Alice came in from the kitchen.

"Bobby," she said. "That dog of yours needs feeding." Bobby's body twitched in irritation. "Now, come on," she said. "He's your responsibility."

"Hello," said Alan. "I love you."

"Now, Bobby," insisted Alice.

So Bobby tottered to his feet. Then tottered to the kitchen, fetched a can of dog food. He tottered back to the dog, who all this time had gazed after his young master in utter adoration. Bobby scooped some of the food out of the tin with his fingers. He bent down towards his dog. And then, very carefully, he smeared it all over the dog's face. He smeared it in good and hard, so that the jellied meat stuck there firm—some of it went into the mouth, and a little on to that hanging tongue, but the majority hung off the face and gave Sparky an impromptu beard.

The Bobby sat down again, picked up his Xbox joystick. He squeezed the controls hard, and the remains of dog food oozed out from his fist.

Alan watched, appalled. "What's wrong with Bobby?"

"Nothing's wrong with Bobby," said his wife. "Bobby's got his dog back. Bobby's happy, the dog's happy, everybody's happy."

"Are you happy?"

"Of course I'm happy. Come into the kitchen. I want to talk to you privately." He followed her, and she smiled as she closed the door.

"What is it?"

"You should sit down."

He did.

"I'm having an affair," smiled Alice.

Alan didn't know what to say. "What?" And then, "Why?" And, "But you said you were happy . . ."

"I am happy. I'm happy *because* I'm having an affair."

"Oh," said Alan. He supposed he ought to have felt angry. Was that what she wanted? But he had no anger left. He'd used it all up, wasted it on loud music and garden rubbish.

"Don't look glum, Alan. I'm not glum. We're going to sort this out. Let me explain how."

"Okay." And Alan felt strangely reassured, actually; Alice always sorted everything out.

She explained how she could keep everything she wanted. And how he could get the same thing in return. That way everything would carry on as normal. It'd just be a *different* normal. A better normal.

He said, very quietly, "Can I have time to think?"

She was very polite. "Of course you can, darling." He'd been staring down at the kitchen table as she coolly told him what she wanted from him, how she saw their marriage surviving, what her conditions were. And now he looked up at her. She was staring at him closely, and there was still that smile, and her head was fixed to one side for the best angle, and he shuddered for the briefest moment. "Oh, Alan," she said. "When we first met, I remember. Trying to work out whether we ought to have just been friends. I think, darling, that we lost our way. I think we could have been such good friends."

"And last night?"

Alice turned her head to the other side, narrowed her eyes, frowned. "What about it?"

That night Alan stayed on the sofa. He played on Bobby's Xbox. He played as Tiger Woods. He beat the computer once.

He went to work. The roads were filled with motorists who'd found love. Old Man Ellis called him in for another emergency meeting, and this time Ellis told him he was a disgrace, and threatened him with redundancy, and Ellis was a short ugly man and body odour clung to him like a limpet, but he'd found love, he'd found Mrs Ellis, he'd made it work, and Alan wanted to ask him what the secret was. Waiting on his desk when Alan came out was an unsigned note calling him 'Wanker.' The man who'd called him a wanker was probably in love too.

He thought about calling Alice. He didn't dare.

He didn't go straight home. He went to the pub. He sat on his own. He drank lager and ate crisps.

By the time he reached the house, Alice was already in bed. He undressed in the dark, and climbed in beside her. She didn't move, not a muscle. He couldn't tell whether she were asleep or awake. Alive or dead. Human or. Or. He wanted to rub against her. In the moonlight her skin looked so smooth.

There was still no sound from next door, and the silence, the desperate silence, began to hurt.

"All right," he said, out loud. "I'll do what you want."

Alan hadn't been on a date in years, and didn't know how to dress. So Alice took him to the wardrobe and picked out a tie, a jacket, a shirt, shoes. She inspected the results critically. "You look good enough to eat." Alice herself was immaculate, she'd never lost the knack, who'd have thought?

"Maybe we don't have to do this then," said Alan. "If this is what you like."

She chewed her lip, just for a second, then laughed. "Come on," she said, and plucked him by the sleeve, and took him downstairs.

Bobby was playing golf with his new friend. "Hello, champ," said Alan. "Hello, *champs*." He thought the boy on the right was Bobby, because that was Tiger Woods.

"Don't wait up!" Alice told the two children gaily.

They stood on the welcome mat. The mat read, "Nostra Casa" and "A Very Happy Family Lives Here!" and "Home Sweet Home Sweet Home Sweet Home Sweet Home." Alan raised the knocker, but at his touch the door swung open.

"We're expected," Alice assured him.

The house was pretty. Everything was clean and ordered and there was the smell of recent polish—or was it something besides? On a shelf with the telephone directory Alan saw his padded envelope, still sealed. "DOG KILLER," it said, and that accusation seemed so spiteful now. We're all good neighbours, aren't we, good friends. Next to it, he saw, there were other envelopes, similarly sized—"Cat Poisoner" read one. "Murderer" said another. Still more: "Child Abuser." "Rapist." "Killer." "Rapist." "Killer."

On a shelf beneath, a cup filled to the very brim with sugar.

"But where are they?" said Alan.

"They'll be in the dining room," said Alice. Her eyes were shining with excitement. "Let's see what they've got for us!"

They'd cooked pasta. Lasagne, fettuccini.

Barbara had really made an effort. Alan had never seen her with her clothes on before, and she looked beautiful, she'd done a really good job. Barbara smiled, a little demurely Alan thought. "Doesn't she look wonderful, Alan?" Alice cooed. "Good enough to eat!"

Eric's smile had no shyness to it, and he flashed it throughout the whole meal. He was wearing a suit. His tie was pure black. Alan thought it made his own striped one look wrong and silly. Eric looked so good he could have got away with a striped tie; even the Santa hat perched on the side of his head looked smart and chic.

The small talk was very small, but Alice laughed a lot at it, and

Alan had almost forgotten what her laughter sounded like. In the background, playing very subtly, was a selection of festive favourites. But there was nothing cheesy about them, they were performed by famous opera singers, and the orchestra was one of the Philharmonics.

It was time for the dessert. "Allow me," said Alice, "you two have worked so hard already," and she fetched it from the brand new refrigerator. "Tiramisu!" she said. "It's my favourite! Oh, how did you know?" And she sat down, kissed Eric gratefully upon the lips.

"Tiramisu, yum yum," said Alan.

Alice scooped a fistful of tiramisu from the bowl. She looked straight at Alan. And her eyes never leaving his, she smeared it slowly over her face. She massaged it into her cheeks, her lips and chin—then rubbing lower, down on to the neck, thick cream and chocolate peeping over the top of her cleavage.

Alan winced. Alice's eyes flashed for a moment.

"If you don't like it," she said, "why don't you come over here and wipe it off me? Come on. Lick it off. Lick it off me, if you dare."

Eric grinned at that, Barbara smiled so demurely. Alan didn't move.

And Alice smiled such a polite smile from beneath her mask of soft dessert. "I think it's time we left you two lovebirds alone." And so saying, she got to her feet. She picked up Eric from the waist, she tucked him under her arm. And they left the room.

Alan couldn't be sure, but he thought as he left that Eric may have winked at him.

"Well," said Alan. He looked at Barbara, who was still smiling, but was it really demure, was she perhaps just as embarrassed as he was? "Well," said Alan. "What do we do now? Just the two of us."

He reached across the table, and took hold of Barbara's hand. It felt like the skin of his dead dog.

Alan said, "I hope we can be friends."

He closed his eyes. He concentrated hard. As if through thought alone he could make that hand warm to his touch, make it take hold of his in turn. As if, by wanting it enough, he could make Barbara love him.

He heard the sound of bedsprings, of his wife shrill and noisy, her screams of pleasure as she reached orgasm. He kept his eyes squeezed tight, and tried to block out all the noise, all the noise there was in the world.

# THE
# BATHTUB

Sarah Anne Rachel Hadley did not like her grandmother's bathtub. Whenever she visited her grandmother, the bathtub was something she took great pains to avoid. She'd try very hard for the duration of that visit not to pee. And if she needed to pee, she'd tap with her feet really quickly to try to drive all the pee away. But sometimes she couldn't help it, she really had to pee. And when she did, she wouldn't look at the bathtub, she would walk straight to the toilet, eyes fixed forward. And after she'd peed she'd have to use the sink, and to do that she'd face the wall, press her feet up right against the skirting board, and she would shuffle around, and that way she'd be as far from the bathtub as could be.

There was hair in her grandmother's bathtub, coming out of the plughole. It looked like they were growing out. They were thick, like spiders' legs, but spiders don't have that many legs, so it was like lots of spiders had been mushed together. They were black. And that was wrong, because her grandmother didn't even have black hair.

Sarah Anne Rachel Hadley really liked her name, Sarah Anne Rachel Hadley. She liked it, because if you spelled out the first letters, S A R H, that was very nearly her first name back again. It was only missing a second A, and she could pretend that it was there. It made her feel secure. And when the kids at school spoke to her, or her mother, or her father (when he was there), when they called her Sarah, she would feel that, yes, she was *doubly* Sarah, she would think, I'm Sarah through and through.

Sarah Anne Rachel Hadley's mother was called Sophie Maureen

Hadley, and that wasn't any good, that didn't spell anything.

Sarah's grandmother was called Eunice Pinnock. Sarah didn't know if her grandmother had a middle name. She'd never asked.

Sarah liked her grandmother well enough, but she would sometimes try and hug Sarah, and Sarah didn't like that. Whenever Mummy told her they were going to visit her grandmother, Sarah would get sad, and she'd ask her Mummy to stop all the hugging from happening, and Mummy said she'd do her best, and she had told Granny, but Granny sometimes forgot. Granny was old, old people forget things. So if Granny hugged Sarah, Sarah would have to be a brave little girl and put up with it, and not cry, and not shout, and Mummy would reward Sarah with a treat.

Her grandmother was always forgetting that Sarah was a special girl, and that her skin was very soft, and that hugging was very bad for soft skin because it would leave marks on it, or even worse, lots of grandmother's skin might get left on Sarah's skin, and then maybe it'd get sucked through the pores, and then grandmother would be inside Sarah. Sarah didn't want that. Sarah wanted to be Sarah through and through.

When her grandmother hugged Sarah, she'd smell of cigarettes and cinnamon. Sarah would sometimes see her grandmother smoking cigarettes, but she never saw her eat cinnamon. Sarah liked the smell of cinnamon, but not when it was on grandmother. And she didn't like the smell of cigarettes at all.

And another thing about the bathtub was the taps. The taps were too big. Something could be hiding inside the taps. Sarah would sometimes look at the taps. Because she didn't want to, but she would sometimes look at the bathtub, she couldn't help it, not for all her precautions, she would just stare at the bathtub, it was like an itch in her mind—she'd stare at those giant taps, those ogre taps, she'd wonder why they had to be so big.

She didn't like the pipes either, which were rusty, bits of rust would get in the water, it'd make the water dirty. She didn't like the cracks in the side of the bath, they looked like dirt too, but they wouldn't wash away. She didn't like the colour of the bath. It was a green bath. Sarah liked green well enough. But it was the wrong colour for a bath.

For that second A, S A R A H, Sarah would make up lots of names. Sometimes she would be Antonia. Sometimes she would be Adelaide, she'd read that in a book once, she thought that was pretty. Sometimes, when she felt bad, she'd be Anne. Sarah Anne Rachel Anne. She'd rattle it through her head, it sounded like a train on the tracks.

Most days Sarah didn't put much thought into which name she'd pick. She was a sensible girl, really. She thought choosing her new name might be silly.

She sometimes wondered whether which name she chose affected anything. Whether she had better days as Antonia or Alexandra or Adelaide or Alice or Agnes or Anne. She'd thought about keeping a diary to see, it would be interesting. She hadn't got around to it yet.

She was trying out a brand new name the day that Mummy gave her the news, she was Amanda, and maybe that had been the problem.

"Pack some toys," Mummy said. "We're going to Granny's for a while."

Going to her grandmother's made Sarah sad, mostly because of the hugging, but also because of the cigarettes and the cinnamon. But she liked the journey to Granny's. She'd learned it by heart. They'd catch the 23 bus to the train station. Then they'd catch the train. Then they'd catch the 32 bus to grandmother's house. Sarah liked the way that 23 was 32 backwards, and that 32 was 23 backwards, and the train bit could be sandwiched in the middle.

She'd sometimes ask Mummy whether they could go to her grandmother's house, but not actually bother seeing her grandmother, they could just turn right round when they got there and go home again, they could get off the 32 bus and get another 32 bus going in the opposite direction, then get the train, then get the 23 bus, and that would be good. And Mummy always said no.

Sarah said, How long are we going for?

Mummy said, "I don't know, as long as it takes," and that wasn't an answer at all, but Mummy sounded cross, and Sarah didn't like it when Mummy was cross. Sarah had only been trying to work out whether they'd be there so long that at some point she might need to go and pee, and Sarah grimly concluded they probably might be. She cried at that.

She cried too when Mummy said they were going to get there by car, because that would miss out the only good bit. Sarah said, I want to go by bus, and train, and bus. Mummy said, "We're going by car, we'll be carrying too much luggage," and Sarah didn't like the sound of that.

And another thing about the bathtub was that it made a noise, a sort of whispering noise.

And another thing about the bathtub was that it smelled of cigarettes and cinnamon.

The good news was that grandmother didn't even try to hug her. Grandmother hugged Mummy, and Mummy held on to grandmother so long and so tight, and grandmother just forgot.

Sarah went into the sitting room whilst Mummy and grandmother talked in the kitchen. Sarah sat down on the sofa. She counted the tiles on the ceiling, and there were fifty-three complete ones, and sixteen half ones, and three which were partially obscured by light fittings. The same as always.

After a while, her grandmother came in to see her. She stood in the doorway. "Do you want to take your coat off, dear?" and Sarah said, No, and grandmother left.

After a while, Mummy came in to see her too. "Take your coat off, Sarah," she said. Sarah did, and Mummy took it, she left the room to hang the coat up somewhere, Sarah didn't know where.

Sarah began to fidget because it was Tuesday and Tuesday was bath night, and they never visited grandmother on Tuesday because Sarah was too busy at home doing ordinary things and having her bath. But she didn't want to fidget too much, she didn't want Mummy to notice, because then Mummy might ask what was wrong, and Sarah was very bad at lying, and she'd have to tell her, and then Mummy might say she'd have to have her bath at her grandmother's. And the idea of missing bath night distressed Sarah, but the idea of grandmother's bathtub with its pipes and taps and spider legs distressed her more, she'd rather have the one distress over the other.

And at seven o'clock sharp Mummy said, "Time for bed, little lady," and Sarah thought she might have got away with it. She'd lie in bed all night and be covered in dirt and the dirt would be soiling the bed sheets but that would be okay. And her grandmother said, "Do you want to use the bathroom, dear?" and Mummy said, "I'd forgotten, it's bath night!" and Sarah hated her grandmother so much.

Mummy went upstairs to run the bath. Sarah thought she would stay downstairs, if she stayed downstairs as long as possible then maybe Mummy would forget who the bath was for, and at home Mummy never needed Sarah to be in the room whilst the bath was being run. But this time she said, "Come along, Sarah," and Sarah had to follow her, and as she climbed up the stairs it seemed to her that her body was getting heavier and heavier and that she was walking through glue. Mummy didn't seem to notice the dangers of the bathtub, she walked straight up to it without even taking a deep breath or anything, and she turned on the taps and the taps whistled and spat out water, spat it out in thick gobbets, then the water began to flow.

Mummy said, "I'm sorry about this, darling, I know this is all very confusing. But you'll understand one day, and I promise you, it's for the best." And Sarah was looking straight at her, and nodding, just so she wouldn't have to look at the bathtub, and hear what the bathtub was whispering.

Mummy turned off the taps. Steam rose out of the water. "You're all set," she said. It's too hot, said Sarah. "It's fine," said Mummy. Sarah said, it's too hot. Mummy said, "You want to wait until it cools down? Okay. Don't be too long, I might need the bath myself! Here's a towel." And Sarah wanted to say, don't go, don't go, don't leave me, don't go— but she'd been having baths on her own now for years, and Mummy left.

Once they were on their own, the bathtub whispered even more. Sarah put her fingers in her ears.

She looked at the bath. She supposed the water in the middle wasn't too bad. The water in the middle wasn't touching any part of the bath. If she could just get into that bit, she'd be fine. If she could just get into the bath, and not touch the bath, not the sides, not reach the bottom, she'd be okay. If she were the size of a little mouse, she could bob about on the surface, safe.

But she was a sensible girl, really. And that might be silly.

She peered over the side, carefully, not too close, in case the bathtub leaped up, caught her, pulled her in. The plug was in the plughole. That was good. Because all the spider legs were in the plughole, and now they were hidden by the plug. But if she got in the bath, the plug might come free. The bathtub would pop it out, maybe the spider legs would *kick* it out, and then the water would be sucked down the drain, and she'd be sucked down too, she'd be sucked into a whirlpool going round and round and down and down. And Sarah didn't mind so much the thought of going down the drain, but she'd have to brush against so many spider legs along the way.

She looked at the ogre taps. She knew what was hiding inside the taps. Fingers. And the fingers would crawl out, once she was in the bath, sitting in the bath and touching it, touching the cracks with her bare skin, the fingers would come out and prod at her. And then they'd pull the plug chain, and out of the plughole would come the plug. And the fingers would be hairy too, probably, with thick black hair, like spiders' legs.

The water had a smell.

Cinnamon. Cigarettes.

She refused to listen to what the bathtub was whispering, but she had to take her fingers out of her ears to stop her nostrils fast against that smell.

She went to the sink. She ran water into the sink. She had no problem with the sink. The sink wasn't cracked. There were no hairs in the sink. Hardened lumps of toothpaste, but toothpaste was good for you. The sink was green, but Sarah liked green well enough.

She got undressed. She splashed sink water all over her body, cupping her hands, and trying to get it on to her before it trickled out through her fingers. She kept her back to the bathtub, she wouldn't look at it anymore.

She dried herself, went down to Mummy.

She knew if Mummy said, "Have you had your bath?" Sarah couldn't lie to her. Sarah was no good at lying.

Mummy and her grandmother were in the kitchen. Her grandmother was smoking. Mummy was clasping on to a cup of tea with all her might. Neither of them were speaking. They didn't notice Sarah standing there for a little while. Then Mummy looked up.

"Are you washed?" she asked.

Sarah said, Yes.

Sarah slept with her Mummy that night. The spare room was right next door to the bathroom, but Sarah wasn't frightened, she knew her Mummy would always protect her.

In the morning, Sarah woke alone.

She went downstairs to the kitchen. Grandmother sat at the table, on her own, and she was smoking, and clouds of blue mist hung around the room. She saw Sarah, and smiled. "Hello, dear. Do you want some breakfast?"

No, said Sarah.

Grandmother got up. She opened her arms. "You poor thing. Come here."

No.

She looked all over for her mother, until the last room to try was the bathroom. Sarah took a deep breath, and went in.

Mummy was there. She was in the bath. She wasn't washing. She was just sitting there, in the bath. She wasn't even using the soap. She was in the bath, and the water was right up to her neck, and she was just sitting there, very still, and staring ahead, and Sarah wondered whether she might be dead, whether the bath had killed her, and she was excited, and not frightened yet, but she knew if she *were* dead she would get very frightened soon.

"Hello," said Mummy. She wasn't dead.

Sarah said, What are you doing?

"I'm having a bath."

Okay, said Sarah.

She turned to leave.

"You don't have to go," said Mummy.

Okay, said Sarah. She stayed a bit longer. They didn't say anything else. So Sarah left anyway.

Sarah Anne Rachel used to be much worse! She couldn't remember now, but Mummy and Daddy once sat together on the sofa, and they told her this story. About how when she was very small, they had all gone on holiday together. They'd driven all the way to Cornwall, and Sarah had been as good as gold, just looked out of the window the whole way, hadn't made a fuss. But when they got to the hotel, oh, it was a different matter! Oh, she'd been a nightmare! She didn't like the bathroom there. She screamed the place down, they didn't know, maybe she'd thought it was haunted or something. They'd booked this hotel months ago, mind. And they had to ask the manageress for another room, on another floor, with another bathroom. And Sarah hadn't liked that one either! They had to leave the hotel, they lost their deposit. And they drove around for hours, checking out all the hotels. And it was tourist season, so most of the hotels were fully booked, and the ones that weren't, she didn't like the bathrooms there any better! So eventually they had to give up, no holiday to be had. They drove all the way back home that night, Mummy and Daddy taking turns at the steering wheel, and all the way Sarah sleeping soundly in the back, good as gold, not a fuss. You'd never have known, they said. You looked so peaceful, you'd never have known.

Mummy and Daddy were cuddled up together, and they laughed a lot at the story, and Sarah laughed too, but she couldn't see really what was so funny.

Mummy and Daddy said they were just thankful Sarah had got so much better.

She *was* better now, it was only the bathtub at her grandmother's house she didn't like. But she never told her parents. She couldn't. She didn't listen to what the bathtub whispered, but sometimes the words seeped into her head anyway. And the bathtub warned her, don't you ever tell your Mummy and Daddy, don't you dare tell anyone. Or I'll come and get you, and make you mine.

They told Sarah to go and play, but she'd already counted all the tiles on the ceiling of the sitting room. She counted them again, and then went to find Mummy. The kitchen door was closed. They had closed it on her. And there were whispers going on behind it. Sarah knew she didn't want to hear the whispering, but she stood outside the door, ear jammed right up against the wood, and the words seeped into her head anyway.

She opened the door, and her grandmother and her Mummy stopped talking.

There was even more smoke in the room now, grandmother was holding a cigarette, Mummy was too, and Mummy didn't ever hold cigarettes. Mummy's face looked puffy like she'd been crying, though Sarah couldn't see any wetness on her cheeks now, and the puffiness made Mummy look old, and wrinkled, and a bit ugly, she looked just like grandmother. She had become grandmother.

Mummy started, looked a bit guilty, and Mummy never looked guilty, she looked less like herself than ever. She'd had a bath and she looked worse, she wasn't wearing any lipstick, her face was dull.

And Sarah understood, it wasn't grandmother who made the bath smell so, it wasn't grandmother who was bad, it was the bathtub, this is what it did to people, it made them ugly like Granny. I'll come and get you, it had said, I'll make you mine. And she knew she must never get into that tub, not ever. Or she'd lose herself, just as sure as she'd lost her Mummy.

"I'm sorry," Mummy said, and put her cigarette in the ashtray, and got up, and came towards Sarah, and yes, she was going to give Sarah a hug, she was opening her arms out wide, and Sarah didn't mind hugs from Mummy, but she minded them now, and Mummy pressed Sarah close to her, and she smelled like cinnamon.

And another thing about the bathtub. It doesn't make you clean. It makes you a different sort of dirty.

Grandmother suggested they all deserved a day out, they should all go to the shopping mall. And Mummy agreed, but then, she would have, wouldn't she? Mummy put on her make-up, and it made her look a bit more like herself, but Sarah wasn't fooled. They went to a department store, and grandmother liked a dress, but it wasn't in her size, and she ordered it, and she gave her name, Eunice Pinnock, and Sarah still didn't know what her middle initial could be, but she didn't much care. And Mummy admired the dress, and grandmother said, well, why don't you get one for yourself? You need a treat, all you've been through. And they didn't have it in Mummy's size either, and so Mummy ordered it too, and gave her name as Sophie Pinnock, and that wasn't right, that wasn't right, that wasn't right. It made her new name Sophie Maureen Pinnock, and that was SMP, and that still didn't stand for anything, but it had been better before. And grandmother said, do you like the dress, Sarah? And Mummy said, you like the dress, don't you, Sarah? Have a treat. You need a treat, all you've been through. And the shop did have the dress in Sarah's size, and grandmother bought it for her, and it looked very nice.

They had drinks in the cafe. Grandmother and Mummy had coffees, Sarah had a milkshake.

And Sarah wondered if she'd have to change her name now as well. She'd be Sarah Anne Rachel Pinnock. A sarp. What was a sarp? A sarp wasn't anything.

Mummy told Sarah to thank her granny for her dress and for the shake, and Sarah did. And when they got back to grandmother's house they hung the new dress in the wardrobe, and Mummy promised they'd put more clothes in there soon, this was only the beginning, and Sarah thanked her too, thank you, Mummy, she said. She wanted to fidget, but she also didn't want to fidget, she didn't want Mummy realizing anything was wrong. Mummy and grandmother went back into the kitchen to make it smell all smoky and sweet. They closed the door on Sarah. Sarah took all the money from Mummy's purse, because she didn't know how much she'd need. And then, very quietly, she went to the front door, opened it carefully, stepped outside, and left.

Sarah went to the bus stop, caught the 32 to the train station. At the station the woman behind the ticket window asked her where she wanted to go, and Sarah gave her the full address. "Which station?" asked the woman, and Sarah told her. Sarah got on the train, and she enjoyed the journey, the tracks seemed to be singing to her, Sarah Anne Rachel Anne, Sarah Anne Rachel Anne—and that was good, because today was an Anne day, today was very much an Anne day.

Sarah got off the train, went to the bus stop, caught the 23, got off the bus, went home.

She rang her own doorbell to her own house, and a woman she didn't recognize opened the front door. She was younger than Mummy. "Yes?" the younger than Mummy woman said. Sarah said that she lived there. The woman blushed. "You must be Sarah," she said. Sarah told her name was Sarah Anne Rachel Hadley. She didn't tell her the whole name, she didn't know her well enough.

The woman seemed frightened of Sarah. Sarah didn't know why. "Come in," the woman said. "Please. Your father's not here. He's at work. I don't know when he'll. He'll be back soon. I'll call him, I'll get him. So. How did you get here? Do you want anything? A coffee, you probably don't drink coffee, there's milk, there's juice."

Sarah said, I want to have a bath. My bath is overdue.

The woman blinked, and said, "All right."

Sarah thought back to some of the whispering she'd heard. Not the nasty whispering from the bathtub, the nastier whispering through the kitchen door. "Are you going to end up my new mummy?"

The woman said, "Well. Well, I. No."

Sarah said, Good.

Sarah went upstairs, and ran herself a bath. The bathtub was pink, the way bathtubs are meant to be, and it didn't talk to her.

Sarah was still in the bath when Daddy got home. "Where is she?" she heard from downstairs. She didn't hear what the woman said in reply, her voice was too feeble.

Daddy entered the bathroom without knocking. This would have upset Sarah once, but she hadn't seen him for a while, she'd forgive him anything.

"Does your mother know you're here?" he said.

Sarah didn't know what her Mummy might know.

"Oh God." He took out his mobile phone, and left the room. He didn't bother to close the door, and it let cold air in, and that was annoying. Sarah heard her father downstairs, and his voice was raised.

When he came back, his voice was softer, kinder.

"What are you doing here, poppet?" he said. "You can't just. You know."

Sarah said, I came home.

"You can't," he said again. "Not for a little while. Okay? Mummy and me. We have things to sort out. Okay?"

Sarah said, Don't you want to see me?

Daddy said, "It's not a question of what I want, poppet."

Sarah said, Don't you want to see me?

Daddy said, "Not right now. Not like this. No. No."

Sarah said nothing.

Daddy said, "Get out of the bath now, poppet."

Sarah said, No. No.

The longer she stayed in the bath the more wrinkly her fingers got. She looked old, like her grandmother.

The water got cold, but to reach the taps and run more hot water in she'd have had to get out of the bath, and Sarah didn't want to get out of the bath.

There was a knock on the door at one point, very gentle, and Sarah thought it would be her father, maybe he'd come to say sorry, maybe he'd come to say he wanted her. But it was the scared woman, the younger than Mummy woman, and she asked whether she could get Sarah a glass of milk or juice. Sarah didn't want milk or juice. Sarah thought the woman seemed rather nice, and probably would have made a nice mummy, but she was glad she wasn't going to be hers.

The water was very cold by the time her real Mummy arrived, and it was dark outside too. Mummy didn't ask, she just said, "Out of the bath, now," and Sarah was happy to oblige.

In the car, Mummy said, "I'm very cross with you. That was a very mean and selfish thing you did."

Sarah thought for a while, and said, I'm cross with you too.

Sarah wondered what the noise was, and realized it was her Mummy starting to cry.

It was gone midnight by the time they got to grandmother's. Sarah was dozing.

"Wake up," said her mother, roughly, but the way she stroked Sarah's hair was gentle enough.

Grandmother was awake, waiting for them, and the ashtray was overflowing. "What happened? Did you see her?"

"Yes," said Mummy.

"What did you say to her?"

"It doesn't matter," said Mummy.

REMEMBER WHY YOU FEAR ME

"What was she like?"

"Oh, for Christ's sake. For Christ's sake, Mum. Stop it. All right? Stop it."

"I only . . ."

"Go to bed. I've had enough of it now. I've had it up to here. All right?"

"All right."

"To bed with you, Sarah. Mummy will be along soon. I'm just going to have a bath."

"Now?" Granny dared to ask.

"Now. I just need to. I want to, I. I need to wash the *dirt* out of me. I want to get rid of the dirt."

Sarah lay in bed, and although she was very tired, she couldn't fall asleep. She was listening to the water as it splashed into the tub, as it thrummed through the rusted pipes. She was listening to the whispering, and it wasn't just whispering now, she could hear every word loud and precise and clear.

Sarah knocked on the bathroom door gently. She went in.

Mummy was lying in the bath. She turned her head. She looked surprised to see her.

"Go to bed," she said.

But Sarah stood her ground.

"Oh, what do you want, Sarah?" Mummy sighed.

Sarah thought. Said, honestly—I don't know.

Sarah then said, He doesn't want me.

"He doesn't want *us*," said Mummy.

He doesn't want me.

"No."

And then: "Sorry."

Sarah said, Is this going to be our new home?

Mummy said, "Just for a while. Not forever. You don't mind, do you?"

No.

"This was *my* home. When I was your age. This house. It makes me feel like *me*."

Sarah wanted to give her mother a hug, but she didn't give hugs. And Mummy was in the bath, the bath was all around her. Sarah didn't know how to hug her without the bath touching her. Sarah didn't know how to offer a hug, so she didn't.

"I want you," said Mummy, quietly. "I promise. I do." And Sarah gave her a hug anyway, just a little one around the neck, and the side of the tub brushed up against her, and Sarah was revolted, and Mummy was wet, and Mummy left damp patches on Sarah's nightie.

"Get in," said Mummy.

I can't.

"Yes, you can. There's plenty of room. It's a big tub."

So Sarah took her nightie off. Mummy sat up to make more room, and the water sloshed about a bit, and the waves seemed big and menacing, and then the water settled down again. Mummy held out her hand, and smiled. And Sarah took it. And Sarah put first one foot into the warm water, and then the other, and both feet hit the bottom of the tub, and then Sarah lowered herself into the water, and her bum hit the bottom of the tub too.

Mummy put her arms around Sarah's waist, pulled her back, pulled her into her soapy body, and it was slippery, it made Sarah want to laugh.

"We'll be all right, you know," said Mummy.

And the bathtub continued to whisper. And it didn't say such reassuring things. But it *was* all right, it was.

And Sarah had such soft skin, and she could feel the water leaking in through her thin pores, swelling her up fat like a balloon. The bathtub had got her now. And she would be her grandmother, she would be her mother, she would be SARP. She would learn how to hug, and to smoke, and she'd smell of sweet cinnamon. And it was all right, all of it. And she put her head back upon her mother's chest, and she closed her eyes, closed them against the cracks and the spider legs and the fingers coming out at her from the taps, she closed her eyes, and she felt safe.

# THE DARK SPACE IN THE HOUSE IN THE HOUSE IN THE GARDEN AT THE CENTRE OF THE WORLD

## i

Let's get something straight, right from the outset, okay? I'm not angry with you. Mistakes were made on both sides. Mistakes, ha, arguably, I made just as many mistakes as you. Well, not quite as many, ha, but I accept I'm at least partly to blame. Okay? No, really, okay? Come on, take those looks off your faces. I'm never going to be angry with you. I promise. I have wasted so much of my life on anger. There are entire aeons full of it, I'm not even kidding. And it does nothing. It achieves nothing. Anger, it's a crock of shit.

Isn't it a beautiful day? One of my best. The sun's warm, but not too warm, you can feel it stroking at your skin, it's all over your bare bodies and *so* comforting, but without it causing any of that irritating sweaty stuff under the armpits. Though I do maintain that sweat's a useful thing. Look at the garden. Breathe it in. Tell me, be honest, how do you think it's coming on? See what I've done, I've been pruning the roses, training the clematis, I've been cutting back the privet hedges. Not bad. And just you wait until spring, the daffodils will be out by then, lovely.

No. Seriously. Relax. Relax, right now! I'm serious.

The apples were a mistake. Your mistake, my mistake, who's counting? My mistake was to set you a law without explaining why the law was being enforced, that's not a sound basis for any legal system. Of course you're going to rebel, right. And *your* mistake, that was eating a fruit in which I had chosen to house cancer. Well, I had to put it somewhere. You may have wondered about all those skin sores and why you've been coughing up blood and phlegm. Now you know. But don't worry, I'll fix it, see, you're cured. Poppa looks after you. As for the apples, good source of vitamin A, low in calories, you just wait 'til you puree them up and top them with sugar, oh *God*, do I love a good apple crumble. I'm not even kidding! Keep the apple with my blessing. As for the cancers, well, I'll just stick them in something else, don't worry, you'll never find them.

Give me a smile. We're all friends. Smile for me. Wider than that.

And so, are we good? Cindy, and what is it, Steve. I think we're good. The fruit is all yours to eat. The air is all yours to breathe, the flowers are all yours to smell. The beasts of the world, yours to name and pet and hunt and skin and fuck. We're good, but there is one last thing. Not a law, ha ha, I wouldn't call it a *law*, ha ha, no, okay, no, it's a law. Don't go into the forest. The forest that's at the heart of the garden, the garden at the centre of the world. The forest where the trees are so tall that they scratch the heavens, so dense that they drown out the light, where even the birds that settle on the branches come out stained with black. What, why, because I said so. What? Oh. Yes, fair point. Because at the centre of the forest there stands a house, and the house is old, and the house is haunted.

Okay.

Okay. I'll be off then. Night, night, sleep tight. Don't let the bedbugs bite.

So they went into the forest the very next morning, man and wife, hand in hand, and they dropped apple cores along the way so they could find a path back again. "Like Hansel and Gretel!" said Cindy, because God had told them all his favourite fairy tales when they'd just been children, he'd tucked them up tight in beds of leaves and moss with stories of enchanted castles and giant killers and heroes no bigger than your thumb; "you can be Gretel," agreed Steve, "and I'll be Hansel!" And the trees were so tall and so dense and so black, and they were glad they were doing the hand holding thing together, it made them both feel warm and loved. And they didn't know for how long they walked, it may have been days, and they worried they might soon run out of apple cores, but presently they came across the house, right there at the forest's heart. And it was a magical house, a structure of red brick and thin chimneys and big bay windows and vinyl-sided guttering. It didn't look very haunted; "it's probably quite nice inside," said Cindy, and Steve agreed, but he held on to her hand tightly, and both hands began to sweat. They went up to the front door, and peered their way through the panel of frosted glass, but they couldn't see anyone, nothing inside was moving. Steve rang the doorbell, and Cindy called "Hello!" through the letterbox, but there was no answer, and they were both about to give up, turn about, pick up their apple cores and go home, when the door swung open anyway at their touch. It didn't creak, the hinges were too good on that door.

Cindy and Steve wondered if they could squeeze themselves into something as small as that house, they'd been so used to the sheer size of the garden that was their world. And they exchanged glances. And they shrugged. And they went in.

In the kitchen there were two places set for dinner, and at each place there was a bowl of porridge. "Like Goldilocks!" said Cindy, because God really hadn't stinted himself in his fairy tale telling; "you can be Goldilocks," said Steve, "I'll be the bear!" They ate the porridge. They both privately wondered who the porridge belonged to. They both wondered if the porridge belonged to the ghosts. They thought they should go home, but it had started to rain. So they decided there was no harm in staying a little longer; they inspected the sitting room, the bathroom, a nice space under the stairs that could be used for storage; "Hello," Cindy called out, "we're your new neighbours!" And they looked for the ghosts, but saw neither hide nor hair of a single one. The rain was coming down hard now, it was a wall of wet, and it hit the ground fierce like arrows and it was so dark outside you couldn't see where the rain might have fallen from, how it could have found its way through so dense a crush of treetops. And the apple cores were gone, maybe they hadn't been dropped clearly enough, maybe the birds had eaten them, maybe they had long ago just rotted and turned to mush. So they had no choice, they had to stay the night together in a haunted house, maybe they could find their way back to their own garden in the morning, maybe.

The bedroom was big. There were two large wardrobes, and there was a dressing table with a nice mirror to sit in front of and do make-up, and there was a huge bed laden high with blankets and pillows. Cindy and Steve got under the covers.

They both listened out for the ghosts in the dark.

"I'm frightened," said Cindy, and reached out for Steve's hand. And Steve didn't say he was frightened too, that his stomach felt strange stuffed as it was with porridge, that his skin felt strange, too: tingly and so very sensitive with a mattress underneath it and sheets on top of it and this smooth naked body lying next to it, brushing against it, tickling its hairs, yes oh yes. "Don't be frightened," said Steve, "I'll protect you, my Snow White, my Rapunzel, my unnamed princess from Princess-and-the-Frog," and he kissed her, and they had never kissed before, and they explored each other's mouths much as they had explored the house, with false bravado, and growing confidence, and some unspoken sense of dread. They pushed their tongues deep into each other's dark spaces. And slept at last. And dreamed of ghosts. And of what ghosts could even possibly be.

## ii

So this is where you are! I couldn't find you! I didn't know where you could be, I thought maybe you were in the maze. You know, that maze I made for you, with all those tall hedges, cylindrical archways, and any number of delightful red herrings. The maze, yeah? I thought, they're playing in the maze, it's easy to get lost in the maze, what a hoot! So I waited for you at the exit, I thought you'd come out eventually, I'd surprise you by saying boo! And I waited quite a long time, and one day I thought to myself, you know what, I don't think they're in this maze at all. The maze I made for them. So where could they be?

I felt a bit of a prawn, I must say, waiting outside a maze for six months all primed to say boo. Getting the exact facial expression right. I got a bit bored. I made a lot more cancers and viruses to keep my mind occupied. Oh, and I made the antelope extinct. Hope it wasn't a favourite.

But, no, you've found the house! And good for you. Oh, did I say that you shouldn't come to the house? Did I? Doesn't sound like me, hang on, trying to think, no. No, I can't imagine why I would have said that. You want a house, with what, rooms and floorboards and curtains and shit, then you go for it. Much better than a maze. Really, *fuck* the maze. I want to hear you say it. Say it with me. Fuck the maze. *Fuck* the maze. That's it, so you can see, I've no problem with the maze at all. I'm not even kidding! You have whatever you like, I never want to hold you guys back, I love you, I'm crazy about you. You have your house, a house with a roof to keep the rain off.

(In fact, sorry about the rain. Not quite sure what that's about. Very frustrating, must be leaking somewhere up there, the sky's cracked, got to be. And yeah, I can hold the rain back, but the thought of that crack, at that poor cowboy workmanship, it makes me a bit cross, quite *angry*, and when I get angry, it seems to rain all the more, and you know what? It's a vicious circle.)

And you've found the wardrobes! Picking through the cupboards as if they're yours, and they *are* yours, of course they are. Look at you, Cindy, no, I mean, *look* at *you*. All those dresses, all those shoes. That skirt, ha, that doesn't leave a lot to the imagination, ha, that really emphasizes your, um, ha, hips, ha ha! And make-up too. Though? If I can? Make a suggestion? The lipstick. Goes on the lips. Hence the name, yeah. . . . And you, erm, Steve, you look nice too.

No, not *all* the house is haunted. Did I give you? That impression? No, the kitchen's fine. The bedroom's fine. The sitting room, fine. Bathroom, ha, there are no bogeymen lurking behind the toilet cistern. No, it's the attic. It's the attic that has all the ghosts in. You haven't found the attic yet? You didn't know there even was an attic? Well, there is. I wouldn't go looking for it, though. No good will come of it. Sometimes you stand underneath that attic, at the right spot, you can feel the temperature drop, there'll be a cold chill pricking over your skin. There'll be a sickness in your throat, your heart will start to beat uncomfortably fast. Listen hard enough, press your ears up to the ceiling, you can hear *whispers*. The whispers of the dead. No, I wouldn't bother, you just stick with your mercifully spook-free lavatory, you'll be fine.

Is that the time? I should go. It's a long way back to the garden, and it's getting late. No, how kind, shouldn't stay for dinner, maybe next time. But how kind. What a kind thought. How lovely. I'll get back to my maze, my silly little maze, that'd be best. Better hurry, it's pissing down out there.

Night-night then. You be happy. Be happy, and stay happy. You both mean the world to me. Night-night, sleep tight. Don't let the bedbugs bite.

It took them four days to find the attic. It was difficult. No matter whereabouts they stood they felt no chill or nausea, and their heartbeats remained frustratingly constant. Eventually it took Cindy balanced upon Steve's finer shoulders, reaching up and prodding at the ceiling—a painstaking operation, and one that took a lot of straining and swaying—before Cindy said that beneath the wallpaper she felt something give. They cut away the wallpaper with a kitchen knife. They exposed a hatchway—small, neat, perfectly unassuming.

It hadn't been opened in a long time. No matter how much Cindy pushed at it just wouldn't move; Steve at last had to help, crouching down with Cindy on his shoulders and then springing up tall, sending his wife fast up in the air and using her as a battering ram.

The rather dazed Cindy poked her head through, and Steve called up, "Can you see anything? Can you hear anything?" Cindy remembered the fairy tales she'd been told, Jack climbing his way up a beanstalk to dangers unknown, Aladdin lowered into the darkness whilst his uncle stayed safe up top. "No, nothing," she said. Steve got up on to a table and climbed through the hatchway after her. There were a few nondescript boxes piled up, mostly cardboard; they contained years old fashion magazines, clothes, toys, a stamp collection, stuff. If there was a chill, it was only because they were away from the central heating. If there was a whispering, it was just the lapping from inside the water tank, or the sound of wind playing against the roof.

And if they were disappointed, neither Cindy nor Steve said they were. They went back to their ordinary lives. Cindy learned how to use the kitchen, she'd make them both dinner from tins she found in the cupboard. Steve found a DIY kit, and would enjoy banging nails into things pointlessly with his hammer.

And in bed they continued to explore each other's bodies. Steve discovered that Cindy enjoyed it when he nibbled on her breasts, but that he should stop well short of making the blood thing leak out; for her part, Cindy quickly learned that sucking at appendages rather than biting down hard and chewing was always a more popular option. They examined and prodded at each and every one of their orifices, and into them would experiment inserting opposing body parts; they found out that no matter what they tried to stick up there, be it tongue, finger or penis, the nostrils weren't worth the effort. And soon too they realized that it was better to do all of these things in the dark, where the ridiculous contortions of facial expressions on their spouse's face wouldn't put them off.

They listened out for the ghosts. They never heard them.

One night Steve woke from his sleep to find Cindy wasn't there. He put on his favourite silk dressing gown from the wardrobe, went to look for her. At last he found her in the attic, sitting on the floor, rocking back and forth as she cried so hard. At his approach she started, turned about, looked at him with startled teary eyes. "Where are our ghosts?" she begged to know. "Where's the chill, the sickness in my stomach? I can't feel anything. Why can't I feel anything at all?"

### iii

You were thinking of a nursery, right? The attic for a nursery, that was the plan?

Oh, sorry, didn't mean to make you jump! Coming round unannounced, very rude, but I tried the doorbell, and there was no answer, and I thought, shall I just pop in anyway, why not, good friends like us don't need to stand on ceremony. I can see why you didn't hear me. You're pretty busy. Pretty . . . entwined, there.

Don't stop on my account. I can wait. You finish off, I don't mind, I'll watch. Oh. Oh. Suit yourselves.

Speaking of which! I can see that you've discovered the joys of sex. Which is nice. I'm a little surprised, ha, by your choice of *partners*, I mean, doesn't it strike you as a bit incestuous? You crazy kids, what will you get up to next! I don't mind. I don't mind at all. I mean, it makes me wonder why I invented the zebu in the first place, you don't fancy the zebu, all those dewlaps? It could have been a baby zebu that's growing inside your stomach this very moment, imagine what *that* would have looked like!

Oh, you didn't realize? Yeah, you're pregnant. Congratulations! Some men don't like women when they're pregnant, but Cindy, I must say, you look *great*, all shiny and hormonal like that, all your body parts swelling every which way. And yeah, well done too, Steve, yeah. And you're going to need a nursery. Which is why, I'm sure, you had only the best intentions when you ignored my *advice* and went up into the attic. And why not, good choice. Babies are great, but take it from me, they're annoying, they cry a lot, there's a lot of noise and sick, keeping the baby up in the attic out of earshot is a good plan. Clear away the boxes, there'll be room up there for all those baby things babies seem to like. It's all just junk, there's nothing in there to worry about.

Except, of course, for that *one* box. The one with the padlock on. Now, you two and I have had a bit of a laugh, haven't we? It's all been fun. But this time I'm really telling you. It's a padlock. That's a big fucking hint. You are not to open the box. You are not to open the box. I forbid it. I absolutely forbid it, and yes it's a law, it's an order, it's a commandment from up high. Leave the box alone. No matter what you hear inside. No matter what the ghosts inside the box say to you.

Lightening the mood!—any ideas for a name for the baby yet? No?

Well, I'm just saying. You want to name it after me, you can. Call it God, or Lord, or Jehovah, or some such, and I'd be honoured.

The daffodils are out. They look beautiful.

Well, I can see you have things to do. Some of which will no doubt make you drowsy, you'll be wanting to sleep soon. So, you know. Night-night. Sleep tight. Don't let the bedbugs bite. No, I really mean it, I'm not sure, but I think I put cancer in a few of them, the bedbugs are riddled with cancer. You see a bedbug, you *run*.

So they smashed the padlock, and straightaway they heard them, the whispers inside—and there were so many, there was so much chatter, the conversations were all overlapping so they couldn't make out what was being said! "Open the box!" said Cindy, too eagerly, and "I'm trying!" Steve snapped back, and it seemed such a fragile little box, but now the lid was heavy, they pulled together and the lid raised an inch, and husband and wife had to prise their fingers painfully into the little gap to stop it from shutting again. And the whispers seemed so loud now, how could they not have heard the ghosts before? And they both felt a bit ashamed of that. Ashamed that they'd been carrying on with their lives quite pleasantly, cooking and hammering and shagging away, and had never paid the ghosts any attention. Cindy looked at Steve, and smiled at him, and thought, *I wonder if I'll find someone new to talk to.* And Steve looked at Cindy, smiled back, thought, *I wonder if their orifices will be prettier.* Because they both loved each other, they knew they did; but how can you tell what that love is worth if you're nothing to compare it to?

They took strength from each other's smiles; they heaved again; the box opened.

The whispering stopped, startled.

Inside there was a house. Not a proper house, of course, but a doll's house. And it wasn't *quite* like their house; it too had red bricks, and thin chimneys, it had windows and guttering, but they could see that the sitting room was smaller, there was less wardrobe space in the bedroom, the toilet had a broken flush.

There was no one to be seen.

"Talk to us!" said Cindy. "Come back!" said Steve.

They wondered if they could squeeze themselves into something as small as that house. And they exchanged glances. And they shrugged. And they went in.

## iv

God didn't talk to them for a long while after that.

There was lots of fun to be had in the haunted doll's house.

Their new neighbours were very kind. Their names were Bruce and Kate. Bruce and Kate knocked on the door one day, said they'd heard people had moved in next door, wanted to welcome them, hoped they'd be very happy. They invited them round to dinner. Cindy and Steve didn't know what to bring, but they found a bottle of old red wine in the back of one of the kitchen cupboards, and Bruce and Kate smiled nicely at it and said it was one of their favourite tipples. Kate made a really lovely casserole, "nothing fancy, just thrown it together," and Bruce laughed and said Kate's casserole was a secret recipe, and it was certainly better than anything Cindy could have come up with. Bruce was in charge of dessert. Bruce and Kate showed Cindy and Steve around their modest house, and it wasn't much different to Cindy and Steve's, only in the bathroom their flush *did* work, Cindy and Steve felt a little bit jealous. And Bruce and Kate had a seven year old daughter called Adriana who was quite pretty and very polite and did ballet and whose drawings from school were hung on display for all to see with fridge magnets. "Can see you're expecting!" said Kate to Cindy, and Cindy agreed she was; Kate said it'd be nice for Adriana to have a new friend to play with, maybe. Bruce and Kate were dead. They were dead, but they didn't seem to know they were dead. Cindy and Steve could see right inside them and there was nothing but ash in there and their souls were spent. They smelled of death, their eyes rolled dead in their heads, they waddled awkwardly as they walked. Adriana was dead, and when at Kate's indulgent prompting she agreed to show the new neighbours a few choice ballet steps it was like watching a broken puppet splaying cack-legged across the floor. "Well done!" said Kate, and clapped her dead hands, and Bruce laughed the most cheery of death rattles, and Cindy and Steve were good guests and clapped and laughed too.

Bruce asked Steve what he did for a living, and Steve said that he was between jobs. And Bruce was very kind, he got Steve an interview at the bank where he worked. And Steve spent the day sorting money and counting money and giving money to people through a little glass grille. He'd never seen money before, but he liked the feel of it, and in return for his hard work he was given money of his very own. Steve determined he would try hard to collect an awful lot of it. And the bank manager was very nice, and congratulated Steve on his efforts, and gave him a promotion, which basically meant that Steve gave more money to different people through a slightly bigger glass grille. And the bank manager was dead, and the customers were dead, and Bruce was still dead, of course, Bruce being dead wasn't going to change in a hurry. And Steve would sometimes after work go out with Bruce to a pub and get pissed.

And Cindy wanted to work at the bank too, but Kate told her she'd really be better off staying at home and looking after her baby. And Cindy could feel it kicking inside, and decided it was high time she let the baby out, she couldn't be sure but she thought it had been kicking inside there now for *years*. She went to the hospital and the doctors were dead and the nurses were dead and all the patients were dead, and some of the dead patients were so ill that during their stay at the hospital they died again and somehow got even *deader*, that was so weird. And a particularly dead nurse told Cindy she had to push the baby out, and that she was being very brave, and that they were having this baby together, and *push*. And out came the baby, and the baby was crying, and still kicking away, and the nurse cooed and said it was a beautiful little girl, and Cindy felt a sudden strange rush of love for her child, a stronger love than she'd ever known before, stronger than anything she'd felt for Steve or, even, God; but the baby was dead, it was dead, Cindy was given it to hold and it rolled its dead eyes at her and burbled and sneezed and Cindy could see there was no soul to it, just ash. "I don't want it," she said to the dead nurse, "I don't want this dead baby," and she thought of how this ashen soulless corpse monster had been feeding inside her stomach and she felt sick. The dead nurse told her again the girl was beautiful, she was such a *beautiful girl*; "You keep it then," said Cindy. But apparently that just wasn't an option, and Cindy had to take the stillborn little parasite home and feed it and pet it and read it fairy tales and give some sort of shit when it screamed.

And Steve didn't like their new baby daughter either—he *said* he did, and he played with it, and sat it on his knee, and asked after it when he came back home pissed from the pub—he didn't say *anything* against the baby at all, come to think of it; but Cindy knew he must hate it, because she hated it, and they were one flesh, weren't they, they were soulmates, they were *one*. And they still had sex, it was a little more routine than before, even a bit desultory—but Cindy didn't mind, she wasn't quite sure what part of the sex process had resulted in this baby growing inside her in the first place; she thought that if they did the sex thing very quietly, almost without passion, almost as if they weren't really there at all, then they wouldn't draw attention to themselves. Then no future daughter would see.

Cindy stayed at home. Cindy felt trapped. Cindy remembered the fairy tales she'd been fed when she was a child. Damsels with long hair locked away in high towers, princesses forced down to sleep on peas. Mothers pressed into bargains with grumpy evil dwarves who wanted to steal their first-born. Cindy didn't meet many dwarves, no matter how hard she looked—not at the supermarket, not at the kindergarten, not at the young mothers' yoga group that the erstwhile Kate had persuaded her to join. Cindy knew that the dwarves wouldn't have been much use anyway, the dwarves too would have been dead.

"I love you," Steve would say to Cindy, each night as they got into bed, and he meant it.

"I love you," Cindy would say back, and she meant it too.

Steve had met someone at work, a little cashier assistant less than half his age. He didn't expect her to like his whitening beard and his receding hairline and his now protruding gut. She fucked him at the office Christmas party, and he told her it had to be a one off, but she fucked him three more times in January, and an astonishing fifteen times in February, she was really picking up speed. "Tell me you love me," she'd say afterwards as she smoked a fag, ash in her ash, and he'd say he did, and he thought that maybe that was even true, just a little bit; she'd wrap her corpse legs around him and her dead matted bush would tickle the bulge of his stomach, and then he was inside her, he was inside something that felt warm and smooth but he knew was really so so cold and was rotting away into clumps of meat. He thought her death would infect him, he hoped it would. He wished he had the sort of relationship with Cindy where he could talk about his new girlfriend, who bit by bit was becoming the very centre of his world, the little chink of garden at the heart of his day. But Cindy had never been one to share things with, nothing of any importance. And some nights he'd cry.

Once in a while they'd try to escape the doll's house. But they couldn't find the exit. They took their dead daughter on a holiday to Tenerife, but there was no exit there, not even as far away as Tenerife. When their dead daughter was older, and wanted holidays of her own, with disreputable looking dead boys who had strange piercings and smelled of drugs, Cindy and Steve took their very first holiday alone. They went to Venice. They drank wine underneath the Rialto. They were serenaded on a gondola. They made love in their budget hotel, and it felt like love too. It felt like something they could hold on to. And sometimes, back at home, when Steve cried at night, or during the day when Cindy stared silently at the wall, they might think of Venice, and the memory made them happy.

This account focuses too much upon the negatives, maybe. They had a good time in the haunted doll's house, and the ghosts were very chatty, and some of them were kind.

## V

"Hello, hello!" Beaming smiles all round. "Well, here we are! Here we all are again!" A clap on the host's back, hearty and masculine, a kiss on the hostess' cheek just a little too close to the mouth. "So good to see you both, I'm not even kidding! I brought some wine, where would you like it?"

They showed him the house. He made appreciative noises at the sitting room, the kitchen, the bedroom. He admired the toilet, Steve pointed out to him the flush, and how he'd fixed it with all the DIY he'd learned. They settled down at the kitchen table and ate Cindy's casserole, and they all agreed it was really good.

"Well. Well! Here we all are again."

God was wearing a sports jacket that was meant to look jaunty, but it was two sizes too big for him; God looked old and too thin; the jacket was depressing, it made him look diminished somehow. The wine he'd brought was cheap but potent. The conversation was awkward at first, a series of polite remarks, desperate pauses, too-big smiles and eyes looking downward. The wine helped. They began to relax.

Cindy asked if they could return to the garden.

"Go backwards?" said God. "I don't know if you can go *backwards*. You crazy kids, what will you think of next!"

They laughed, and shared anecdotes of mazes and apples, of fairy tales told long ago.

God mused. "I think the idea is. If I think about it? I think, the older you get, and the more experienced you get. And the more you realize how big the world is, and how many opportunities are in front of you. Then the smaller the world becomes. It gets smaller and smaller, narrowing in on you, until all that's left is the confines of a wooden box." He coughed. "You could say that it's a consequence of maturity, of finding your place in the world and accepting it, of discovering humility and in that humility discovering yourself. Or, maybe. Ha. It's just a fucking bad design flaw. Ha! Sorry."

He drank more wine, he farted, they all laughed, oh, the simple comedy of it all.

"But," God said, "this world isn't all there is. It can't be. There must be a way out. At the very centre of the world, there's a dark space. Don't go to it. Don't go. It isn't a law. I'm not, ha, forbidding you. But I think," God said, and his voice dropped to a whisper, and he looked so scared, "I think there are ghosts there. I think the dark space is haunted."

"Well," said Steve, eventually. "It's getting late."

"It *is* getting late," said Cindy.

"No doubt you'll be wanting to get back home," said Steve. "Back to your garden and whatnot."

"Back," said Cindy, "to your maze." She took away God's wine glass, put it into the sink with a clatter.

God looked sad.

"I'm dying," he said.

"Oh dear," said Steve.

"That's a shame," said Cindy.

"I've been mucking about with too many cancers. I've got nobbled by the Ebola virus, I've come down with a spot of mad cow disease. It's all the same to me. I've been careless. Too careless, and about things that were too important." He coughed again, gently wiped at his mouth with a handkerchief, looked at the contents of the handkerchief with frank curiosity. He blinked.

"Shame," said Cindy again.

"And I wanted to see you. I wanted to be with you, because we're family, aren't we, you were always my favourites, weren't you, you're my favourites, did you know that? I'm crazy about you crazy kids. I miss you. I miss you like crazy. We never had a cross word. Others before you, others after, well. I admit, I got angry, plagues, locusts, fat greasy scorch marks burned into the lawns of the Garden of Eden. But I love you guys. I love you, Cindy, with your big smile and your deep eyes and your fine hair and your huge norks and your sweet, sweet smelling clit. And you, what was it, Steve, with your, um. Winning personality. If I have to die, I want to die with you."

His eyes were wet, and they couldn't tell if he were crying or rheumy.

"This world can't be all there is," he breathed. "It can't be. I have faith. There *must* be a way out." He opened his spindly arms wide. "Give me a hug."

So they did.

"Because," said God. "You loved me once. You loved me once, didn't you? You loved me once. You loved me. Tell me you loved me. Tell me you loved me once. You loved me. You loved me. You loved me."

They buried their father in the back garden that night. It wasn't a grand garden, but it was loved, and Cindy and Steve had planted flowers there, and it was good enough.

Then they went indoors, and they began looking for the dark space at the centre of the world. They'd been to Tenerife and to Venice, they'd seen no dark spaces there. So they looked in the kitchen, they cleared out the pots and the pans from the cupboard. They looked in the bathroom behind the cistern. They looked in the attic.

They decided to go to bed. It had been a long day. And Steve offered Cindy his hand, and she took it, a little surprised; he hadn't offered her a hand in years. They both liked the feel of that hand holding thing, it made them seem warm and loved. They climbed the stairs together.

They looked for the dark space in the bedroom too, but it was nowhere to be found.

They got undressed. They kicked off their clothes, left them where they fell upon the floor, stood amidst them. They came together, naked as the day they were born. They explored each other's bodies, and it was like the first time, now there were no expectations, nothing defensive, nothing to prove. He licked at her body, she nuzzled into his. Like the first time, in innocence.

She found his dark space first. It was like a mole, it was on his thigh. He found her dark space in the shadow of her overhanging left breast.

She put her ear to his thigh. Then he pressed his ear against her tit. Yes, there were such whispers to be heard! And they marvelled that they'd never heard them before.

She slid her fingertips into his dark space, and they numbed not unpleasantly. He kissed at hers, and he felt his tongue thicken, his tongue grew, all his mouth was a tongue. They both poked a bit further inside.

They wondered if they could squeeze themselves into something that was so small. They looked at each other for encouragement, but their faces were too hard to read. They wondered if they could dare. And then she smiled, and at that *he* smiled. And they knew they could be brave again, just one last time. They pushed onwards and inwards. And they went to someplace new.

# Afterword:
## Merely a Horror Writer

The editors of this volume have asked me to give a brief overview of the life and works of R___ S_____, and I shall say at the outset that I have misgivings about the enterprise. The enterprise being not merely the introduction itself, but the very publication of this collection. I do not think S_____ would have wanted to have seen his books back in print; indeed, I am quite sure not. And I do not think that the motives behind their reissue are of the best either; the letter I received this morning urging me once again to change my mind and write about S_____ speaks—and I quote—of "the public's fascination and appetite for the 'Master of the Macabre.'" I put it to you that the fascination is not with the stories themselves, which I suspect to be no better than the rest of their genre, but with the author himself, and a rather prurient curiosity about the manner of his death. I put it to you, too, the reader, holding this book in your hands, that the aforementioned appetite is sensationalism of the worst kind, and I say, shame on you, sir, shame on you.

But nonetheless, and much to my surprise, I find myself writing. There is a storm outside; there is a draft in my study that I cannot locate nor still; the very candle by which I work is guttering. And I am not without a sense of humour, no matter what my students claim, and I can see the irony of a night like this, the very setting of so much of S_____'s work, a setting which lets the mind fancy about ghosts and witches and wendigos. So, here I put this before you, if not with my blessing. And this way I may at least hope, with the book on sale, that Margaret may be given some money.

I do not say that S_____'s interest in writing supernatural fiction was beneath him. Every man must have a hobby. I myself am quite a keen golfer, with a handicap of sixteen above par, and I take great pleasure in that, but would also venture that it in no way intrudes upon my academic reputation. The same was not true of S_____, and that was his curse. He was a scholar of some undeniable merit, and although many critics would claim that his analysis of fourteenth century poetry yielded little fresh insight, I've never heard anyone suggest that his research was anything less than thorough and his theories anything less than cogent. But there is surely no question that whatever his academic prowess, in the last few years of his life any renown he had was for his ghost stories. It wasn't even as if he had published that many; he wrote one a year, as I understood it, always performed on Christmas Eve during the university celebrations. This was the sum total of his literary fame, or shall I say, notoriety: no more than three thousand words per year, and all three thousand melodramatic mumbo-jumbo.

I attended his final ghost story reading. There was an undeniable excitement in the air, and I allowed myself to share in it in spite of myself. The undergraduates all dressed in their gowns, and drinking wine and ale, and eating pork and steak, and singing Christmas carols and songs of an altogether more secular nature. S_____ sat up on high table, of course, and looked shrunken in on himself, not conversing, not eating, barely taking part in the festivities at all—but then, when the port was served, and cigars were lit, the lights were lowered, and S_____ got to his feet—and it seemed to me that he was suddenly *transformed*. He seemed much taller, much younger, and at once the room fell silent in ready anticipation; there was no need to call for silence, this performance is what we all had been waiting for. And S_____ read, and we all shivered in the hope of something frightening that would put our nerves jangling and let reel our darkest imaginings. I do not think S_____ was a natural actor. Even as a lecturer he had a propensity to mumble, and as a reader, merely reading the words in front of him, he was inclined toward halting monotone. And I do not think that the story was a good one, even by his standards: the tale of a ghost in a hotel preying upon the residents within seemed to me rather stale and obvious, and painfully lacking in theme or subtext. But what could not be argued was the *authority* with which S_____ spoke, the way there was no other sound to be heard save his voice for the full half hour, in a hall large enough to fit five hundred (and had done so, easily, to bursting) and had only so recently rung loud with the unfettered boisterousness of youth. As S____ read of his ghosts and demons, there was a change in the atmosphere. It seemed to grow colder. It seemed to grow darker. There was an almost preternatural stillness to the air, I fancied that time itself had stopped, or at least *slowed*, that I would look outside the window and the branches would only be inching in the wind and the snow would fall at half speed. And by the time he had finished, the world seemed a more mysterious, and unsettling, and more *remarkable* place to live.

I only discussed his horror writing with S____ on two occasions, many years apart. And his answers were contradictory, and I like to think that the first time was the *correct* answer nonetheless—back before he'd made a name for himself, even so, back before he'd been defined and limited by his own peculiar imagination. I asked him, simply enough, why it was he put such focus upon his tales of the uncanny, and I asked, I think without judgment—and he blushed (as well he might) and told me that it was really all about trying to make people *laugh*. That was it. He thought that within his flights of fancy there was something so absurd that it would amuse people, that delight could be taken in the dissonance between what they expected and what they received, like the way a child giggles in a hall of mirrors seeing himself fat or tall. But something always went wrong with the punchlines to his jokes, he said. What he'd hoped would elicit a chuckle would instead produce a gasp; the tightrope, he argued, between comedy and horror was really very narrow, and his problem was he just kept falling off it. As a little boy his attempts to make his parents laugh only made them recoil; he gave his sisters nightmares with the jolly adventures he'd dream up for their dolls to entertain them. And pretty soon he realized that if he couldn't win anyone's heart with ready wit, he wouldn't try; he'd let that dissonant way he looked at the world—a way that deep inside still would make him chortle, he alone still found full of jest—be as unnerving and twisted as one could wish. If he couldn't make them love him, he'd make them fear him a little. And at this he blushed even deeper, and of course I knew the reason why.

The reason why was Margaret. Of course he loved Margaret, just as I did; she was an outsider. We were all of us outsiders there, at a university which was based upon privilege and rank, where most students could trace back their family's college attendance as far as their great grandfathers. S____ was the first person in his family to go to university; so was I; his father was in trade; so was mine. And it sounds an unlikely contrivance now that we met on our first day there, but it was true; it was as if we wore badges telling the other undergraduates that we didn't belong, they smelled out we were frauds at once, and the way they so blatantly excluded us made it all the easier for us to find each other.

We became firm friends immediately.

And very soon, once we'd found the nerves to speak to her, Margaret was part of our group too—a female student, back in the times before that became a point of fashion, and from the middle classes as well. S_____ was very shy of her, I recall, and it was hard for him to introduce himself, as soon as he even got close he'd wring his hands and start to stammer so he looked less like a first class academic in the making than a babbling simpleton—I was, I think, much smoother with her, I was able to say hello and tell her my name and comment upon the weather and ask her the time. But it was to his credit that it was S_____ who invited her to go punting with us—he came back to the halls one day, and threw himself down on the chaise, and he looked so red I thought he was having a seizure. "I've done it," he said, "I've asked her out. She'll go punting with us on Sunday afternoon at two o'clock sharp." I pointed out to him that I didn't know how to punt, and nor did he; at this he turned even more red, he hadn't thought of that. So for the next four days we neglected our studies, we spent our time on the river trying to master how on earth one can steer a wooden boat with a pole. I fancy by the time Sunday came both of us had achieved a certain halting proficiency; we had stopped falling in, at any rate; and we both had the blisters on our hands to prove it. But when Margaret came to join us, all of S_____'s training went in an instant, he didn't know what to do with that pole, whether to push it or pull it or wave it about like an idiot—and I must admit, I too, I was tired and the weather was warm and I was not at my best. Margaret watched us struggle with the pole; we were both getting irritable with it, and with each other. "May I?" she asked, ever so gently, and we stepped aside, and *she* took the pole, and *she* took control, and S_____ and I sat in the back and enjoyed the afternoon as she punted us up and down and all over the river.

I would say, where S_____ and I were concerned, that I was the more attractive. I was more confident; I was taller; I had dark hair, where S_____'s was wispy and blonde like a girl's; I was specializing in John Milton, who is the greatest poet of the English language, and S_____'s interest lay in Geoffrey Chaucer, who had palpable talent, of course, but was rather too inclined towards bodily function jokes, and has always struck me as something of a dilettante. It was understandable that it was me that Margaret fell in love with. But this in no way affected our friendship with S____, and indeed, we became an inseparable trio; Margaret and I would walk the streets of the city hand in hand, and S____ would bound about us good-naturedly like an amiable dog trying to amuse. It worked. Margaret called us "the Three Musketeers"—and I didn't like that, I thought that as students of English literature we should really avoid a reference to Dumas and concentrate instead upon our own heroes. I suggested we be called "the Three Metaphysicals," after the great poets, Donne, Herbert and Marvell; but it didn't catch on; no one could agree which one was Donne, which one was Herbert, which one was Marvell; after a while I gave up trying to persuade them and let Margaret and S____ have their way.

It occurs to me now I can't recall which poet was Margaret's own area of specialist interest. I'm sure it was one that I didn't disapprove of, however; I would remember.

Later that term we celebrated our first Christmas together. There was a formal dinner on the Christmas Eve, and we wore our gowns, and ate, and drank, and looked quite the picture of academia, I think. And Margaret had had an idea; that we should have our own private party afterwards, in her room, and each person would bring along an entertainment to perform. There was wine, and I think it was where I smoked my first cigar; I'm pretty sure it was S____'s first cigar, and he cried through the smoke, and we laughed; it was Margaret's first cigar too, and she puffed away quite proficiently, and I felt very proud of her, I remember thinking that she was my girl. There was a dozen of us in all; Margaret's social circle was rather wider than ours. One student sang a ballad, another played his violin really very reasonably indeed. I read aloud my own translation of one of Virgil's Eclogues, and it went down very well, and afterwards I was given a round of applause, and I remember making a little bow. It was S____'s turn. "I'm going to read a story I've written," he said. "Can we have the lights off, please?" Someone laughed and pointed out that if it was dark he wouldn't be able to see to read; he hadn't thought it through! S____ said quietly that he'd rehearsed it a lot, he knew his story by heart.

And I remember how different it was in the darkness. Some of our number made jokes, but they were uneasy jokes, and Margaret called for silence. And S____ began. As I've said, he was not a natural performer, but I think his nervousness did something to lighten his shy monotone, it gave the piece a wavery inflection. "What stuff is this!" said one student, Baines, halfway through, and Margaret rounded on him; she told him bluntly that he had to shut up or leave. Baines' interruption had sounded scornful, of course, but I knew where it had come from; a desire to break the atmosphere, to emphasize that what we were listening to was really just nonsense, there was nothing to be afraid of. And Baines didn't leave, he couldn't leave, none of us could.

I can't recall the details of the story now, and I see it isn't one that S_____ ever collected for publication. Quite possibly it lacked the sheen of the more practised stories he would later write; quite probably he lost it. The plot naturally enough sounds ridiculous, as most plots do when boiled down to synopsis: even Milton can't escape that. It was something about an old curse, and a man who awakens it by reading a book, and the book (I think) was found in a crack in a wall of an abandoned church, or an abandoned monastery. And the hapless man is pursued by a ghost who drives him to suicide, setting himself on fire. S_____ was the last person to perform that night, because after the lights were turned back on no one was quite willing to continue; I was just glad I'd got my Eclogue out first. S_____ apologized. He could quite see he'd destroyed the party. He hadn't meant to.

It had hardly been an auspicious debut, but it was astonishing how its reputation spread. By the beginning of the Trinity term, S_____ was being approached by students who had never deigned to speak to us before. They were asking whether he would perform it again. I knew S_____ didn't want to. He was, as I say, a naturally shy man. But he found it hard to say no, especially when it seemed that friendship (or, at least, acceptance) was being offered to him at last. He asked Margaret what he should do, and my girlfriend said she thought he should try again—and if it would make him feel better, she would be there too to support him. At this he agreed. He performed the story another four times, I think, and then he added another story, and then a third, and it was a cold Winter that took its time to thaw, and everybody seemed to be in the mood for something dark and creeping. And S_____'s name became something that was known on campus—even though, as I warned him, it was for his frivolous fictions; his Middle English prowess, by anyone's standards, left much to be desired. By the time Baines killed himself S_____ had an identity—and, as his best friend, so had I.

Student suicide was a fairly common phenomenon around examination times, but what made Baines' one unusual was that it occurred in March, and mid-term at that; with fewer opportunities to distract us, his death occasioned no little interest. He left no note. His friends said they were quite surprised, because he hadn't even hinted taking his life was under consideration. And it was the manner of the death that really caused comment. Most students liked to hang themselves, or took poison, or, if they were of an especial melodramatic bent, threw themselves off the bridge. Baines had set fire to himself.

It was clear where he'd got the idea from, of course. And S_____ was appalled. He came to me one night, and he was shaking, so Margaret and I didn't turn him away, although I must confess I was a little put out. He asked us whether we thought he should write to Baines' parents to apologize. (We said no.) He asked whether he should confess his involvement to the police. (Definitely not.) He asked whether he should stop his ghost stories—and at this Margaret and I disagreed; I felt it'd be inappropriate for S_____ to write any more of them, even ones that didn't involve self-immolation of some kind or another. In truth, I was rather tired of having a reputation based upon my knowing a spook writer—I felt it was high time I found a reputation all of my own.

It was around this point that Margaret and I broke up. S_____ came to me and asked if he could step out with her instead. His hands were wringing and he was stammering, he looked as pathetic as he had when I'd first met him, he was that frightened. And I told him that he was welcome to try his hand. That I'd had enough of her. That I'd used her up. But I suggested he might not have much luck knocking against that particular door. "Oh, no, you don't understand," he said, and he looked truly wretched. "Margaret's asked *me* out. I just wanted to make sure you didn't mind."

I didn't see much of S_____ or Margaret after that. It really wasn't personal, and I still regarded them as friends. But I don't think they were quite as subtle in their love as they might have been; on a Sunday you could see them kissing on a punt, and I thought that lacked a certain class. And at Christmas S_____ was asked by the senior staff whether he would perform a ghost story. No longer something hidden behind the doors of drunken undergraduates, but as a part of the formal celebrations. I can only imagine how terrified he was. I imagine Margaret got him through it. I wasn't in attendance at the revels that year, I agreed to go home and spend the holiday with my family.

We rubbed alongside each other quite comfortably over the next few years. Whenever we met, we would greet each other affectionately enough, with protestations that it had been far too long, that we should all get together again soon, the Three Musketeers forever, that we were still all so close and dear. And when I had an invitation to the wedding, I genuinely considered going. But of course I'd found new friends, and I didn't need S_____ or his girlfriend any longer, his fiancée, his happy little wife. I won a first class honours for my degree, of course, and was offered any place I wanted to go and study for my doctorate and teach: I chose Oxford. S_____ got his first just barely, I understand, and was kept on right where he was. I think they took some pity on him. I think they liked his Christmas ghost stories. And there was no need for us to meet again. He was fourteenth century, I was seventeenth; we were kept apart by entire centuries of difference.

I didn't speak to S_____ again for a very long time. There were the Christmas cards for a while, of course, but I rather think he stopped writing to me before I stopped writing to him. It was fifteen years before I had a letter marked "Shearman" again—and that was surprise enough, before I realized it was initialled M J, not R S. I still didn't think of Margaret having a surname like that. I couldn't.

Margaret told me she was passing through Oxford the following week; would it be possible to have lunch with me for old time's sake? I wrote back at once, and assured her I would; and I followed her request that I should be discreet, not to mark the envelope so that it was clear it had been sent by me, and I would normally have found such fuss rather irritating, but I decided to indulge her. It led me to believe, of course, all sorts of idiotic things. That for fifteen years Margaret had loved me, and only me. That finally she had worked up the courage to say so. None of this chimed with the Margaret I knew, of course, the woman who had taught us how to punt, how to smoke cigars, how to (yes) love. But it was a happy fantasy all the same.

We agreed to meet on a Thursday, in a cake and tea shop that one of my undergraduates recommended, somewhere quiet. I was shocked when I saw her. She hadn't aged well. I could see the resemblance to the girl I'd known, but it was a resemblance one would find in a *mother*— she had always had a fleshy figure, with cheeks so plump they dimpled when she smiled, but now she'd thinned, and it made her look hard and plain, and when she smiled the smile had nowhere to grow. Her eyes were dead. We had tea. I asked her how she was. She said she was well. I asked her how S_____ was, and at this she sighed. She said he was well too, she believed. She stressed the 'believed', as if there were some cause for doubt, as if she might not be the best person to judge. I asked her why she had come. I told her I did not believe she was passing through to anywhere, and I was right. She told me that S＿＿＿ was a different man. I asked her if he hurt her in any way, and at this she looked rather offended. She said that he had days of mistemper, but the mistemper was always with *himself*; he was remote; he seemed, if anything, and she picked the word carefully, haunted. I laughed and told her that would seem appropriate for those little spine chillers of his, and she attempted a laugh back. And all the while she wouldn't look me in the face, and at first I thought this was out of shame, that she wanted to apologize, and my heart went out to her, her embarrassment was apology enough. But as our time wore on, and she still wouldn't look at me, and she still wouldn't tell me she regretted the way we had parted, I rather decided I wanted a spoken apology after all. "Could you go and see him?" she asked. "He wants to see you. He needs an old friend. And he's too proud to ask." I told her that I would think about it.

But that was in August, and I had a new term's lecturing to prepare, and a new paper to complete. In December I received my annual invitation to the high dinner on Christmas Eve at my alma mater, and as always I threw it into the dustbin. But something made me pull it out and reconsider.

I saw S＿＿＿ perform that last time. I didn't recognize him at first. If Margaret had aged, that was nothing to her husband. He was a man in his late thirties now, but he didn't look a day under fifty. And a badly worn fifty at that—his hair had greyed, he wore a drooping beard that did nothing to hide how his face sagged. And he was hunched—as he sat at dinner, he seemed bowed over the food, as if in some grim obeisance towards it. I didn't let him see me, of course. I kept my distance.

And I decided that this was all a mistake. That I should get out before I was identified. Get out before Margaret saw me, and made it impossible for me to leave. But no one looked at me, and I searched the room for her, I looked hard, and Margaret wasn't there. And then S＿＿＿ read his ghost story. He performed. As I say, I don't think he performed it well. I don't think it was a good story. But the world seemed to shift, and I decided I had to explore what this new world was before I got back on the train to Oxford and lost myself once again within the old one.

It was strange. After the impact his story had made I would have expected S＿＿＿ to have been flooded with well-wishers, students and academics alike congratulating him. That had certainly been the way when he was an undergraduate performing his ghost stories for the first time—and how shyly he had received those compliments, how he had blushed. But now, though he was a bona fide celebrity, everyone ignored him. The lights were turned back to full, he sat down morosely, stared at his food, prodded at some vegetable matter with a fork.

I went to see him.

"My God," he said. "Is it you? Is it really you?" And his face lit up, and years fell off it in an instant—not enough, I should add, he was still pushing fifty, but it was an improvement. "Did you like my story?"

"I'm afraid I arrived too late to hear it," I said. And at that his face fell so glumly, and I wished I could call back the lie. I wanted to reassure him, I promised I'd come to the next year's.

He indicated I should lean in, he wanted to say something to me in confidence. "There won't be another year's," he said. "I'm getting out of it. I'm getting out of the ghost story racket."

I told him I was pleased to hear it, and he nodded seriously.

"Can we talk in private?" he said. "Can you come to my rooms?"

And I said yes.

He seemed properly affectionate towards me as he showed me in. As if all the years of silence hadn't mattered a jot. He showed me around his study, waited for my approval.

"More than serviceable," I said.

"I'm sure your rooms in Oxford must be . . ."

"Well, yes," I said. "But that's Oxford."

He nodded.

I told him that academia would be delighted he was giving up his spook stories, that he had become something of a laughingstock. And he smiled and said, "Indeed, indeed!" and nodded, like a crusty old don, like the crusty old don he'd become, wanting to make a good impression on his bright young pupil.

"I should have listened to you in the first place," he said. "That's the truth of it."

I asked him why he'd written horror stories in the first place. And I expected the same answer he'd given me so many years ago. But it was different.

"Because," he said, "horror has to find a way out into the world."

I didn't quite know what to say to that. He looked apologetic. Wine, would I like some wine? To ease the mood, I said I would. A cigar? Why not, I said. We lit cigars, and as always, he never looked comfortable with a cigar, it looked ridiculous jutting out of his mouth like that, his eyes watering all the while. "This is good," he said, "this is fine, having you here again, yes, yes." I asked him how he was, generally. Like Margaret, he said he was well. I asked him how Margaret was. Well, he believed. I said I was pleased.

"They're not stories," he said suddenly.

I asked him to repeat himself.

"They're not stories," he said. "They're all true."

I scoffed at that. Asked him whether some sort of ghoul scaring hapless hotel patrons was *true*.

"No," he said. "I'm not saying it happened. But it's true all the same." He poured me another glass of wine. "But," he said, "I'm stopping that now. Before it's too late. And there's nothing they can do to me worse than what I've done to myself and to Margaret."

He asked how I was. I said I was well. He asked if I had a wife, was she well? I said I didn't have a wife, but if I had one, I'm sure she would be well, well. I told him to explain what was going on, I told him to stop dancing around the matter like a student who hasn't prepared his tutorial.

"The stories don't die," he said.

Wait, I asked, his ghost stories? I understood the print run had been rather small.

"Any stories. Do you know why Chaucer wrote? Do you know why Milton wrote?"

I said I'd spent an entire lifetime discussing why Milton wrote.

"So they'd never die," said S_____. And he grinned at me then, and he showed all his teeth, and at that moment I had a flash of fear, I had the most certain knowledge that my old friend was quite mad.

"They're kept alive in the books," he said. "In *all* the books, they live on. And they come to me, you know. They stand over me. They stand over me at night, when I'm alone."

I asked him whether Chaucer came to him, and he said he did. I asked him whether he could talk to Chaucer, and he said he could. I told him that must be useful for a lecturer in Chaucerian studies, he could ask him for all sorts of tips. But S_____ wasn't listening to me, and couldn't be chivvied along by my good humour.

"They're all trapped in the books," he said. "And they've had enough. They want to die. I've got to set them free. Posterity just isn't what it's cracked up to be."

I asked him then about Margaret. He told me he didn't see much of Margaret anymore, he slept alone in his rooms. I asked him how Margaret felt about that. He said it didn't matter, he had to help the ghosts, they wouldn't come unless he slept alone.

"The stories make you write them," he said. "They tell you they want to be let out into the world. Let them out, and they promise they'll leave you alone. That's what they told Chaucer, and Milton, and the rest of them, that's what they tell me. But they're liars. There are always more of them. Always more, filling your head, blocking out the light."

But I reminded him he only wrote one story every Christmas.

And he gripped my hand, and I recoiled at the touch, it felt like old man's skin, it felt like thin paper. "I write one *every day*," he said. "I write a new story *every single day*."

He asked me where I was sleeping that night, and I told him I had a hotel in town. He said I should stay with him and Margaret, and I replied that I wouldn't want to put them out at Christmas. He made me promise I would visit him the next day, and I said I would.

I went then and got on the next train back to Oxford. It was a long wait, and it was snowing. But I felt better for it.

As I left him, and wished him a happy Christmas, he said to me again, "I should have listened to you. I should always have listened to you. You were my best, my dearest friend."

And he said, "I'll do my best to last as long as I can."

S____ didn't even last the year. "Ghost Writer Dies in Blaze," said the newspaper of December 29th. It went on to report that the 'Master of the Macabre' R____ S____ had burned to death in the great libraries of the university where he had made his home. They suggested it was suicide, that he had set fire to himself whilst gazing out on all the great works of literature he held in such high regard. There was no note. The article went on to say that he is survived by his wife, Margaret, and two children, John and Abigail. I never knew he had children.

The article of course doesn't explain many things. Why kindling was found all around the library itself, as if he'd wanted to set fire to the whole collection. (Not a single book was even scorched. The university reported that this was a stroke of luck.) Nor did it explain why, had S____ wanted to kill himself, he'd not doused his body with a flammable agent like alcohol or gasoline first, that might have hastened the process. Self-immolation otherwise would be such a slow and painful way to go.

I wasn't invited to the funeral. I wrote to Margaret offering my condolences. I told her in the kindest of terms that she would be welcome to visit me in Oxford, at any time, for tea and cake. She hasn't written back yet.

There has been renewed interest in S_____'s fiction. I understand why the publishers have wanted to get his complete ghost stories back into print, in one easy volume like this one. As I say, I am not sure it is what the author would have wanted.

And I had said no. I wouldn't write this introduction. For that reason, and more. Because although S_____ called me his best and dearest friend, he was wrong, as he was about so very many things.

But the publisher keeps writing to me. They won't take no for an answer. Every day I receive a new letter, longer, more insistent than the last. I have never heard of the publisher before. I do not even know where I can send this introduction. They have not furnished me with a return address.

I can only hope that now I have written this out, that they'll keep their promise, and will leave me alone.

S_____ suggested to me he had hundreds more stories he'd written secretly. No one in the press has made mention of them, so I'm assuming they were not found amongst his personal effects. Maybe S_____ managed to destroy them in time. Maybe he never wrote them at all. Maybe, as I suspect, they are hidden—and for his sake, they should remain hidden. For pity's sake, leave the man alone, let him rest in peace.

As for these, now back in print—I'm sorry, Robert. I'm truly sorry.

# ACKNOWLEDGEMENTS

The new stories in this collection were written whilst enjoying a year's residency at Edinburgh Napier University, attached to the Creative Writing MA course. For all the friendship, support, and meaty literary discussions (and food! and expeditions in the snow!), thanks to Sam and Stuart Kelly, and to David Bishop. And also to the wonderful talented students, who sometimes took what I said with great seriousness, and just as often, when I most needed it, laughed at me.

These new stories are part of my hundred stories project, in which one hundred bold people have volunteered their names as characters. So thanks to Jason Zerrillo, Laura Marshall, Steven Baird, Craig Boardman, Simon Harries, Andrew Kaplan, and Sarah Hadley for allowing me to do terrible things to their namesakes—and Edward Wolverson, whose own name got cut from this edit! If you want to read the rest of the venture, it's being showcased as justsosospecial.com.

Thanks to all the past editors who worked on these stories—but, in particular, to Xanna Eve Chown and Steve Jones. Xanna has ploughed her way through no less than three complete books of mine now, and greets all of my stupidest schemes with cheerful diplomacy. She's back for more soon. She's nuts. Steve keeps on commissioning me for horror stories, no matter how rude I am to him personally, and introduced me to this whole genre with such great generosity. He also wrote the introduction to this book, for which I am very grateful—even though everything within it is a specious lie.

To Helen Marshall, who's edited *this* book—and besides being a smashing editor, is also one of the very best short story writers I know. She worked with me on this whilst polishing off her frankly rather brilliant collection, and I felt a strange mixture of guilt and relief that I was taking her away from her own work, and yet that there was someone looking over my words who so innately understood them and got the rhythm. For the past couple of years she's been the best and most loyal of friends, always encouraging my ideas and inspiring me with her own. Helen, I am at once hugely jealous of how good you are, and even more hugely proud that I know you. You're one in a million.

To Suzanne Milligan, my agent and pal. Always supportive, always patient, Suze has the remarkable ability to listen to all my little writing paranoias and make me feel I can beat them all. I've had quite a few agents over the years, and some of them were really good, but Suze is the first one that I really *want* to impress. She's also the first one to introduce me to the joys of Argentinian red wine. (Which reminds me, we must really share a bottle of Malbec again soon, preferably somewhere very swanky and tall with an impressive view of London.)

And lastly—but, really, never lastly—to my wife, Janie. We first began dating fifteen years ago, when I cast her in a play I was directing. It wasn't a very good play, actually, but she was very good in it, and made it seem better. She's always been great at that, making the bad things better. Over the years she's seen me change from someone writing domestic comedies for the theatre to writing—well, *this*—a bunch of weirdy wobbly horror stories. And she's never minded, and has trusted me all the way. I write obsessively, and sometimes that makes me grumpy, and more often, rather distracted and selfish—and every single time she forgives me. Especially if the story I turn out has a good scare in it. She likes good scary stories. I hope she enjoys these.

# ABOUT
# THE AUTHOR

Robert Shearman has worked as a writer for television, radio and the stage. He was appointed resident dramatist at the Northcott Theatre in Exeter and has received several international awards for his theatrical work, including the Sunday Times Playwriting Award and the Guinness Award for Ingenuity, in association with the Royal National Theatre. His plays have been regularly produced by Alan Ayckbourn, and on BBC Radio by Martin Jarvis. His two series of *The Chain Gang*, his short story and interactive drama series for the BBC, both won the Sony Award.

However, he is probably best known as a writer for *Doctor Who*, reintroducing the Daleks for its BAFTA-winning first series, in an episode nominated for a Hugo Award.

His collections of short stories are *Tiny Deaths*, *Love Songs for the Shy and Cynical*, and *Everyone's Just So So Special*. Collectively they have won the World Fantasy Award, the British Fantasy Award, the Edge Hill Short Story Readers Prize, and the Shirley Jackson Award, celebrating "outstanding achievement in the literature of psychological suspense, horror, and the dark fantastic."

Several stories in this collection have been compiled in annual anthologies as diverse as *Best New Horror* and *Best British Short Stories*. "Damned if You Don't" and "Alice Through the Plastic Sheet" were shortlisted for a World Fantasy Award; "Roadkill," "Alice Through the Plastic Sheet," and "George Clooney's Moustache" all for the British Fantasy Award. Robert has also been nominated for the Sunday Times EFG Private Bank Award, the most highly prized award for the form in the world.

# PUBLICATION HISTORY

MORTAL COIL © 2006. First published in *Phobic*, edited by Andy Murray, and subsequently collected in *Tiny Deaths*, both published by Comma Press.

DAMNED IF YOU DON'T © 2007. First published in the collection *Tiny Deaths*, published by Comma Press, and shortlisted for the World Fantasy Award.

SO PROUD © 2007. First published in the collection *Tiny Deaths*, published by Comma Press.

FAVOURITE © 2007. First published in the collection *Tiny Deaths*, published by Comma Press.

PANG © 2008. First published in *The Lifted Brow*, issue 5, edited by Ronnie Scott, and subsequently collected in *Love Songs for the Shy and Cynical*, published by Big Finish.

ROADKILL © 2009. First released as a novella by Twelfth Planet Press, and subsequently collected in *Love Songs for the Shy and Cynical*, and shortlisted for the British Fantasy Award.

GEORGE CLOONEY'S MOUSTACHE © 2009. First published in the *British Fantasy Society Yearbook 2009*, edited by Guy Adams, and subsequently collected in *Love Songs for the Shy and Cynical*, and shortlisted for the British Fantasy Award.

COLD SNAP © 2010. First published in *The Lifted Brow*, issue 7, edited by Ronnie Scott, and subsequently collected in *Everyone's Just So So Special*, published by Big Finish.

FEATHERWEIGHT © 2010. First published in *Visitants: Stories of Fallen Angels and Heavenly Hosts*, edited by Stephen Jones, published by Ulysses Press; subsequently reprinted in *The Mammoth Book of Best New Horror 22*, and collected in *Everyone's Just So So Special*.

GRANNY'S GRINNING © 2009. First published in *The Dead That Walk*, edited by Stephen Jones, published by Ulysses Press; subsequently reprinted in *The Mammoth Book of Best New Horror 21*, and collected in *Everyone's Just So So Special*.

ALICE THROUGH THE PLASTIC SHEET © 2011. First published in *A Book of Horrors*, edited by Stephen Jones, published by Jo Fletcher Books, shortlisted for a British Fantasy Award and World Fantasy Award.

GOOD GRIEF © 2011. First published in *Haunts*, edited by Stephen Jones, published by Ulysses Press.

THE DARK SPACE . . . © 2011. First published in *House of Fear*, edited by Jonathan Oliver, published by Solaris; subsequently reprinted in *The Best British Short Stories 2012*, edited by Nicholas Royle, published by Salt.

ELEMENTARY PROBLEMS . . . © 2012. First published in *Hauntings*, edited by Ian Whates, published by Newcon Press.

The remaining stories are all new to this collection, and are © 2012.